THE SHAMAN'S KNIFE

Mysteries by Scott Young

Murder in a Cold Climate
The Shaman's Knife

THE
SHAMAN'S
KNIFE

SCOTT YOUNG

VIKING

VIKING
Published by the Penguin Group
Penguin Books USA Inc., 375 Hudson Street,
New York, New York 10014, U.S.A.
Penguin Books Ltd, 27 Wrights Lane,
London W8 5TZ, England
Penguin Books Australia Ltd, Ringwood,
Victoria, Australia
Penguin Books Canada Ltd, 10 Alcorn Avenue,
Toronto, Ontario, Canada M4V 3B2
Penguin Books (N.Z.) Ltd, 182–190 Wairau Road,
Auckland 10, New Zealand

Penguin Books Ltd, Registered Offices:
Harmondsworth, Middlesex, England

First published in 1993 by Viking Penguin,
a division of Penguin Books USA Inc.

1 3 5 7 9 10 8 6 4 2

PUBLISHER'S NOTE
This is a work of fiction. Names, characters, and incidents
either are the product of the author's imagination or are used fictitiously,
and any resemblance to actual persons, living or dead, or events
is entirely coincidental.

AUTHOR'S NOTE
All place names in this book are real—except one,
Sanirarsipaaq, where most of the story takes place.
The word means "on the edge of." The fictional Sanirarsipaaq is on the
eastern edge of Victoria Island, almost due north of Cambridge Bay.

Grateful acknowledgment is made for permission to
reprint excerpts from the following copyrighted works:
"She Ain't Rose" by Gary Vincent and Ken Gray. © 1987 Temi Combine Inc.
All rights controlled by Combine Music Corp. and administered by
EMI Blackwood Music Inc.
All rights controlled by Music City Music Inc. and administered by
EMI April Music Inc.
All rights reserved. International copyright secured. Used by permission.
"Base Details" by Siegfried Sassoon. By permission of George Sassoon.

LIBRARY OF CONGRESS CATALOGING IN PUBLICATION DATA
Young, Scott.
The shaman's knife / Scott Young.
p.   cm.
ISBN 0-670-83555-2
I. Title.
PR6075.085S48   1993
823'.914—dc20   92-29873

Printed in the United States of America
Set in Times Roman
Designed by Virginia Norey

For MARGARET BURNS HOGAN

THE SHAMAN'S KNIFE

ARCTIC OCEAN

ALASKA

ARCTIC CIRCLE

Victoria
Island

Herschel
Island

Banks
Island

Sachs
Harbour

Aklavik   Inuvik

Holman

Paulatuk

Saniraгsipaaq

N O R T H W E S T

Cambridge
Bay

YUKON

Artillery Lake

Yellowknife

Great Slave Lake

PACIFIC
OCEAN

BRITISH
COLUMBIA

M

ALBERTA

C A N A D A

SASKATCH−
EWAN

UNITED

CANADA ◆ AND
ITS NORTHWEST
TERRITORIES

GREENLAND

Pond Inlet

Boothia Peninsula

Igloolik

Baffin Island

Spence Bay

Melville Peninsula

Dew Line Site

Iqaluit

T E R R I T O R I E S

Gjoa Haven

Cape Dorset

Frobisher Bay

King William Island

Southampton Island

Hudson Bay

LABRADOR

ANITOBA

QUEBEC

ONTARIO

STATES

Map by Virginia Norey

O N E

Just before I flew out of Goose Bay in Labrador early that Monday morning, I heard a brief news item on a radio another passenger was carrying. "Two brutal murders have rocked the Arctic Inuit settlement of Sanirarsipaaq, northeast of Cambridge Bay on Victoria Island," the announcer led off, and went on to say that a middle-aged Inuit hotel cook and her grandson had been murdered during some kind of a drunken brawl. A possible third victim was a very old Inuit woman whose role in the matter was not immediately known. She had been found unconscious in an icy ditch just outside what the news reader called "the murder house," and had been flown to hospital in Yellowknife with a possible fractured skull.

The young Inuk carrying the radio turned. I'd been testifying in a murder case in Nain and had been described rather colorfully on local radio. As an RCMP inspector who was also a full-blooded Inuk, I was bound to get a lot of attention in Nain, which was almost entirely of my own people. Speaking in our tongue, Inuktitut, the young man with the radio said, "That sounds like a job for you, Matteesie." If I'd had a little more time I would have called headquarters. We'd been on the same light plane earlier, starting from the gravel runway at the Inuit settlement of Nain and flying south to the big air base at Goose Bay to catch this fast charter I'd heard was going directly to Ottawa, due there in three hours or so. But I'd be home before eleven. Then I could get details.

In Ottawa I took a taxi to my home in the old Glebe district intending to take on a quick infusion of tea, change my clothes, and go to the office.

A note on the door read: "Getting my hair done. Back soon. XXOO. Lois."

In the kitchen the light was flashing on my answering machine. I pushed the button. The message instructed me to call my office immediately. I made a pot of tea, put milk in my cup, waited a minute for the tea to steep, poured, sipped, and was about to call the office when the phone rang. An operator said, "CBC News, Inuvik, person to person for RCMP Inspector Matthew Kitologitak."

"Speaking."

"Go ahead, miss."

Then the jolt came. "Inspector Kitologitak?" Maxine asked.

I knew her voice better than almost anyone's. I thought of her as she would be now, just starting work in her cubbyhole at CBC Inuvik, two hours behind our time zone. The streets there would be just beginning to liven up after several hours of mid-April's long daylight. Her grandfather had been Scottish, other ancestors Slavey Indian. Her long black hair had a little gray in it, her skin was dark, and she was getting a little thick in the body, as I was. About five feet six, as I was. In all the years we'd been close to one another, Maxine had never before called me at home.

"Do you have a minute?" she asked, her voice ultra-impersonal. "It's about the murders in Sanirarsipaaq."

The case in itself couldn't be the reason she was calling me. There is a distinct pecking order in such matters. Local RCMP detachments tend to feel proprietary about their own murders. They like to provide the news media with their own versions of enlightenment, evasion, or nuances between. They often managed this without help. Usually I wasn't called in until normal procedures had been exhausted.

But through Maxine's attempt at impersonality I could hear an emotional note in her voice. "I wanted to tell you in case nobody else had, that the . . ."—shaky pause—"uh, old lady who got hurt outside the house where the murders happened is your mother."

I choked out, "How in hell . . . ?" then gave silent thanks that she hadn't said *was* your mother.

"She was medivacked to Yellowknife Saturday night," Maxine went on. "She's in hospital now. When I got her name yesterday and only then knew she was your mother, the doctor looking after her, a guy I know, Quinn Butterfield, told me there's no actual fracture but it's a bad concussion, maybe some minor internal bleeding but anyway a mighty headache . . ." She hesitated. "I tried your office and was told you were in Labrador. I just wasn't sure you'd heard . . ."

I had a strong feeling that there was another line she thought but didn't speak: "or you'd have been here by now, Matteesie."

"What held up anyone else getting to you was that I guess the police in Sanirarsipaaq didn't know from her name that she was your mother. Especially her being a stranger there, a visitor."

My mother's travels were a family joke. She'd been on the move much of her life. Like a lot of the old nomadic Inuit, or Eskimos, as she still called herself, travel was in her blood. At mother's ninetieth birthday party in the settlement where she lived near Holman there were about eighty of us in all, five generations. When I spoke about this party later to a rather lofty anthropologist of my acquaintance in Ottawa he told me kindly that when describing such gatherings I should use the term "kin group," which I do like the ring of. At the party one of my half-sisters said, "Now that you're ninety, you'll *have* to stay home where we know where you are!" Mother just cackled.

If she'd been hurt there in the Holman area, over on the west side of Victoria Island, where I often visited, someone would have got in touch with me immediately. Anywhere else—well, I am Matthew Kitologitak. She is Bessie Apakaq. The Inuit system of more or less picking our own surnames baffles some people, especially the whites, but it's one of our traditional ways that we've been able to hang on to. It's not based on patronymics, like in Russia, or matronymics, if that's a word, but simply allows the

individual to take the name he or she wishes. My uncle Jonassie
Kitologitak had been a famous hunter in the western Arctic, an
idol of mine, so I took his name as my own. It was not the kind
of tidy arrangement that governments, at least theoretically, dote
on. This name business naturally confused the authorities. Amazingly enough, those in charge resisted the natural temptation to
set up expensive new government offices staffed with party hacks
and defeated candidates to work out genealogical tables in an
attempt to keep things straight. Instead, in 1941 some deputy minister must have ruled that the simple way would be to print numbered metal tags and give each Eskimo one to be known by. If
old number E5-9 died, his number would be retired, just like
Gordie Howe's. . . . In a few decades the system went back to the
old puzzle of surnames, which is where we are now.

None of that really went through my mind, except as a ping
from one of those microchips that each of us carries in mind and
memory, a mere flash in time before—back to Ottawa, kitchen,
telephone, my tea getting cold.

In Maxine's work for CBC News, no doubt in her first checks,
she'd been talking to the detachment at Sanirarsipaaq. Steve
Barker was the corporal in charge there, not a guy I liked a lot.
He saw himself as sort of the great white father. I heard him say
once, "This is my town. What I say goes." An attitude that natives
never warm to.

"Steve Barker got any idea who did it?"

"Well, you know him. Doesn't trust reporters. He told me I
could quote him that they were *working* on it. Expecting to make
an arrest soon. The usual. Great headline, right? 'They're working
on it.' He spelled B-A-R-K-E-R for me so we'd pronounce it right
on the news . . ."

My smile was a little rueful. I didn't relish what might lie ahead
if Barker and I had to work together, as would likely be the case
if the phone message to call headquarters was what I expected, an
order to get up there fast.

"But I know another guy there," Maxine said. "Alphonse
Bouvier. He's a corporal sent in to take over when Steve Barker
goes on his holidays to Hawaii, which he's going to do as planned,

or his wife would kill him. She has all her new bathing suits bought . . ."

"When does this happy event come about?"

"Right away."

"No kidding?" A nice sense of relief.

"No kidding. Anyway, when I phoned Steve back to check something and got Bouvier he told me they didn't have a clue at all, yet. Everybody they'd checked out right after it happened had an alibi. But about your mother, to be fair, when I'd been talking to Barker first late Saturday he was in a big rush, getting rid of me fast because the medivac plane was just about to land and a storm was blowing outside . . .

"Neither of us knew then that she was your mother, of course. When I asked her name he said he wasn't even sure yet but gave me the name of the relative she'd been visiting for the last few weeks, um, Annie Kavyok. I phoned Annie and that's when I knew it was your mother who was hurt."

"Anything else you can tell me?"

She said there wasn't.

I keep flight times to the north in my head. There was one by Canadian Airlines to Edmonton at noon and on to Yellowknife after a stopover in late afternoon. I could catch it if I moved fast. "If you hear anything more, I should be at the Yellowknife Inn or the hospital around ten or a little after."

"How be I call you after you've seen your mother? Something for the morning report?"

"Sure."

Lois had appeared silently (we have thick rugs) in the kitchen doorway. She must have heard some of what I'd said. Probably the part about me being at the Yellowknife Inn that night. She was dressed to go out, wearing a suit that showed her off very nicely. The skirt just touched her kneecaps and her hair had been sculptured the way she liked it. She was holding her gloves. She never drives without them. Then I remembered where she might be going. This was Monday, the day some of the RCMP wives got together for lunch, drinks, sometimes bridge, a lot of gossip.

"Yes," she'd often say after I got home and told her the office news, "I knew that yesterday."

"What's that call about?" she asked now. "Obviously something in the *bloody North* again," speaking in audible italics.

"Yep, it's something in the '*bloody North*' again," I said. Lois had met my mother once soon after we were married, but apparently didn't really warm to a toothless old Inuit woman with a tattooed face and only one eye. Anyway, in all these years, nearly twenty of them, Lois had never campaigned for a rematch.

I told her what had happened to my mother. In the middle of it Lois shook her head and winced as if she were hearing her own words again, bitter words spoken most likely from habit when she might, even briefly, have given me a chance to explain before she spoke.

We had once cared for one another very much, and maybe, in a way that only seriously disaffected but still-together married people could understand, we still did. She said, "Oh, Matty, I'm sorry I was bitchy about it." She hesitated for several seconds, shaking her head. "It's just that . . . it seems you're always *going* somewhere . . ."

"I know," I said soothingly. "It's *okay*, Lois."

But she had regained her equilibrium. How dare I tell her what's okay, right? She doesn't need a pat on the head, right? "Don't patronize me!" I rolled my eyes, knowing how much she hated it when I did that. That line about patronizing—I couldn't help it. Civilization has come a long way since I was a kid, if a five foot six Inuk from Herschel Island could legitimately be accused of patronizing anybody. Even if it is just a dumb buzzword. Why is there no such word as *matronizing*? If there were, would it ever be used as an epithet? I wondered sometimes if it would have been better if we'd had children. But the time when we might have, the right time, had passed years ago without us really noticing. With modern means of contraception there are not many accidental births that in time become blessings. Each other was all we had. That had turned out to be not enough.

I thought of putting the phone down and making peace the Canadian way (peace at any price) by saying I was sorry, too; sorry for what I wouldn't know for sure, and it would take too long to figure it out, and anyway it would be for something I really had no control over.

So to hell, I'm not *that* Canadian.

I shrugged and began to dial. She turned away. As the airline answered, I was hearing our front door close. I booked a seat on the noon Canadian (it was 11:22 now), then called a taxi. Luckily, my big unpacked bag from the Labrador trip had what I'd need. I didn't have time to call the doctor, my first impulse, or the office.

When I got to the airport's departure lounge and did call, the doctor was unavailable. Then my office confirmed that I'd been right in suspecting that I'd be assigned to the case. I told them the flight I was on, didn't mention that I would have been going anyway because of my mother. That would have taken time. As it was, I was the last passenger to board.

On the flight west I didn't feel like reading or drinking or talking, and this left me with a lot of time to look out of the window and think. I was a kid again on the shore watching my mother in a kayak fighting a whale she had harpooned. I was out on the winter trail getting ready to move, the komatik overturned to repair and smooth out the mud on the runners and then, if we had warm water or tea left from breakfast, wiping the mud with what would become a slick thin layer of ice to make the komatik run easier for the dogs. If we had no warm fluid, my pee would do. "Why do you think boys are constructed as they are?" my mother once asked, and answered triumphantly, "It is for peeing on sled runners." I had a friend. Some mornings we used to stand at opposite ends of a fourteen-foot runner and try to have our streams meet in the middle.

Tears came to my eyes at the thought of her injured head, hating to think of her in pain and danger. There'd been the scare a few years ago of the cataract operation on her single eye, but that had worked out all right. I'd been there for the operation in Inuvik. When the doctor said it was successful, Maxine had put a brief item on the news and on the "Northern Messenger" radio program so that all through the north relatives and friends would hear that Aunt Bessie, as dozens or maybe hundreds affectionately called her, was still in business, and would be home near Holman soon.

Never in my whole life had my mother been anything but all right. I prayed both to God and, just in case, also to the goddess Sedna, who in our ancient tribal beliefs lives at the bottom of the sea and is sometimes visited there by shamans looking for direction.

For a while I thought about the exchange I'd just had with Lois. Some people, when faced with a choice between a bickering marriage and a conflict-free relationship outside of marriage, head for divorce. I don't know about Lois, but I had never seriously considered that way out. I'm not very profound on the subject, but on one level our marriage still bound me. Maybe it was partly because when I thought of Maxine, I couldn't imagine us married.

I remembered Maxine's younger sister Gloria, somewhat in her cups, her own life a serial disaster of disappearing lovers, mostly white, who just wanted to get her into bed, demanding to know why Maxine and I went along year after year as we did. Maxine had met my eyes and laughed. It may sound simpleminded, but I felt more comfortable evading the issue than going through the torture I'd seen in some others who tried to shuck off the remains of one marriage and head for another in what might seem to be love—but might not work either. If Maxine had been demanding I might have felt differently; but she never campaigned for more than we already had. In that, we were alike. Sufficient unto the day?

I thought of mother and Maxine, the first time they met, years ago. I was in Inuvik with a prisoner locked up and his statement being typed as to why he had killed one of his cousins (he hadn't liked this cousin, and besides they were sleeping with the same girl). Anyway, I had a couple of clear days. Maxine had time off coming to her. We were in her kitchen having coffee, talking about what we might do when she suddenly exclaimed, "Hey, Matteesie, two days! Why don't we go see your mother?"

We'd flown over to Holman. It was a risk. Not a risk on the married side of my life as it might be for a white man who would have to fear some sharp-eyed do-gooder hastening to call and tell the dear little wife at home what a faithless bugger she'd married. That was a different world entirely. The risk was that Maxine was

part Indian and my mother was from a generation where relations
between Inuit and Indians, especially among elders, had not quite
recovered from earlier centuries of territorial warfare, fighting,
murder, ambushes, bloody encounters almost every time the twain
did meet. The north's distant history was full of such events.

Mother had been wary, at first, as if accepting Maxine only
because she was with me. Then Maxine had taken over. After
asking Mother's permission, she had mixed flour, salt, baking powder, and water into a stiff dough, fried in lard, browned on both
sides—bannock. She had eaten muktuk, the edible part of beluga
whale found between outer skin and blubber, with every evidence
of enjoyment, while exclaiming as she listened to mother's blow-
by-blow account of the successful beluga hunt that had produced
enough muktuk for the whole settlement. She had scrutinized carefully and admired the tattoos on my mother's cheeks and chin and
upper lip. Braided my mother's long unruly hair that she couldn't
get her arms up to do by herself anymore. Tied ribbons around
the ends of the braids. Asked my mother many questions and then
listened as one should to the elders of a people, treating my mother
as I imagined she treated her own grandmother.

There was also the matter of the pipe. Normally Maxine smoked
many, many cigarettes. But on that trip she smoked a pipe that,
with an excited (for her) call of "Hey, this oughta help!" she'd
resurrected from a drawer just before we left her townhouse in
Inuvik. Claimed it had belonged to some man who had stayed
overnight sometimes with Gloria. She even had boiled the pipe to
get rid of germs. "Germs must live to a hell of an age, especially
that bastard's!"

There was an almost holy moment, for me, like watching a one-
on-one for an Olympic gold medal, when Maxine produced her
pipe and accepted some of the ferocious cut plug that my mother
smoked. They lit up. Mother inhaled happily. Maxine went pale
and her eyes bulged at her first puff but she did not gasp or choke,
only wiped her eyes a lot from time to time. Images . . .

Maxine and I are about the same age, middle forties. Years ago,
when we had just become lovers, both single, she a probationary
bedpan jockey at the Inuvik hospital and I an RCMP special con-

stable in the Inuvik detachment, we laughed a lot and figured our lowly lives were not that bad, especially in the loving part. But we never talked about a future, even then. The Mounties didn't encourage their men to marry and thus become less transferrable. As for Maxine, not long before we met she had almost married a young white doctor with whom she had a summer affair largely on the banks of the Bear river and who, in the grips of some mad delusion, had asked her to marry him. In preparation, he had taken her to his ancestral home in doggedly white Kingston, Ontario, to meet his folks. By the time she told me about it—"This is how crazy I was . . ."—she had made a funny story out of the first silent, strained family dinner in their grand old stone house at a long table with a white linen cloth bearing a puzzling number of silver forks, knives, and spoons. A few nights later she had sneaked out of the sleeping house to escape from Kingston forever by Greyhound bus. Four days later she'd landed in Yellowknife and worked as a waitress to get the money to fly to Inuvik and the hospital job she'd had when we met. She liked being single.

When we eventually parted I don't remember any long farewell or fervent promises for the future. I had applied and was sent to the RCMP training facility in Regina. A few years later, when I was working in Edmonton, my first posting "south," I met Lois, naturally fair-haired, lissomely beautiful, and in love with me, as I was with her. A while after that, we married.

I do remember, will not forget, how good it was until in a few years the physical part began to fade. A lot of people handle that, but with us it led to fights, recriminations, accusations that I was getting sex elsewhere, which at first I wasn't.

Next time I met Maxine she was in a journalism course at Arctic College. On graduation she got a job as a free-lance interpreter in English and her tribal tongue, Slavey, mainly in court work but increasingly in radio. When there was a CBC staff opening, she got it. By then I'd made sergeant in the RCMP and we seemed to be ready for each other, but as we were, she in her living space and I in mine.

Landing in Edmonton a little before five and facing a two-hour wait, I phoned the hospital in Yellowknife. I knew the switchboard operator and she knew me. "You want Dr. Butterfield, Inspector," she said. "I'll find him." As I waited, I could hear hollowly in the distance, "Dr. Butterfield, pick up a phone, please."

Quickly, one word, "Butterfield."

I said my name and that I was in Edmonton on my way to Yellowknife. "I'm calling about my mother, Bessie Apakaq."

"Ah, yes. You'll want to know all about it? Do you have a few minutes? I guess you do, being between planes. Reason I ask is I have to fly to Fort Reliance and won't be back until late tomorrow. I've been concerned that I wouldn't have a decent chance to talk to you before I left. Right. Okay. So far so good. I'll get right to it.

"To start with, we're pretty lucky so far. From there on, it gets a little technical, if you'll bear with me . . ."

I cherished the phrase *pretty lucky so far.*

"When I say lucky, this or almost any ninety-year-old woman has to be pretty osteoporotic, meaning bones get porous and therefore weak. In ordinary circumstances the kind of thing your mother experienced, let's say falling five feet on her head after being pushed quite hard, might very well crack her dome. Skull fracture. Add to that the greater likelihood of injury to her cervical spine and the arteriosclerotic vertebral arteries encased therein and we could have a very sick old lady . . ."

Some of the medical terms I knew from other cases and my reading in forensics.

"But those things didn't happen," he went on. "Which is not to say that the concussion she did suffer isn't painful. It is also not entirely free of danger. Her headache now comes from both the superficial trauma, bruising of her scalp, as well as a slight, we now believe, increase in intracranial pressure resulting from the severe bump on her head. This usually settles within one to five days with no residual side effects, and as it is now something like three days from when she was hurt, we are justified, I believe, in thinking that she is through the worst part. If she hadn't improved she would have had to go to Edmonton, probably, for a CT scan to look for a subarachnoid hemorrhage, which would have required intracranial surgery to arrest the bleeding, a perilous undertaking indeed in a lady her age. Are you with me so far?"

"I think so," I said rather faintly. "As long as I don't have to spell, uh, *subarachnoid,* is that what you said?"

"Right!" He laughed. A human laugh that made me feel good. "Now, just so you'll know it all, luckily the Sanirarsipaaq nursing station is in the charge of a very well qualified woman who called the doctor in Churchill, got instructions, and did everything right in the twenty-four hours before your mother was moved—had her on what we call a serious head injury routine. Her blood pressure was checked hourly, along with her pupillary reflexes. She had an intravenous to guard against shock and, to deter her falling into a coma, a danger in such cases, she was wakened every fifteen minutes.

"Once on the medivac plane, and after she arrived here, she was wakened hourly and from time to time her eyes were inspected with an ophthalmoscope—a small but penetrating light you've probably had used on yourself if you ever had eye trouble. But the fact is, now her headache is receding and if she is as well tomorrow as we expect, she'll be moved out of the hospital into a convalescent facility we have, Franklin House, which you probably are familiar with."

"I appreciate all you've done for her," I said, an inadequate line, but deeply heartfelt. "And for telling me about the last few days in such detail. Thank you very much."

"Not at all, not at all," he said. "I'm just glad the news is this good, so far." He hesitated, then I think I heard a sigh as he went on more slowly. "I would be remiss if I didn't add, however, that in a case of this sort, taking into account age, nature of the injury, and so on, there is always the chance that some condition we haven't detected could cause a relapse."

I took that in. "I'll either be in Yellowknife or the RCMP will know where to reach me, if needed."

"You mean you might be going to Sanirarsipaaq?"

"Probably," I said. "Not sure when, depending on mother's condition, but at the same time that I heard about her being hurt, I'd been detailed to Sanirarsipaaq."

"I'll make sure everybody here has instructions to find you, if anything happens."

T W O

When I reached the Yellowknife Inn that night, a message at the desk asked me to call Erika Hall from the *News/North* group of newspapers and news services, giving her home number. Erika's interest I understood. Although the murders by then were becoming old news, as soon as Maxine made the name connection and CBC Inuvik broadcast that the old woman hurt in the Sanirarsipaaq murders was my mother, the story had taken on a different aspect. She wasn't just any elder, she was Matteesie Kitologitak's mother. I'd picked up the Edmonton papers in my stopover there. The *Sun* covered it on the front with a photo of me in fur hat and parka and knee-highs from some other Arctic case, a red caption screaming, "Mother of the north's most famous cop roughed up during Sanirarsipaaq murders."

Erika Hall and I had known one another for years. Sometimes she'd helped me—reporters occasionally hear things that cops don't. I liked her, would call later, but dropped my bags, told the desk that I'd be back to check in, and took a cab to the hospital.

"Your mother is still dazed sometimes," the tall young duty intern told me matter-of-factly and went on with more or less a condensed version of Dr. Butterfield's report. "She's improving amazingly fast, for her age, but if she's asleep when you go in, wake her, it won't hurt."

I didn't have to. When I walked in with the nurse, a small and tidy Inuk who told me she was from Baker Lake and had heard a lot about me, mother was awake. She looked confused for an instant, then with her eye gleaming joyously reached out her arms to me. The nurse smiled approvingly, no doubt a story to be told later, then asked in Inuktitut if she wanted anything.

Mother reached into a glass for her upper denture, then said yes, she wanted her pipe and tobacco.

The nurse smiled politely but shook her head. Smoking in the room was forbidden, she said. Hospital rules. That's why the pipe and tobacco had been taken away . . . But what are sons for? I said, aw, come on. Without much persuasion, the nurse relented. I went into the corridor for a wheelchair and lifted my mother into it—so light now, this woman I could remember long ago walking straight and fast beside me while she carried a caribou carcass as easily as I was now carrying her.

The patients' lounge was nearly empty. We nodded around. I loaded her pipe, puffed on it, got it going, and handed it to her, rewarded by a thousand smiling wrinkles and the gleaming eye. If any passing hospital staffers noticed the clouds of pipe smoke, they looked the other way.

We talked quietly, with long pauses, some about family things, some about the trouble in Sanirarsipaaq. There were brief times when she fell silent and seemed disoriented. During one of those times she muttered something about "the shaman" and distinctly said "the shaman's knife is lost." When she was lucid again I asked her to explain what she'd meant by the reference to the shaman and a lost knife, but she didn't remember that at all, so I dropped it. There were also times when she moved her head suddenly, forgetting, and winced. After one of those times she had me feel the bump at the back of her head and explained that her braid, that thin braid that used to be a thick rope, and the thick hood of her second-best parka, which she had made herself long ago, had helped cushion the blow when she fell.

It was near one when I got back to the Yellowknife Inn, checked in, and was handed another message from Erika, saying to call her no matter how late. I thought about asking her up for a drink. I could use one, and some company. In the end I voted no to drink and company but did call and while the phone kept ringing I thought of Erika, white, thin, in her midthirties, sexually predatory in a pleasantly friendly kind of way, and originally from Edmonton.

At nineteen, a junior at *News/North,* she had married another reporter. She later referred to him only as "that shit," but the marriage did produce two sons. About all else I knew was that a year after her husband moved to a job in Vancouver they were divorced and she went back to *News/North* and was raising the children herself.

After the first sleepy hello she was wide awake. "Is your mother going to be okay, Matteesie?"

I still had reservations, but ignored them. "I think so." At the same time, I had a sudden worrying thought, a cop's thought, that mother was the only witness known to have seen whoever ran from the house, perhaps the murderer. Such a person would certainly realize that any witness could be a threat. I'd have to do something about that. For some reason I thought again of my mother's mutterings about the shaman and a knife he had lost, something that I could not connect to anything.

"First word we had was fractured skull."

"Yeah. But now it looks like bad concussion and a big headache."

"I understand she's being moved to Franklin House today if she keeps on improving." Franklin House was like a hospice for Inuit unlucky enough to be away from their far north homes while taking hospital treatment. "They told me they think she'll be better off convalescing outside of the hospital atmosphere for a week or two. And the hospital is short of beds."

"They told me," I said.

"Any chance to go see her at Franklin House with you and maybe do an interview with you both?"

I thought it over. I couldn't see why not. "If she gets upset, I'll just say so and you blow," I said.

We talked a bit more. When I hung up I called the hospital, got the nurse from Baker Lake, and told her that no one was to be allowed into my mother's room unaccompanied. I went to sleep with the worry somewhat receding. My mother was tough. That I knew from other things that had happened in her long life, some while I'd been there.

First phone call I got in my room that morning was from Maxine, at work, mostly brief and businesslike. I told her about Mother being well enough to move into Franklin House, and said I'd call her later when I knew what I'd be doing next.

The second call was from the Justice Department of the Northwest Territories, housed in a downtown building near the hotel. Justice wanted a taped account from mother because of the very concern that now kept nagging me; that she was the only witness, even though she'd told me she'd hardly seen a thing except someone big hurtling at her, running her down.

When I hung up from that call I made one of my own, to Corporal Steve Barker in Sanirarsipaaq. He did not sound happy to hear from me. He nosed around to find out if Ottawa had sent me to help him out—even though he must be expecting some sort of reinforcement from somewhere, with his holidays imminent and his temporary replacement, the Bouvier whom Maxine had mentioned, fairly new on the ground. He sounded a little more friendly when I told him I'd come mainly because of my mother being hurt. I was certainly going to get in on this case, with or without his invitation or Ottawa's orders, but he didn't have to know that yet.

"You got a suspect?" I asked.

"Well, just a few hunches," he said, and let that trail off.

"Tell me about your hunches."

"There's nothing clear enough, yet."

I said, "For Christ's sake! You must have something!"

He got the implication, which I guess wasn't all that difficult. "I can't tell you what I don't know!"

"This happened Friday, right? Like eighty hours ago? What've you been doing?"

"Maybe you better read my report."

"I can hardly wait." I hung up.

I let RCMP headquarters in Yellowknife know where I was, said I'd be over later, then went downstairs to eat breakfast at the street-level restaurant. It didn't have quite the atmosphere of the eating place that used to be there, called the Miners Mess. Still, the mainly male clientele at the long crowded tables was almost entirely native—Inuit, Dene, Metis. There were a few nonnatives as well. Some, both white and native, wore business suits. Parkas were hung on hooks or slung over chairbacks. There was a constant filing along the cafeteria line and people carrying trays looking for an empty chair. Some joined people they knew and took up conversations about last night's hockey games, weather, work. They took on sausages, pancakes, eggs, bacon, toast, English muffins, jam, honey, coffee, juice, a few pots of tea. I had the sausages, pancakes with butter and syrup, grapefruit juice, Earl Grey tea. Some men stopped briefly to talk. Some who didn't know me but had read or heard about my mother, asked about her. Two or three wondered if I was headed for Sanirarsipaaq.

It was a pleasantly sunny morning, about minus seven Celsius. I walked to the hospital and rode with Mother in the ambulance the few blocks to Franklin House, where Erika and a lanky young man from Justice, Al Hopkins, were waiting. Mother seemed to have continued to improve overnight. When she was settled in her wheelchair in the lounge with other Inuit nearby sewing, talking, reading, watching a game show on TV, I explained to her why the man from Justice was there (he'd told me he was normally a court clerk), and who Erika was, and that we just wanted to hear her recollections of what had happened.

Fairly quickly she warmed to the idea. She spoke in Inuktitut. I translated. I could sense that Al Hopkins from Justice, although white, hardly needed the translations. When I asked how come, he told me that his parents had been schoolteachers in Gjoa Haven. He'd learned in schoolyards and on the street and at the weekly all-Inuktitut service at the church to speak Inuktitut fluently. Later he had gone to high school in Iqaluit, earned a scholarship to Lakefield College School in Ontario, and intended to go back to school in Alberta and study law. He taped both the Inuktitut and the English (in case the tape had to be used later in a court where lawyers wanted to split hairs about meanings in either language). Erika was also taping and making notes.

All this took place under the shyly watchful eyes of other Inuit

waiting for operations or to give birth or, like my mother, convalescing after a stay in hospital. Franklin House is all Inuit, including the cooking (or lack thereof, in cases where some older
ones, from habit, might prefer their fish or caribou raw and frozen).
For people from settlements and hunting families far to the north
Franklin House helps smooth the heavier aspects of culture shock
and loneliness for home and family. All seemed to listen, but
unobtrusively, as my mother got to the part about hearing screams
and shouts and other sounds of fighting next door to where she'd
been staying in Sanirarsipaaq. She told how she had pounded on
the wall and when that brought no results, had gone outside and
was slipping and sliding across the hardpacked snow and ice to see
what was happening when someone burst out of the door and
knocked her down and ran over her.

I had a sudden idea. "A man?" I asked.

All the earlier reports had said, or seemed to assume, a man,
but in the north men and women often wore the same type of
clothing. She started to answer, then paused, shrugged, and said
she thought so, but wasn't certain.

She demonstrated with waving hands that the running person
was just a silhouette against the light from the doorway, so she
really hadn't been able to see clearly.

I asked what happened next. She shook her head hazily, didn't
know. Erika took up the slack. "According to the story we had,
a man who lives out that way was coming home and saw her lying
there outside the open door. He didn't know how long she'd
been there. He went into the house a few steps and saw a lot of
blood then ran next door to your relative's house, Matteesie, where
she'd come from, and called police. Then he helped your mother
to her feet and back home. When the duty Mountie got there and
went inside the house he found the young guy dead, badly beaten,
in his upstairs bedroom. The guy's grandmother was on a sofa
downstairs, everything covered with blood. She died before she
could be moved."

I told my mother this in Inuktitut. Then she took over again,
quickly skipping over the next time period until she used the word
for a medical evacuation which is the same in both English and

Inuktitut, *medivac.* When she said that and I repeated it in my translation, her eye flicked briefly from me to other members of the audience, touching her head and murmuring, "*Aannipaa,*" the word for "hurts," and paused to light her pipe before she went on.

In that way, from her account and interjections from others, the bare bones of what was known so far emerged. My mother had been staying in Sanirarsipaaq with a great-niece, Annie Kavyok, one of my more educated relatives, an Arctic College graduate in social work. Her work in that line for the government of the Northwest Territories meant she qualified for one of the subsidized houses that the government was building in settlements throughout the Arctic.

Mother had gone to Sanirarsipaaq on Annie's invitation for a gathering of elders for feasting and drum dancing and throat singing as well as modern dancing for the younger folk—the usual community celebration to mark the end of what we called the dark days, the five or six weeks in December and January when the sun never got above the horizon. Then she'd stayed on, enjoying the rapidly lengthening days and the company of Annie Kavyok, who had never married but had borne two kids, not an unusual situation among some of our people.

That Friday the plane had brought the weekly liquor and beer orders for those considered by Sanirarsipaaq's alcohol committee—Corporal Steve Barker, chairman—to be respectable enough to order booze from outside. That same night, while no doubt a lot of the newly arrived alcohol was being consumed, Annie had gone to a meeting at the rec hall and left my mother with her young ones, a girl thirteen and a boy fourteen. Mother digressed there to say, with frowns and grimaces, that she would have gone to the meeting herself, the kids were old enough to stay alone, if the meeting had been for bingo or almost anything except yet another palaver about what to do with Annie's committee on drunks, drugs, single-parent families, and so on, stuff about which she'd heard too much already. In what appeared to be a favorite, well-honed complaint, she noted that in her early days drunks were entirely seasonal, corresponding to when the people she was with visited the trading post to deal furs for guns, ammunition, tea, sugar, flour and the like. Usually someone around the settlement had a store of *immiugaq* (home-brew). Now booze came in by weekly planeload and everybody got drunk. Her face said she didn't like that at all.

As to single-parent families, she only said, "What's that, anyway?" I had to smile. Obviously the very phrase bugged her. She'd come from a nomadic time all across the Arctic when people moved together according to the seasons, sharing hardships, food, hunger, responsibility for children, and sometimes sex partners.

Anyway, as she told it, that night she had stayed home with the kids. When Annie came in tired and went to bed, my mother and the kids were playing cards, finishing one more game before bed. They'd been hard at it when this almighty ruckus started in the house next door, thumps and screams and voices sounding through the thin common wall to the next unit. Annie grumbled sleepily in her room upstairs but didn't wake up. As the uproar went on, Mother finally went next door to check, with the results we'd already heard. That, she said, was about all she knew about the matter.

The young man from Justice waited a minute to see if there was more, then shut off the tape.

When he left, Erika stayed, making occasional notes as she went to talk to the quiet and shy Inuit women who'd been watching and listening. I could see her getting names and taking pictures, for whatever she was going to do with this. Mother sat quietly, smoking her pipe, looking quite content while she and I chatted about matters of the moment, the impending springtime, her thoughts about whether she should go home to Holman or back to Sani-rarsipaaq. I didn't advise her on that one way or another and after a few minutes other thoughts took over.

I knew I should report in person to headquarters here, Yellowknife being the administrative centre for the RCMP's huge G Division, covering detachments large and small, mostly small—a man or two—throughout the whole Northwest Territories. Then I should call Ottawa to see if they'd heard anything new on the case. I was rising from Mother's side when I caught, across the room, a look from Erika as she returned from a phone call she'd been called out to take.

"This might be nothing," Erika said, "but we've got a young Inuk, Byron Anolak, graduate of Arctic College journalism, can't get a regular job but strings for us in Sanirarsipaaq.

"He just called. Of course, everybody's talking up there about who could have done it, and so on, but he said on the phone— said it in a low voice, actually, I had to get him to repeat it—that there's some talk that shamanism has something to do with the murders."

I don't think I showed it, but I felt a jolt. There hadn't been a shamanistic-connected murder in my lifetime, that I'd ever heard about. Of course, the reference was to men and women who, as shamans, were the chief instruments of the fairly complicated set of tribal beliefs and legends that all our people once lived by. That was before Anglican and Roman Catholic missionaries spread through the Arctic building churches and teaching the Christian version of what life was all about. Harvesting souls, they saw it as. "Bringing in the sheaves . . ." I remembered the hymn.

But whatever the missionaries did, or thought they did . . . well, you can't wipe out ten or twenty or thirty centuries of beliefs, including shamanism, just by teaching a lot of people to sing "The Old Rugged Cross," "What a Friend We Have in Jesus," and the like. There were shamans around still. Their activity certainly didn't exist anymore on the old scale, but in most communities the elders kept in touch.

It was true that a lot of our people, even most of them, did go to church, or mass, for reasons that ranged from real Christian belief to just the idea that most of the missionaries did help people in various ways, and it was only polite to show gratitude. Going to church and listening to a priest or lay reader denounce booze (easily agreed with) or find fault over sex or whatever, pleased the missionaries, so why not?

Still shamans remained, more active in some communities than in others. One Anglican priest had told me on my last trip north that there was an upsurge of interest among the young—even a worrying rumor that, in some places, Satanism had been involved, imported from the south, a frightening perversion of what the old shamanism, mostly helpful, had meant to our people.

Defensively, to Erika: "But shamans—I knew some when I was a little kid, and not such a little kid, and still know a few now—are almost always trying to help somebody. Drive out sickness or madness, bring changes in weather, improve the hunting. Except in some of the old stories people tell I've never heard about shamanism being connected to killings, unless it was to help people who'd asked for help and were being threatened in some way."

"What about Sanikiluaq back in the early forties? The famous Belcher Island murders? What was it, nine murdered? Or eleven?"

I sighed. Once I had dug out and read the transcript of the 1941 trial of the Belcher murders, as well as microfilm of stories written by a *Toronto Star* reporter, William Kinmond, who had flown in to cover the case. That terrible few weeks in the Belchers, an island group in the southern part of Hudson Bay now called Sanikiluaq, was a black blotch in the north's history, a terrible reminder of what a tiny sampling of a new (to them) religion can do to primitive people.

What happened was that a missionary had come in, holding revival meetings, thundering away about the second coming of Christ, the holy trinity, and so on. Then the missionary had left, never to return, the damage done. In the dark days of that winter one man, hallucinating, gone mad, whatever, had convinced himself that he was Jesus, back to save not only the sinners of the Belcher islands, but the world. Another had got on the bandwagon with the red-hot news that he was the Holy Spirit.

These and their few followers were steadily and sanely opposed by people who knew these claimants to such high estate were not holy spirits at all but ordinary humans who somehow had become full of shit. These opponents were methodically, madly, shot or beaten to death or both by the new deities and by their followers. One woman left her husband's bed (he was an unbeliever, later killed) in favor of the new Jesus's. She subsequently led other women and children out onto the ice, exhorting them in the name of the Lord to take off all their clothes, that they did not need clothes when going to meet their Maker. Some argued and turned back but others died, frozen, out on the ice.

"The Belcher murders had nothing to do with shamanism!" I said, raising my voice. I saw Mother turn her eye to me, puzzled at my tone. She could not have understood the words—in her time and for many years later there had been none of the boarding schools that took kids away from their families and insisted that we all learn English. "That was nutty Christianity! Or black Christianity!"

But abruptly I thought, there is at least one shaman that I've heard of in Sanirarsipaaq, a famous carver named Jonassie. Also, somebody had told me that almost all the Sanirarsipaaq carvings and drawings even these days had shamanistic themes; a much greater proportion than was found in the many other communities where Inuit art flourished. That didn't necessarily mean anything, but . . .

"How did your stringer link shamanism to what happened?"

"I don't know. I don't think he knows. I asked him. He just said some people around town were talking like that . . ."

Even the mention of shamanism having some evil intent had made me feel uneasy. I was usually easy with Erika. She quickly noticed the change and changed gears, saying hastily, "I just thought I'd tell you . . . As I said, maybe it means nothing.

"Anyway, mostly what I want is"—and she said it very simply— "to know more about your mother. Often when I interview elders they're shy, or the translator is shy, I have the feeling I don't get it all. I don't have that feeling with you and your mother. I'd just do *anything* for another few minutes with her!"

I laughed. She was like that sometimes, a whiz at overstatement. "*Anything?* What d'you have in mind?"

She flushed, then laughed. "You can go to hell! But I *would* buy you lunch."

Another few minutes' delay in making my rounds wouldn't hurt. Our people are wonderful storytellers. Until we had a written language, telling stories was the way our culture survived. As a boy and young man I'd been in many a snow house redolently jammed with fur-clad bodies and ringing with laughter and sighs and groans as stories were told and centuries of the real and imagined unfolded, including accounts of shamanism. Now here at Franklin House in downtown Yellowknife, an alien city far from their roots, we were in a room of Inuit waiting in deep boredom and loneliness for life to begin again when they could go home to their relatives, children, open spaces, their real lives. Some talk about our people's past might help some feel that this too, their stay in Yellowknife, would pass. A lot of old Inuit women had stories. I felt love for this particular one. Every time my mother spoke about the past I knew a little more about both of us.

"Okay," I said to Erika, and told my mother that Erika wanted to ask some questions, not about the murders, and we began.

Erika asked politely what life was like among my mother's people when she was a girl. I translated. Mother's level husky voice began.

In the earlier questioning, she had caught the rhythm of speaking, pausing, me picking it up and then pausing when it was her turn again. I didn't always translate verbatim . . .

"When my mother was a child, she says, she used to travel with her family and friends or relatives on the ice or land or water, depending on the season, along the coast of the Beaufort Sea and Amundsen Gulf and sometimes inland, always pursuing food. When the children were hungry they cried, so if there wasn't enough food for everyone, adults went without, because when they were hungry they did not cry. When there was lots of food they ate when they felt like it, not at any set time. When she became older and had a man, in the summer she would rise each morning and prepare what food they had, in good times any kind of meat, whale, seal, caribou, musk-ox, Arctic hare, ptarmigan; in bad times little or nothing until a hunter was successful. Then she would do other jobs left to women in a camp, cleaning seal and caribou and other skins to sell or sew into winter clothing that could be used or sold, making mukluks (boots), fetching water in summer or melting snow in winter to make tea.

"In the fall when the cold weather came they would freeze caribou, seal, sometimes bear and other meat by cutting it in strips and laying it on top of the tent or igloo. If there was tea they would have it to drink, but if they had run out of tea the women would make tea out of berries. In those days almost all the time was spent hunting or traveling to find places where there was food to hunt."

"Ask her more about what the hunting was like," Erika said.

"When she was a young girl, before almost all hunters had guns and ammunition from trading furs at Hudson Bay company posts, the most dangerous hunt was for the polar bear, using spears and knives . . ."

I interrupted myself to say to my mother in Inuktituk, "Most dangerous? What about the barrenground grizzly?"

That is the fiercest Arctic animal of all, now dwindling in numbers, endangered. This question, which I then translated, was entirely for Erika. I knew the answer.

"No hunt!" my mother burst out. "Run!"

In the ensuing laughter, mother went on about polar bears, squinting her single eye not only at Erika and me but at others around the room who had stopped everything to listen.

"If the hunters had no guns or ammunition, the dogs would get the bear stopped by circling him. When he swatted at the dogs on one side, others would dash in and out nipping and biting, so he was always whirling, but for a hunting party with no guns the hard part was getting close enough to stab the bear. They would try various means. Such as, tie a knife or spear to a pole and try to stab the bear on one of its front feet with that or a long-handled spear. If the bear was stabbed on a front foot, it would be unbalanced and not as good at swatting with the other foot."

She thought for a minute and then continued.

"Or a hunter might dive under the bear and stab it from below . . ."

I couldn't quite imagine anybody being that brave, or foolhardy, but who was I to say? Anyway, my mother had stopped, shaking her head as if she did not blame anyone for not believing that, and after a minute she went on, changing the subject.

"A lot of time was spent having babies and looking after them," I translated. "She gave birth to fourteen, of which two died . . ."

At this point my mother jerked her head toward me, smiling as she spoke. I smiled back. Erika asked, "What's that about?"

I said, "She said that I was one who didn't die."

"Ask her more about giving birth out there in the tent or igloo or wherever. It must have been pretty, ah . . ." I think she was going to say primitive.

I asked, but knew something about the answer. I'd been at birthings a few times out on the trail, although none were hers. I had been her last child, born when she was forty-five.

"She says she always preferred to give birth alone except for a woman or two who could help," I began rather pedantically, but while I spoke my mother, not pedantic at all, moved slowly and painfully out of her chair and kneeled on the floor, legs spread wide apart, with her hands braced against her chair, looking at me expectantly.

"She is showing you the most comfortable position for giving birth," I explained, grinning at Erika's wide-eyed reaction, then hurried to catch up with the flow as my mother kept talking while laboriously getting back into her chair.

"When the baby came out and started crying," she said and I repeated in English, "then someone in the family, or a friend, would cut and tie off both ends of the umbilical cord. Sometimes cutting the cord would be done with an *ulu* or even a snow knife . . ."

The *ulu* was the sharp crescent-shaped knife blade women used for everything, including scraping hides; the snow knife was much bigger, and used for cutting blocks to build igloos.

"When she got pregnant the only way she would know was because she wouldn't menstruate. Then she would get bigger, of course, but never knew for sure when the birth would come until she started to have pains."

At that point I had to stop and smile when she was talking, before I went on in English. "Her last child was born when the family was on a long move to a winter camp," I said. "The pains came on so suddenly and so close together that she was still trying to get her pants off when the baby was born."

Mother was laughing at the memory, looking around at us with her eye flashing, her mouth open, the ruined lower teeth showing below the upper dentures and above her heavy lower lip as she laughed, her hair straggling over her dressing gown with the two thin braids hanging one over each shoulder. She was pointing at me and nodding meaningfully.

"Matteesie!" Erika said. "You?"

"That's what they tell me," I said. "I always figured that having to fight my way through a pair of caribou-hide pants to get born was what made me so short."

I translated that for mother and the place was rocking with laughter, the story going from group to group around us.

I was thinking that this laughter was not a bad way to exit—I didn't want to tire Mother—when the huge middle-aged Inuit woman named Sophie from Cape Dorset, who managed Franklin House, came in. "Matteesie, you're wanted on the phone."

"Will you ask them to hold a minute?" I asked. "We're just finished here." Erika caught the cue and rose immediately. "Can I get a quick picture of the two of you together? Then I'll get out."

I stood beside my mother and put one hand on her shoulder. She covered it with her own. The photo was taken. I said in Inuktitut to Sophie that maybe my mother should have some rest now in her room, then to my mother that I would be back in a minute. When I left the lounge, some of the other women, the young and pregnant and the sick and mostly old, were chattering among themselves about stabbing a polar bear on the foot so it couldn't fight as well.

They didn't believe that any hunter would dive under the bear and try to get it from below. But, pointing at me and laughing as I left, they certainly did believe the part about me being born on the trail to winter camp before my mother could get her pants down.

T H R E E

The telephone was in the entrance hall. I picked it up and said
hello. The voice at the other end was the RCMP commissioner's
motherly, even grandmotherly, Québecoise secretary at headquarters in Ottawa. "Buster wants you, Matty." She was the only
person at headquarters who openly called the commissioner
Buster. In turn, her nickname among the rest of us was Old
Ironsides, mainly because she still wore massive "foundation
garments."

"Tell me what it's for, so you can tell him you couldn't find me
if I don't like it."

She said, "No, but what he has in mind I think you're going to
like." Pause. "Oh, he's just picked up another line. I'll put you
through when he's finished. Anyway, I wanted to say I'm real sorry
about your mother and we've been wondering how she is this
morning?" I told her what we'd been doing and she said, "Darn,
that's good, great that she feels up to it, sounds like fun!" And
then, abruptly, "He's taken another call. I'll have to put you on
hold."

She had started with the RCMP as a teenage typist from her
French-speaking home across the river in Hull, and had stayed
through the reigns of several commissioners before Buster. One
of her sons was in the force, too, which might have been why I'd
got in the habit, whenever Buster called me directly, as he did

from time to time, of trying to get an advance tip from her as to what it was about. Often enough it seemed she'd feel that a cop out in the blue somewhere, faced with God knows what, might benefit from a little preparation before dealing with the force's highest of the high.

Also, she knew that Buster had practically invented me, in my present role. In my late twenties, after being an RCMP special constable in the north for years, I'd been accepted to take the full officer's course at the RCMP training establishment in Regina. He was commanding officer there and from the start took a special interest in me.

Turned out, I found later, that after several stints in the Arctic himself, he'd written a lot of memos urging that more natives should be recruited and trained for general police work. A natural place to look for candidates had been among us specials, whose main work was not so much policing as helping white officers, doing the joe jobs around detachments, a dead end. When Buster's memos bore fruit, I had been asked if I was interested and had jumped at it. In Regina, there were thirty in the class, and I was the only native. If I didn't do well, I knew that I'd have to go back, maybe forever, to being a special.

I was determined not to forfeit this chance and as it turned out, I didn't. At graduation, when Buster called us up, he did it as usual in reverse order to our final marks. As the marks got higher and higher and I still hadn't been called, my tension and joy rose—and I was the last one he called to the podium. I remember that as I walked across the stage he watched me with an oddly quizzical look. When I stopped in front of him, hardly believing that I'd passed with the highest marks in the class, I came just to his malletlike chin. He'd played college football for Queen's and then briefly pro for the Ottawa Roughriders before joining the police. I felt like a boy scout meeting a giant. Everybody was applauding except maybe a few who thought natives in the force should forever be there for chopping wood, cooking, doing dishes, hunting or fishing for dog food, translating on occasion, doing real police work only when there was no white man around to take charge.

But there was no doubt about Buster's beaming "Way to go,

Matteesie!" Then he added something I didn't fully understand at the time: "We'll be seeing one another as we go along."

All I thought was, sure, we're national police, we do police work right across the country. We tend not to be left in one place long. We're bound to meet occasionally. I figured that was what he meant.

What I didn't know was that he'd already got his next posting to become officer commanding the big Inuvik subdivision, with about five dozen all ranks from specials on up. He told me years later when we got to know one another better: "When you were walking toward me on that platform in Regina, I had a sudden thought that with all the territory we cover in the Arctic we should have a unit that specializes in native crime, and that you were the first guy who seemed to have the qualities to make it work."

Actually, whether a native investigative unit was a good idea or not, it never really came about except in a somewhat different form—establishing at headquarters in the late 1980s the Community and Aboriginal Policing Directorate, a mainly aboriginal group to advise on setting up separate aboriginal police forces. As Buster went on and up to bigger jobs, we often met and discussed cases in accord with one of his specialties, talking man to man. But if anything was needed to finally cement the relationship, even move it to another level, it came late one night in Inuvik a couple of days before a royal tour was supposed to arrive. I was a sergeant by then, assigned to local security. He, with the rank of deputy commissioner, was in charge of security for the whole tour. He'd come early to Inuvik because a protest by western Arctic Inuit showed signs of erupting into militance, not against the visiting royals, but to use the media throng covering the royal visit as a vehicle to draw attention to a long-delayed land-claim settlement.

He called me to his room at the Mackenzie Hotel. "Would you go and talk to them, see what you can do?" he asked.

I did. It turned out to be actually not all that difficult. The protesters included many Inuit that I knew well and respected, and they knew this. On the night before the royals were to fly in, at the meeting the Inuit held to plan their strategy, I managed to get to a microphone. Speaking in Inuktitut, I told them what I believed, that we as a people generally speaking didn't have much to beef about. We had schools, medicare, social assistance; there was not an aboriginal people anywhere in the world who had been treated as well as we had.

"I support what you are trying to do, getting the land claims settlement, and would like to see it done faster, but I'm just asking that you find some other way than this to put pressure on the government. As you know, I am an Inuk. You are my people. But part of my police job is to see that whoever wants to see the royals in this once-in-a-lifetime visit to our land should get to see them, without violence or difficulty or anything that would damage our reputation as reasonable people.

"What I am asking is that you call off the public protest you have planned, which no doubt will get out on a lot of TV news programs but I don't think will do anything to speed the land claims. What I am offering is that I will sign the document you have drawn up and hope to present to the royals. I will sign it as Sergeant Matthew Kitologitak, RCMP, senior native officer in charge of security."

There was a deep silence, then murmurs for and against.

What really turned the tide was when I said, "It took me ten years to get to be a sergeant! You are my people. I'm signing your protest and maybe risking my job by doing that. You wouldn't want to do something, some real disruption, that would have me broken back down to special constable, would you, back to being just Matteesie, the special?"

I don't know whether that should have worked, but it did. My people like to laugh. They laughed! They came up and said, "Hey, Matteesie, what a comedown to be a special again! Maybe you'll be lucky and get assigned to Paulatuk!"

Many reporters assigned to the royal tour had covered the meeting. My plea got a lot of mileage across the country. The idea that I had put my job on the line to support my own people had a sort of romance that the media loves—especially, I found, the English press, which has lots of experience in covering royals among distant tribes and falls gratefully on any change from the rather boring respectful norm.

On the appointed day the visit, including handing the royals our petition, went off without incident. When the press, the royals, the welcoming and farewell committees, and stray dignitaries gathered at the airport to fly out, Buster pushed through and stood in front of me with a little grin twitching at the corners of his mouth. All he said, shaking hands, was, "Well done!"

But the other effect was that the whole incident, the well-reported meeting, the flourish with which I signed the petition, the TV film of my people laughing and pushing forward to joke at me, made me a name, however briefly. In Cece MacAuley's *News/North* column she termed me "a native who stood up to be counted, without turning his back on his people." And she is Metis, not Inuit.

All of this, I think, also made it easier for Buster to push me along, give me breaks that I might not have got otherwise. Over the years, as he rose higher and his influence grew, he pushed courses at me that the force paid for, forensics at University of Toronto, criminal psychology at Michigan State, even a year at Princeton studying, as I used to say, the morning paper.

What he had in mind—laugh if you want to, some in the police did—was to make me a well-rounded native cop by moving me along in a way that made use of my Inuit beginnings but equipped me to operate in the white world. Whenever there was a case that he saw as being specifically Matteesie Kitologitak's, quite often he jumped in personally instead of passing things along through deputy commissioners or superintendents or anyone else. I thought of him in command of the vast fortresslike headquarters in Ottawa, a huge job, but the Arctic, it seemed, was still his baby. When something up here sounded like me, usually it would be his voice I heard on the phone. We talked often. This time, after I had stood a while at the phone in the corridor at Franklin House, finally I was put through to him.

"Matteesie! How's your mother?"

I told him what I'd told Old Ironsides.

"You want to stay there for a while, see her out of the woods? I know we had you ticketed for Sanirarsipaaq, but that was before we knew she'd been hurt in that damn thing. But I've just been looking at the preliminary report from the detachment. Not much in it. Whatever the reason, we sure as hell need somebody else on the scene fast."

He was giving me the opening, and I knew it.

I took a deep breath, and said my piece honestly. "Tell you the truth, sir, there's nothing much I can do here. I can always get back in a hurry if . . . if I'm needed. And one more thing . . ."

"What's that?"

"I'd go crazy here if we kept on getting zeros out of Sanirarsipaaq. What I mean is, yeah, I'm on my way, quick as I can."

"Good man! That makes me feel a lot better." Brief pause. "Ah, one other thing. I know you left in a hell of a hurry after getting back from Nain. Is there anything that needs doing around your house that I can send somebody to help Lois with?"

A kid shovels the walk and the drive. She's got a car. Maybe somebody who would kiss and hug a lot as we once did, who would send her flowers and take her to bed would help. "Can't think of anything," I said.

At that moment I heard another phone ring in his office and he said, "Look, I'll be out for a couple of hours, but get me for sure again before you leave, I've just got a note handed to me saying there's some other stuff on the case coming in." Abruptly, he hung up.

I saw my mother to her room, a single, and into bed, and touched her sore head gently and told her I was going to Sanirarsipaaq. She just nodded as if that was no surprise, no more than she had expected from her son the policeman. Tiptoeing out, waving back at her from the door, I then skipped an invitation for lunch with Erika, who had hung around waiting. We walked down the street together. She kissed me warmly when we parted in front of the Yellowknife Inn.

"Good for my image," she said, "neckin' with the great Matteesie in public."

"Not bad for mine, either."

"Thanks for the help, Matteesie."

A few yards down the street she turned and waved. I like people

who do that, rather than marching off as if that's that. Sometimes
the way Erika acted made me thoughtful about where we might
go from here if I didn't already have Lois and Maxine. But I know
that although men and women being attracted to one another
outside of marriage is a fairly well known human condition, usually
not acted upon, out in the open it looks like a bad thought, like
that line in one of Leon Redbone's songs, "She ain't Rose. But
she ain't bad. And Rose ain't here."

For shame, Matteesie.

In downtown Yellowknife, RCMP G Division headquarters, Justice Department offices and courts, other government offices, the
liquor store, drugstore, hotels, bars, the Wildcat Cafe, the ram-
shackle *News/North* building, bums, shopping, travel agencies, you
name it, are all a short stroll apart.

I checked in at headquarters and went straight to Superintendent
Abe Keswick, with whom I'd worked often over the years. When
I requested a guard put on my mother twenty-four hours a day he
stared at me, startled, and then got it.

"Sole witness," he said.

"Right."

"We'll start it right now." He picked up his phone.

From his office I went to records to read whatever was on file
about the last few days in Sanirarsipaaq, including the same file
Buster had received by fax. I learned little I didn't already know,
except that the young man who had been murdered, Dennis Raakwap, had a couple of hundred dollars in his pocket at the time.
Meaning on the face of it that robbery didn't seem to have been
the motive. There was also a mention in an internal memo from
someone in G Division personnel that with Barker going on leave
and Corporal Alphonse Bouvier having been there only a few
weeks from Spence Bay as his replacement, the detachment could
use someone else, pronto. Buster and I had solved that one in our
phone call. I read also that a forensics specialist would be moving
in as soon as possible, maybe a couple of days, to check out the
house. The file said that the bodies would be flown out under
guard and turned over to forensics, all of that being procedure,

by the book. Unless I got there before they left, I wouldn't have a chance to look at them myself and maybe see a few things Barker and Bouvier hadn't noticed—so I should get there today. Fast.

There's one thing I didn't do right then, but only realized later that I should have: send an order that the bodies were not to be moved until I'd seen them.

I looked at air schedules. Not good. Regular commercial flights by First Air went to Sanirarsipaaq a few times a week, but from Iqaluit in the eastern Arctic, not from Yellowknife. There was one today, west from Iqaluit with stops at Igloolik, Pelly Bay, Spence Bay, Gjoa Haven, Cambridge Bay, and Sanirarsipaaq before terminating in Inuvik. Meaning that to catch that flight I had to get to Cambridge Bay, with no scheduled flight that I knew of that would get me to Cambridge from Yellowknife.

I went to the headquarters dispatcher, a sergeant I knew well. He asked about my mother. I told him, hurriedly, then asked, "Anything flying today to Cambridge quick? Charter, medivac, anything?"

He looked at me sharply the way some people do when dealing with a problem that must be solved fast. "You wanta get to Sanirarsipaaq. Just missed a Twin Otter charter from here straight in there a few hours ago. Well. We still got one chance." He picked up his phone and dialed. "Shit. Busy." Immediately he began to dial again. "If this works it'll be very sudden. Get your luggage into the hotel lobby. I'll call you there in a few minutes."

The hotel was only a minute or two away. I was in the lobby checking out when the desk clerk said, "Matteesie, call for you," and passed me the phone. It was my friend the dispatcher. He'd known when he spoke to me that a Cessna Citation had been chartered to fly the Supreme Court of the Northwest Territories out to begin a trial in Cambridge Bay starting tomorrow morning. What he hadn't known was whether there was a spare seat, or someone he could bump. Whatever he'd done, there was room for me. The Citation would drop the court in Cambridge but couldn't go on with me to Sanirarsipaaq because it had to head back right away for another charter somewhere else. It was due to leave in less than an hour. I should get to the airport right away. He gave me all that very fast.

"It'll be a tight squeeze at Cambridge," he said, "but I'll get on to First Air to hold their Sanirarsipaaq flight there for you."

"Thanks, pal."

"No problem."

Some busy guys are like that. Work their ass off and then shrug. All in a day's work.

I passed the phone back to the hotel clerk, thinking, Buster had asked me to call him back. In case it took time to track him down I'd be better calling from the airport. If I didn't get him from there I could call from Cambridge Bay.

On the taxi ride to the airport I pored over again in my mind what I knew of the case so far, coming to admit that the stakes were partly personal, even a lot personal. I'm normally objective about my work, but I had a totally unobjective hatred for whoever hurt my mother. The murders weren't all that nice, either, and I would pay attention to that, but also I wanted to look into the eyes of whoever had knocked my mother on her back ninety bloody years of living after she'd been born in an igloo on the shore of Herschel Island. My intent did not involve beating hell out of someone. If it came to that, I might get the hell beaten out of me, which would be counterproductive. I wanted it to be cold turkey, looking into guilty eyes, letting whoever it was know that retribution would be swift.

Not a hell of a lot to ask. Especially when I knew deep down that if my mother's frail condition had got worse and she had not lived, I might be tempted to kill whoever was responsible. Tit-for-tat murders do not all happen in Northern Ireland, or in the hills of Kentucky. Blood feuds were part of many an Inuit settlement's past.

The Citation was on the tarmac. Its pilot, a fit-looking middle-aged man with silvery hair under his cap, was watching for me in the terminal. Somebody else (it turned out to have been Erika) had been bumped from the flight, Buster's emissaries being very high in the priority line. "The court hasn't arrived yet," the pilot said crisply. "When they get here follow them out right away and we'll go. Weather is chancy as hell around Cambridge right now."

I went to the pay phone and called Buster. Old Ironsides said she'd find him. A minute or two later Buster came on.

"Matty! Look, I have something else to tell you. Might be important. Our press relations officer has had a lot of calls from media people in the east asking who they can call in Sanirarsipaaq for an update on those murders. He's been giving out the detachment's phone number because as we both know, some officers on the scene like to get their own names in the paper. This morning one of the reporters called Sanirarsipaaq with questions about shamanism. He specifically asked Bouvier about a rumor that the murders had a shamanistic connection. You know reporters. Two murders and shamanism too, they'll be peeing their pants. This guy wouldn't say where the rumor came from."

I wondered if Erika Hall was maybe stringing for an eastern paper and had raised the shamanism matter.

"Anyway," Buster went on, "Corporal Bouvier stonewalled the guy but did call our information officer to say that sometime overnight a note addressed to Barker was found pinned to the notice board at the rec hall. Nobody saw it being put there. The note wasn't signed, but named and blamed a shaman named Jonassie . . . know him?"

"Jonassie Oquataq, yeah. He's a shaman, all right, and a master carver. He did that green soapstone polar bear and walrus item in your office. Has stuff in the best Inuit art collections in the world—Winnipeg Art Gallery, UBC, National Gallery, and others."

I didn't mention right then to Buster a rather light note, when talking about shamans: that this shaman's twin brother was an Anglican priest in some other community, I wasn't sure which. The Anglicans had opened their ranks to Inuit, with a good deal of success that the Catholics couldn't possibly counter because Anglican priests can get married, or whatever. To your average Inuit, that makes some sense, while they feel that Roman Catholic celibacy rules are not quite of this world. Which might, of course, be the idea.

"Anyway," Buster went on, "this note said that this Jonassie had used his shamanistic powers to cause the murders. Not sure whether the media knows about that yet, but" . . . drily . . . "no doubt they soon will."

Two things you could say about anyone trying to hook shamanism into the murders. One possibility was that the note-writer was Inuit and believed that shamans had that kind of power. The other was that if a guy involved in the murders was trying a red-herring game, bringing in the threat of voodoo-type shamanism was a way to go. Even people who didn't believe in shamanism have been known to feel a shiver at the idea that shamans can influence the relationship between humans and their environment, and cause a man to die without ever feeling ill, or a woman to rise from a coma.

I shrugged. A crank note, what the hell? But on second thought maybe not from a crank. There was what Erika had said about their stringer hearing rumors. If someone was writing accusatory notes, they could be spreading rumors, too. Or what they believed to be facts.

Buster went on. "One more thing I see in my morning report came in from Sanirarsipaaq on a bad line, or whoever transcribed it didn't seem to get it right. It *seems* to say that the guy who was murdered, and who worked at the hotel, had just been paid, but that the money we found on him was more than his pay. Of course, he could have had the extra on him when he was paid.

"But that's where the stuff gets puzzling—saying something not clear at all that there actually might have been more money than that in his pocket when he was killed, or being killed, because some bills were bloodstained and others not, as if somebody took some money but not all, screwing up the bloodstain patterns."

Luckily, I didn't have to solve that puzzle right then. Across the lobby I saw the Citation pilot storm in from the tarmac and glare around. When he saw me at the phone he came toward me jabbing his index finger meaningfully at his watch. The gesture was an unmistakable, "Come on, for Chrissake!"

Buster was still talking. I interrupted. "Sir," I said, "I've gotta go, plane's leaving, pilot's going nuts at me."

The pilot was right beside me and heard that as I hung up. But

I needed another minute or two. "Look, I'm sorry, but it's murder business, the judge'll understand," I said. "I'll be right with you."

He stamped off and didn't look back. The next call was still at least partly murder business. I was giving the Inuvik CBC number to the operator, praying that Maxine would answer on the first ring, which she did. "I'm off to see the wizard," I said. "If you hear anything meaningful from your million sources, will you call me in Sanirarsipaaq? Either the hotel or the detachment."

She laughed. "Million sources, sure," she said.

I trotted out to catch up to the pilot. "Sorry about that," I called, tucking my head down against the driving snow and taking two steps to his one. "I saw the sheriff, court clerk, court reporter, crown attorney, defense lawyer go out, some others with them, but I must have missed the judge. Didn't know I was the last."

Letting me go up the Citation's steps first as if otherwise I might disappear on him, he growled, "That's what they all say."

F O U R

As soon as we had reached cruising altitude and the Supreme Court people had settled into their various ways of passing the time, Mr. Justice Charles Ferguson Litterick, fifty-five, known in the trade (to crooks, lawyers, court officials, and police) simply as Charlie, ambled back toward me from his seat by the flight deck. He had been away from the western Arctic for a year, working in Ottawa as an adviser on land claims matters. I'd read in *News/North* about him coming back by choice, saying in an interview that this time he was here for keeps and Ottawa could find its way out of its own tangles. He had a shock of thick white hair, black eyebrows, a hooked nose, and a limp that, as he once explained in a bar association speech, had been caused by jumping out of a second-story window to get away from an angry mob of defense lawyers.

This Citation seated eight comfortably, four to a side. The triangular spaces between each set of back-to-back bucket seats had doors and were used as lockers for inflight supplies. The charter companies were responsible for stocking serve-yourself in-flight food and drink, as ordered by the client.

"Well, now," said the judge to no one in particular, bending to open the locker door he'd been heading for, "I wonder what we have here?" He pulled out a six-pack of Heineken and put it on the floor. Reaching farther, he produced cans of Coke and 7-Up and packaged sandwiches, put all beside the six-pack, and eyed rather longingly a small box packed with a couple of dozen minis of vodka, Scotch, rum, rye, gin, plus a few liqueurs; but he settled for a beer and offered me one, which I accepted.

"Anyone else for beer or pop?" he called along the cabin.

There was some desultory reaction. Cans were passed. He sat on one of the seat arms near me as we opened the beers. "You seem to have a lively one going at Sanirarsipaaq."

I nodded, swallowing my first mouthful.

"Tough about your mother," he said. "How is she?"

"Still fairly frail. Not quite out of the woods yet."

"She got any idea who she saw, the guy that ran her down?"

That touched what had become my raw nerve. "No. And I sure as hell don't want anybody to get the idea that part of her recovery might be to remember who it was." I paused, then told him about my worry on that score, and the guard I'd had posted.

His quick shrewd glance into my eyes told me that he understood. I knew that now, when that particular point came up in the legal fraternity—did she or didn't she see anybody she knew?—Charlie would shoot it down.

We sipped our beer. I'd been in his court from time to time and we'd had a few drinks together here and there across the north. This happened usually in privacy, in a hotel room or an aircraft. There are very few bars in the north outside of Yellowknife, Inuvik, and Iqaluit. Even if there were, we try to discourage the idea some people have that the police and courts are one and the same thing, or at least on the same side.

Still, some fraternization was by mutual consent or impossible to avoid. On this flight the crown attorney and defense lawyer were going into their briefcases only a few feet apart. Lawyers in the Northwest Territories might battle in a courtroom by day, but they couldn't easily keep it up while riding on the same aircraft to the next case, or playing cards or talking shop over drinks on layovers. When the court was on one of its almost weekly circuits into the hinterlands, everybody shared what jokes came along.

Once, for instance, Charlie had woken up in the hotel at Cambridge Bay with an urgent need to go to the bathroom down the hall. His red judicial robes had been the first thing grabbable to cover himself (he slept naked), and he had neglected to take his key when he hurried out of the door, which blew shut and locked behind him.

The image of Charlie naked except for his robes of office knocking on the manager's door with this flimsy story of needing her keys was a story that went through the north like wildfire. She was a known target (so far believed to have been impregnable) for lustful males, skilled at beating off even the most plausible male attempts at making a pass. Describing this event for me the last time I was in Cambridge, she had added her own dry touch. "I would never have expected a judge to be so inventive."

I know he enjoyed that aspect of the story himself, and sometimes would add, "Nearly made it, you know."

I asked, "What's the case you've got tomorrow in Cambridge?"

"A charge of abduction. The father and mother shared custody of the children. Last summer when the father had the two kids and was supposed to get them to Edmonton at a certain date, he didn't show up. She called the police and he was picked up in Manitoba going home from work, he's a roofer, to where his sister was looking after the kids on a farm. He'd been offered a week's extra work, money he needed, and figured it was no big deal. He'd been late before and so had she without either taking it to court. White people's malice. Natives wouldn't have been so stupid." He waved around, taking in the aircraft, Cambridge Bay ahead, Yellowknife behind, and a lot of tundra in between. "So there's all this expense. Pity the poor taxpayer . . ." He sighed. "Anyway, you know any more about the Sanirarsipaaq murders than the rest of us?"

I still didn't know much, I told him.

"I had a trial there a few years ago, you know," he said. "I gave a guy named Davidee Ayulaq four years for raping his sister. Nasty bastard, obviously, but very plausible. Might have got off, or a lighter sentence, in some courts. Apparently they'd had sex when she was younger, more like fooling around, more kids than there were beds. Then when she was older and smarter, about fourteen or fifteen, it happened again. She fought but I guess she wasn't any match and he tied her hands behind her and raped her."

I sighed. There was nothing much to say. I hate the incest and other rough stuff, but it exists. Booze and sniffing glue or gasoline or whatever is available can contribute.

Charlie shook his head and sipped his beer. "Of course, various kinds of sex abuse in families happen, not only in the north. But not many have this kid's guts. She decided to hell with her parents and went to the police, who questioned the parents and Davidee, all of whom denied everything. When it became obvious that the police were going to let it drop, she set fire to her parents' house. One of those plywood jobs, went up like wildfire."

He laughed. "Sorry, I have to laugh," he said, explaining. "So she gets charged with arson! Her case was on one of my circuits. She pleaded guilty but seemed like a decent kid. I asked her why she'd set the house on fire. She told me it had been set so someone would listen to her about the rape. So I did listen and after a lot of questioning and some other kids backing her up, I acquitted her of arson and charged him with rape. All on the same circuit. It seems he'd been sexually abused himself before being adopted. Something like that. Anyway, there wasn't only this one instance with him. Later I gave him four years and stipulated that he couldn't go back there when he got out."

When Charlie went back to his seat I thought about it, more or less idly. Charlie's ruling that Davidee could never return to his home settlement had the weight of long custom behind it. Long before white man's law arrived, when a person in a nomadic community did something bad enough—murder, theft, some other serious breach of the community's rules and customs—it was the elders in the community who sat in judgment. The most serious penalty they could enforce was banishment. The offender would simply be turned out of the settlement. Could freeze, starve, whatever, but couldn't return. Modern judges in our Arctic, Charlie and others, tend where possible to make some kind of a marriage between Canadian law and native customs; in this case Charlie added permanent banishment to the four-year sentence.

We had long since swung easterly out of Yellowknife, banked to the northeast, and crossed the treeline. No longer could I see open spots marking rocks or clearings, where the snow and ice melt faster. Sometimes I could distinguish certain landmarks, Artillery Lake for one, I knew the shape of it from the air; a few places in the Thelon game sanctuary; and when we swung north, the Back River.

I thought idly that if I were down there traveling by dogsled or snowmobile, not too cold, I'd see the tracks and know what animals had been by, would think about them and watch the trails they took, maybe stop to inspect some droppings, or where scattered feathers had been left behind by a fox eating a ptarmigan or bits of fur from a rabbit; the signs of how life went for animals. The longer the hours of daylight the more they moved around; now, in spring, the days were getting longer and longer.

Yet it's not my favorite time of year, early April, as the spring breakup nears. Soon the ice would become suspect; in a few weeks some would be too rotten for aircraft to land on. Trappers coming in with their winter furs sometimes left it too late and were stranded with their dog teams (rare now) or snowmobiles beside open water until an aircraft with pontoons responded to a radio call and went looking.

Today, with a howling wind on the surface raising clouds of ground drift, it was still winter. In that wind I'd be hunting for a ridge, the bank of a frozen stream or lake, anything that would help me make camp at least slightly protected. Then I'd get myself all snug and tucked in and maybe wake up a few hours later to a sodden tent and water dripping from that same ridge. A spring thaw could be like that.

I was still staring down at the ground drift like swirling fog below, when the crown attorney, tall, thin, young, came back to where I was. He held a sheaf of papers in his hands, possibly so he wouldn't be leaving them where the defense lawyer could get a glimpse of what an airtight case he was building. He helped himself to a sandwich and regarded a mini of rum thoughtfully, but put it back. He asked about my mother and a few questions about the murders. "Any leads?"

"I should know better in a couple of days."

He smiled. "You should be able to pick up a clue or two by

keeping track of who leaves town when they hear who's arriving to take charge."

A jokey compliment.

He finished his sandwich, ducked so his head wouldn't scrape the ceiling, went back to his seat.

The defense lawyer then paid his courtesy call. His manner struck me as being like that of a cocky schoolboy. No hesitation about whether *he* should have a drink. He poured a mini of vodka into a plastic glass, added 7-Up, sipped it, then laughed. I didn't like the sound of the laugh. Couldn't say why. I just instinctively thought that some mockery was about to come.

"This place Sanirarsipaaq, the murder place, I was there once," he opened. "Great case! Appointed by the court to defend an old lady charged with cashing her husband's old age pension checks after he froze to death out on a hunt. Turned out she didn't know he was dead and just was waiting for him to come home! She'd been saving all the money for him! Case dismissed."

He laughed, shaking his head at the comedy of it all. I couldn't see what was funny, the poor old lady.

"And the hotel there, four to a room, Jesus! I laughed the first time I saw the Sanirarsipaaq hotel ad in the yellow pages: 'Accommodation for sixteen in four rooms!' Four to a room!"

What the Christ did he think a hotel in Sanirarsipaaq was going to be like, the great old Chateau Laurier in Ottawa?

"Where you from?" I asked.

"Vancouver," he said, still chuckling. "Why?"

I considered saying that I'd thought maybe he was from Toronto, the deadliest insult you could hand a guy from Vancouver. Instead, I tried an indirect route. Sometimes that works with his kind.

"The hotel suits me all right," I said, looking him in the eye without a flicker.

Dismissively, "Well, I guess you'd be used to it. I wasn't."

"It isn't that entirely," I said. "But, you know, when I'm in Sanirarsipaaq I have three women I sleep with. Four to a room cuts out a lot of travel time, you know, dragging your ass back and forth between the igloos."

He stared at me, thought I might be kidding, looked uneasy in case I wasn't, decided not, cleared his throat and seemed about to say something, then to think better of it. Back in his seat he took some papers from his briefcase and looked back at me searchingly.

Among the other court people, one was a very thin woman, I'd guess around fifty, who chain-smoked. As I had everybody else pigeonholed, she had to be the court clerk, her job to read charges and generally manage court routine and traditional procedures. When she wasn't smoking or talking, and briefly held the cigarette away from her mouth, she nervously chewed the inside of her lower lip.

The sheriff's office guy I knew slightly. He was sleeping, or at least had his eyes closed and his head against the backrest. He was stocky, maybe midfifties. I knew at least his first name, Bob. One of his jobs was to keep order in the court, make sure the Canadian flag was on a stand behind the judge, and other court niceties.

One other woman, youngish, sturdy (she probably would call it overweight), with really a nice face, was the court reporter. When I caught her eye she smiled, waved, and called, "Hi, Matteesie!!" and I called back, "Hi, Deborah!"

She came from south, Edmonton, or somewhere, and had a cousin who'd been a pro hockey player.

The sky was fairly clear, even sunny at times, showing up the increasingly active ground drift. One thing for sure, the signs of spring that I'd seen this morning in Yellowknife, the salty slush in front of the hotel, the foot or two of open water around the frozen bay down in Old Town, hadn't made it yet into the Barrens.

I went back to what Buster had said about the note blaming shamanism for the murders. Soon I went into a sort of reverie, or trance. This sometimes happens to me. Once in a quiet time with my mother, just the two of us, when I was trying to explain something that I had dreamed, or daydreamed, and was sure it was important if I could remember it, my mother told me that this happens with shamans, that they listen to what a problem is and then go far, far away in their minds and learn something that no one else knew.

I began thinking of carvings. As far as I knew, carvings had nothing to do with the problem I had to solve, but the shaman in

Sanirarsipaaq was a master carver. My mind kept struggling to come up with carvings I'd seen from time to time. What I was seeking seemed to be a particular carving. I couldn't visualize it clearly but was getting *something,* maybe a memory from childhood.

I stared from the porthole and tried to *will* that particular carving into revealing itself to me. For a brief few seconds, a moment, I thought I was getting it, some kind of an angry-looking bird, and then the beak dropped off and it all became fuzzy and was gone and wouldn't return. Passing the endless procession of frozen lakes I refused to let their outlines register, instead registering an endless procession of shamanistic carvings, calling up anything I'd seen or heard.

But what I sought eluded me.

Then I began to think of shamanistic masks I'd seen, the kind a shaman might don when going into his trance as he tried through his helping spirits to bring our people better hunting, better fishing, a healing power that would drive out sickness or madness. Not that would lead to murder.

Then I fastened on the passages in the report I'd seen in Yellowknife that mentioned the amount of money found on the murdered man. The later information I'd received from Buster, not in the report, that his bankroll had been larger than the money he'd been paid that night, might take us somewhere. Meaning someone had paid him a debt? If so, who? What debt?

I must have dozed. When I woke we were coming into Cambridge Bay, landing, wheeling in beside two other aircraft. One was the First Air milk run Hawker Siddeley that I would catch for Sanirarsipaaq. The other was a Twin Otter from Adlak Air. The Hawker Siddeley was parked as close as possible to the terminal building.

As I gathered up the bag of winter clothing that I'd packed— was it only yesterday?—in Labrador, had not unpacked in Ottawa, again had not unpacked in Yellowknife, our pilot up front could be heard swearing into his radio about whoever had parked "that goddamn First Air blocking the terminal entrance so that nobody else can get near, for Christ's sake."

There are social distinctions among aircraft in the north. Citation pilots look upon themselves as deserving precedence, like a Mercedes in a flock of Fiat 850s. So our pilot beefed, but in vain. As I looked outside I wished I was wearing something warmer than my Ottawa clothes. The court people, carrying their own bags, fought their way out of the aircraft into the wind. Even though dressed for the cold, they were wincing from the stinging whip of ice particles blowing almost horizontally off the winter banks of snow and ice lining the runway. The official start of spring was two weeks past, but official is one thing, actual another. The radio that morning had given a Celsius temperature of minus thirty for Cambridge Bay. The thin woman and the lawyers protected their faces by walking backward as they ducked around the offending Hawker Siddeley. The judge had his parka pulled low over his face but didn't walk backward, as if to say "to hell with it."

With all those impressions fighting for attention, it wasn't until I got inside the little terminal building and the wind slammed the door shut behind me that I found that the whole place was packed with weeping people. The court party had stopped dead, astonished and abashed at the scene around them. Deborah, the pretty young court reporter, ran back to me. "Matteesie! What is it? Why all this?"

I said, "It must be for someone who has died. Maybe for the murdered people. I'm not sure."

Then among the mourners I saw the thin and wasted figure of Lovering Oquataq, the Anglican priest who was twin brother of Jonassie the shaman in Sanirarsipaaq.

He seemed to have shrunk since I saw him last, years ago. His clerical collar was several sizes too large under his open parka. He sat with his arm comfortingly around the shoulders of a very old lady, maybe of my mother's generation, who was making a steady heartbroken sound, stopping only for breath. Another old Inuit woman sat at her other side, tears running down the deep lines in her cheeks. Many other women, especially the old, wailed as they wept. Some alone, some with the women, were somber, set-faced men with tear-filled eyes. Little kids stared, upset and wide-eyed. Some teenagers were trying to keep the little ones calm, holding their hands, talking quietly.

I knew what was happening. I had been part of it from time to time myself, long ago.

"Father Lovering," I said, leaning over to him.

"Matteesie," he said, looking up, unsurprised.

The old woman he was holding to him was oblivious, her wails uninterrupted.

"This is for the boy and his granny killed in Sanirarsipaaq?"

He nodded and briefly met my eyes. "The young man murdered, Dennis Raakwap, was young and bright, much beloved," Lovering said quietly. "Good schooling, more planned . . ."

So my guess had been right. It was always this way for the young and treasured, not so much for the old. Deaths of the old by sickness, accident, drowning, freezing, starving, are seen as natural, inevitable—they have lived their lives. When a young person dies, cut off almost before the real life begins, it is a wound to the survival of our whole race, our culture, our language. The worst losses are those suffered through suicide or murder, unnatural ends. A young girl's suicide through lack of job opportunities, a perceived hopelessness, an unwillingness to keep on in the world she sees, of drink, unemployment, serial welfare, so that she chooses death instead, brings such an outburst as I was seeing now.

There were tears in my own eyes. All the brothers, sisters, uncles, aunts, cousins, grandparents, loved ones, of the vastly extended family that is common to Inuit life were here. "They're from Pelly Bay, Hall Beach, Gjoa Haven, Spence, Cambridge, Igloolik," Lovering murmured, looking up at me. "Even Iqaluit, Inuvik. Gathered here to mourn. It is the double blow, Dennis and Thelma . . . not only the loss of a good young man, but Thelma was the mother to some here, granny, aunt, cousin."

I turned away. No doubt some would come on to Sanirarsipaaq, others would not. The old taboos against touching the dead or anything that had belonged to the dead are no longer so strong as they were, but the Inuit always would rather remember the live person than mourn over the body emptied of its soul.

When the boarding call came and I moved with the wet-eyed mourners who were continuing to Sanirarsipaaq, I felt part of them more than just in the physical sense. The last time I had grieved among others this way was when a sixteen-year-old girl in Paulatuk, my first cousin, had hanged herself, apparently out of deep despair that what she saw around her was all she had to look forward to. She was wrong, she was special, but it is the special people who most often fear that they are not special *enough*. Among the weeping people gathered with me in that other airport I had heard a kindly white woman, just wanting to say something to show sympathy, ask among the mourners, "How old was she?"

A middle-aged Inuit woman with a ravaged face had replied calmly, but too fatalistically, a common trait among my people, "Old enough to make up her own mind."

The plane was not very crowded for the fairly short flight on to Sanirarsipaaq; there were perhaps fifteen of us in all. As usual, the passenger part of the plane ended at a partition behind which freight would be stowed. The partition, movable depending on the size of the freight load, had a small door on the left hand side for access to the freight and flight deck.

As soon as we were airborne the stewardess stopped in the aisle beside me. She was tall with long fair hair and a very womanly figure, and wore little or no makeup.

Leaning over to speak, she said, "You're the only new one, except the ones who are crying, and I don't think we have to disturb them. Would you mind if I just explained the safety measures to you personally instead of me getting up in the aisle at the front like we're supposed to do?"

"Go ahead," I said.

She explained seat belts, oxygen, exits, the usual. All in about fifteen seconds. With that over, I said, "I want to change to heavier clothes. Could I do that behind the partition?"

She gave a radiant and amused smile. "I won't peek."

I had to bend my head and turn sideways to get through to the freight compartment, where I stopped with my bag beside big boxes strapped into freight racks. Some were addressed to Sanirarsipaaq, many to Inuvik. Others were for transshipment to Arctic Red, Fort McPherson and Norman Wells. I dumped out the warm clothes I'd worn a few days earlier in Labrador, when I helped the sergeant from the local detachment get a few caribou for his freezer.

I pulled on a thermal undershirt due for laundering as soon as I could arrange it, caribou-skin pants with the fur side against my body, wool socks, knee-high mukluks with white felt liners, and over it all a long brown oversweater that Lois had knitted for me long ago. Into my parka pocket I stuffed an old woolen balaclava that I carried more out of habit than anything else. Then my hat, very official RCMP, the force's badge in front.

The co-pilot emerged from the cockpit just as I was finishing. He stared. "Back to nature, is it, Matteesie?"

Even before he spoke I had presumed he was Irish (the name badge on his left chest read: Kieron O'Kennedy). Many foreign nationals are part of the scanty population (some fifty-five thousand at last count) of our North—Germans, Americans, Vietnamese, Russians, English, at least a dozen nationalities co-existing with, and working alongside, the much greater majority native population of Inuit, Indians, and Metis. The newcomers, including many from southern Canada, go north for all kinds of reasons, from leaving trouble behind to looking for a new meaning in life. I could not even guess what had brought Irish Kieron O'Kennedy to fly co-pilot on an Arctic airline. Whether he was from Ireland's Protestant-dominated north or Catholic south, the thousands of sectarian murders committed by terrorists of both religions bothered good people in all parts of Ireland. Drove some out. He had the Celtic red hair and a very fair skin and backed up the Irishness by talking like a cast member of a sometimes ribald Irish play I'd seen once in Ottawa, *Playboy of the Western World.*

"Some kind of a disguise is it you're puttin' on now?" he asked. "Somebody's husband after you, then? I thought you Inuit fellas didn' worry about technicalities like that . . ." He laughed at his own joke. "Anyway, what I came back to tell you is that we're laying over in Sanirarsipaaq for an hour or two, in case you want to solve the murders fast and come back with us."

"Very funny," I said.

"Well, we're concerned about time. I mean, if yer man up front there"—I deduced he meant the pilot—"doesn't get to Inuvik tonight his girlfriend says she's going to look for a bank clerk or somebody with regular hours."

None of this really affected me, but what he said next did.

"We're lucky the weather has changed enough already, thanks be t'God, to let us get down with this crowd of sad people. The Otter guy we saw in Cambridge, I know him, he can fly anything in near any weather. Still, he said in normal circumstances he would have just laid over in Sanirarsipaaq waiting out the weather, but he had the bodies to take out."

Bodies? I had a sinking feeling.

"If he hadn't got out, they would have had to put the bodies back in the cooler. Otherwise, they might have thawed if he'd had to lay over and leave them aboard and then the weather changed. He said people were pleading with him to hurry and get away while he could or they'd never forgive him and the whole economy of the town would be ruined. He told 'em he'd give it one try and if it was too dangerous they'd just bloody well have to put the bodies back in the cooler. As it turned out, though, once was enough, he made it."

He was laughing. I wasn't. Gradually dawning on me was the fact that the bodies that were my main concern in coming here, and that I'd intended to see before they were moved, had been on that Twin Otter we'd seen on the ground at Cambridge Bay. But I still didn't have it all.

"Put the bodies back where?"

"Oh, I guess you couldn' know. When they had those two murders last Friday, y' know, the weather was away too warm for them to be just left, like, in the shed at the Mountie detachment, so they put the body bags in the freezer at the Co-op. They were stacked away at the back, out of the way, nobody even had to look at them if they didn't want to, but the Inuit guy who manages the Co-op knew both of them . . . Superstitious, y'know? He just refused to open the freezer door again as long as every time he went in he had to look at them body bags."

I groaned. This all figured. Nobody who understood Inuit fears and beliefs about death would have used a public freezer for body storage. That goddamn Barker!

O'Kennedy was going on. "No freezer being opened meant nobody could get anything out of the freezer until the bodies were gone. Meaning no nine-dollar cheeseburgers or four-dollar ice cream bars or other stuff for the bingo players. The entire economy of Sanirarsipaaq was grinding to a complete halt. So now with the bodies out of there, the joint's back to normal. At least until somebody else gets murdered."

I went back to my seat, swearing.

"Okay?" the stewardess asked.

Okay? Not really. "Yeah, thanks."

Gradually I accepted what I'd heard. Couldn't do anything about it. A few deep breaths and I forced myself into less stressful thoughts. We were flying over places I remembered, the deep bays and fjordlike inlets. I'd traveled these parts often with nothing on my mind but where to make camp. When I was young and on the move sometimes we'd be forced to swing wide offshore with our dogs or snowmobiles, slowing to a crawl where the sea ice had been tossed and tumbled against the island, then frozen.

I thought ahead. I had never met Jonassie Oquataq, but was remembering something about him that had not crossed my mind for years. One of my assignments in the 1970s was to tour Inuit settlements in the eastern and high Arctic with what was called a vice-regal party, led by Canada's governor-general, who was officially, but mainly ceremonially, the queen's representative. At the time, our government was in one of its periodic paroxysms of showing the flag in the Arctic. There are a lot of ice islands far to the north that Canadian sovereignty freaks claim are ours. Scientists of the old Soviet Union and their successors prefer to believe they are at the very least jointly owned. Both sides take care not to get tough about it—while the Americans send in submarines and icebreakers from time to time, more or less in the peaceful spirit of, "Hey, fellows, remember us?"

The Inuit, tenants for thousands of years? No vote.

Anyway, never mind the politics, the governor-general's trip was seen by the media as exotic enough to cover. Among those zigzagging from one set of inhabited snowbanks to another, sometimes two or three in one day, were representatives of *Time* magazine, *The Times* of London, *The New York Times*, the *Ottawa Journal*, the *Globe and Mail*, the *Montreal Star*, CBC, and CTV, in addition to the governor-general's wife, male secretary, and a few other civilians. The media people no doubt got what they wanted, but my people on the ground waiting for the big event were plainly puzzled. They had envisioned the queen's representative as someone in a grand uniform, chest covered with medals, maybe carrying a sword and wearing a cocked hat (with earflaps?). When this friendly former politician wearing a parka over a tweed suit stepped down from the vice-regal aircraft our people kept looking over his shoulder to see where the real guy was.

I'm almost ashamed now to remember what was a really *serious* showing-the-flag stop on that trip: the distant early warning (DEW) line station near Hall Beach. The DEW line had been built with U.S. money and for years was operated and controlled by U.S. forces. At lunch, the U.S. major in command presented the govgen with a nice but not spectacular soapstone carving. I had to smile. It was like, "Sir, this here carving is a souvenir of your own country we'd like you to keep as a memento of how our two nations get along together."

The press people were not exactly riveted by the obligatory speeches, but were obliged to sit through them. Sight of the carving made some of them think of their loved ones at home, who would be expecting presents not bought at some United Cigar store. Some asked me to find out if there were any more carvings around, for sale.

While the lunch was still going on I obediently scouted around among the GIs and was steered to the workshop of a middle-aged and squatty Inuk carver named Simeonie, who took me to a room where a dozen or so pieces, a few his but mostly not, were set out on a simple wooden table. I stopped in front of a carving in dark gray stone of a crouching hunter with his spear poised at a sealhole. I could not leave. A little card leaning against the carving read: "Hunter at Seal Hole, Jonassie Oquataq, $55." (This was long ago.) All I had was sixty dollars, six tens. Simeonie couldn't make change. "Gimme the fifty," he said, shrugging.

The media people and others were to come in later and buy, but as I put my carving in my knapsack Simeonie laughed. "You beat the white men to the best piece." It now sits on a mahogany table in my own room in Ottawa. Lois loves the piece as well. She occasionally moves it to the living room, but soon I move it back. Family law has some fine points on joint ownership, and if Lois sometime decides she could do better in the way of a husband, which I wouldn't blame her for, I sure as hell don't want to wind up with a judge saying, "Okay, you get first chance with the saw, Matteesie. It was your fifty bucks—you takin' the hunter or the sealhole?"

One recent Jonassie that I had seen, and so had Lois, was a larger-than-lifesize gyrfalcon of the same black or very dark gray stone. It was at a show in Ottawa, priced at three thousand dollars. For some reason Jonassie had chosen to withdraw it, not to sell. There was a story in the art sections of Toronto, Montreal, and Ottawa newspapers speculating on why, with a lot of stuff about the gyrfalcon having a special place in Inuit tribal and shamanistic beliefs, and mentioning in passing that Jonassie was a shaman.

Thinking this way, it occurred to me that if any old-time shaman of my youth had donned his mask and rattled his bones and charms down there below us on the ice of Padliak Inlet or Albert Edward Bay and proclaimed that one day an Inuk dressed like a Mountie inspector would be passing overhead three miles up, he might have been regarded even by the faithful with at least mild suspicion.

Then my thoughts came back to the present. The bodies in that Twin Otter. It hadn't occurred to me before, but did now, that RCMP regulations called for bodies in murder investigations to be under police guard at all times, when being moved. When the thought did strike me, I actually wondered who was guarding them on the way out . . . the other corporal, Bouvier, whom I'd never met?

Meantime, every time I thought of the way the shit was going to fly when I got Barker alone, it was very good for my mental health. I never once thought of the other possibility, that Barker had gone out with the bodies himself. That is what turned out to be true.

F I V E

Suddenly the flight got bumpier. O'Kennedy's voice came on the intercom: "Seat belts! This might get worse. We're in descent, coming in to land." For minutes we pitched and yawed around, losing altitude. The mourners gripped their seat arms and hung on. I could still see nothing. It was like flying through gray soup. Then suddenly the cloud got wispy and I saw the landing strip feet away, much too close. The engines roared us back up out of there. On the second try we came through the cloud the same way, saw the landing strip about twenty feet away, bumped down, braked like hell, and I realized that I hadn't been breathing a lot, if at all, in the last few seconds.

We turned to taxi back. O'Kennedy appeared through the cargo-compartment door and strolled through the cabin. His smile made even some of the mourners look relieved. "Never in doubt," he said, then laughed and paused by me to say in a low voice, "Just about wore out my prayer beads."

"No wonder you're not going to take off in this stuff."

"Dead right. But like I said, we've been told this weather is movin' through, so we have, although they've been wrong before. A couple of hours, they say, three at the most—just time for a flutter at the roulette tables, ha ha. Or maybe take the stewardess to the hotel and fool around a little." He caught Father Lovering's disapproving gaze. "Just a joke, father."

As we taxied back through the heavy ground drift I was remembering a lot. The other time I'd been here, when our RCAF Hercules rumbled deafeningly out of the sky on the governor-general's trip, we'd landed on a small lake a bit inland and pulled up to where a dozen natives had tramped out a place in the snow.

When we got to town then on a fleet of snowmobiles the only buildings were the Hudson Bay post, the community hall, and some prefab houses called 512s because that was their square footage, thirty-two feet by sixteen, among a scattering of caribou-skin tents. The official reception was in the community hall, built on pilings that went down to the permafrost, so that the area under the building was open. One Inuk, caught by a call of nature, calmly and naturally had ducked under the overhang, whipped his pants down, and defecated. I noticed the shock that ran through the official party. The journalists normally had been great on making notes about clashes in culture. I later learned that only one, from the *Toronto Globe and Mail*, had written the story of the man relieving himself in full sight of the vice-regal party. His editor had cut it. Apparently some culture clashes were just too strong for southern comfort.

Over the years I'd seen all the changes, here and elsewhere. Now we bumped along toward a real terminal, a building exactly the same as others throughout the north, all brought in by sealift barge, factory-built with everything including electric lights and toilets.

I pulled on my parka, looking around at others standing up and reaching into the overhead rack for their belongings. Once during the flight I had thought, what if the murderer had fled out of here and now for whatever reason was coming back? I looked around carefully but there was no way of telling. O'Kennedy stood by to get the door open while our pilot wheeled the Hawker Siddeley in a half circle in front of the building like a reckless kid parking a bicycle. Maybe he was mad about having to hang around here a bit instead of hightailing it for Inuvik. A toothless little old Inuit granny behind the terminal window ducked out of sight as the wingtip swung by and stopped a few scant feet from the glass. She rose into view again, a laughing mass of wrinkles and an extended arm pointing out this close call.

The instant we stopped, a big man in a blue RCMP parka strode out of the door into the storm. I knew he wasn't Corporal Barker. I'd met Barker years ago in Inuvik; his build and gait had reminded me of a football player I used to know in Edmonton, bowlegged and pigeon-toed, almost impossible to knock down. This one was a good deal taller and heavier than Barker, moon-faced, wearing round-rimmed glasses and somehow exuding vigor. I'd never seen him before.

I was first off. "Bouvier," he introduced himself with a nod of his head, almost a bow. "Welcome, Inspector."

He reached for my bag as O'Kennedy handed it down, then grinned, gesturing to the wingtip's proximity to the window. "That would've been just what we need!"

I wasn't sure what he meant. Having this aircraft crippled by bashing up a wingtip couldn't have any effect on the murder investigation, that I could think of.

"What do you mean?"

We were hurrying for the terminal. He looked at me strangely.

"If the wing had been damaged it would have meant Sadie Barker couldn't get out!" he called over his shoulder as we got through the door and out of the wind.

"Why's she going anyway, ahead of Steve?"

He stopped so quickly that I ran into him. Earlier I had half-assumed that Bouvier had been inside with the bodies locked up in the Twin Otter at Cambridge. I was just about to ask who had gone with them when Bouvier looked at me with a mixture of surprise and amusement.

"He's already gone. Went out as guard on the bodies. Saved himself an airfare. Sadie's going to catch up to him via Inuvik and another flight to Yellowknife."

I had a moment of righteous fury that the guy who'd been in charge when the murders took place, the guy with all the local knowledge, now obviously had *chosen* not to stick around and give me a few hours of his valuable time. I wanted to know more, but that could come later. In only a few more steps I progressed to a guilty feeling of relief that I was not going to have to deal with Barker. As simple as that. Now the job was just to find out who had committed murder.

Inside the terminal Bouvier greeted some of the others there with a minimum loss of progress toward the door, until I touched his arm and said, "Not so fast. I want to look around." I moved over against a wall where I had a good view of the dozens of people who had come to meet the plane, and also those who'd got off. Most of them were greeting mourners, but not all. One man came out of the men's toilet and looked directly at me and then quickly away. He was wearing a Toronto Blue Jays baseball cap. When he took it off briefly to adjust it, he had a very high forehead ending about halfway up his scalp in well-trimmed hair that covered his ears neatly, like half a skull cap.

I said to Bouvier, "Who's that half-bald guy?"

He saw the direction of my gaze. The man had turned away and was heading for the door with a cheerful-looking young Inuk wearing the kind of hard hat that construction workers use.

"Don't know. Never saw him before that I can remember. The other guy, Donald Thrasher, everybody calls Hard Hat because he's never without it."

Then, out of the ladies' came by all odds the most noticeable female in the crowd, not only because she was tall, maybe five feet ten or eleven, and strongly built, but because under her open parka she wore a thigh-length skirt and patterned tights that showed a great deal of long, shapely, well-groomed leg above classy winter boots. She looked around and immediately headed toward us just as I was asking, "Who's that?"

By then she was standing beside me. "Hi, Maisie," Bouvier said, then the obvious, because she sure as hell wasn't dressed for Sanirarsipaaq or environs. "You look as if you're going somewhere."

"Just out for a few days," she said. I think her voice would be called contralto. Anyway, pleasantly low. She seemed more than a little distracted. "I wanted to see you and ask that if anything happens about the murders, will you make sure Mother phones and lets me know?"

"Sure . . ." He introduced me and she reached out and shook my hand. She had a strong grasp, a large hand. Her nervousness was plain, and her words came with a rush. "I thought this plane was going to turn right around and go again! Mother told me I was crazy to come out so early but I've got a job interview in Inuvik and it drives me nuts sitting around the hotel, everything reminding me . . . I didn't want to miss the flight because of this damn weather and now I hear it'll be an hour or two, maybe more." She looked from Bouvier to me and back. "Anything new at all?"

Bouvier shook his head. "Want a ride back in with us?" She shook her head. "I'll wait, I've got a book." She moved through the thinning crowd to a chair where she sat and lighted a cigarette, inhaled deeply, fiddled with trying to pull her skirt down a little over her legs and sat staring at the wingtip so close to the window, obviously lost in thoughts of her own. She wasn't pretty, far from it, but striking. Large nose, generous mouth. Her hair was short and fair with tight curls. A woman no one was likely to ignore.

"Her mother runs the hotel," Bouvier said. "She and Dennis Raakwap were pretty close, working around the hotel together."

"Close?" I asked.

He shrugged. "As friends, it seemed. But maybe more. Worked together, sometimes played together, about the same age."

"You interview her after it happened?"

"Yeah, but not much more than asking did Dennis seem worried lately, or did he have any enemies that she knew of . . ."

"Did he?"

"Not that she knew, she said."

"You believe her?"

"Not entirely. But we sort of filed her away in case something came up that we could ask about specifically. At the time she seemed pretty rattled, naturally."

"She got a lot of boyfriends? I'd guess so."

"I don't think so. A few passes by hotel guests, maybe, but nobody local that I know of. She'd tower over most of them—except Dennis, he was five nine or ten, just a little shorter than she is. Anyway, they worked together. I got the idea that was about it."

I looked at her again, filing it away, and kept on checking the others. Any who did meet my eyes did so without reaction. Then there was a quick exodus, head-down dashes through the wild wind to board snowmobiles, Honda all-terrain vehicles, pickups, vans.

The half-bald man revved up a yellow snowmobile while Hard Hat climbed on behind.

About then a short, stocky Inuk with thick, graying hair and a drooping moustache rushed in, glanced around, and walked quickly to Father Lovering. They embraced. Looked to be in their sixties.

"Is the man with the priest his brother?"

"Yes. Jonassie the carver."

"And shaman."

A quick look at me, then, "Yeah."

They left together with the tail end of the mourners, a group of them crowding into a dirty brown van, with Jonassie getting into the driver's seat.

I took one more look at Maisie, settled into a corner with a book that she was not reading. I'd be talking to her, for sure, but I'd have to do some homework before I'd be likely to get anything out of her that Bouvier and Barker hadn't. The next plane back would be Friday. If it seemed seriously warranted, I could get her back faster.

I figured by then I'd seen what there was to see. "Let's go."

Outside we ducked our heads into the wind and headed for the blue police van with the RCMP crest on the side, parked with its engine running. In a few seconds we were skidding out of there, the heater fan roaring.

"About Barker taking off!" Bouvier roared over the noise from the heater fan.

"Yeah?" I said.

"You're probably thinking that he shouldn't have."

"Right."

"He couldn't help it, entirely. Really wanted to stay around until we'd got somewhere in the investigation, but . . ."

"But what, for God's sake?"

For a moment he had to concentrate on his driving, the slippery road. A snowmobile suddenly appeared out of the murk, going too fast. Bouvier swore, swinging the van to the right, then came back to Barker.

"At first he was going to stay. The morning after the murders,

we'd been up all night of course, he told me and told Sadie, his
wife, she'd come to the detachment with some sandwiches, that
he was going *nowhere* until we got the guy who'd done it. Sadie
went ape, right there in front of me, about how they'd had these
reservations for six months, Yellowknife to Vancouver to see a
sister she has there and then on to Honolulu. And how she already
had a substitute teacher to fill in for her at the school, and *they
were going!* Period."

An oncoming Jeep-type vehicle skidded, spun around, and
straightened out, the driver waving at us cheerily as he kept on
toward the airport.

Bouvier said, "Anyway, all day Saturday, we were interviewing,
checking, chasing people, a lot of stuff you can read in our notes,
and Steve was still holding out against Sadie, and she was still
screaming at him. On the phone and in person."

Bouvier looked at me, as if expecting a reaction. I had none.
He turned back to watching the road, steering carefully on what
was sometimes glare ice. Once when he had to brake, the van
turned two complete circles. After that he pulled over to the side
of the road, turned down the heater fan, looked at me, and sighed.

"May as well stop and get it all off my chest without having to
drive, too . . . So he kept on swearing he wasn't going anywhere.
Then late Sunday or early Monday he got the word from Ottawa
that you would be coming to take charge. Natural enough, because
he was going out and I was new. But that's when Sadie got the
upper hand, with a lot of stuff about how would he feel taking
orders from you." He said the next words carefully. "You, a goddamn native, she said. Maybe you know about the way he talks
—this is his town, what he says goes, all that stuff. Great white
father. It can be really irritating, but that is Steve Barker. Half
the people in town will be laughing now, making jokes, like Steve
might be tough but what Sadie says goes."

He paused. "That would really hurt him, the snickering."

We sat there at the side of the road, other vehicles passing both
toward the airport and away from it. I thought we might as well
clear the decks from my side, too. I was still bothered, plenty,
about what had been done under Barker's orders, or at least his

jurisdiction, letting the bodies out of here before I arrived. It might never be a factor again, but I wanted Corporal Bouvier to know something.

"Let's get off Barker. That's history. But I sure as hell wish those bodies had been held until I got here."

He replied mildly, "Well, the way Barker saw it, he and I both had had a good look at the bodies, saw what there was to see."

I didn't let up. "I might have seen something neither of you saw! I just like to start at the beginning, and see what I'm dealing with. Also, sometimes when the bodies are natives, with me especially, I might see or sense something that white guys don't."

He said softly, "White guys . . . You think I'm white?"

Oh, hell, I thought, and looked at him again, noticing his color, more than just ruddiness. Our people are usually smaller. His size had put me off.

"Tell me," I said.

He grinned sideways at me. "Small Inuit mother, great big goddamn French-Canadian father."

"Sorry." I really felt a lot more than just the one word, sorry. Here I'd been doing something to him that I'd hated when it was done to me. When I was a kid working my first year or two as an RCMP special around Inuvik and Sachs Harbor and expressed an opinion above my station, I had often been dumped on by white cops, some of them okay, really, but others like Barker, the king-of-the-hill types. Some of the reasons for dumping on me might have been valid, but when someone said openly or even implied that, being a native, I couldn't really be expected to act like a real policeman, I would keep an impassive face. I thought at first maybe Bouvier now was doing the same, letting any resentment at my dumb mistake go away.

Actually, he was doing more than just letting it go. I could see the corners of his mouth twitching. Suddenly he shook his head and laughed aloud. "Wait'll I tell my wife! Jesus! Will she enjoy that about you thinking I'm not native."

"Be sure to tell her I said I was sorry."

"Oh, I will." He laughed again. "From a goddamn racist white guy to a goddamn racist Inuk! What next?"

We rode in silence, both now smiling.

"Anyway," Bouvier said, pulling out onto the road again. "About holding the bodies here until you arrived . . ."

I interrupted. "You gotta admit you sure got the bodies out of here fast."

Bouvier said mildly, "Not fast enough for the Co-op. When we heard that you were in Yellowknife and on your way here, I did raise that point, that you'd want to see the bodies, and what difference would a day or two make in getting them out? He yelled at me for second-guessing him, so I backed off. He was really pressured, knowing a lot of people would joke about him leaving a big case. That made him determined to get everything done that he could do, like getting the bodies to forensics . . ."

The outskirts of the settlement showed fitfully ahead through the ground drift. I thought of the Twin Otter and its murdered cargo.

"When I brought that up about waiting for you, what he said was what the fuck could you see that we didn't? He also said that he didn't figure there was some royal fucking highness that moving the bodies had to be cleared with."

It was about then that I began to come to my senses. I say, began. I still wasn't really thinking rationally. I'd got myself stoked up too high, in too short a time. It was Tuesday suppertime and since Monday breakfast I'd flown from Labrador to Ottawa and then to Edmonton and then to Yellowknife, where I was up half the night talking to my mother with her head hurting, and then to Cambridge Bay and then to Sanirarsipaaq. But there was something else—and it was my fault.

If I'd made one more phone call from Yellowknife to order that the bodies remain undisturbed until I got here, and if Barker had argued that crap about the Co-op freezer, I could have said to him loud and clear, "Clean out somebody's goddamn home freezer and put 'em in there until I have a look! Why is it that half the goddamn spouse-murderers you hear about in a year stash bodies in home freezers practically forever or at least until new tenants move in or some innocent visitor looking for the ice cream opens the freezer and raises the alarm? Yet I can't have *my* bodies stay in one place

for even an extra goddam day or two! Why? Answer me that?" I
didn't actually say any of that. But it sometimes helps, making up
speeches that I never actually get to say.

My angry reverie was interrupted by Bouvier. "You okay?"

Suddenly I was back in the police van on the road into town.

"What do you mean am I okay?"

"You're squirmin' around."

I stopped squirming and wiped the frosty condensation off the
window on my side. We were passing houses with chained dogs
curled up, backs to the wind, beside old komatiks that maybe once
in a while were still pulled by dog teams instead of by the snowmobiles and all-terrain vehicles parked at every door. In all the
ice and snow and wind I suddenly had a random thought that I
still liked this better than spring in the south, with crocuses coming
out and empty beer and rye bottles and Big Mac containers beginning to peep shyly through the other crap in the ditches. And
people on my street thinking they'd better get the snow tires off.

"You got a family, Bouvier?" I asked.

He was making a turn and almost blew it, maybe surprised to
hear from me. "Yeah. Four boys. Why do you ask?"

"When the ice goes out do you take 'em fishing?"

"Well, I've never had a springtime here, you know, but around
Spence Bay in the summer me and the wife and kids would pack
a cooler with beer and food and take a tent and lots of fly dope,
and go out to a lake a few miles inland and stay out until we had
enough Arctic char to fill the freezer."

My belligerence was gone. Probably we were both glad. He
slowed almost to a stop and let the momentum carry the van a
few yards in neutral before he turned the wheels a little. When
they caught he eased back into four-wheel drive to get up a small
rise before he skidded, again in neutral, this time to a stop alongside a solitary terraced row of townhouses.

They stuck up like sore thumbs, looking laughably out of place,
the only dwellings of their sort in town.

He waved one arm in that direction. "That's where your mother
was staying with Annie Kavyok. Annie's probably home from
work. The kids'll be home from school either now or soon. I've

got the key to the place next door where the bodies were. Turned the heat way down or it'd be smelling pretty bad. Still ain't no hell as it is. Wanta have a look?''

I thought about it. "Maybe. Better give me the keys, just in case. I'll leave my bag in the van and pick it up later.''

I got out. I think Bouvier was glad to see me go. I would be, in his place. But look on the bright side. Barker was gone, about to enjoy, if that's the word, a holiday lumbered with a wife who for some reason had him by the balls. Not to mention missing his big chance to solve a couple of murders all by himself and show Matteesie the big-shot Inuk that this really was *his* town. The dumb bugger.

Bouvier reversed out of there and disappeared in a cloud of snow particles. I stood for a few seconds and just looked. There was no one around outside, but suddenly I felt very good. The weather was getting worse instead of better. I didn't care, I was headed for family.

The older I got, the more my relatives meant to me. Maybe if I'd been born a lot sooner or a lot later I never would have left the north. But then maybe I'd never have had the other times, good and bad, making my way in the police, going on courses to universities, loaned once for a couple of years to Northern Affairs. I thought of a battered old book I'd found secondhand and still had; one of those old orange-colored Penguins. It's called *An Anthology of War Poetry,* published around 1942, one chapter per war, poems going back centuries, from the "heigh ho, off we go," stuff of old wars right down to the last two chapters covering World War I and part of World War II. Names went through my head: Robert Graves. Wilfred Owen. Siegfried Sassoon . . . And fragments. "Scarlet majors from the base . . ." (I've met civil servants like that. And some policemen.) There was one about a soldier being scolded for his uniform being dirty and replying, "It's blood, sir," and being told, "Blood's dirt."

I wondered where those thoughts came from—"blood's dirt"— and walked slowly toward the terrace of five two-story townhouses where there had been a lot of blood, some of it related to me. Maxine rented one in a row like this in Inuvik. I walked toward the unit with a brass number 2 on the door, and knocked. Immediately within there was a rush of footsteps. The door was flung open by a boy, behind him a girl a little younger, both yelling, "It's Matteesie!"

Then I could see Annie coming from the kitchen at the rear, bulky and broad-hipped, with long gray-black hair parted in the middle, an old-looking wool cardigan unbuttoned and hanging loose, a skirt of some heavy material, embroidered sealskin slippers on her feet.

Without a word, she clasped me to her, a person of my own blood making me welcome.

"Come in, Matteesie! Come in!" she said. I followed her back into the warm kitchen where she set out tea things and biscuits, soon pouring tea and pushing the milk jug and sugar bowl toward me. I hadn't felt so much at home for a while.

"And your mother, our dear *anaanak*?" she asked, using the Inuktitut term for grandmother. I told her a little of what had happened that morning and that mother still had the bad headache, but at least had been moved to Franklin House.

From there, we spoke in Inuktitut. Nothing of what was said about the murders differed in any important detail from what my mother had said. The kids acted out the thumps and shouts, falling over one another to get the message across. Annie's voice and expression were full of regret as she said, "I missed all that part, fell right asleep as soon as I got home. I keep thinking if I'd been not so tired, this terrible thing might not have happened."

Strangely enough, as we talked on and on, comfortably, I had a strong feeling that Annie was holding back something and that perhaps eventually I would hear more. I didn't press it. I had no more than skimmed the reports made by Barker and Bouvier, when they had originally questioned Annie and her children. Rather than go over the same information twice, I thought I would read or listen to everything available. There would be lots of time to come back to her on some points.

"We have room if you wish to stay here," Annie said. "That blizzard outside is getting worse, instead of better."

Very politely and reasonably, I explained, "Phone calls, official stuff, it'll all be handier if someone is trying to reach me and I'm at the detachment or the hotel."

"Well, at least have supper, you have to eat!" My stomach was saying yes and my head was saying no, droning away less and less convincingly that I had so much to catch up on, and should get at it.

She took out four caribou steaks, put on a frying pan with the heat on high, dropped in what seemed to be the last of her butter and leftover fried potatoes, kept turning them, moved them to the oven with bannock when they were hot, heated canned corn, dropped frozen peas into boiling water, threw the steaks into the smoking pan. It was wonderful. We kept talking as we ate. When I took my last bite of caribou I'm pretty sure I seemed wide awake. I still was intending to go . . . and then, while we were drinking tea, my eyelids went closing, closing, closed.

She led me upstairs like a sleepwalker and showed me a turned-down single bed. I didn't ask whose it was.

"I'll phone Bouvier," she said, I think, or I dreamed that, as well as her saying, "The murders will still be here for you to-morrow."

Vaguely hearing the storm pounding against the walls and windows, I almost got my clothes off. When Annie closed the door and I lay back on the bed to struggle out of my pants, my head hit the pillow by mistake and I don't remember any more. When my eyes opened again the sun was shining through the uncurtained window and no doubt had been for hours. Sunrise was at about five up here at this time of year. I must have got my pants the rest of the way off in the night. Annie had breakfast ready, strong tea, fried Arctic char, fresh-from-the-pan bannock, margarine, and strawberry jam from a two-pound can. I was thinking that it had been a long time since I had lived like that, eating when hungry, sleeping when tired.

It is hard to describe how I felt outside in bright sunshine. The blizzard had blown itself out during the night. I put on sunglasses against the white glare as I ran through what I knew versus what I should know. Yesterday I'd been a zombie. Now I was getting the feeling I always had in the early days of a case, weighing everything, turning over what I knew and looking for a door to go through, a crack that needed widening.

I would go to the murder house. I would question Annie about the habits of the two who had been murdered. I would poke around the edges of what more there was to know about the striking Maisie. Maybe I shouldn't have let her go until I talked to her myself. The half-bald man, the way he had turned his glance at me so quickly away . . . why? The fact that Bouvier didn't know him was mildly surprising. The cheerful guy with the hard hat who had driven him away stuck in my mind for no good reason. Instinct I paid attention to. I needed logical suspects. If the case had been open-and-shut it would be over by now. Usually if you don't get on a fresh trail right away it is hard slogging, hard digging, looking for lies and evasions and things that don't match.

For now, I walked, sometimes on traveled roads, sometimes cutting through between houses, mostly laid out in streets with a comfortable amount of room between them. One street was all A-frames, six of them, the roofs alternating between red and brown. In front of each was a rusty barrel for garbage, painted with the house number. Caribou skins hung from one clothesline. Here and there sealskins were stretched on frames or bits of plywood. Besides snowmobiles, most houses had Honda all-terrain vehicles, usually the old three-wheelers now outlawed in southern Canada as being accident-prone. One of the newer four-wheelers (safer but twice the price, so not so plentiful) had a pile of caribou skins on the back.

Living next door to the murder house, Annie should have a lot to tell me. She would know the comings and goings, and some might be important. Mother, what would she want to do when she was ready to leave Franklin House? I didn't want her coming back here with that she's-the-only-witness thing lurking in somebody's mind, especially if the somebody was still here.

Now I was walking past houses painted blue or yellow or a washed-out brown, all with snow banked up against their walls. Here and there the bow of a boat or a carelessly dropped ladder or pile of building materials, poked through the snowbanks. Every house had its two-hundred-gallon fuel-oil tank close by the kitchen wall. At one a komatik still hitched to a snowmobile was almost hidden by the carcass of a musk-ox, which no doubt soon would be skinned, and the tender and flavorful meat divvied up among the families of the hunters who had brought it in.

No matter how often I saw all this, being not often enough, the scene meant much to me. Children were on their way to school, obviously having left themselves enough time to play en route, the way I had sometimes done as a child, slipping and sliding here and there, enveloped in warm clothing, laughing a lot. In the bitter dark days of winter's minus forty or fifty, kids rarely played outside. It was still plenty cold, I'd figured minus twenty today, but the important change was to long hours of daylight. The kids could catch up.

Yet into all this, last Friday night, someone either with murder in his heart or anger that could lead to murder had walked between these houses . . . Murder in his *heart? I stopped myself there. Did it have to be a man? It had been easy to slip into the idea that a man had done the murders. A tall-built woman could hurtle through the night as well as a big man. Now that I was fully awake I knew that I should have asked that tall one, Maisie, a few more questions.*

I found myself among kids again, more and more pouring out of houses with a yell, some still chewing on whatever they'd carried away from the breakfast table. Wherever there was a slope they were riding toboggans or bits of cardboard, sliding to a stop and getting off to trudge back up to do it again. Two boys on mountain bikes were pedaling like mad down a road where two or three feet of glassy ice had been packed all winter by big snowplows and graders. They fought to steer through the skids and slides until they hit maximum speed, before easing on the brakes and trying to stay upright while whirling and inevitably falling—to get up laughing and do it again. There would be two months yet of gradual thawing until in June the ice retreated a few yards from the shore of the bay and on sunny days the more daring, these ones on the bicycles and their like, would swim in the icy water. In early July the ice would go out of the streams and fathers and mothers would take the kids and picnic inland and pick the swift-growing flowers.

A smiling girl walked by. "Hi!" she called. She had a hockey stick over one shoulder with skates and a hockey bag hanging from it; the skates bumping her back with every step. I called back, "Hi!"

I was almost at the shore of the bay when the road I was walking turned to the left just short of the two-story hotel. More houses lay to my left over toward the town's main buildings. Due west of the hotel was the rec hall and rink, the trading post, the Co-op, and the school (near a small building bearing a tattered old sign reading INTERNATIONAL LITERACY YEAR and a neater one reading LIBRARY). One side of the rec hall was two stories high, with office windows facing our way, and a sign reading HAMLET OFFICES. In there would be the settlement administrator and an office for the mayor.

Across the street and beyond the rec hall a small building bore a familiar insignia and flag, the RCMP detachment's one-room office. I walked in. There was a bathroom off to the side, door open. Near the bathroom door was a table with a coffeemaker, toaster. Underneath was a tiny refrigerator. On the wall behind Bouvier was a calendar and beside it a printout from the Climate Information branch of Environment Canada, showing sunrise and sunset times in this area. Bouvier was busy at his desk against some filing cabinets. He was wearing his parka. He looked up, smiling, pecking with two fingers at an old Underwood typewriter and smoking a cigar.

"This is a smoke-free zone," he said. "Got a sign somewhere says that, but you can never see it through the smoke." He got up. "Did you know that the plane was weathered in here last night?"

I was startled. Had I just assumed it had gone, or been so unconscious I didn't even assume? Second option rang true. "No, I didn't."

So Maisie was still here. I'd been thinking maybe I shouldn't have let her go, and she isn't gone yet, and I'm a lot more awake.

"Weather never let up until around dawn, four-thirty or five," Bouvier went on, and laughed. "Sadie was fit to be tied—her kind of nightmare! Barker loose in the fleshpots of Yellowknife!" He grinned. "And, of course, Maisie worried about her job interview. Anyway, they're leaving right away. Sadie just called. I'll drive her to the airport."

"The redoubtable Sadie," I said. "I'll come with you."

"Redoubtable," he said, grinning. "Wish I'd said that."

She was waiting on the snowy steps leading from the door of her house, bags ready, a woman probably thirty-five, well formed, with dark hair and brown eyes that radiated both defiance and a kind of awareness that she'd stuck her neck out by interfering in her husband's job and everybody in Sanirarsipaaq knew it.

Could she possibly have another reason for getting out of here fast, away from the murders? She's a teacher. Could some of her kids have been involved somehow? I couldn't imagine how.

But even if that idea is for the birds, she's been here a few years and is married to the cop who'd been on the case first. She looks sharp, intelligent, sure to have some ideas. But one thing is for sure . . . two things, actually. One: asking Sadie to postpone this holiday would start World War III. The other: when I talked to Maisie now, if she struck a false note at all I would *hold her.*

While driving to the airport, I tried to make conversation with Sadie that might lead to a question or two. I struck out entirely. She just wasn't having any. "That's police business, not mine," she said.

I thought of replying, "But I hear *everywhere* that you're quite influential." Instead, prudence prevailed. Maybe I'm getting chicken in my old age.

At the airport I drove out on the tarmac and stopped alongside the Hawker Siddeley. Everybody else had boarded and there was plainly an air of let's-get-the-hell-out-of-here as O'Kennedy hurried down the steps to help. I thought of Maisie and her distracted manner, and of the pilot with the girl in Inuvik, and I thought, well, they'll have to stand a little more.

O'Kennedy must have read at least a bit of my mind. "You saw that lady longlegs in the crowd yesterday," he murmured, out of earshot of Sadie. "Well, she's aboard. Wouldn't mind that one throwin' me over her shoulder and carryin' me off to some cave." I had an idea from the way he spoke that he might have tried to make that happen and had struck out.

"She say when she's coming back?"

"She said something about seeing us again Friday. That's the next scheduled plane in."

"Can I have a couple of minutes with her before you go?"

He looked amused. "Sure, General."

I climbed in, noticing many I'd flown with yesterday. There was no sign of anyone new, like the half-bald guy. The layover had been a break for the mourners, getting out without having to wait for the Friday flight.

Maisie had a window seat. One beside her was empty but I sat on the chair arm, fielding her reaction—which was a surprised, "You going out again already?"

I trotted out my heavy artillery. Watching intently for reaction of any kind, I shook my head, kept my voice low. "That's not why I'm here at all. I've been thinking overnight that I shouldn't have let you go and now I've got a chance to remedy that. I have a feeling I should get you off this flight so you can tell me about Dennissie. Everybody says you were close. I want to know a lot that you must know—people he spent a lot of time with. Anyone who had tended to push him around or anyone he had pushed around. And especially . . ."—I paused—"your relationship with him."

In swift succession she registered shock, dismay, disbelief. At the mention of relationship I thought I saw a shadow, a flicker, like a memory going by at speed and then suppressed as she wailed, "But my job interview! I'm going to be late as it is! I told the police everything I could think of . . ."

"But that was right after it happened," I said. "You've had a lot of time to think since then. Were you ever in his house?"

Tears came to her eyes. They were real tears. "Yes, twice." Her voice was even lower than usual. "Both times Thelma was there, too."

"What were your visits about?"

She seemed nonplussed. "Just visits!"

"Were you in his room?"

She hesitated a split second. "No."

"You sure?"

"Yes."

I stared at her, almost believed her, and noticed the fascination with which others nearby were trying to hear her low voice.

I thought for a few seconds, weighing what she had said, and then abruptly changed my mind. I sometimes do that in interrogation, plant a small bomb and then defuse it. It's a matter of instinct. I had scared her. Letting her stew for a couple of days might produce more results than going on now, when most of my information was secondhand, or guesswork. Her home was here, with her mother. She'd said she was coming back. And if she didn't, with her looks she sure couldn't get far unnoticed. Might win the Wanted Poster of the Year award and become a collector's item.

"You're definitely coming back Friday?"

She nodded. "That's the next flight in."

"All right. I'll be ready for you then. And you be ready, too."

She was dabbing at her eyes when I left.

Outside, I watched Sadie as major domo, telling O'Kennedy to be very careful with a bag marked FRAGILE and getting the reply, "Oh! *careful!* So that's what *fragile* means!"

When she boarded and O'Kennedy was about to follow, I stopped him. "Something you said about Maisie," I began. "A suggestion that she'd be a, um, real asset in fun and games, and I assume this isn't the first time you've run into her. Ever get close?"

"Once, for about five seconds." I had an idea he didn't often look really rueful, but he did now, shaking his head. "She's a riddle. You take a look at her and think, hey, here's a live one . . . That's what I thought. One night at the hotel when we were on a layover we had the radio going in the dining room after dinner, some people dancing, nothing much else to do, and I danced with her and it was fine until I started to hold her closer and make a pitch and she just froze. In no time at all she's headed for the kitchen. A real surprise to me, I'm tellin' you. I don't generally get brushed off so fast, if at all." He thought for a few seconds. "I heard about her and Dennis Raakwap being close before what we Irish call 'unrest' hit Sanirarsipaaq and he got snuffed. He must've had something I didn't." Another pause. "As you can tell, I've thought about her a lot. Sounds crazy with a looker like her, but the only answer I can come up with is that she's really inexperienced and Dennis knew the way around and didn't push. I mean, in my opinion Maisie just doesn't know how to handle the effect she has on men . . . What a fookin' waste!" He sighed. "Gotta go."

I wheeled the van back toward town. I'd been thinking about giving mother time for breakfast, tea, a smoke, before calling Franklin House. Back at the detachment I got big Sophie on the phone and then mother, feeling soothed by mother's slow voice saying she was getting better every day, her head didn't hurt so much. I told her Annie was fine, the kids were fine, we had good caribou steak last night. The ordinary family things.

Then, it seemed, Dr. Quinn Butterfield had just dropped in to see her and wanted to talk to me.

All was well, he said, except, "I should mention, we had a call at the hospital last night that was a little strange. The night nurse who took the call said she was pretty sure it was a man, or anyway a person with a low or muffled voice. Wouldn't leave a name. Asked how your mother is and when she'd likely be well enough to be discharged. Hung up when the nurse asked for identification or a number she could call back on."

The caller could have been anybody, of course. Erika or Maxine would have left their names, and they didn't have low voices. It occurred to me that Maisie did. I called my brother Jopie in Holman.

"Did you phone the hospital about mother last night?"

"No, why?"

I told him about the call. "Might be nothing, just somebody curious, but I'm worried. We all have to remember that she's the only one to see who charged out of that house after the murders. We *all* have to watch what we say about her and her movements from now on. She might be in a lot of danger—"

"How about getting a guard?" Jopie asked.

"We've got one, RCMP, posted at Franklin House. But this call I'm talking about was not to Franklin House but to the hospital, where they'd know more than anybody else about her condition, and when she might be discharged."

S I X

Bouvier had been making tea. As he poured for me I was pacing and worried. A man, the nurse *thought*. But couldn't be sure. Voice muffled. I picked up the phone and called RCMP Yellow-knife. The corporal on the switchboard put me through to Super-intendent Abe Keswick's office. He wasn't in. I was transferred.

"Inspector Sutherland," a female voice said.

"Matteesie," I said, and told her what was worrying me: "In fact, she wouldn't know the killer," I explained, "hasn't a clue, except that he, she, or it knocked her down. Would you put out a memo to that effect, so that our own people won't be talking as if she's important to the case? Abe Keswick arranged a guard at Franklin House to check visitors. Could you get a report? Has anybody been nosing around?"

"Right. You getting anywhere there?"

"Just plugging along, so far."

"I'll get back to you about Franklin House, but I was going to call you this morning. Two things. Forensics will have a man there either tonight or tomorrow, as soon as he's looked at the bodies."

I was surprised. "He didn't look at them last night?"

"They were held up in Cambridge by that storm you had, too. They're just on their way here now."

So much for Barker's goddamn speed at getting the bodies out of here. "You mentioned two things. What's the other?"

"Inuvik picked up a guy drunk and carrying drugs who came in from Sanirarsipaaq Saturday. Don't know any more details yet."

"Any bloodstains on his money or anywhere else on him?"

"I don't think so or it would have been reported. I'll tell Inuvik to have a good look. If there's any I'll call."

"Okay. I'm going to put out a memo, copied to everybody in G Division, to search every arrest looking for bloodstained money, and look hard, because attempts might be made to wash it off."

"Right."

"Oh, one other thing," I said. "Will you tell Inuvik there's a woman due in there this morning from here. Maybe a material witness. Named Maisie Johanson. Tall, um, white, noticeable legs—"

"Why, Matteesie!" she snorted. I got it. Noticing legs is sexist, of course.

"It's just what you'd notice first," I said firmly. "Anyway, she knew the murdered guy well. I'm going to talk to her Friday." I figured Inspector Sutherland would be wondering how come I let Maisie go today, so I said, "She lives here, her mother runs the hotel, and she said she'd come back. You gotta believe somebody."

Bouvier had been listening. I told him the Yellowknife end of the conversation.

"What was the money Dennis had on him, anyway?" I asked. "I mean, what kind of bills?"

"Mostly twenties and tens, it's written down somewhere how much of each, all covered with blood." Suddenly he grinned. " 'Covered with blood!' When I'm typing the report Steve is looking over my shoulder and I keep using 'covered with blood' this and 'covered with blood' that and Steve explodes—" Bouvier did an imitation—" *'For Christ's sake . . . everything's covered with blood! Whaddaya expect with people bleedin' upstairs, downstairs, and in the fuckin' kitchen.'* "

I wanted to stay on the track. "If there's more about the money tell me when we get to it. Go back to the beginning."

Bouvier opened a file folder and consulted some notes, then left the file open but didn't read from it directly. "Well, back to the night, last Friday when the weekly liquor came in. On booze days we always had one guy on duty right here in the office, usually me.

"Okay, at twelve sixteen a.m. I get a call from a guy who lives out past that row of houses. Byron Anolak. He said he'd been heading home and had found an old lady, didn't know who she was, lying outside one of the houses. I grabbed the camera and jumped in the van and got out there—"

"Grabbed the camera?"

Bouvier looked rather pleased. "Yeah. It's a habit I developed in Spence and a couple of other places. Amazing how many times a photograph stimulates the memory when some guy gets up in court and says he was home sound asleep when whatever he's up for happened. . . . Now, to save time I'll tell you not only what I got right then from Byron, but also what he added later." The second mention of Byron's name rang the bell. I remembered Erika telling me the *News/North* stringer here, Arctic College journalism grad, was Byron Anolak.

"One door, number three, was open. Byron said he thought the old lady was from there and had just fallen or something, so he started in to number three to see if he could get help and was just a step or two inside when he saw all the blood. He ran home, maybe a hundred yards, and called here and then he went back and hammered on the door to number four on the north side of the place your mother was found. The people there came to the door and said no, she wasn't from their place, she was from number two. Said they'd been watching television and had heard some noises but nothing they thought was serious considering that it was booze night.

"The man there seemed either deaf or confused, but the woman and Byron carried her in to number two, Annie's place. The two kids were playing cards, and Annie was just coming downstairs, the noise had roused her.

"The kids said that your mother, their granny, they called her, had gone next door to check some noises and hadn't come back."

"What about Annie?" I interrupted. I'd heard this from Annie herself. But sometimes recollections differ in detail.

"She said she'd come home earlier and told the kids to finish the hand they were playing, which they were doing when she went to bed. Must be a good sleeper . . . Anyway, I called Barker from there. He got over fast on his snowmobile. I heard it coming and met him outside. When we started through the door . . ." He actually shuddered.

"Okay, so you're going through the door," I prompted. He pulled himself together and went on.

"There were no lights on but we could hear a low moaning to our left, that's where the TV is."

"On or off?"

"Off. We turned the hall light on, pushed the switch up with my flashlight so we wouldn't be lousing up any prints. First we found old Thelma on the couch in the living room. She was still alive then, but seemed unconscious. The moaning was mixed with a sort of bubbling in her throat. Bleeding all over, godawful mess. We tried mouth to mouth but no good. She never did come to. We went up to the bedroom, where we found Dennis's body. As far as we could see he'd been stabbed or kicked to death, or a mixture of the two. Blood all over . . ."

"How long were you in the house that time?"

"Me, five minutes, max. Then we didn't want to disturb anything by using the phone there so Barker sent me to Annie's house to phone and get the nurse to come see your mother. He stayed in the other house because somebody had to . . . and he thought I could talk to your mother in Inuktitut."

Bouvier shook his head with a sort of sorrowful clucking sound, and let out a long breath.

"On the way there I suddenly thought of what I'd just been doing, the mouth to mouth, the bubbling noise, and threw up all over my goddamn boots, which didn't improve things a hell of a lot." He was in control again, talking with no more emotion than a guy giving the hockey scores. "I cleaned them off in the snow and went in. Your mother was sitting at the kitchen table, very groggy and confused, kept saying she just wanted a cup of tea." He stopped. "A really game old lady," he offered, and looked at me. I nodded.

"I did try to talk to her but I don't really talk her dialect, I guess, or she don't talk mine. But the kids and Annie listened to her too and we made out that she didn't remember anything after being knocked down. I asked, 'Who by?' 'Don't know,' she said."

"Exactly that? In English?"

"No," he said, exasperated. "Would she suddenly start talking English? She said '*Mi.*' It's the same in some dialects. Meaning 'I don't know,' right? I went back to tell Barker. There were people from other houses hanging around by then, packing down the snow so that there was no way we could separate them and compare them with the tracks inside. He told them to go home and nobody try to go in the house or he'd lock them up and throw away the goddamn key. We asked Byron Anolak to stand guard, he's a responsible guy, and I'd relieve him later. Meanwhile we figured next thing to do, and fast, was check around town and see who was still up." He thought about that, with a ghost of a smile. "Thought we might get lucky, I guess, find a guy staggering along covered with blood."

"Did anybody outside the house at that time know what had happened, that people had been murdered?" I was thinking, could the word possibly get around enough that whoever did it could hide his tracks?

He shrugged. "Must've guessed whatever had happened was serious, but nobody spoke up when we asked if they'd heard anything, and if so, what? The people in number four were saying 'No hear 'em, no see 'em.' Number one is empty. There's a big white woman in number five, gets paid to take in orphans and strays, kids like that. Said she didn't hear a goddamn thing, her exact words, because she'd been asleep until all the uproar got her up.

"That's when we went separately, me in the van and Barker on the snowmobile, to see what we could see. Covered the town. Saw nobody. Of course, whoever done it had plenty of head start. It was no more than eight or ten minutes before we both arrived at the detachment. When I'd hustled out of there after Byron's call, there were still lights on at the rec hall. It's supposed to close at eleven, but on booze nights that rule is relaxed a bit. Helps keep the drunks in one place so if anybody is falling-down drunk at least they won't freeze to death in some snowbank.

"When we got there the superintendent, he's not that old but not that husky, either, not the bouncer type, was just sitting in his chair, watching some guys play pool. Said when he'd tried to close up at twelve thirty some guys who'd been drinking got ugly and said they'd beat the shit out of him. We asked him if anybody had come in with blood on him, or anybody at all after midnight."

"What did he say?"

"That they were in and out, he couldn't remember specifically. Anyway, finding the rec hall open was a break in a way. Nobody there seemed to know what had happened. Of course, somebody could have been faking that, but they kept asking what the hell were we doing anyway, what right did we have to search them, and take pictures. Barker told them they'd better fuckin' well stand still and answer the questions or he'd get 'em for something, sometime, and they knew he would."

"So you took the names."

"Right. Ten of them. Listed right here." He tapped his folder.

"Blood?"

It was rather a basic question. Bouvier told me that with a look and then went on. "No blood. Several had knives, but most people carry knives. From our list and photos at least we'd know who was there right then and we could check where they'd been earlier, if we had to."

He paused for a minute and then said, "Barker told me later that one guy there, Thrasher, the one you saw in the airport wearing the hard hat, woulda been a sure suspect, crazy bastard sometimes, except we wind up giving him a goddamn alibi by listing him as being at the rec hall, a little stoned, but clean. I mean, his clothes were clean."

Bouvier rubbed one hand over his big face, then took off his spectacles and wiped the lenses with Kleenex.

"Seems this Thrasher once did a little time for beating up a girl after she'd brought a rape charge against him, but before it got to court. Don't really know the details. Anyway, the fact that the superintendent at the rec hall couldn't say for sure when anybody had come in meant we couldn't narrow that part down at all. If he was going to remember anybody arriving you'd think it would be Hard Hat, most noticeable."

"Unless Hard Hat wasn't wearing his hat."

"But he was. I've got him in some of the pictures."

I thought about it. Of course, he could have come in not wearing the hat, put it on after he got there. Also, the murderer could have run somewhere, maybe even home, ditched one set of clothes, put on others, then mingled with the crowd at the rec hall.

"We asked each guy separately how long he'd been in the rec hall. Thrasher said he'd been watching the hockey playoff on television until it was over, and then he decided to go to the rec hall. Two guys backed him up on when he arrived. Others named other places they'd been. When we checked, all those stories stood up."

"Did you check alibis together or what?"

"We took five each. We've got a list of them, with notes. I took the first five and Barker took the rest."

I thought it over. It sounded like everything possible had been done according to the book, the name-taking, checks on where guys had been if they weren't at the rec hall all evening. The photos were an extra.

"How long before you get back prints of the pictures you took?"

"Should be on the Friday plane. I got that Irishman to take them with him and give them to a guy I know at Inuvik who works for *News/North.* I phoned him this morning and he said he'll print 'em fast, and give blowups to O'whatsisname to bring back."

I was respecting Bouvier more and more.

"I take it they're group shots."

Bouvier shot a sharp glance at me. "Yeah." Then sardonically: "Of course, if I'd known you wanted portrait-type stuff . . ."

I got up and wandered around the room. It was only eleven, and I'd had a big breakfast, but already I was thinking about lunch. Time changes sometimes do that to me. It was past lunch time in Ottawa.

I turned back to Bouvier. "When I was talking to Judge Charlie Litterick on the court flight to Cambridge he told me about a case a few years ago when he'd sent up a guy for four years for raping his sister. Davidee Ayulaq. Do you know who he'd hung out with around here, I mean other guys big in the violence line, including rape?"

Bouvier looked thoughtful. "When I was going through the back files, there's a transcript of the Davidee case somewhere . . ." He pulled open a door and took out a folder. "Yeah." He glanced at what was obviously a transcript, but went on to other papers. "Here's some of Barker's stuff at the time. Davidee was apparently big with the women, no names mentioned, but the guys he hung out with were, let's see, Donald Thrasher, that's Hard Hat, uh, Tommy Kungalik, and here's a surprise, Byron Anolak! Byron isn't that class of guy at all, not now, anyway. In fact, his girlfriend then and now is Debbie, the sister Davidee was convicted of raping."

He looked up. "I didn't know this stuff! Byron is the father of the little girl called Julie you might see around here, she's nearly two now, real cute, her mom is Debbie, who really looks after her . . ." He laughed. "If you see a little toddler in a squirrelskin parka with pink sunglasses with the frames made heart-shaped, you know, like valentines? That's Julie."

"Where do they live?"

Bouvier walked to a window, not the south one that faced the rec hall but a smaller one facing north. When he pointed, I could see a row of three houses straggling up a small rise.

"The one farthest from us of those three is his family's house, the new one they got after Debbie burned the other one. The judge tell you that story?"

"Yeah." I looked up the snowy, icy hill. Two of the houses were the kind you see more often than any other in the north, the 512s. From here, these were indistinguishable from one another. Davidee's family's house was one of the newer models, bigger, with a peaked roof. A woman was out at the side scraping a sealskin. A man who looked a lot older was standing by, watching her and smoking a pipe.

I turned away from the window, back to the present. "Okay, the money found on Dennis's body," I said. "Where does it fit in and how much was involved? What I was told from Ottawa was sort of confused."

"He'd just picked up his weekly pay that night, according to Margaret Johanson at the hotel, two hundred bucks, mostly in twenties and tens. But something else we haven't been able to get a handle on yet could be important. When we were doing the check at the rec hall before anybody there knew that Dennis was dead, I asked if Dennis had been in earlier.

"One of the guys said yes, maybe around ten o'clock, and he was sure because Dennis had loaned this guy fifty a week before, and that night had collected the fifty, a fifty-dollar bill, and ten dollars' interest. Anyway, when we moved the bodies into the freezer on Saturday we found this roll of close to four hundred, mostly twenties, most stuck together, but there was no fifty."

Of course, that could have gone in another transaction. Or whoever killed Dennis, maybe panicking, had grabbed some money but not all. What about the loan-sharking, though? If Dennis had been doing it on that cottage-industry level it wouldn't likely cause a murder. But maybe somebody could have been into him for a lot more. Maybe someone who had been in the rec hall for Bouvier's photo opportunity.

I said, "Okay, let's have the list of the guys in the rec hall. With your comments."

He looked a little doubtful. "Trouble is, two months here, I don't know a hell of a lot about some of them. But Barker did keep a file of guys who'd either been under suspicion or actually charged in the last few years. I'll get it out. At least he kept it in alphabetical order." He hunted, took out a folder, opened it, and nodded.

We worked at it for half an hour. I wrote down names and comments. Bouvier said he'd type it out later. It took up only two sheets of paper, the comments identified according to what Bouvier knew plus what Barker had on file.

   1. Byron Anolak. Bouvier: Seems like a clean guy, has a bad limp from a birth injury, works part-time at the Co-op, did journalism at Arctic College and gets a little work stringing as a local correspondent with *News/North*. Seems a good father to Debbie's little girl, but lives with his own family so far. He and Debbie have applied to Sanirarsipaaq Housing to rent the empty house, number 1, next to Annie's. If either of them had some kind of government job they'd probably get it. Or poor old Thelma's house when it gets cleaned up.

2. Noah Akpaliapik. Barker: Works summers for Northern Transportation, an engine-room oiler. Once charged with drunk-driving a snowmobile, hitting a house. Sentence suspended.

3. Andy Arqviq. He's only fifteen or sixteen, Bouvier thinks, school dropout, hangs around the rec hall and Co-op a lot, runs errands, has a room with the fat white woman at number 5 in the row of houses where the murder took place. Does some crude carving and hangs around Jonassie Oquataq's house a lot watching Jonassie work at stone carvings. Barker file: "Juvenile delinquent." Bouvier: "Not a bad kid in the circumstances. Our version of a city street kid."

4. Ambrose Aviugana. Barker: Used to hang out a lot with Davidee Ayulaq, Donald Thrasher, and Tommy Kungalik, sometimes in trouble, all four charged but not convicted in 1987 sexual assault on a young female, Luci Kunnuk, who refused to testify, maybe because she was intimidated either by those charged or by disapproval of other girls who hung out with the same four. Bouvier: Since I got here Aviugana and Kungalik haven't been in trouble but spend a lot of time together, drinking, hanging out with girls. Make a little money hunting seals around here and caribou from a camp on a lake south of here.

5. Paulessie Goose. Bouvier: Big kid around nineteen or twenty. Took the heavy machinery course in Yellowknife. Works at house construction in summer and some road work and carpentry. Not noticeably a big drinker but had a skinful the night of the murders.

6. Jack Kritaqliluk. Son of Sanirarsipaaq mayor. No previous trouble on the record.

7. Tommy Kungalik. See Aviugana. Short and slightly built.

8. James Nirlungayuk. Nothing known by either Barker or Bouvier.

9. Simeonie Pakkiiuq. Charged three different times with assault on Davidee Ayulak. Beat him up each time. Always due to differences over girls. Regular churchgoer. Most sober person in rec hall on the night of the murders.

10. Donald Thrasher (Hard Hat). Barker's file: Has not been in trouble with the law since Davidee was convicted, but until then was considered to be Davidee's closest friend. Competed with Byron Anolak for Debbie's favors. His testimony for the defense at Davidee's trial was that Davidee was not to blame: "Debbie was always asking for it." Also see 4 and 7 above.

I looked at Bouvier. He looked at me. I had the feeling we both were thinking, okay, we've got a list, so what?

"You see any signs of a natural-born murderer there?" I asked.

He shook his head. "Could really be almost any of them, or none."

I felt the same. Thumbnail sketches. Could have been part of a football team. Or an all-male musical.

Grasping at straws, I said, "Is any of those on the list the half-bald man we saw at the airport yesterday?"

"The guy who rode off with Hard Hat? Naw. I'd remember if he'd been there."

So the sum total of the day so far had left me no closer to any solution, or even real suspicion. Only one thing is worse than having several equally likely suspects. That is having no suspects at all.

My unreasonable hunger drifted into my head again. I consulted the wall clock, which was closing in on eleven forty-five. I would check in at the hotel and then eat.

"I'm thinking of lunch," I said.

Bouvier grinned. "It used to be funny. If noon or six o'clock came and Barker was still here the phone would ring and it would be Sadie, asking if he was here or should she try the hotel. He'd grab his parka and get out of here and I'd say, 'No, he's just left here for home, Sadie.' " He shrugged, with the merest hint of a smile. "Every time he was late for a meal she'd be sure he was at the hotel."

"She didn't like that?"

"You haven't met Margaret Johanson, the manager, yet?"

"No."

"Well," Bouvier said, as if no further explanation were needed. "Anyway, I'm ready to eat. How about you?"

"I'll go when you come back so I'll be around if somebody calls up and wants to confess and throw himself on our mercy." He lit another large black cigar with a wooden match. The flame glinted on his so round, smooth, and fully packed cheeks, and reflected cheerfully from his spectacles.

"Where are you staying? I forgot to ask."

"I've been at the hotel but Barker asked me to stay at their house and look after things. After you get back I'll go have some soup and see whether the dogs have eaten the side out of the house. The detachment phone rings in at Barker's too, if you need me."

Afterthought. "Where does Jonassie live?" I wanted to talk to him about the shamanism rumor and anything else he might tell me about Dennis and Thelma and life at Sanirarsipaaq.

"Up behind the library." I knew where the library was.

I thought about Debbie. Such names for Inuit girls always struck me odd. Her Inuit name would be something else. But right through the north many girls, even most, adopted names that the mostly nonnative teachers could handle more easily. So far there'd been nothing much to suggest that Dennis might have been sexually involved in a major way (it was hard to be sure about Maisie), but any Inuit girl in the community would know, or have an opinion. He'd been by all accounts bright and enterprising (to judge by the loan-sharking), and certainly something else had caused tears to come to Maisie's eyes when she talked about him.

I'd talk to Debbie. I had to find a trail that led *somewhere*.

An unrelated thought: Charlie the judge had made clear that Debbie and Davidee had lived in the family house after the rape and until the fire and subsequent trial. Rapist and rapee living in . . . what? Harmony? Almost incredible. Hatred maybe. But strange things happen, not only in the Arctic. There were the parents. Stoical whites were not the only people who faced what there was to face and still got up in the morning. From the detachment window I looked at their house, the usual fuel-oil tank alongside, a yellow snowmobile and a Honda three-wheel ATV parked nearby, an old forty-five-gallon barrel out front smoking from a load of burning garbage. No human in sight. Children from those and other families would be in, sitting down to eat, maybe in front of television, maybe never thinking any more about the old Davidee nightmare.

Taking it all in, I suddenly got the special feeling I sometimes have when I'm hunting something or someone, and getting close. It came on me like a sudden shiver along my spine.

S E V E N

I left the detachment in bright sunshine. The day actually felt a little like spring. Coming off the detachment's steps I ran hard and set my feet and slid along, waving my arms for balance.

Bouvier called from the doorway, "Not bad! Not bad!"

An old Inuk woman was coming the other way, laboring up the slope. She clapped her hands and called out something I couldn't hear and we smiled at one another, passing a few feet apart.

There were a few houses to my left, the rec hall on my right, the squatty shape of the Sanirarsipaaq hotel ahead. Early April, a lot of winter ahead yet, but fifteen hours of daylight helped. I'd looked at the climate chart for today: sunrise 04:46, sunset 19:47.

The noonday sun glittered off a line of boats overturned for the winter along the shore of the settlement's little bay. A half mile or so out on the ice I could see a hunter crouched immobile at a seal hole. I couldn't see it, but his rifle or harpoon would be ready. The stillness was essential. The slightest movement, a change of shadow—result, no seal at that hole, it would go somewhere else for air. Beyond the hunter the jumbled pressure-packed ice of the McClintock Channel lay between this eastern shore of Victoria Island and, a hundred miles or so away, the western shore of Prince of Wales Island. One summer when I was a boy we traveled with two other families across the channel to Prince of Wales in an umiak—a good-size boat—looking for whales and walrus. We found some and had a good summer there, eating regularly.

As I neared the hotel a woman in a red dress towed an embarrassed-looking city-type man toward the middle of the road. He wore a yellow toque perched on top of his head, and under his open parka showed a scarf, shirt, necktie, and three-piece suit. A shyly smiling Inuit girl followed with a camera, focused, clicked it.

"There, now you can put that along with your huge expense account," the woman said as the three of them laughed, slipped, and slid toward the hotel's plywood door. The other two entered. The red dress and its occupant stopped at the door. "Hi there, Matteesie!"

Obviously, Margaret Johanson. We hadn't met before but she would know who I was and what I was here for. So, by now, would nearly everybody in town. Because I once had been one of their own, they tended to know not only my name and rank and successes and failures but also to have taken sides in debates as to whether I was the great brain of Arctic crime or just dumb lucky.

As for Margaret, well, every Arctic settlement has its reigning beauty, or sex symbol, as the case may be. I thought she would be a bit of both. There was just enough weight on her that even the Inuit elders would approve, their traditional belief being that the fatter the woman the better. I figured her to be in her forties, with the ripeness that some women get when older. She'd probably look good in anything. Or nothing. That last was not a prurient thought, simply an observation.

She smiled, eyes lively, teeth as white as any in a toothpaste commercial but just crooked enough to provide a tiny clue about a nonyuppie background: no money for braces. "Well, do I pass?"

I smiled. "Caught looking."

"Just leave your bag here, unless it's full of secret codes and classified information. Or even if it is."

I put down the bag and dropped my boots among others whose owners had obeyed the sign over the dining room entrance that read, LEAVE BOOTS HERE, THIS MEANS YOU!

The city-dressed man had disappeared to the left and down a

couple of steps to join a group of others who were kidding him about what they'd tell his wife.

"What was the photo opportunity all about?" I asked.

"Polaroid proof that everybody up here doesn't wear caribou."

Following her down the steps, I was hit by a mixture of aromas: fresh baking, rich meat, coffee. Tables were scattered about. Three were full, two white and the other Inuit, probably all of both backgrounds being either government people or construction workers. Somebody told me once that seventy percent of all air travel in the north was by government people, which besides including me tells you a bit about civil service and native-organization expense accounts and why hotels like Margaret's can charge $185 a day, including three meals and four to a room.

They had finished eating and were drinking their coffee or tea. Another table had one man at it, the hefty, gray-haired Inuk with a huge head whom I'd seen at the airport yesterday: Jonassie the shaman and carver. He looked somewhat apart from the others not only in appearance but in what he was doing: drinking tea while reading Monday's *News/North*, where the front-page headline read, NO ARRESTS IN DOUBLE MURDER. He glanced at me, upended his teapot for a final few drops, drank that unhurriedly and folded his paper.

"Margaret," he said as he passed her. "Matteesie."

But he didn't stop, as might have been natural. She looked after him, shrugged, turned back to me, and waved toward an oilcloth-covered table set against one wall. "Help yourself. I'll see about the soup situation." I was being frankly inspected by those at the other tables. Some smiled at me, some just nodded briefly and went on cleaning up the last of their pie and ice cream. On the serving table were several two-cup teapots, the stainless steel kind that inevitably spill tea in several directions when you pour, along with mugs, saucers, assorted teabags, a jar of instant coffee, a jug of milk.

Unless a miracle had occurred, the milk would be from Milko milk powder, the only kind most Arctic people ever had unless they were in one of the big settlements. I never had fresh milk until I was twenty. I remember way back there sometime there was a rock song with a line, "I believe in miracles." Hearing it improperly, I had thought the line was, "I believe in Milko." I had thought that was nice for the Milko people, that kind of approval from a rock group, and wondered how much the plug had cost. Even now, some northern youngsters, getting real fresh milk for the first time, whine that it tastes funny.

There were baskets of sliced fresh bread, raisin-studded scones, a single doughnut, the remains of four pies, a tall plugged-in urn of the sort that dispenses hot water, a small glass-fronted cooler full of soft drinks in cans. A handwritten sign on the cooler door read "$1.50." I took bread, still warm, scones, hot, and carried my plate to the table Jonassie had just left, which Margaret was clearing. The girl who'd carried the camera a few minutes earlier brought me soup, thick and peppery.

I was finishing the soup and my third hot buttered scone when Margaret emerged from the kitchen with a plate of steaming potatoes and a thick slice of musk-ox pot roast, all of it covered with rich brown gravy. She brought cauliflower with a cheese and curry sauce steaming hot in a separate dish, creamed corn in another.

The other tables emptied, guys sticking toothpicks in their mouths, taking drink cans from the fridge, one wit calling in an artificially prissy voice, "Anyone for tennis?"

Margaret had got herself some coffee and wandered over to look from the window beside me. It wasn't a scenic delight: some plywood covered by tattered plastic, a pickup truck that apparently had been snowed in for a winter or more. A pair of snowshoes stuck into a snowbank had fallen over.

"I suppose you grow your own cauliflower," I said.

Well, she did smile, and turn to me. "Behold the smartass Inuk." She left the window and, on the way by, stopped by my table. "Want some company?"

"Sure do," I said.

"Jesus," she said, dropping into the chair opposite, "how come you didn't say, 'Especially in your case,' or something to make a woman feel good."

"Especially in your case," I said.

"That's better."

Oddly enough, with that she immediately seemed to sag, as if her "Especially in your case" line had been something she did from memory and couldn't be bothered building upon. For a little while, as I ate, she just stared into her nearly empty cup. From what I'd been able to see of her public manner, bouncy and provocative, I imagined that she didn't often show the expression I was seeing now, as if her mind were miles away. When she looked up and caught my eye for an instant she seemed flustered, vulnerable.

"With Thelma and Dennissie running the kitchen, doin' every damn thing, I've got soft," she said. "Hard to get going again." Pause. "Son of a bitch, eh?"

I didn't reply, except to nod. I wanted her to keep talking. I wanted more about Sanirarsipaaq and its people from a nonpolice angle. If I didn't get it soon I'd have to wring it out of somebody.

She mused, "I keep thinking that if I'd been able to give Thelma a room right here so she didn't have to share a house with somebody who couldn't protect her when it counted . . ."

"But Dennis worked for you, too."

She raised her eyes. Looking into her shrewd, suddenly judgmental gaze, I felt that this wasn't just a casual unloading; that maybe ever since she had heard I was in town she'd been weighing what she knew and how much she should tell. "Hiring Dennis was just me trying to help Thelma."

"How do you mean?"

"She was worried about some of the people he hung out with. He'd done pretty well at school, saved some money from a job in Yellowknife, but then started to drift. Except for some part-timing, he was sort of bumming with the wrong kind of company. Of course, she didn't know the half of it. But when my handyman took off for Edmonton last fall and I needed somebody else, Thelma asked me to take Dennis. Her idea was that if I would go for, like, hiring him, she would make sure that he didn't goof off. God knows she did enough work for both of them, but he wasn't bad, either, no trouble to me, Thelma saw to that. He'd wait tables and vacuum and clean rooms and run errands . . ."

"Who was he was mixed up with that she didn't like?"

"She didn't know. She just had an instinct. For instance, she didn't know about how much he dealt with Hard Hat, Donald Thrasher, at all."

"What about him?"

"I don't know all of it. What I do know is that Dennis got paid two hundred a week at the hotel. I don't know when the loan-sharking started, I've got an idea Hard Hat was in on it. Anyway, people would borrow money from Dennis, a week at a time, high interest, and Hard Hat—"

"—would help collect the money," I said.

Surprised, she said, "How did you know?"

"If Dennis was the kind of basically harmless guy that everybody says, he'd need an enforcer."

She nodded. "Yeah. The way I first suspected was that Hard Hat sometimes called Dennis here. I don't think he ever showed up at Thelma's house, at least not when she was aware. She'd go home after work every night, you know, turn on the TV, half the time fall asleep, wouldn't know who was going in and out . . ."

She stopped there. I was wondering a little about how she knew all this. Where she stopped was not where her thoughts stopped, I was pretty sure. Somebody running a hotel, especially in a small settlement, comes to know most of what there is to know. Like the closeness between Dennis and Hard Hat, which Bouvier hadn't mentioned at all, even when we were looking right at Hard Hat at the airport. If Barker had known, surely it would have been on the record, especially after the murders. Meaning that, in public, anyway, Dennis and Hard Hat must have been very discreet. Barker was the man who had said so often, "This is my town," with the implication that he knew everything that was going on. Or did he just not care about Dennis's loan-sharking, thinking it was just loans between friends, too small-time to worry about?

"Did Thelma ever indicate to you that she was worried, either for herself or for Dennis? Anything else that bothered her a lot?"

Quietly, "This thing with Hard Hat would have, if she'd known about it."

By now we were alone in the room. I didn't push. If I was right that she simply wanted to talk to me as a policeman, eventually she'd get to her main reason.

She started out, "You really wanta listen to, well, guesses?"
"Yes."

She took a deep breath. "Well, you met my daughter at the airport. She got pretty emotional about Dennis being killed. When the flight had to lay over and she came back here, she told me about meeting you, which led to other things. That's when I started to think about talking to you. Maisie doesn't really fit in here . . . What I mean is, totally different kind of person, different interests. She doesn't hang out with the local kids maybe as much as she should, or could, but through Dennis got to know some of them and learn or guess things, like about the Hard Hat connection—which incidentally, sometimes resulted in beating up guys who couldn't pay but were scared shitless to let the police know why they were beaten up."

A lot here was new. But so far, how could it lead to Dennis and Thelma being murdered? The enforcer doesn't usually bump off his meal ticket.

I'd try another tack: Dennis and Maisie. "For him to let her know, or guess, all that, they must have been pretty close."

She considered one more time what she was saying and where it was leading, made a face, shook her head, let out a long breath.

"That's what stopped me! If I'd told all I know to Steve Barker he'da been out with all guns blazing and it woulda got all over town, what was going on and who'd blown the whistle. Next thing Maisie would be involved, or might be involved, other kids treating her like shit, which they can do. She doesn't deserve that."

I didn't quite get it. This sounded like more than just the loan-sharking.

There was another long pause. Then new territory suddenly arrived on the agenda.

Margaret gave a sigh, then her eyes met mine. "One of the things she told me after the murders was that Dennis sometimes took girls home with him at night after Thelma was asleep. The way Maisie knew this was that he'd tried to get *her* to go with him."

Margaret's eyes were angry. "It started right here in the kitchen! Maisie liked him in that sort of, well, I hate to say it this way, but it's the way I think of it, that sort of heiferlike way she has. Pay no attention to how she looks, like the miniskirt at the airport, for God's sake, it's just she craves attention, and when she gets the wrong kind, well . . ."

I thought she started something there then abandoned it.

"But she's inexperienced. Tall women have trouble anyway, unless they're models. In Calgary before she came up here she spent more time running marathons, competing, doing the high jump damn near onto our last Olympic team, than dealing with men. Strong as a horse, physically, but I don't know how I could wind up with a daughter so clueless about men. Dennis was a happy-go-lucky kind of a guy and she liked that. When he propositioned her, not in so many words, she didn't believe he was serious." She looked at me wryly. "Or says she didn't. I guess I don't really know everything that goes on in her head."

"She told you about him asking her to go home with him?"

She looked surprised. "Yeah. That's the only way I could know." After a thoughtful pause, sarcastically emphasizing some words, she continued, "After he mentioned it the first time and she thought he was kidding, a couple of days later he came back to it, in Technicolor. There was *no* problem, his granny *always* went to sleep watching TV on the *downstairs* couch, his room was *upstairs*, if Thelma did wake up she *always* just went to her own room, she *never* even heard him come in, *never* woke up until morning, and they could thump away with some music up there, have some fun, so how about it? Dennis was a pretty confident guy in a lot of ways, even if he was also stupid in this deal, seeing Maisie as just another stray piece of tail. Especially *Maisie,* for God's sake."

Piece of tail was an expression I hadn't heard for a while. Used to be popular when I was younger—and when Margaret was younger.

"Anyway, she just laughed it off, but then began to hear around that not everybody, I mean, not every other girl she knew or knew of, did turn him down. Especially on booze nights, he'd get a couple of drinks into some girl and take her home with him."

"I thought the booze committee was pretty tough about who could bring stuff in. Was Dennis considered an okay guy?"

She shrugged. "Once in a while, maybe once every few weeks, he'd apply and they'd let him bring in something, a case of beer or maybe a bottle of something. He never pushed it or applied every week or showed up drunk. Thelma didn't even know he drank. Thought he just got it for friends who couldn't."

I thought of a way Dennis could have worked it. Maybe on the nights he did get something to drink it was when he had a girl lined up for his we'll-sneak-past-Thelma game. But it couldn't have been that way, at least involving a girl, on the night of the murders. No ordinary girl is going to work Dennis over the way he wound up dead. Then again, I thought, how ordinary is Maisie? Not very.

I kept on. Could Dennis possibly have taken *two* people home with him that night, a girl and another guy? Or just another guy? It didn't come clear, to me. He's going to take a guy home with him and they're going to get stinking and start fighting? I wondered if maybe the guy in the house with Dennis that night hadn't been a regular at all, but a first-timer, or maybe not there for sex or booze, but for some other reason or for a combination of reasons. Not for robbery, or Dennis wouldn't have been left with a fair amount of money, even if what we did find on him did not include the fifty that Bouvier had mentioned. We didn't know how much more might have been taken.

Margaret and I had both stopped talking.

Suppose that, for some reason I hadn't yet come up with, some guy just wanted to beat hell out of Dennis, wound up killing him, and then, coming downstairs, had heard a sound and realized that there was somebody else in the house?

Or maybe the noise upstairs had wakened Thelma. Two guys fighting to the death are almost certain to be much noisier than a guy and girl making love (the exceptions being those rare occasions, of sometimes treasured memory, when the reverse is true). If, for whatever reason, she had staggered half-asleep off the couch and yelled something, maybe even recognized the guy, and if he had thought of what he'd done with Dennis upstairs, he would have know that he had to shut Thelma up, too.

"It opens up an awful lot of possibilities," I said finally, not naming them.

Suddenly Margaret yawned and looked at her watch. "God," she said, rising quickly. "I've got to clean up in here and set tables for tonight." I stood up, too, suddenly feeling a little surprised that she'd let Maisie fly out of here when she could have used both help and company. Whose idea had it been for Maisie to get away from the heat for a while?

"Had she planned this trip for long?"

Margaret shook her head. "Applied for a job and got called in for an interview."

"What kind of job?"

"Librarian. She took library science in Calgary."

Margaret was on her feet, looking rather forlorn. I have these impulses sometimes, with people I like—wanting body contact, nothing necessarily major, just touching a hand or whatever.

She was looking at me, smiling, guessing. "Don't," she said.

I took a can of ginger ale from the cooler on the way by. We walked along the dining room and up the two steps to the half-door leading to her tiny office. The lower half had a slice of shelving on top, a flat place to hold the register she gave me to sign.

"None of what you said will come back on you," I said.

"I'm counting on that. How'll you manage it?"

"I'll manage." Bouvier and I could ask around, starting with girls Dennis hung out with, put some heat on them if we had to.

Handing me a key with the number four on it, she said, "This opens the front door, too. I lock it when I go to bed. As for the rest . . . an Irish friend of mine sometimes says, the height of good luck to you."

"The friend's name wouldn't be Kieron O'Kennedy, would it?"

"Jesus," she laughed. "And he overnighted here only once!"

I walked up six steps to the landing, turned, went another six steps to the second floor. Number 4 was at the end of the building. The room door was wide open as is usual in the north when a room has been cleaned but not occupied. What was not usual was that in a chair by the window was Jonassie. He must have come upstairs after he left the dining room. That was nearly an hour of patient waiting, figuring that I'd either come up or he'd see me from the window heading for the detachment and follow me. Whatever the case, obviously he was serious about wanting to talk to me.

"Hi," I said.

He was smoking a pipe. The smoke hung in the room. He shifted the pipe from his right hand to his left as he rose and said, "I'm Jonassie, the carver."

I'd been familiar with the name and reputation, but until yesterday not with the face. I could imagine him wearing the carver's mask against the stone dust while working inside, or outside bundled up in the cold working with axe and crowbar and maybe wedges on a piece of stone until he found the shape he was looking for, the stone's inner spirit that told good carvers what to aim for. I knew carving better than I did shamanism, but I'd heard a Winnipeg Art Gallery curator say that Jonassie's carvings always had a shamanistic content and that this was regularly remarked upon by curators and collectors.

"You are also a shaman," I said.

I saw a glint of humor in his eyes.

He nodded. "And I hear," he said, "on the radio, no less, from Yellowknife and Inuvik and other places, that police are proceeding on at least a rumor that there is some shamanistic connection to these murders. So I thought I should introduce myself and say that I know you by reputation and would be happy to help in any way I can."

I looked around. There were four glasses on the dresser. I fleetingly remembered the cocky young defense lawyer on the court's flight to Cambridge, and his scorn for four to a room. It also occurred to me that Jonassie could be a suspect, a man very strong in his body. At this point anybody in Sanirarsipaaq with the size and strength had to be among the suspects. Still, the rumors about shamanism being involved in the murders could be best checked out, for now, with the shaman himself.

"I would like to talk to you," I said.

He jerked his head toward the open door. I read that as telling me that our talk should be more private. "Maybe if you would drop in to my home a little later?"

That suited me very well. "I'll stop at the detachment for a few minutes, then come to see you."

As it turned out, that meeting turned out to be considerably delayed. When I got to the detachment the door was locked and the phone inside was ringing. By the time I picked up the receiver, Bouvier was doing the same at Barker's house.

"I got it," I said, and he hung up.

"Matteesie," a familiar voice said. "Charlie Litterick. You making any headway there?"

I thought of Hard Hat's involvement with Dennis, and the unfocused feeling I now had about Maisie and Dennis. "Certainly nothing more than circumstantial," I said.

"Well, here's some more of the same. Circumstantial, I mean. After the court recessed for lunch I was doing a brisk walk out towards the old DEW line site to work up an appetite and clear my head about the case I've got here. On one of the back streets who do I see but the guy I was telling you about when we flew in here, Davidee Ayulaq! I'd told you he was tucked away in the pen at Prince Albert, so I thought I'd better let you know he's around. I don't know any more than that, yet. But he was eligible to apply for parole after serving two-thirds of his sentence, meaning thirty-two months. That would be five or six weeks ago, and he must have got it. When I saw him he was fifty, sixty yards away starting a snowmobile, not looking my way, but when he was pulling his helmet on I couldn't mistake that half-bald head."

Half-bald head!

"I'm running a check right now to see what happened. I'll hope to call you back in a few minutes."

In less than five minutes, just as Bouvier arrived, the phone rang again. "Damnedest thing," Charlie sighed. "I told you Davidee is a great con man. Conned his parents about the early rapes, conned the police there—Barker, I guess—the second time. If that girl hadn't burned the house down, he . . . well, anyway, he did the same con job in the pen. Read some law books and convinced some fruitcake prison psychiatrist that never mind the way the old Inuit used to do it, in modern Canada it was cruel and unusual punishment not to let him go home after paying his debt to society, as the saying goes.

"This psychiatrist spread the word around to a few other bleeding hearts in the civil liberties game. They got a lawyer. When the parole was granted and he was still bound by his sentence not to return home, he had to name where he would be living so he could report weekly to a parole officer, in this case RCMP. He told them Cambridge, because it was the closest RCMP to Sanirarsipaaq, as close as he could get legally. Meanwhile his, uh, support group took my banishment stipulation to court on the grounds that this was discrimination, an extra penalty applied only to one group, natives, and they won. I guess that means that when the paperwork of transferring his parole from Cambridge to Sanirarsipaaq goes through, you'll have him there."

I said, "I did see him, a few seconds only, at the airport here Tuesday. I wondered who the guy was who was half-bald."

"But Barker would know!"

I spoke again the immortal words, "Barker ain't here."

Bouvier got in on the last of the conversation. I filled him in on what I knew, and phoned RCMP Cambridge. Anybody paroled has to check in regularly at a designated parole office and cannot leave town without permission. Reporting is commonly once a week at the start, rising to less frequent periods if he keeps to the schedule and keeps his nose clean. It turned out that, originally, before the banishment thing was settled in his favor and Davidee was paroled to Cambridge Bay, he'd reported faithfully. Now that the court had ruled that he could return home, the paperwork was being done to transfer his parole point to Sanirarsipaaq.

"In fact, it's supposed to come through today," the corporal at Cambridge said. He was a Six Nations Indian from Ontario and a tough cop. "We'll be faxing it up and then he'll be your baby."

I said, "While you've had him did he ever ask for permission to leave Cambridge at all? Like to come here?"

"No. Not to Sanirarsipaaq. He knew he wouldn't have got that, of course. He did get leave every week to go to a camp north of here at a place called No Name Lake, to do some trapping and hunt caribou. He said he wanted to make some money, instead of depending on welfare. I even liked him some for that attitude."

The good con man at work. No Name Lake is about halfway between Cambridge and Sanirarsipaaq. My guess was it would take no more than a few hours of fast snowmobile travel to get from there to either place. So every time he'd had leave he could have been coming here from No Name but not showing his face.

I was on the point of saying that I'd seen him here yesterday, but changed my mind in time. Obviously, he had broken parole at least that once. But I didn't want him picked up on that technicality. I'd rather have him here where I could talk to him. I wanted to know where he'd been last Friday, when murder had been done and he was supposed to be in Cambridge. I wondered about times before last Friday, when he might have been here taking up again with the guys Barker's files identified as being his special buddies.

I said to Bouvier, "Find out how long it takes a fast snowmobile to get from here to No Name and from there to Cambridge."

"Will do."

I told him about seeing the shaman at the hotel.

"I'd better go see him or he'll think I'm not coming."

I was halfway to the door when the phone rang again. Bouvier called, "Inuvik. For you."

"Constable Joyce, sir," a youngish voice said. "Uh, maybe I overstepped something here, but you know, your call to sort of keep track of this woman, Maisie Johanson?"

"What about her?"

"I was doing some work on the computer, running the name of a guy here we caught with drugs. When that was done, just for something to do I ran Maisie Johanson. Got it on the screen now. Used to live in Calgary? Well, I'll read it to you . . . 'Charged with assault causing bodily harm—' " He laughed and said, "Sorry, sir, I have to laugh at this . . . 'Bodily harm, in the savage beating of Calgary Stampeders football player, Jerome Radalafski, whose collarbone was broken in the affray. She pleaded self-defense, that Radalafski had tried to have sex with her against her will, which he'd been charged with, too. This happened during a victory party after a game. While she was defending herself vigorously, by her account, Radalafski fell through a window of the second-story motel bedroom where she'd been taken not knowing they were going to be alone in there.' "

"So what happened?" I asked.

"Judge gave 'em both probation."

E I G H T

I would have called Jonassie to tell him that I'd be delayed, but after talking to the judge and to RCMP Cambridge and the constable in Inuvik with his revelation about Maisie's prowess in fighting the good fight for virtue, Maxine phoned from CBC Inuvik. The Davidee case—it had been on the news wires that he was now free to return home. Had he arrived yet? Not that I knew of, I said. Would he move back in with his family? I didn't know; I told her to try me tomorrow.

Anything else new on the case? "We're working on it," I said, meaning that as a joke because it was the same response that Barker had given her days ago.

She didn't laugh. She had something else in mind, off the subject. "Did you see the piece in *News/North* about a new course for natives as news directors and producers?"

"No."

"It's going to mean a couple of months each in Ottawa, Toronto, and Edmonton CBC, but the graduates, they say, will go on to greater things."

My immediate thought was that such a course would be perfect for her: she had done journalism at Arctic College, had done well at CBC Inuvik, was ready for a step up. Turned out that's what she was thinking, too. "I've applied," she said. "Keep your fingers crossed for me." Then, innocently, "In Ottawa I might even get to meet Lois."

The next phone call was from Lois. She asked first about my mother. I reassured her, based on what I knew that minute. Then she went on to the murder case. "I wish you'd get everything settled and get back here with me," she said with a quiet warmth. When she hung up, I was left wondering, as I often did, indecisively but with a nagging concern, about our future.

The mention of my mother made me think of calling Yellowknife again. It must have been a hunch. I couldn't get through to Dr. Butterfield but he'd left a message with his nurse that my mother seemed to be having a delayed reaction that wasn't good, and he would phone me in an hour. He phoned in twenty minutes, said he didn't know for sure yet what was happening but she seemed dazed. "It's too soon to be more specific, but we've moved her out of Franklin House and back to the hospital."

"Should I come?" I asked. He thought that over, then said, "I'll call you back in the morning," and left me worrying. I called my older brother Jopie in Holman at the musk-ox meat co-op. Told him she'd had a setback and would he pass it on. Other dozens of our relatives live in or around Holman. Already, it seemed to have been a long day.

In the end, around four, I walked north past the library toward Jonassie's house. He was outside of his back door, dressed in a long smock, fur hat, swinging what looked something like an axe, and wearing a face mask and goggles on his huge grizzled head. He was just starting to hew away at a chunk of stone, the preliminary stage in getting a stone ready for carving. When he swung the heavy mallet above his head and crashed it down on the stone, chips and splinters bounced off his upper body and the mask. Then he noticed me.

"Ah, Matteesie," he said. "Come in."

He nodded that huge head at me, pushed up his face mask, and led the way up a few steps and through the cluttered vestibule into his cluttered kitchen, like no other kitchen on earth except maybe that of another master carver. Stones of various shapes and sizes littered a rumpled canvas laid on the floor, along with chisels, files, sandpaper, and other aids to carving. Bits of stone lay here and there on the wooden floor. A pile of white dust had been shoved into a corner by a push broom, which had been left on the spot, leaning against the wall. The stove was gas, not lit. Chairs and table were of unpainted wood, appearing to be hand-hewn. I was curious about where they'd come from. Perhaps done from driftwood, I thought, although not much driftwood got this far north —not like on the shores of the Beaufort Sea where I'd been brought up. Driftwood discharged from the Mackenzie River often had been used there to make our homes or summer shelters.

The table, also canvas-covered, held work that already had been started. He pointed out some shapes to me, explaining what he saw in them that he would develop. When I stared hard I could see, only crudely yet, what he saw in the stones: a polar bear killing a seal, a hunter dwarfed by a giant Arctic hare (it is not uncommon in such carvings that something people can eat will be depicted as larger than its hunter), a little stone igloo with a sled beside it and tiny shapes of dogs.

In the next room a kettle steamed lightly on a table beside a casual array of mugs and milk and sugar. Jonassie picked up a half-full teapot, filled two mugs, put them in the microwave, and turned the dial. As digital numbers ticked and we waited for the final ping, I remembered my mother many times in camp trying to coax a few twigs or bits of dried grass into enough heat to boil water and make tea.

"Sorry for being late," I said.

He smiled, watching the microwave's timer. "So now you're on northern time," he said.

"Right," I said. In the north, the prudent understand that making a date is mainly to register an intention that might have to be postponed due to other matters, as had happened to me.

He put the two tea mugs on the table where there was canned milk and a bowl of sugar. We sat and stirred. His eyes were boring into mine.

When the tea had been poured and we were sipping, he said, "I have heard on the radio that Davidee has *just been cleared* to come back. That *just been cleared* surprised me. I'm not really up

on the ins and outs of the law on paroles, but does that mean that
if he was here before now it would not be legal?"

I nodded several times, a habit I have. Overkill. "That's right."

"But he's been here a lot lately! Off and on for weeks."

I was really surprised by the "off and on for weeks," but didn't
show it. Like every shaman I'd ever known, Jonassie struck me
as someone who ordinarily played cards close to his vest. The
shaman character known to us through our tribal beliefs was rarely
a gossip, and I'd say *never* one who would go against the customs
and instincts of his people; meaning he simply would not volunteer
information to police, as he had just done to me. The only variation
would be some kind of a ruse, but a ruse in aid of what?

I trod carefully. "I saw him in the air terminal Tuesday, but
didn't know who it was because I'd never seen him before or really
heard him described. Didn't know about him being half-bald."

He listened impassively. I wondered how much I could press.

"Can you tell me who saw him, where, and doing what?"

Wrong button. He shook his head. Someone back in Ottawa
might contend I could have pushed harder. But you don't get rough
with a shaman. There's no, "Okay, wise guy, let's me and you go
downtown and see how tough you are there." I smiled to think
of it.

Then he did react, an almost imperceptible flicker of the eyes.
If his mind worked even partly the way I thought it might, he
would be wondering why the smile. I didn't explain.

"I know the restrictions you feel you must obey," I said. "But
do you know if Davidee was here at the time of the murders?"

"No," he said.

"He wasn't here or you don't know if he was here?"

"I don't know if he was here at that time."

My turn again. The rumor a few days ago that shamanism had
something to do with the murders, I simply didn't believe. But in
a sense Jonassie had brought that matter up himself in my room
at the hotel. Now he was loading his pipe from an oilskin pouch,
tamping down the tobacco with a huge callused forefinger. He
struck a wooden match, puffed, tamped the hot coal with the same
finger, and almost disappeared in a cloud of smoke.

"Did you know that Davidee once aspired to become a shaman? Came to me about it?"

I shook my head, again surprised.

"Even then, and this was some years ago, he just wasn't the type. Bright enough, but with no principles. Still, some of the worse aspects had rubbed off on him. In your files you'll find, or should find, that in a sexual assault case a few years ago, before the rape incident, a girl said he had threatened her with a shamanistic curse of blindness if she didn't, uh, I believe the slang is, come across."

"I haven't gone through the Davidee files yet because it was only today I found out, and from you, that he'd been around here at all."

Jonassie dropped the matter cold, but then did go on to something that I later came to believe was his main reason for talking to me. He was almost hidden by his pipe smoke, speaking through it. This was a shaman speaking, simply, not in logic or in any way related to any rules of evidence or intent to enlighten me if I did not find the enlightenment myself.

"On the morning after the murders I was working at my new carving when I went into a sort of daydream, as I sometimes do when I'm working, and in the daydream saw a knife with a handle that was a small carving of a falcon, done in black stone of the kind found around Povungnituk, a knife handle I knew well because I carved it."

I had a strange feeling that he was acting toward me as if I myself were a shaman and would understand about daydreams that could have hidden meanings. I am not sure that he was wrong in that assessment, but what I really understood was that there was an eeriness to his story that I could not read precisely, and that I was transfixed by the eyes looking at me from this huge head and by the words coming to me through smoke that swirled all around him.

"The knife blade itself"—his words came through the smoke—"I found on the road near the rec hall a year ago, this time of year, winter but nearing spring. It was the first sunny-day thaw. Ahead of me I saw a glint, a reflection of sun from this blade below the ice.

"On digging it out I found it was an excellent steel blade five and a half inches long with an unworthy"—he stressed the word—"handle."

"Unworthy?" I asked.

"Plastic made to look like bone."

He had asked around looking for the owner. A few weeks earlier there had been some construction workers in on some job or other. They had gone. One of them might have dropped it. Anyway, nobody had claimed it, so he had smashed the plastic handle with his rock-axe and carved the small falcon from black stone as a new handle.

"The falcon," he said, "as you of course know, is one of the earth spirits that if offended can be dangerous, even cause death."

I waited respectfully. He did not go on. "I would like to see that knife if you will allow me," I said.

His face was somewhat shadowed, but there was no doubt about his regretful expression. This was the carver talking, not the shaman. "I had put it on a shelf of carvings that I might sell even though stone and steel together are not in our tradition. On the morning after the murders when I had that daydream about the knife I became very upset even before I hurried to look for it. I could not find it. And then I realized that I hadn't noticed it for a month or more."

A memory: my mother mentioning the shaman, a knife, lost.

"You mean, it had been mislaid, somehow lost?"

"Neither," Jonassie said. "I do not lose, or mislay."

"Stolen then?"

"Anyway, gone." There were no locks on his doors, he said, but he had never lost a carving before. "The people on buying trips from the galleries don't start coming until later, in better weather, so no stranger I know of has been in the house since the last time I saw that knife maybe a month or two ago."

He sighed. "But it did exist. That was no dream. I had shown it to Lewissie Ullayoroluk in case he knew of a buyer, because he travels a lot. He was away on a hunting trip when I searched for it and couldn't find it. When I told Lewissie on his return that the knife was gone, he immediately told me that he had seen that boy, Andy Arqviq, around here one day, near my house.

"Figuring that I was home, Lewissie had not thought more about it at the time. We figured out the day. I had not been home that day, I was away buying stone. So if Andy had been in my house, he'd been in here by himself."

"Did you ask him about it?"

"No. I do not want to accuse him of theft, even indirectly. I thought he would be around, he often is, but for weeks now I believe he has been avoiding me."

"But generally speaking, if it was stolen it had to be by someone local?"

He shrugged, simply not inclined to talk more.

Walking away down the slope past the library and through the school kids romping, sliding, shouting, laughing, I thought about the knife all the way. Could it have been connected to the murders? Even used against Dennis and Thelma? There is a saying about a ghost walking over a grave. I shivered.

The day got stranger and stranger. When I got back to the detachment Bouvier was not there but the van was. There was no note of explanation. It was too early for dinner at the hotel. Besides, I wasn't hungry, and the earlier word about Maisie versus the football player was not something I was ready to discuss with Margaret, yet. Then I saw that there was an incoming message on the fax machine. It was from Yellowknife and read: "Forensics has examined bodies, report being prepared. Constable Joe Pelly will arrive tomorrow morning, weather permitting, to complete forensic examination of house where murders occurred. Hi Matteessie, hope you're having fun. (signed) Max McPhee, Duty Inspector."

I put that on Bouvier's desk along with a note that I would be at Annie's house. Leaving Jonassie and walking down the hill, I had finally stowed the matter of the knife in the back of my mind, on the shelf, to be brought out when required. I'd gone on to think about finding girls who had gone home with Dennis from time to time and might tell me something I didn't know. I'd done a fair job of talking myself out of that: I could talk to probably defensive girls for days and maybe still be a panting virgin as far as real progress went. What I needed was a big, significant break. Now

I changed my mind again and was thinking that if anybody could tell me more about Dennis and his girlfriend habits, it would be the people in that same row of houses. Most of them should be home now.

I left the note telling Bouvier what I was up to and took the van. I knocked on the door of number 5 and was told by the huge woman who answered that cops were a pain in the ass, and to fuck off, she'd told Barker and Bouvier all she knew, which was nothing. In number 4 a thin and evasive Inuk with untidy hair and mustache just stood there shaking his head and saying he and his wife also had told police all he knew, which was nothing. Number 1 was empty. Number 3 was still locked on the grisly aftermath of the murders that the forensics guy and I would open tomorrow. That left one house in which, all along, I had pinned hopes for more information. I knocked on Annie's door.

"I thought you might come and see us!" Annie Kavyok said happily. Big hug, and surely I could stay for dinner, she urged. Sleep here again too, any time I wished to get away, relax. She was talking as if I was going to be here forever, which with all due respect I hoped would not be the case. And my mother? she asked. I told her the disturbing news, but that I hoped it would be better tomorrow. Her boy and girl hung back, smiling at me in the warm kitchen. Tonight she was serving a baked Arctic char stuffed with bread crumbs mixed with fennel. We ate fish, rice, bannock, pie, drank tea.

If she'd been someone I knew better, things might have gone faster. I might have mentioned that I had spent some time that day with Jonassie the shaman, might even have mentioned the missing knife in case she ever heard or saw anything of such a knife; but I did not. In talking of the food at the hotel I did mention Margaret, and thought I noted a brief darkening of Annie's determinedly upbeat manner. Why? Or did I just imagine that?

Eventually, when the kids had gone to the TV set and we were drinking tea in the kitchen, I had to face that I had come there for a purpose. There was a lot to like in Annie, as if I hadn't judged that already, and now the time had come to learn more of what she knew.

I said, "I'm wondering if you can help me with something."

Her smile evaporated. Her face was full of regret.

"Not much about that night, as you know. I was right out of it. I keep thinking if I hadn't been, none of this might have happened."

Without mentioning that the information came from Margaret, I told her that I understood that sometimes Dennis brought girls home and sneaked them in past Thelma when she was asleep.

"That's right," she said quietly. "I sometimes saw them. I don't always sleep like the dead."

"You saw some well enough to know who they were?"

She nodded several times, slowly, even reluctantly. "You know, my work here, a lot of it is with families with troubles at home, money or drink or kids that get into trouble. I've been here three years now. There's hardly anybody in town I don't know. Also, I'm a member of the Inumerit."

I felt a flash of interest. The Inumerit. In some settlements committees going by that old Inuit name were making a comeback. In the old days, before northern courts began to travel more and more to try cases where they had happened, if someone offended the rules or taboos of a settlement the Inumerit would deal with the case. It was like a loose committee of a dozen, more or less, of a settlement's most mature and respected people. They would gather in one place, summon the miscreant, and simply talk turkey.

I'd often pictured it. There in the middle would be some miserable male or female offender facing the entire power structure of the settlement. They'd be talking quietly but insistently and the accused would be listening, maybe arguing, but vastly outgunned. In a court case I'd once been part of, a defense witness, a psychiatrist, had summarized the Inumerit process as "continuing confrontational counseling," with the emphasis on "continuing." The message from the elders would be that their community could only exist in comfort and safety if certain rules were obeyed by all. The rules and ethics of decent Inuit life would be hammered home by elder after elder, world without end, the aim being to get the offender to promise to go straight. It worked more often than not, the prize being that without involving the official law at all the offender would be allowed to reform among his own people. At the same time the community would keep a person that some of them, relatives, friends, did not wish to lose no matter what he or she had done.

Cheaper and better than penitentiaries by a long shot.

Should this fail, however, the Inumerit of old could and sometimes did exercise its final solution: ban the accused from community life, tell him or her to get out and make a life elsewhere. This was a step that, in the open tundra in cruel weather and with little or no food available, sometimes had fatal consequences.

With the coming of police and courts to even the smallest settlements, the Inumerit system vanished for a time; but in recent years it had arisen again in some communities, using modern counseling methods to head off trouble, if possible, before the law got involved. Some judges now routinely sought opinions from the Inumerit, the opinions usually being to go easy on jail terms and let the community have a go at rehabilitating one of its own.

When a judge does go easy, sometimes the prosecution appeals and then legal arguments about the status and effectiveness of the Inumerit make it into court records. If a defense lawyer thinks he can make some yards by invoking the Inumerit as a traditional form of counseling by elders that has proved more effective among native people than putting people in jail, he uses Inumerit witnesses in seeking a lighter sentence. If a crown attorney thinks his prosecution case can be helped by pooh-poohing the Inumerit as being just a way of avoiding the punishment the law calls for, he'll argue that way.

When Annie Kavyok told me she served in the local Inumerit, then, it meant that she would know in individual detail those local people who got into trouble, what kind of trouble it was, and how they reacted to insistence that they must reform.

I told her what I had in mind, that it would help me if I could learn what usually happened when Dennis led someone, innocent or experienced, up those stairs next door; what inducements he might have used; whether other men were ever involved. To learn that, I had to have names. "The whole idea is to bring me closer to understanding what happened that night," I said. "How it could have happened. Who could have been involved."

"I don't know . . ." She faltered. "I don't know whether the effectiveness of what I do here, both in and out of the Inumerit, could survive . . . I've spent these years trying to get the people to trust me, let me help."

She paused, thinking it out. Silently, I tried to lead her thoughts and responsibilities a step or two past her apprehensions. Whether I succeeded, or whether she got there all on her own, I don't know. But she got there.

"On the other hand," she said, thinking aloud, "by getting this murderer even at the cost of hurting some people, maybe others will be saved."

I let out a long breath. "Could you give me a list of girls or men you've seen Dennis bringing home?"

She paused for one more instant, then reached for a notepad near her telephone and began to list the names. I read them as she wrote, hesitantly, pausing to think: Sarah, Agnes, Leah, Maisie . . . Maisie!

She might have caught my surprise. "Maisie was a little different," she said, looking up. "I was still watching only a few minutes later when she came running out, which was not really a surprise to me. Some others I saw a lot more than once. I only did see Maisie the once."

Which, of course, was more than Maisie had told Margaret about. Or had Margaret been telling me less than she knew because it might place Maisie among the murder suspects? She also hadn't told me about the flying football player in Calgary. I wondered if there was more untold about Maisie.

Around eight or a little later, still with daylight outside from the setting sun, Annie's phone rang. "I didn't want to call and interrupt something," Bouvier said. "But I thought you'd like to know. Davidee rode in on a snowmobile a little while ago, pulled up at his parents' home, went in, and hasn't come out. So I guess he's staying there."

It was hard to avoid some sense of shock that he would be moving back in with the family whose life he had damaged so much. There might be places in the world where such a prodigal son would come back and be accepted again, but I didn't know any.

"I'm coming in," I said. "See you in a few minutes."

When I got there and parked the van I walked over to the window that faced up the misty hill to the house that Bouvier had pointed out to me earlier, which now once again housed Davidee.

Bouvier, watching me, said nothing.

Still, Davidee. I had to start somewhere. I kept hearing his name but so far had never spoken to him—or seen him except that once, so briefly. Now he was so close to the detachment that if he did stay there Bouvier and I and anyone else in here would often see him coming and going. I was thinking of incidents, habits that might tell me something. Did he usually walk fast, slow, run, amble? Was he usually alone or with people? Would he be ever, never, or often seen with his father or mother or sister or sister's little daughter?

I thought about it a little more as I looked out of the window at the house where some kind of drama would be going on now, quietly or otherwise. A dim light showed through the kitchen window at Davidee's house, with an occasional shape moving around inside.

"I think I'll go up and meet the famous Davidee," I said.

Bouvier got up immediately, thought he should come, too. I said no. I pulled on parka, hat, and mitts. When I stepped outside and headed toward the house the sky was darkening and a cold wind rising.

Bouvier would be watching. All he would see was me trudging up the slope. A dog chained outside one of the other houses set up a frantic barking. When I got to the house the outer door wasn't latched. In the vestibule there was the usual jumble of clothing on wall hooks. I could hear voices from inside. I moved some boots out of the way and knocked. The voices ceased and the door was opened a few seconds later by a young woman carrying a child.

I took her to be Debbie. She looked to be around twenty, not especially pretty but smiling, cheerful-looking, with thick spectacles, her hair in neat plaits, wearing jeans and a beaded vest over a clean yellow blouse. The table had not yet been cleared after their meal. Davidee was not in evidence. Sitting at the table behind Debbie were the man and woman I'd seen only from a distance. Both looked old far beyond their years, which couldn't have been much past the late forties, being parents of Davidee and Debbie.

The man was particularly wasted-looking, thin, showing ruined teeth when his mouth dropped open. He looked scared. Maybe this was his permanent expression. He was dressed in filthy pants, shirt, layers of pullover store-bought clothing, and slippers of worn sealskin. The woman at the table had not turned her head but was glancing at me sideways from under thick eyebrows. She was wearing a neat handknit sweater with a pattern of caribou and polar bears and foxes across the breast. A ribbon was tied around thick graying hair that hung, not untidily, to her shoulders. Her sleeves were folded back on painfully thin, almost fleshless forearms. Large veins stood out on the backs of her long-fingered hands.

The bright-looking very young girl Debbie had been carrying I figured to be Julie, the one Bouvier had told me about, the one with the pink sunglasses (not now in evidence, of course). She had a round and well-fed look, bright eyes, the kind of apple cheeks that shine out of glossy government-produced tourist publications purporting to show the happy real people of the north. The table was strewn with remains of their meal: teapot, a plate of bannock, margarine, a milk jug, mugs, a platter with still one piece of fried fish on it.

Until then, no one had spoken. I said in Inuktitut that I was a visiting policee and had come to speak with Davidee.

The girl I'd taken to be Debbie looked at me sharply and went back to the table with the young child in her arms. Where was Davidee? Had he gone out unnoticed? Then there was a sleepy groan back in the house and the sound of feet hitting the floor. I thought maybe he'd been asleep, roused by my knock on the door, or my voice. A straggling curtain to one of the back rooms was pulled aside. Davidee stood in the doorway in jeans, a singlet, and thick gray woolen socks. His expression was that of someone whose sleep has been disturbed and who didn't particularly like it, but there was nothing overtly antagonistic in his manner. The half-bald head showed hair brushed over his ears on both sides from where it ended in mid-scalp.

"Looking for Davidee?" he asked.

"Matteesie Kitologitak, RCMP," I said. "I'm working on the murders. Thought you might help with a couple of things."

"I'm not Davidee," he said. He had an open, assured smile beneath a thin mustache that curled down past the edges of his lips. "I'm Byron Anolak, Debbie's boyfriend, and I don't know anything about the murders."

"He *is* Davidee," Debbie said, quietly.

For an instant, Davidee glared at her. Then he sighed in an exaggerated way, but still smiled. "Just joking."

"Don't joke with me about these murders," I said. We locked eyes. He did not drop his. Neither did I drop mine. If Debbie hadn't walked between us waving her hands and saying, "Oh, for Christ's sake," maybe we would be there yet.

"I've got a few questions," I said.

"So ask ahead," Davidee said in English.

First I studied him. Even though I wouldn't have been fooled into taking him as Byron Anolak, Debbie had stuck her knife in. And it was a knife. Whatever he felt about her, he seemed to hide it. What she thought about him, I could see from her eyes, was open contempt. What would ever make him think that she, of all people, would go along with the gag that he was not Davidee?

She spoke again. "If you had believed that he was Byron and had asked if we had any idea where you might find him, we would have answered, 'Who ever knows where Davidee is?' The real Davidee, I mean. Which is true, as you can see." A reference, I thought, to his companionable manner.

At this point the mother rose hospitably and set out an extra cup, I assumed for me, and was carrying the teapot toward the kettle steaming on the stove. Davidee almost imperceptibly raised one hand in her direction. He had only been here a short time, not much more than an hour, but he was in charge.

She stopped and went back and sat down.

I had only moved a step or two into the room. Davidee's father was still staring at me without speaking. I have rarely seen a man in such open distress.

"We'll talk outside," Davidee said.

I moved out of the doorway. He went past me, grabbed a parka off a hook, and stepped into his knee-highs. I followed.

What came next was the confusing side of Davidee. A few feet away from the door he stopped. "Look, you can see how it is in there," he said, shrugging. "It's the old story, give a dog a bad name . . . What is it you want to ask me?"

"I want to check where you were on the night of the murders."

"Not here, that's for sure."

"Tell me."

"I was at No Name Lake, I had permission to be there."

"So I've heard from the RCMP in Cambridge. But No Name isn't all that far from here."

"You don't think I could have been here and not be noticed? Davidee, the local pariah? You must be kidding. I've heard about what happened, sure. I also know that the police checked the whole town, took the names at the rec hall, and I simply wasn't there. Couldn't have been."

"And you stick to that story."

"I do."

Again he was meeting my eyes with every sign of honesty, concern, and even a little bit of pleading. For the first time I could imagine a prison psychiatrist getting to know him, believing perhaps not in his innocence, but that he didn't deserve to be canceled out of the world he'd been brought up in. Anybody not knowing the background at all might be at least unsure as to whether at any given time he was telling the truth or led the league in acting out a lie.

I wanted to shake his composure, but so far didn't have the ammunition—and, I admitted to myself, maybe I never would have.

"Okay," I said.

"You mean that's it?"

"For now," I said, and as I turned away I thought I could see a sudden change in his eyes. Not fear. Rage.

When I was walking back down the hill through the steadily darkening night I realized I had nothing new on Davidee, except impressions, and Jonassie's words about his one time interest in shamanism.

At the detachment Bouvier appeared in the doorway to meet me, a walking question mark.

"You like a drink?" I said. "I've got some rum and as long as

Margaret hasn't put somebody else in my room, we can at least sit and stare at one another."

He grinned. "Not often I get an invitation like that." I waited while he turned out the lights and locked the door. He was singing a tune I knew, but with different words.

"I've got nerves that jingle, jangle, jingle," he sang, "as we go riding merrily along."

N I N E

The next morning at seven thirty the bathroom was empty and the whole place quiet. Everyone else had eaten and vanished. I must have been sleeping like the dead to have lasted through the boots, mostly those of construction workers, going up and down the halls. I shaved, brushed my teeth, and conducted my daily debate with myself as to whether to attack my gums with a little rubber pointed thing that made them bleed, as the dentist in Ottawa had told me I must do.

"You don't want to get gum disease, do you?" he said accusingly.

I said, "When you ask that, does anybody ever say yes?"

He didn't laugh, too bad, but I really did not want to get gum disease, so I obeyed him every morning until the gums bled. I spat and cursed and hoped no native would come in and ask me why I was making myself bleed, and should they call the shaman?

Margaret was not around the kitchen when I came down. The Inuit girl served me oatmeal porridge, fried fish, toast, and honey. She asked how my mother was and looked solemn when I told her I was about to call and find out the latest. I finished my tea and went outside into the frosty morning. The spring sun was already two or three hours into the sky, visible through a cold mist that softened the outlines of houses and what lay around them. A few kids were heading by circuitous routes to be early for school, some dressed Arctic-style in caribou-skin pants and mukluks with seal-skin soles, others getting the jump on spring, as kids tend to do, with lighter clothes, store-bought anoraks, even a couple in Nikes. Most were getting in some sliding and wrestling on the way.

When I walked in, Bouvier was putting down the phone. "The forensics guy just phoned from the airport. Got in by chartered Beaver from Cambridge Bay. Wants to get at it."

After a moment's thought I said, "Pick him up and bring him to Annie's." In that I had a slightly ulterior motive. Bouvier and I both were very short on local knowledge, people, personalities. Annie already had been helpful. I thought the more she was personally involved, the better off we'd be. Her insights might point us in one direction or head us off from another.

When he was gone I called the hospital and got Dr. Butterfield. "No change," he said. I walked up the hill to where the police van was parking outside Annie's place.

In the kitchen, Annie poured coffee for Bouvier and Constable Joe Pelly, tea for me. Pelly was tall, thin, fair-haired, with an Adam's apple that bobbed up and down when he spoke or swallowed. As a graduate of the RCMP's tough forensics course, he would be well educated about fingerprints, footprints, material from under fingernails, minuscule shreds of clothing, weaponry, rigor mortis time spans, everything that might have a bearing on a case.

When we shook hands I noticed that his were chapped across the knuckles, as happens when someone works outside a lot in cold weather. I mentioned that.

"My girlfriend and I are building a ski cabin."

"Where?"

"In the Gatineau." It was a region in northwestern Québec, not far from Ottawa. "Our cabin is one of those jobs where logs are cut to a pattern and numbered, with lots of directions, arrows, and so on, so that any fool is supposed to be able to put one up." He laughed. "But it ain't easy. For me anyway. I feel more at home doing what I've been doing so far on this case."

"About the bodies," I began, and stopped, because at the mention of bodies Annie got up and said she had to get to the office.

Hastily pulling on her parka and boots, she declined Bouvier's offer to drive her to work. "With all due respect," she said drily, "I don't want everybody to think I'm part of the police force."

The door closed behind her. Pelly looked at me with a mild flick of the eyes. He'd noticed the abruptness of Annie's departure. "You were saying?" Pelly asked me.

"Did you find anything new, looking at the bodies?"

"Well, two things I could mention. Even before I got them out of the body bags they were starting to thaw a little." Bouvier, leaning against the sink, suddenly looked sick, but if Pelly noticed he showed no sign, went on matter-of-factly. "Because of the weather delay night before last at Cambridge the dry ice the bodies had been packed in hadn't lasted all the way to Yellowknife. But basically what I could see was pretty close to what anyone would see right after they died. We'll need an autopsy to determine exact cause of death on both of them. The old lady, she was stabbed so many times it'll be a tossup which one did her in."

Bouvier looked sicker. I didn't feel so good myself. I hated to think of an honest old lady carved up like that just for being alive and in the way.

"Any idea what the knife was like?"

"I'd think about average size for a hunting knife. There was one wound in her right thigh where the handle bruised the flesh, meaning the knife had gone in full length. But it didn't come out the other side of the thigh. Of course, there was pretty thick flesh there. Say a blade five, five and a half, six inches."

Jonassie had said the blade was five and a half inches on his knife with the gyrfalcon handle.

"You said there were two things you could mention."

"Yeah." He looked thoughtful. "The money in Dennis's pocket had been put in there, like, laying flat. I mean, you take a stack of bills and pile them neatly and slide them into a pocket loose without folding, get what I mean? With all that blood, some of it was in that pocket. The bills that I saw had a lot of blood spread around, but mostly on what would be the bottom end, the end deepest in the pocket. There must have been half a cup of blood there. However, the top bill of what was left had a smear on one side consistent with somebody sliding some of the blood-soaked bottom stuff out and across it."

He looked pleased with that deduction and had a right to be.

"Meaning if we do find money with a smear of blood on it, you'll be able to match it with what was left?"

"Well, the person who took it might have had time to wash the blood off when it was fresh, but there would be traces." He stopped briefly, finished the last of his coffee, and looked baffled. "Thing I can't figure out is why only *some* of the money was taken."

I'd been thinking about that and had one possible answer. "Maybe whoever it was thought that leaving some of the money would make it look as if there'd been no robbery at all."

Whatever the case, our wondering about why Dennis had more than his pay now had another dimension. He'd had even more, and some of it would be bloodstained.

I looked at Bouvier. "I'll get on it," he said.

I said, "First make a list of people in town who handle a lot of money and can keep their mouths shut."

I meant, people who would not go blabbing around that the cops are looking for bloodstained money. We didn't want some kind of a general alarm to spook somebody into getting rid of the evidence.

Bouvier pushed his lips together into a tight straight line, reading my mind.

All this hadn't taken long, about long enough for Pelly to drink his coffee. He got up, put his cup in Annie's sink, and looked at me. Time for action. I couldn't put off any longer going to look at what I didn't really want to see. Each new scene-of-the-crime I had faced over the years had had its own horrors. I knew this one wasn't going to do much to help me fall asleep at night, either. I tidied the table, moved dishes to the sink and margarine and milk to the fridge, thought of Lois's compulsive neatness, of Maxine's more relaxed attitude. In microcosm, the story of my life.

"Well," I said finally, "let's go."

"I think I'll pass," Bouvier said, not unexpectedly. "I'll go back and start on the money-with-blood-on-it angle."

"One other thing," I said, passing him the names that Annie

had given me last night. "See if there's anything on those and tell them we want to talk to them."

He glanced at the list thoughtfully.

"Dennis's night visitors," I said.

"Yeah," he said. "Maisie is a surprise. We did talk to them all briefly."

I thought of Margaret's remark about Maisie being "strong as a horse" but clueless about men.

I had an afterthought. "If Corporal Barker phones to give us a pep talk from Waikiki, read the list to him and see what he says, especially about Maisie."

When Pelly and I stepped outside, Bouvier was gone; nobody was in sight. I didn't know how curious the neighbors might be, this long after the event, but all adjoining windows faced out, not sideways, and there were no other homes close enough for me to see if anyone was watching. I shoved the key into the lock and opened the door, Pelly right behind me.

The house's heat had been at minimum since the night of the murders, so although there was an odor it was more musty, cold, and clammy than repugnant. Dried blood looked black against the cheap gray carpeting, especially black in what appeared to be footprints. If somebody spilled a pail or two of blood on a floor and it splashed and then you struggled in it, fought through it, and killed some poor woman who might have struggled a bit until she fell back, it would look like this.

Pelly's instant cursing seemed private, almost inaudible. "I didn't get the idea that she had had this much chance to fight back," he said finally. His professional reaction quickly followed the human one as he put down his bag of tools. "There's a real goddamn mother lode of tracks here, though," he said. "We should try to step where the, um, others didn't."

We took off our shoes. He padded over toward the kitchen, turning on an overhead light on the chaos there, and then dropped to his knees in the doorway and unlimbered his camera, taking endless close-up photos as he slowly traversed the downstairs rooms and entrance hall.

I don't really have a system in a killing where there isn't much to go on. I rarely take notes. I listen and smell and see. Leaving Pelly working in the kitchen, I turned on more lights and climbed the steps to the second floor.

By staying close to the left wall I avoided the crazy pattern of splotches and stains on the stair carpet and wall on the right side. When I reached the second-floor landing and faced its three door-ways, left (Dennis's room), center (bathroom), and right (Thelma's room), it was easy enough to figure the pattern of the bloodstains there: anyone hurtling out of the lefthand bedroom, Dennis's, would naturally wind up on the other side.

The bathroom, directly ahead, looked undisturbed. Whoever had made that mad dash away from Dennis's body had certainly not stopped to clean up. Clean towels, folded neatly, hung from a metal rack screwed into the wall beside the washbasin.

The bedroom door to my right was open. From where I stood, the hall light showed Thelma's neatly made single bed. It had no headboard, simply a mattress on a boxspring that had short screw-on legs, the bed covered by a multicolored and cheerful-looking patchwork quilt. I pushed the door wider open and stuck my head in. There was no sign that anyone had been in the room since the last time Thelma made it up. A nice Inuit doll of a sort made in the north and sold in souvenir shops had been placed on the pillow so that it leaned against the painted drywall.

Dennis's bedroom door was closed. I couldn't remember anyone saying whether it had been open when Barker and Bouvier first walked in last Friday night. If so, it had been closed after they removed the body. Tracks leading from that room to the landing were not complete footprints, as was the case on the ground floor, but looked more the way mud or dung, or blood, for that matter, anything that tracks, might look if someone had been slipping and sliding, in a hurry.

I opened Dennis's door and closed it again quickly. The smell in there was not like it had been below; this was human excrement, and urine, and general foulness, along with a lingering aroma of stale beer and wine or whisky. I opened the door again, turned on the light, and walked in, stepping carefully. I had seen animals killed, caribou torn to pieces by wolves, once a dog being torn apart by a wolverine, polar bears harassed by dogs and finished off by Inuit hunters, but never anything like this: tangled sheets and blankets on the double bed dried into weird shapes by the blood and excrement that stuck this part to that part and then dried, clothes and bedding torn and flung around, foulness everywhere. Hanging over a full-length mirror on the wall beside the dresser was a shirt that seemed to have been hung there clean and ironed and then splashed and fouled from below but not all the way up. One sleeve and the collar were as pristine white as when Thelma, presumably Thelma, had ironed the shirt.

From downstairs, Pelly: "How you doing up there, sir?"

"Coming down."

Pelly was kneeling in the blood-splashed hall, flashlight in hand, now engrossed more or less impersonally. "I've never even heard of a case with stuff like this," he said, waving at the mess around him in a kind of awe. "If the people who did it are still here and still wearing boots, maybe we've got them."

"Them?" I said.

"Some of the boots were big but there are smaller prints, too, maybe a woman or a boy. Here, look." He knelt carefully on a bit of carpet and pointed to an unmistakably small but smeared shoe print. "I'd say there are three or four distinctly different prints, including a faint one not associated with blood, one of the smaller ones—could have been just wet, as if someone came in out of the snow."

Even not-so-good prints in the right hands could yield details of size, make, extent of wear, and the way a person walks as indicated by where the wear occurs. Finding out where a specific piece of footwear was sold might take some doing in a city, but it would be easier to trace if it had been bought here or hereabouts.

I asked, "Any of the prints look like sealskin?" Our women still make boots in the age-old style, with warm caribou uppers and maybe insoles, but outer soles of sealskin, which doesn't react to damp the way caribou skin does. It also would not have a manufacturer's brand name helpfully stamped into the sole.

"It's hard to be sure with all the sliding around but I'm not thinking sealskin, yet, except maybe the one that didn't get into the blood. When these prints get the full treatment they'll tell us some things I can't get at just yet."

He glanced at his watch. "I'll photograph the upstairs and take up a lot of the carpet samples before I get out of here, but if I could make it to Yellowknife tonight I could have at least some preliminary stuff back to you tomorrow."

I said, "How long do you need here?"

He looked around thoughtfully as if working out aspects I couldn't even imagine. "Gimme a few hours. Let's say three o'clock. The goddamn cement they use to stick this carpet down is hard to handle."

He went upstairs. I could hear him gasp and swear in a low voice. Then he came back down. When I left for Annie's kitchen phone he was on his knees prying up a section of the kitchen linoleum with an instrument resembling a short square-ended spade, and using heavy curved-blade clippers to cut the tile into a manageable chunk.

I called the Yellowknife hospital again, got the same answer, no change. "I'll call you as soon as I have something," the doctor said. "Depend on that."

The other calls took a while. Pelly's Beaver pilot had gone to the hotel for a sleep. Margaret told me she'd have him out front at two forty-five, or sooner if we called again. I asked Bouvier to check the airport to make sure the Beaver was gassed up and ready to go, and told him to be ready at two forty-five to pick up the pilot and then us. The Cambridge Bay airport line was busy, but the RCMP line there wasn't. There were two more flights to Yellowknife that day, the sergeant told me, one scheduled and one charter. If Pelly's Beaver could get there by late afternoon, getting to Yellowknife that night should be a cinch.

When I walked back through the door, Pelly was putting chunks of stained and smeared carpet and linoleum into plastic bags and was getting ready to collect more. He glanced up and I told him the travel details.

On the way to the airport a little after three, with the sun high in the sky, I sat in the back of the van with Pelly. I liked both his youth and his professionalism. They went well together, as usual. Allied with open ambition.

"It's a break for me, getting a job like this," he called over the roar of the heater. "Funny, we spend most of the forensics course on fingerprints. Miss a fingerprint match on a comparison exam and you're out, man, off the course! And then I wind up with this! Beats hell out of fingerprints!"

After a minute or two I said, "You mentioned a girlfriend, back in Ottawa."

He nodded.

"See her often?"

Hint of a smile. "She says not often enough."

"You know," I said, "in the old days and not so old a man had to get RCMP permission to marry. They liked to keep a man single. Single guy could be moved around on short notice and cheap, without having to move a wife and kids, too."

He glanced at me, grinning. "Well, my girlfriend and I haven't talked about marriage, so far, just about building us a ski cabin."

I realized I'd said enough about the old days.

At the landing strip we drove the van out to park beside the Beaver. I could see some people in the terminal watching curiously. Pelly climbed in. Bouvier and I carried and lifted in to him the bags of what we hoped would be useful evidence.

"See you," Pelly said. "I'll call."

When Bouvier and I drove back into town the day was warming. There were quite a few people around, mostly kids playing. Bouvier said, "Corporal Barker called from Vancouver. I read him the list you gave me, the four girls. He didn't seem all that impressed. Said we'd already talked to them. Also mentioned what I already knew, of course, that two of them, Sarah and Agnes, were in his wife's grade-ten class at the school."

Their being schoolgirls didn't rule out the main aspect that I was concerned about—sex as a motivating factor in murder. These girls plus Leah and Maisie were the only people we knew about who could tell us whether what happened in Dennis's room *might* somehow produce revenge motives which *might* in the end have led to dead bodies.

"In the first interrogation with these girls did you or Barker get to the point of asking, frankly, what their relationship with Dennis involved? I mean, about sex. If they'd had sex, for instance, were they willing? If unwilling, scared, or whatever, did they try to fight? Did they complain later to one another or to anyone at home?"

Bouvier was smoking one of his cigars but through the cloud of smoke I could see his amusement. "We just didn't get that deep into it. Sadie was upset about Sarah and Agnes even being questioned. Maybe some of that rubbed off on Steve. Anyway, he wants you to call him. He's a little pissed off, leaves here on Tuesday, gets weathered in at Cambridge so they miss one flight and he's still only in Vancouver . . . although he did say they're getting out later today."

I called. I wasn't going to, but then decided it was a courtesy I could afford. Theoretically he would rather be here than there. In years to come when people talked about the case he would not relish having to um and ah and admit that he'd been in Honolulu at the time.

Barker picked up the phone on the first ring. I could imagine his big and burly figure, pug-nosed face, the paunch, and had the idea that his wife was sitting there all set to listen to him running his empire from afar, but he started off just like any tourist, "Great weather here, Inspector! Seventy-five today, sunny, shirtsleeves, now if we hadn't missed our goddamn airplane, sorry honey . . . not you, Inspector! . . . Anyway, Bouvier told me what you've got in mind about these girls and sex and so on and I just thought I should put in my two cents worth . . . that isn't the kind of thing we're looking for."

He rushed on. "So what if Dennis had been banging, sorry honey, some of them or at least trying? If you're thinking of some girl's boyfriend going over there and bumping off Dennis because he'd made a pass at their girls, there's not a chance! The picture we've got of the guy that did the murders is that he's gotta be big enough to beat the shit, sorry honey, out of Dennis, who was big enough to fight back and obviously did, and then out of old Thelma. She might have slept a lot but was strong as an ox, and certainly wouldn't have taken the kind of beating she did from some high-school kid mad about Dennis cutting in on his girl."

He did have a point. Even several points. But they weren't necessarily at odds with what I thought was important.

"How about some father or big brother?"

"Well, you gotta find a girl first who'd been getting laid," he began, forgetting to say "sorry, honey." "Then even if she got pregnant, that kinda thing happens and if every time it happened we had a murder or two out of it, there'd hardly be anybody left in town. That just *isn't* the kinda thing that leads to murder . . ." —he finished with a flourish—"around my town, anyway!"

Polite is polite, but I was becoming tired of polite. I didn't raise my voice. Didn't have to. But I laid it on the line.

"Considering that it is now nearly six days since the murders happened and we haven't got a goddamn thing"—I thought of saying sorry honey, but didn't—"I want to know who Dennis made it with and whether it had ever caused any arguments or fights and whether anybody knows anything, from earlier, about going into that house after Thelma had gone to sleep. When we find out a few of those things we'll know more than we do right now."

"Okay," Barker said grudgingly. "But when we do get a break I'm goddamn sure it's not going to be through those kids we've been talking about. More likely to be somebody we haven't even hit on yet."

"All right," I said, belatedly soothing. "You know the town. As you sometimes say, it's your town. So what's your opinion on this: Could anybody from the rec hall with a cooked-up alibi leave there, commit the murders, get cleaned up, and then get back to the rec hall without anybody knowing he'd been gone?"

Barker, flatly: "How can anybody know for sure? To make it stick someone would have to have seen the guy somewhere that contradicted the alibi."

"In lieu of a better idea, I still wouldn't rule that out," I said.

"Well, that's up to you."

"I didn't get a chance to talk to you before you and your wife had to leave"—a little dig—"about that list of the guys Dennis was loan-sharking with, guys that must have been paying up, maybe more substantially than we know yet, maybe one with a money-based grudge against Dennis."

"So what about those guys?"

"I don't find any record that they were interviewed."

"It's there somewhere, all small-time stuff, tens, twenties, one fifty. No reason for some big grudge."

"All right," I said. "We'll check harder, and maybe get more." The mildest rebuke of my life, but he'd get it. "That brings us to something else. I don't get the idea from anything anybody has said that Dennis was the kind of guy who could strong-arm somebody who didn't pay up."

"That's right!" Barker said. "I mean, whenever there've been fracases around the rec hall or anywhere else, Dennis might be on the fringes but in all the assaults and that kind of thing due to boozing or whatever, we never had to lay a glove on him."

I guessed that years ago, before Davidee did his time, he might have been both the loan shark and the enforcer. If so, when he left he might have turned the business over to Dennis. Or maybe it was just a matter of Dennis filling the void and arranging with someone (Hard Hat?) to be the enforcer. But Davidee, being Davidee, here secretly off and on for the last few weeks, might have felt the business was just on loan, there for him to pick up again now that he was back.

"If Dennis was that clean, it might mean that he had somebody else doing his enforcing for him," I said. "Who do you think? Name or names. Somebody to put the heat on."

Bouvier had been mainly studying his half-finished cigar, glancing at me from time to time with an encouraging smile. Now he came over and stood writing a note that read, "Hard Hat. Maybe in recent weeks Davidee taking over?"

Barker, slowly: "I've thought about Hard Hat. I mean, he's a real asshole, sorry honey, but it shouldn't be too hard to find out what connection he had, if any. And to get back to the murder night, we did check him out first. He'd been at Davidee's parents' house watching the hockey game most of the evening and then went to the rec hall. Davidee's parents backed him up, and never mind the kind of son they had, they are decent people."

Davidee's parents backed up Hard Hat? I had assumed that Hard Hat's own family had backed his alibi. I came close to blowing up.

"For Christ's sake, Barker! Don't you think that in this place everybody, including Davidee's parents, maybe even especially Davidee's parents, are so scared shitless that they'd say anything either Hard Hat or Davidee told them to say?"

Bouvier voted by nodding vigorously. Motion carried.

But one more question suddenly, to me, seemed vital. "So when Davidee's parents gave Hard Hat the alibi, how about Debbie? Did she back them up?"

"She wasn't there when I talked to them," Barker said. "She was out somewhere and didn't come back until later."

"Oh, shit," I said, and hung up.

I put down the phone thinking that for a lot of that conversation I hadn't been getting anywhere, like at one of those police seminars where nothing new comes up but everybody does a lot of show-off talking and then a lot of eating and drinking, after which I'd go to bed thinking, what a bloody waste of time. But in this case, Davidee's parents turning out to be Hard Hat's alibi was like a pinpoint of light in a dark tunnel.

I tried the hospital one more time. No change. "I'll call you as soon as there is," Dr. Butterfield said.

Bouvier said, "What now?"

"I'm going looking for Hard Hat."

"He might not be too easy to find. Want some help?"

We checked the rec hall first, on foot. Not there. Then we drove the van to his house, a good-size A-frame, one of the newer ones, down the shore from the hotel. A three-wheeler Honda was parked outside. The usual trash barrel languidly trailed some acrid smoke into the otherwise clear air. The door was answered by a lively looking young woman with a woolen toque perched on top of her head.

"Hi, Sarah," Bouvier said. "We're looking for Hard Hat. He here?"

Sarah shook her head.

"Do you live here, too?" I asked.

She smiled. "Just when my parents are away—they're out on a hunt. But cousin Donald isn't with them. He went sealing with Davidee."

She was the first one I'd met in all of Sanirarsipaaq who didn't call him Hard Hat. Also, I noted, she had spoken his name fondly.

"They good friends?" I asked.

The slightest of shadows showed in her eyes. "Sometimes, but when I came here about noon Davidee said something and Donald yelled something back at him." There was no use asking her where they'd gone or when they'd be back. Hunters came back when they finished hunting, not by any schedule.

She didn't look especially apprehensive; in fact, it was more as if she wished to please. "Don't know where they went," she offered, "but it was on Davidee's Skidoo. Maybe if they kept on arguing they won't be gone long. Want me to tell him you're looking for him?"

"Will you do that?"

"Sure."

When we were driving away, Bouvier asked, "You looking for him for what I think you're looking for him for?"

"Wouldn't be surprised. I want to know who was into Dennis for more money than he could pay."

An hour later at the detachment, I *was* surprised. The door opened and Hard Hat came in. I thought, it's strange the way that hat suits the rest of him, sort of a feisty-looking welterweight. The first time I saw him at the airport I'd thought that he had a particularly cheerful expression. He didn't look all that cheerful now. I wondered what he and Davidee had been arguing about.

"You get anything?" I asked. I meant, on the hunt.

He shook his head. "Nothing but a lot of shit from Davidee."

"I thought you were friends from away back."

"We used to be. Then I smartened up."

I took a shot in the dark. "What were you two arguing about today?"

"Who told you we were arguing? Oh, Sarah, I guess. Anyway . . ." He paused. "I was going to come and see you even before I got the message."

"What about?"

"Well, it seems to me . . . ," he said, then stopped. "You would hear that him and me were good friends . . ."

I waited for the rest.

"We're not, anymore. I don't want you thinking that anything he's mixed up in, I'm automatically in it too."

"What's he mixed up in?"

He paused as if wrestling with himself about what to reply. "Just that we're not friends anymore," he said stubbornly.

"Okay, I'll tell you what I wanted to see you about. I understand you used to help Dennis collect what people owed him."

"That's true. But I never done anything wrong. I'd just tell 'em, pay up or I'll beat the shit out of you." He smiled very faintly. "That was always enough."

"Always?" I asked.

"Always."

"Was there anybody who owed Dennis a lot of money who might have got into an argument about it with him, enough to beat him up? Enough to get into the fight he had before he got killed?"

He was shaking his head even before I finished the question.

I tried another tack.

"Your alibi on the night of the murders . . . ," I began.

"Was that I was watching hockey at Davidee's parents' place and then went to the rec hall."

"You went straight to the rec hall and stayed there until after Bouvier took the pictures, and then you went home?"

"That's it. The other guys there would back me up, I was playing snooker with some of them. When you guys, I mean the corporal here, and Barker, came in and did the searches, I didn't know what it was all about. None of us did. I didn't even know about the murders until the next morning."

"Was Davidee in the rec hall any of that time? We know he wasn't when the pictures were taken."

"All I know is, he wasn't there when I was there."

I couldn't think of anywhere to go from there. "Okay," I said, "and thanks for coming in."

He nodded. "I just don't want you to think of me and Davidee any more as being friends. In fact, I beat the shit out of him this morning."

I couldn't believe it—for about three seconds. Then I looked into Hard Hat's hard eyes and did believe it. "Why?"

"Something he said about my cousin Sarah. That she'd fuck anybody."

Abruptly, he walked out of the door and slammed it behind him, leaving two very surprised cops staring at each other.

"You believe him?" Bouvier asked.

"Most of it," I said.

T E N

I hadn't been paying much attention to the fact that we'd been closing in on Easter and that in our part of the world nobody, or very few, would be working that day, Good Friday. The hotel was very quiet when I woke up. I lay there counting, not sheep, but fragments of thought. Hard Hat: Was he grinding an axe, trying to distance himself from Davidee? Had he really beaten Davidee up? Mother: It was too early to phone Yellowknife and get the latest. That nagging only-witness worry wouldn't go away. Money: I wished we'd known earlier about the chance that money might be around with blood on it. Laundering money was not unknown elsewhere in the world, but not the way someone might have tried it in Sanirarsipaaq, believing the TV commercials and going at it with New Improved Daz. "Out, damned spot!" hadn't worked for Lady Macbeth either, and in those days there had been no forensic science to pick up traces no matter what kind of a cleaner was used. I could only hope that none of the smoking garbage barrels around town was burning money that someone knew would be incriminating.

After Hard Hat's visit, Bouvier and I had got into the money matter. Okay, we'd agreed, what people had in their pockets was beyond us, but money does tend to move out of pockets fairly fast. Most spenders aren't really into checking every little splotch. We'd start with cashiers at the Co-op and ticket takers at the bingo, food, and pop counters in the rec hall.

Some places would be closed Good Friday. "We can get them Saturday," I had said, sounding a little like one of the hockey coaches often seen on TV in these days of spring and the constant playoffs.

Bouvier had picked it up, twinkling. "How about the collection plates Easter Sunday? Should be a real haul there."

I rolled my eyes.

"Okay," he had grinned. "For starters I'll see if the Co-op is still open."

He hadn't called me later and I'd been tired, had gone to bed early. Now I thought again about Dennis's night visitors: Hard Hat's cousin Sarah, whom Hard Hat protected, Agnes Aviugana, Leah Takolik. Maisie.

The first three likely would be, at most, accessories, witnesses.

Maisie was different. I went over again what she had told her mother, and the fact that Annie had placed her as being there only briefly one night and that before the murders. But "briefly" to one person could be translated as "long enough" by another. I remembered one of Margaret's lines, delivered fondly: "In some ways she's her mother's daughter." That could have some bearing here. I saw Margaret as having been a chance-taker; perhaps she still was. In our occasional conversations, she'd mentioned a lot of places she'd lived when she was married. She hadn't got into and out of a marriage by playing everything safe before she wound up in Sanirarsipaaq.

Also, of the four on Annie's list, only Maisie's size and physique were unusual. This was no happy-go-lucky Inuit kid. She might have been the only one wary enough (crafty enough?) to make sure that she *usually* (except that once when Annie saw her) would not be observed when she was taking a chance. She wouldn't be roaring up on the back of a snowmobile giggling and falling over her feet. That thing in Calgary might have been isolated, the only time that she took that kind of a chance with a man. But who was I kidding? There wasn't much on two legs that she had to be afraid of physically. And not one of the other kids had beaten up a full-size Calgary football player, as far as I knew. "Strong as a horse," I thought again.

I ate a leisurely breakfast, almost alone in the dining room. No sign of Margaret. The sun was well up. When I came out, I looked across the almost empty settlement. Even the kids seemed to be sleeping in, no school today. At the detachment the van was parked outside, meaning Bouvier was on duty. I walked down the hill from the hotel to the jumbled ice of the seashore. Out a mile or more I could see an almost daily sight, the man motionless at a seal hole. He was too far away for me to see whether he was using a rifle or a harpoon. If it was a rifle, as the seal's head broke water it would be an instant goner, a floater, the man hauling it out. If he was using a harpoon there'd be a line on it. Either way the seal meat was food, and the skin became clothing: taking from nature only what was required, the rule of thumb that most natives at least *tried* to live by.

I leaned against one of the overturned snow-covered boats and for the moment decided that work could wait. Looking out at the seal hunter, I thought about the seasons for hunting in the sea: seals could be anytime, geese when they came back in the spring to nest (natives weren't bound by the game laws banning spring hunting), walrus, various kinds of whale from the beluga and nar-whal to the mighty bowheads. I grinned, remembering once when I was a constable, soon to be married to Lois. I was checking something in the main library at the University of Alberta when I'd happened across a reference to bowheads. Bowheads, I read, had been known to reach a length of sixty feet and a weight of fifty tons—one hundred thousand pounds! I had laughed aloud, couldn't help it. Everybody in the otherwise silent library had looked up, some glaring.

But I couldn't keep it in. "Some bowhead whales," I said loudly, "grow to be sixty feet long and weigh one hundred thousand pounds!"

"My God!" exclaimed a huge man far along the table from me.

"Are you *sure?*" This a cry from a handsome woman with mixed gray and blond hair, parted in the middle.

"Quiet, please!" hissed the librarian.

"Godalmighty," came a voice from far back in the stacks. "Imagine two like that making love!" This being followed by shouting, laughing, hooting questions and comments about tidal waves and the size of sexual organs.

So I could laugh about bowheads. Killer whales were the ones that gave me a shiver even now. They traveled in gangs. All creatures great and small hid when they approached. In igloos at night long ago there'd often be stories about how in summer killer whales would tip an ice floe from below to send basking seals or walrus or polar bears or Inuit hunters into the sea. When this happened near shore they'd been known to follow their prey right into shallow water; then, more than half-beached, they would wiggle their way back into deeper water and play with their catch like cats with mice, flinging seals and walruses (and perhaps a few stray members of the Save the Whales committee) into the air and catching them again before they actually killed and ate.

It was nice sitting there in the April sun, the Arctic world silent all around me except for the sound of an aircraft over by the landing strip and the snore of a couple of snowmobiles far away on the tundra. Then I gradually noticed a shrill and piercing whistle, the kind that some people make by joining their first and fourth fingers at the tips, placing them against the folded-back tip of the tongue, and blowing hard.

I had no idea the whistling was directed at me. The thoughts of long ago, of bowheads and killer whales, story time in the igloo, and me as a young constable laughing aloud in a library, had insulated me, briefly, against the fact that so many parts of this murder investigation were going around and around like a perpetual-motion roulette wheel, the ball never stopping on a number.

When I stood up I could see in the sky an approaching black cloud that meant the sun wouldn't be lasting for long. On the radio last night there'd been warning of a bad storm heading our way, with a caution for pilots and hunters that conditions would make any kind of travel hazardous. As I stretched, turned, and registered again the shrill repetitive whistle, I saw Bouvier leaving the detachment steps and hurrying toward me. When he saw me move he stopped. His hand came down from his mouth and the whistling stopped. "Hey, Matteesie!" he yelled. "Phone!"

When I got there the receiver was on the counter. Bouvier was studiously not looking at me. I picked it up and said, "Matteesie here." The sergeant who was secretary to Superintendent Abe Keswick, top man at G Division headquarters in Yellowknife, said quietly, "Just a minute, please, Matteesie."

Abe Keswick came on immediately and said, "I'm sorry to bring bad news, Matteesie."

I knew. I had had it in my mind when I picked up the phone. "Your mother died very suddenly just an hour ago," he said.

I can't remember in detail what was said from then on, only that Abe Keswick's voice was gentle. She had had a seizure that morning and simply died in a matter of minutes, her frail old body unable for once to fight back. Dr. Butterfield had tried to get me but couldn't get through, and he had an operation scheduled so he'd called the RCMP. "The doctor told me there was no doubt that the seizure was related to her head injury," Abe said.

Caused, my own mental voice taunted me, by someone I was making little or no progress toward identifying.

He let a silence grow, then went on. "As soon as storm conditions allow—it's okay here but they've got a doozer blizzard going at Cambridge, all flights cancelled, and it's heading your way—we'll send an aircraft to pick you up."

I put down the phone. Bouvier said, "Your mother?"

I nodded. I felt numb. Tears were running down my cheeks. Bouvier's voice had a break in it too as he put his arm around my shoulder and said, "I'm awfully sorry."

I walked out of there through the growing storm and down to the shore again and then along to where I could sit with my back against a huge slab of ice that hid me entirely from anyone else's sight. All flights cancelled meant that Maisie wouldn't get in today, and neither would Bouvier's photos, but those were the least of my worries.

I wept painful tears during that next hour or so, but also made decisions. Grief is a strangely nonexclusive emotion. Sobbing would give way to a fairly cool appraisal of what I had to do next. Then I'd lose control again. Gradually the grief left me more and more space to think of the job so far not done. Getting my mind back to work wasn't lack of respect, awareness, remorse. I wasn't some college kid crying over the loss of someone who in that social structure might be known as "my mom." My mother's soul no longer was in her thin old tattooed body, the single eye would never glitter with amusement again, and for that I grieved, even as I thought that, as far as I knew, the only RCMP aircraft available to pick me up would be the Beaver that Pelly had left on yesterday, not fast, not great in really bad weather.

Well, I could only hope. When I pulled myself together I'd make a few calls, simple enough: Maxine, Lois, brother Jopie in Holman. That one call to Holman would do for my half-brothers and half-sisters and other relatives there.

Holman was the principal settlement in the region where our mother's dialect, Kangiryuarmiutun, was spoken, and where she had lived among other Kangiryuarmiut since her nomadic days. Jopie and I would meet in Yellowknife, I thought (in the end it didn't happen that way) and do what had to be done. Then I'd come back to finish the case that had resulted in her death. I did not know when the finish would come, tomorrow or a month from now, but it would come.

Maxine I'd call because she had cared about my mother.

Lois, well, certainly Lois, because if I did not call Lois she would know why and would feel even more deeply wounded because she would know deep, deep down that essentially her wound was self-inflicted. Twenty years of lack of interest do not a high priority mourner make. My brother at Holman wouldn't be working today at his job in the musk-ox meat co-op. Maybe I could catch him at home, if he wasn't using the holiday to do some hunting.

For some reason I can't explain, now that my mother had died, my emotional wish for revenge had abated. I would find out whoever was responsible for her death, but it was her being hurt that had bothered me so much originally, and she didn't hurt anymore.

I'm not sure how long I sat on that slab of shore ice. Certainly for an hour or more. The sun was gone and the weather had turned sharply colder, the sky growing heavier with the storm approaching. Even under ideal circumstances ice floes are not made for sitting. What made me get up was growing discomfort from the cold.

Rising and stamping to get the feeling back in my legs, I remembered speaking at a seminar in New Mexico on the similarities between Navaho and Inuit customs and tribal beliefs. Along the way I'd talked some about living in an igloo as a child. At the end the audience had been invited to ask questions.

"Mr. Matti, uh, oesio," an earnest middle-aged man had said, "how can you people possibly live like what you've talked to us about, sittin' on ice or snow ledges in th'igloo all the time while the storytellin' is goin' on, an' that, without gettin' hemorrhoids?"

I had explained earlier, but apparently in vain, about the layers of skins insulating us from such a painful fate.

"An excellent question," I groaned, and shuffled off as if in pain, imitating the hemorrhoidal two-step.

The memory brought a smile and helped. A little.

I walked along the shore and turned up the slope. Through the blowing snow I could see Bouvier on the steps of the detachment, looking my way. I had the feeling he'd been there off and on all this time, watching for me. I kept on going past the hotel and rec hall to the detachment. I wanted Bouvier to know that I was back in the real world. He might have wondered. Although we didn't know one another all that well, just his waiting and watching conveyed a sense of caring.

Neither of us spoke. As we walked into the detachment together the phone on the counter rang. He reached for it, but I shook my head and he left it. I didn't want a phone call. I'd answered the "what next?" question in my mind, and wanted action to start now. "You've had some calls," Bouvier said. "Your mother's death has just been on the radio, CBC Inuvik. What the guy said told me things I didn't know about you and your mother."

Probably meaning that Maxine had written the item.

"The calls," he said. "None of them gave full names and all said you had their numbers—Maxine, Lois, and a woman from headquarters in Ottawa who said she and someone called Buster were very sad about your mother and will call again. Who's Buster?"

"The commissioner."

Bouvier looked as if he didn't believe it, then did. "No kidding! Buster! Sounds almost human!"

"There was another call from Yellowknife," he said, reluctantly. "The transport guy said that according to the weather people this storm will pass across our part of Victoria Island late today, and that it looked like the best they could do was get an aircraft to Cambridge tonight, weather permitting. It'll fly here and get you to Yellowknife tomorrow, and you could get back here on a regular flight Monday."

Monday before I could get back here? For an instant I hated the idea of three days away. But only for an instant. What could I do about it? If the rest of it happened as he'd said, and the aircraft to be sent for me did get as far as Cambridge tonight, it probably wouldn't fly here until after first light in the morning. Let's say I'd be taking off from here around eight. Then it would take a few more hours to get to Yellowknife.

I thought, well, at least the liquor store will be open after being closed today. If it looked as if I'd be further delayed getting there, always a possibility in the capricious Arctic, I could phone ahead and get someone, Erika Hall came to mind, to pick me up something. I could have stood being dry as long as I had to be in Sanirarsipaaq. When I got to Yellowknife and did what needed to be done, all I could do now for my poor mother, I would want a drink, for sure.

All those ifs and buts were getting me down. I knew I had to snap out of it.

"Okay," I said aloud, but to myself, "okay." I picked up the telephone directory because I had no idea where to call and get the sad process started.

In the yellow pages under the heading "Funeral Directors" there were only four names, two in Edmonton, one in Inuvik, and the fourth in Yellowknife, the advertisement for that one reading: "Territorial Funeral Homes."

I called the number. A suitably quiet voice answered. I identified myself and said that my mother had died there that morning and . . .

"I heard it on the radio," the quiet voice said. "We're very sorry, Matteesie. It's a shock to us all." Pause. "Now, what can we do?"

I was taking a lot of deep breaths again. "I would like to have everything arranged as quickly as possible for burial near Holman, where most of our relatives live. I'd like to let them know today when the service will be."

Sometimes when someone died an air charter would bring mourners to wherever the service would take place. I didn't want that. In Holman many of our friends and relatives were too old to contemplate, or be comfortable with, any such trip. We'd go to them.

"It's Friday now," the quiet voice said. "We could arrange that your mother could be ready to leave tomorrow or early Sunday. We could also make arrangements for the burial Sunday or Monday. Ah, would it be a Roman Catholic or Anglican service?"

I had a random impulse to ask if there was such a thing as an Inuit service with a shaman present, but I answered, "No church service, just one at the burial site. If possible with Father Lovering, he's Inuit, conducting the service. He's visiting in Sanirarsipaaq right now. I could check with him."

"Fine. Will you call back and confirm that with me? And will you be going directly there, or coming here to accompany your mother to Holman?"

"I'll come there," I said. "The weather forecast is bad right now, but I should be there by tomorrow. I'd like to get a flight to Holman with my mother Sunday morning." Then one detail bothered me. "About the grave . . ." Digging graves in the Arctic in winter was difficult, sometimes impossible, sometimes could only be done with a jackhammer. Or a body was stored for later final commitment to the ground. "I'll have to check with my brother in Holman about a grave . . ."

"I think we can save you that," he said. "Some settlements now have pre-dug graves, you know. Quite a few do that, knowing that they'll be needed." He added drily, "They always are. They dig half a dozen or so before freeze-up. I'll check the present availability."

A nice word, availability. What if too many died? Or not enough? I could imagine a city council somewhere else, Ottawa or Toronto, wrangling about the waste of money in unused graves, demanding that the planning officer resign. Maybe the contract had been let to the mayor's brother-in-law. Maybe the mayor's wife owned the backhoe.

But that was that. Unless I was told otherwise, a grave would be ready at my mother's settlement near Holman, certainly readier than any applicant for occupancy.

I slipped and slid up the hill to Jonassie's home. He met me at the door. I stepped just inside. "I heard about your mother on the radio," he said gently. "I'm very sorry, of course. She and I talked often when she was here, about religion and our people's beliefs. I remember she was interested about the knife I had carved with the gyrfalcon handle that I told her had been lost." He sighed. "Still lost," he said.

I was momentarily elsewhere, back with mother the night I arrived in Yellowknife when she'd sometimes seemed dazed and disoriented. "She mentioned something to me about a knife that had been lost," I said. "She was not being very rational, right then, but I heard distinctly . . . 'The shaman . . . the knife is lost.' "

He stared at me fixedly, then shook off whatever he was thinking about and said, "I was just going to come and tell you that when I heard of her death I thought about her deeply, and what I knew of her, a fine old lady." He stopped. I had a feeling that what he was telling me, indirectly, was that after hearing of her death, or maybe before, he had consulted his own shamanistic sources. I was right. He went on after a pause, "I believe that my familiars . . ."—by that he would mean his helping spirits—"will be tending to her soul."

I was glad he had spoken as he did, giving me solace about my mother's soul.

Father Lovering had appeared behind him. He said yes, he would fly to Inuvik when the weather cleared, and on to Holman.

In all that time I had been performing automatically, keeping my grief at bay. As I walked down the hill my eyes flooded with tears again and were still there when I called the funeral home to say that Father Lovering had said yes, he would conduct the service.

After that call came a time when I realized that it was still only midmorning. I had the day to put in. I could not let myself be immobilized by what was going endlessly through my head. I heard later that some people thought I was callous to keep working on the day that my mother died, but that was what I did.

I doggedly made a list, organizing my thoughts. Keeping in mind that, if the weather should suddenly clear so that I could take off sooner it would be a good idea to have talked things out now.

So Bouvier and I talked, drank coffee, acted as close as we could to normal.

Bouvier hadn't been able to check the Co-op last night for money with blood on it. He had just arrived as the manager had put the safe on a time lock, impossible to open until Saturday morning. So that had to hang fire. He'd checked the snack bar at the rec hall. Nothing. The airport. Nothing.

"I'm obviously here for the day," I said. "Let's use it. First, try to get a handle on the whereabouts of Davidee now and anybody who hangs out with him, close. Hard Hat, Ambrose Aviugana, Tommy Kungalik, anybody else you can think of who I could talk to. I know the obvious has been done. Now we have to try for the less obvious, identify any guys ever involved with Dennis, borrowing money and so on, whether they were around when the murders happened or not. Might haul some in on warrants, if we have to."

He hesitated. "What grounds?"

"Accessories to murder might get their attention."

Bouvier nodded, rather happily, I thought, although in the circumstances he didn't let it show with a smile. I recognized the reaction. Futzing around the edges of a crime in a preliminary way is okay in its way, necessary, but when it's getting nowhere there's no substitute for doing something real, preferably something that is not going to come back on you through the complaints bureau or a lawsuit. Muscle comes in many forms, some of them legal. I had some pretty good friends in the force who would have used legal muscle on Davidee before now, based on what we knew of his illegal movements while on parole—just to see how he reacted.

Bouvier was making notes, his own list.

"Also, talk again to the girls Annie saw. Except Maisie. She was due back tonight, but won't get here in this weather. I'll talk to her when I get back unless something happens that means you should see her before that."

I would rather be doing all four interrogations myself, but I simply wasn't in shape. Questioning properly takes quick wits, the readiness to seize a loose end, jump on it. Even the little I was doing now came hard. From our talks Bouvier knew what we wanted to know from the three girls: details, the sex side. As for Maisie, I wanted to be there when she was hit with that business about the football player in Calgary.

Wind-driven sleet began to hammer the detachment windows.

Bouvier said, "The three native girls together or one at a time?"

"One at a time, but warn them not to talk to anybody else. Don't want them to get their stories homogenized. Tell them they'll be in trouble if we find they have been talking to one another about questions and answers."

I made some coffee, good and strong, and drank it. Then I picked up the phone and called home. Lois must have been sitting there with her hand on the receiver. We talked. What was there to say? Not much. Funeral arrangements, bad weather, the shock that I hadn't quite mastered yet.

Lois said, "I want to come for the funeral."

I wasn't brusque. I did appreciate what she was thinking, there at the phone in our kitchen wishing she could do something to help, but I told her definitely no. My thinking was that it would be bad enough, complicated enough, with just the people who really had loved my mother.

I felt a little mean, in effect flatly turning down her well-meant wish to help me through a bad patch. Couldn't help it. I told her about the arrangements for Holman, the reasons why I wanted to push things along so I could get back to Sanirarsipaaq right away without any more complications than I already had.

She still hadn't quite given up. "What's right away?"

"Sunday if possible." Even while knowing that it might not be even remotely possible. But Monday *would* be possible, if the weather cooperated and there weren't too many other complications.

"Oh, well, then," she said, and let it trail off. "But I'll be thinking about you." I heard her sigh. Maybe she was even in tears. "I haven't been very good about your mother, all these years."

I made no reply. What's done is done. This wasn't a weep-in to me, but a sad, sad end to a good life. When we hung up I called Maxine. I couldn't get her either at the office or at home. I left a message on her machine that I would be going to Yellowknife early tomorrow and later, I didn't know when, to Holman.

After that call Buster was on the line, exuding sympathy, commiserations. Maybe it's always the same, there are so few things to say that have not already been said, or thought.

"We'll send someone in to replace you if you wish," he offered.

"No," I said. "Bouvier is good. And I won't be away long."

I caught Bouvier's quick, pleased glance.

Buster had something else on his mind. He fumbled a bit, then spoke bluntly. "Look, I probably don't have to tell you this, but this is police work now, not vengeance."

He certainly would have sensed my vengeful tone when we talked while I was in Yellowknife, on my way here. But I'd already worked that matter out. I was thinking more like a policeman than I had been at first. That's what I thought, anyway. Later, it turned out, I did feel vengeful, but it didn't count in the end. "Don't worry," I said.

When I hung up I said to Bouvier, "I've got to get out of here. The phone will keep ringing."

Outside, wind-driven sleet was bouncing in waves across the frozen open space. I could see only one other person braving the wildness. Jonassie was heading toward me. We stopped in the shelter of the detachment. He had to shout over the noise of the storm. "I forgot to say I saw two snowmobiles going south this morning, right after the bad news came on the radio. Davidee and two others." He said nothing more, but turned back into the wind and walked back toward his own place.

I still needed something specific to do. The morning already was dragging toward noon. I had to find ways to get through the afternoon and evening. Then sleep was going to come hard—but it would be even harder if I didn't get the hell moving now, occupy my mind.

Oddly enough, it all worked out. It was too early for the noon meal at the hotel, so I walked through the rec hall to that part of the building taken up by the ice-skating rink and watched swarms of kids, mostly Inuit, a few whites, using the day off from school to play pickup hockey. The yells and sounds of skates cutting the ice and pucks bouncing off boards and sticks crashing together sounded hollowly in the big rink. Half of them wore number 99 sweaters—Wayne Gretzky's number. They bumped, fell down, got up, slashed, tripped, hooked, wound up for big slapshots— playing a game they'd never even heard about until the National Hockey League's tough playing style became almost nightly fare on satellite television.

From the rink I went to the hotel. No one was around; it was still too early. The holiday emptiness was like a dead hand on life. I shaved and showered. When I came down, there were a few earlybirds in the dining room and I could hear Margaret's voice in the kitchen. I made myself a pot of tea and sat by myself near the window. The sleet had changed to snow that melted into blurred streams on the window. I looked through the crazy mush thinking about Margaret. A lot of things must have crashed before this in her life, and now she might be in for another.

How could anyone prepare her? Certainly I couldn't logically tell her what I was thinking, straight out. Still, if Maisie had been one of Dennis's regular playmates, I wanted her reaction to my new information directly from her, not after she and her mother had had time to cook up ways of dealing with it. At the same time, Margaret had been my first real source about the girl side of Dennis's life. She either had taken Maisie's story as gospel or had laundered it for my consumption. Either way, trying to protect her daughter was natural. I didn't want to repay her with a slap in the face. But was there any other way?

People began to straggle in for the noon meal. I had mine,

caribou steak rare. The dining room was in the tail end of the lunchtime routine when Margaret came in. She winked as she went by my table. I sensed that she hadn't been listening to the radio. Maybe she had slept in, hadn't heard about my mother yet. Like many another person preoccupied by personal shock, I had tended to feel that the whole world knew of it.

Some diners staying at the hotel were signing their tabs. A group at one table, however, was paying cash—the standard fifteen dollars per noon meal. Margaret had to make some change, and went back to her desk to do so. I followed and watched her open a metal cashbox she'd pulled from under the counter.

"How often do you send money out to the bank?" I asked.

"First flight Saturday. Why?" She smiled. "Planning a holdup?"

"Meaning you've still got everything you've taken in since the murders?"

"Right." She looked puzzled.

"Could I have a look?"

She laughed. "You an income-tax guy on the side?"

But she handed over the cashbox and watched me silently as I looked carefully at every bill, both sides. Besides a few checks and credit-card slips, the cash was in hundreds, fifties, twenties, tens and fives. Some bills were old and worn.

None had anything that looked like a bloodstain.

"What are you looking for?"

"Blood."

Her eyes went wide.

I told her that, according to the forensics guy, some money had been taken from Dennis's pocket at the time of the murder or soon after. For some reason whoever it was hadn't taken it all. Maybe pulled some out and saw a lot of blood.

"You mean, there was blood in Dennissie's money pocket?"

"Slathered with it."

"Jesus!" She looked at the money as if it might reach out and bite her, then locked the cashbox and leaned to put it back on its shelf under the counter.

"So don't faint if you see money with blood on it," I said. "Just call me, if I'm here, or Bouvier."

"I'm not the fainting kind." The guy waiting for his change came by and she handed it to him abstractedly. Others behind me were pulling on their boots and leaving.

"What do you mean *if* you're here?" Margaret asked. "You leaving? You got it all solved?"

By then we were alone again. I told her about my mother.

"Oh, hell!" she wailed. "Oh, Matteesie, I'm so sorry . . . I slept in, just got up, didn't hear anything!" There were tears in her eyes. That talk we'd had about life as she knew it in Sanirarsipaaq had made us . . . well, not instant close friends, but friendly. She kept shaking her head, her eyes brimming.

My own numbness hadn't quite worn off. Maybe that was just as well. There is a kind of clarity of purpose in being numb, getting bothersome things over with.

"I have to go to Yellowknife first thing tomorrow. When I get back I'll have to talk to Maisie."

At first, Margaret thought I meant about my mother's death.

"Oh, she'll be phoning, I'll tell her," she said. Then something in my face made her doubt her first reaction. "Talk to her about Dennissie?" she asked incredulously.

I nodded.

She said, "But you know what I told you. That he tried but she didn't fall for it."

I don't generally feel miserable about doing my job.

"It's necessary," I said.

"How *can* it be?"

I told her straight, except I didn't mention Annie. "Girls were seen going in with Dennis from time to time. Maisie was one of them. Maybe it was only the once, who knows, but going in at all, she'll have something to say about it. I've got four names in all to question."

"Who are the others?"

"Sarah, Agnes, and Leah."

She nodded without speaking, her eyes thoughtful and . . . what? Angry? If so, at whom? I don't know why I was feeling defensive, but I was. Certainly not because Maisie was white, the others native. With me being native too it might easily have been the reverse, even had been from time to time, giving natives any break they had coming.

I didn't mention the other thing I was thinking about, Maisie's physique and the Calgary case.

"Well," Margaret said, in a train of thought that hadn't occurred to me, "if the others know that Maisie *was* in there, for whatever reason, and you question them and not her, they're going to think she was the one who told you. Those kids aren't gentle when they think they've been double-crossed. Oh, God!"

For a minute she seemed to have forgotten I was there. I guessed she might be thinking about Maisie and the football player, and the complications therein.

"I'm coming back here at the latest Monday on the regular late flight," I said. "I'd like to see Maisie as soon as I get back—say late Monday here in the hotel? Do you want to be there when I talk to her?"

She let out a long sigh. "Okay." Whatever she might have added, she didn't. Then she did add something. "That sonofabitch!"

I couldn't be sure which sonofabitch she was referring to.

"Who do you mean?"

"The guy who did it." I thought of the common assumption that whatever had happened had to have been done by a man, and I thought of the size and strength of Maisie, and of how surprised the Calgary football player must have felt flying out of a second-story window.

"God, Matteessie," Margaret said, her eyes again full of tears. I didn't think they were for my mother, this time.

I walked back to the detachment again, looking for ways to fill the day. Pelly had had time to reach at least some preliminary conclusions about all that blood-tracked stuff he'd taken out for close inspection, but hadn't called. I called him and found him in. He knew about my mother's death and spoke of it subdued and sorry, then said, "I've been feeling guilty about not getting back to you sooner, but it's sort of complicated."

"In what way?"

"Well, there are really two categories of prints, the stuff with blood on it and something else, sort of latent prints, no sign of blood, undoubtedly made before the murders—but maybe important. The way I figure it, a lot of the floor that didn't have blood on it was pretty clean, as if it had been scrubbed before the murders took place. I'd imagine old Thelma was a pretty good housekeeper, and anyway I'm making that guess. So anybody coming in let's say just before the murders with shoes wet from the snow, the track would dry into a very faint mark. I'm going to say 'very faint' a lot. There's a couple of different sets, one just maybe one size bigger than the other but I'd say both were made from women's shoes or boots, a little smaller and narrower than what we take to be a man's prints, the main ones, but not as small as the real small bloody ones, get me?"

"Go on."

"As I say, there were two types of them, hardly visible, trademarks, but we can get a fair outline. One set, the smaller ones, show up on the stairs as well as, almost invisibly, I can't even be sure yet, in Dennis's room. Could have been done anytime before the murders, that set, but not after or they would have been in blood instead of faint, faint watermarks. Know anybody who was in the house before the murders and might have made those prints?"

"Nobody," I said. "I mean nobody we've found, but we'll go at that."

I hung up thinking, maybe Maisie for one set and some other girl or woman—Sarah, Agnes, Leah, or someone we don't even know about, for the other?

A little later that afternoon I was drawn to see the shaman again for reasons that at first I didn't try to figure out. I walked up there with my parka hood pulled over my head, slipping and sliding where the sleet had turned to ice. I found him sitting alone at his kitchen table, listening to his radio. "My brother is out visiting his flock," he said drily. He made tea. After some silence I asked him about the state of shamanism, whether people still consulted him when they were in trouble, whether young people were interested or was it just the old.

There was a long pause before he answered. "Attitudes of young people, not only about shamanism, depend a lot on what they have heard. To some of the young, everything about our old beliefs is a joke. To others, it is not. The jokers like the story, a true one, about an old shaman at Spence Bay. If you know Spence Bay you will remember that on one side of the harbor there is an overhanging cliff. That's where this old shaman lives. Some time ago his wife developed tuberculosis and in the end became so sick that an aircraft was sent in to take her to hospital, where she died and was cremated. But the old shaman did not accept that she had died. When he heard an aircraft coming in he would don his mask and go to the edge of the cliff dancing and shaking his leg rattles, thinking that because an aircraft had taken his wife away, he could make one bring her back."

He stopped for a while, then added, "This was the joke, people laughing at an old man trying to cast a spell that would bring his wife back to him."

I knew the cliff. I could imagine the rest. Young people who watched all kinds of amazing things happen on television, and saw them as real, were cautioned in church against the kind of superstition the shaman's antics would suggest to them. On television, if the shaman did bring his wife back, it might be merely another happy ending to some sitcom, but in real life in their own familiar community they would see such an attempt as a joke.

"Really both a joke and a tragedy," I said.

He nodded his huge head and poured me more tea. "But that is not the worst. Some of the young do accept shamanism, but not for the good. In movies and television they see or hear about Satanism, black practices, devil worship. To some of the young the stories told by the elders are not unlike some of the concepts of Satanism. There have been instances of young people blending the two, shamanism and Satanism. Some person attracted by Satanism announces that he is a shaman . . . That can be very bad, and has happened."

"Like the murders at the Belcher Islands long ago," I said, thinking of the discussion Erika Hall and I had had when the rumor first surfaced that shamanism had something to do with the murders here.

Jonassie simply nodded. "I told you Davidee tried to become a shaman once."

We sat in silence for a while again. Then I had a thought.

"Have you found out any more about the missing knife?"

He looked at me sharply. "No," he said.

When I came out the storm was almost imperceptibly abating. The sun showed fitfully through the scudding clouds. I was getting through the day.

Around eight I followed the dinner crowd to the rec hall. The hockey playoff was on TV, two of the three pool tables were busy, coffee and soft-drink machines thunked and clattered from time to time. Near the door a noticeboard was jammed with notes. I read about jobs wanted, workers wanted, free French lessons available, gun for sale, dogs for sale, camera for sale, wedding dress for sale (unused). Below that a joker had written, "Condoms for sale (unused)." Beside the noticeboard was a large and well-made poster headed:

!!!!!!! NEXT FRIDAY, DON'T MISS !!!!!!!
SANIRARSIPAAQ'S WELCOME TO SPRING!
DRUM DANCING, THROAT SINGING,
KNUCKLE HOPPING
MODERN DANCING TO COUNTRY AND
ROCK 'N' ROLL TAPES

The rec hall was where the settlement's young, especially the males, gathered every night. Tonight most clustered around the television. Hockey playoffs were on every night at this time of year. Mixed with the cheers and groans from that corner of the room was a constant roar—from the Winnipeg Arena a couple of thousand miles to the south, where the Winnipeg Jets were playing on home ice.

Byron Anolak was playing snooker against a tiny Inuk, no more than five feet tall, one of the government people staying at the hotel. Whether Byron had been nervous all along or just got nervous when he saw me enter, he began to blow easy shots, lost badly, and moved over to a stool against the wall to watch his opponent massacre somebody else. I carried a stool over and sat down beside him. He looked as if he'd prefer I hadn't, but eventually asked in Inuktitut how we were making out in the case.

I didn't answer directly. "I still haven't caught up with the people who know the answers. Including Davidee."

"You probably won't see him for a few days anyway. You know he's out hunting. He left right after the radio report about your mother dying. He'd figure that meant you'd be getting a lot tougher. He's good at disappearing when he knows he might be in trouble."

"Was the hunt trip that sudden a decision?"

He shrugged. "I don't know. He and his pals don't tell me."

After a pause I said, "That's a nice little daughter you have."

His face lit up. "Debbie, she's a good mother. When we get a place of our own it'll be better."

I liked him. He seemed to be a straight arrow. "Erika Hall was telling me you did journalism and were stringing for *News/North*. Any chance of getting on staff there or at the CBC?"

There was sudden hope in his eyes, but then he shrugged. "I've tried. Tell the truth, I haven't tried as much since Julie was born. I wouldn't want to leave her and Debbie behind." He thought about that. "Wouldn't like to leave here for other reasons, too, my family." He dropped his eyes and stared for a while at the floor. "I've got a real close family, but once Debbie and I get straightened around, maybe get married, I really do feel I've got the stuff, especially with things changing so fast in the north . . ." He let that trail off.

I told him about Maxine, how her journalism course had led to free-lance translating in court cases, then to the CBC. "Maybe there are things you can do here to earn a shot at the kind of jobs you want. You know these parts. There are all those committees involved with northern ambitions. Self-government is going to come eventually. The settlements need people to write speeches, negotiate, use the kind of languages background you have. Get noticed so when a job comes up somebody will think of you."

His eyes brightened. "I've filled in once in a while to help Lewissie in the hamlet offices. Did okay. But that's Lewissie's job, and if there's one man in town who can do it better than anybody else, it's Lewissie. You know him?"

"Just by name."

He nodded his head in the direction of an Inuk I'd noticed in the crowd around the TV: taller and heavier than me. His neatly trimmed hair was parted so that a strand fell across his forehead. He had a thick mustache above a small beard, and his eyebrows were so thick that they almost met in the middle. "That's Lewissie," he said. "He helps me out when he can, any job that's going."

A scruffy boy smoking a cigarette, never still, was among the youngest there. Sometimes he mingled with the hockey crowd and other times I thought he might be panhandling. He was approaching people, speaking sometimes jokily, sometimes being turned away, sometimes seeming to be involved in some transaction.

"Who's that kid?" I asked.

"Andy Arqviq," Byron said. That was the boy who'd been seen near Jonassie's house before the unsolved disappearance of the shaman's knife.

"Younger than the rest," I said.

"He's fifteen," Byron said, and immediately left. I wondered whether his leaving was coincidence, or whether maybe he felt uneasy sitting with me in the sight of everyone. Some might suspect that whatever we were saying would not be casual socializing.

Or maybe my innocuous question about Andy had made him think that this was question time about things he didn't want to answer. If he'd stayed I would have tried to put names to some of the others, young men especially, but also to some of the middle-aged and old Inuit. Usually when one of those happened to pass me he'd nod briefly but distantly, and not stop to pass the time of night.

Andy Arqviq did it differently. He came up to me grinning, a wiry boy in a thin jeans jacket. He projected calm insolence.

"Want cigarettes, policee?" he asked. "Fifty cents each. Or anything else, soft drink? Gimme the money and I'll get."

"No thanks."

He shrugged and moved on. Then there was a break in the

hockey action, and the big man Byron had pointed out to me came over and sat where Byron had been sitting.

"I'm Lewissie Ullayoroluk," he said affably. I knew from what Byron had said that he was the town administrator, the custom in many settlements being to have someone who spoke English well handle correspondence and other matters, assisting the mayor.

"Matteesie Kitologitak," I replied.

He smiled. "Everybody here knows that. And wonders."

He left it at that. "Wonders." I wondered how many people here knew some of the things I wanted to know.

We talked. It turned out that Lewissie coached the Sanirarsipaaq hockey team, sat on the liquor committee, and was married to the librarian, who had been Jane McLeod before she came here from Nova Scotia. She had arrived to teach school and stayed to marry.

"How you making out?" he asked finally, the question the whole settlement was asking.

I told him not great.

"That boy you were just talking to," he said, "if anybody knows what goes on around here, including in the rec hall that night, he'd know. He try to sell you something?"

"Just a cigarette," I said.

"That's not all he deals in," he said. "Whether he can deliver or not, I don't know, but once last winter a men's hockey team from Inuvik was in here for a game. The coach is a man I know. He told me that young Andy there was offering to get girls for his players. When one guy strung him along to see how far he'd go, Andy said he knew where he could get booze, too, and the player said how about hash, and Andy said he could get that, too, and then, maybe just boasting but maybe not, sometimes cocaine."

I was not especially surprised. Part-time dealers could get in and out undetected, with some legitimate job as a cover. There had been at least one cocaine bust in Sanikiluaq, some woman bringing it in from Great Whale on the Québec coast, and other busts in Iqaluit and elsewhere. I didn't think any fifteen-year-old would be running deals himself. He'd have to be a runner for someone else. But as the Arctic version of a street kid, with access to a lot of things, Andy looked the part.

"If there's anything I can do, just ask," Lewissie said. "Those murders and then your . . . your own other sad thing, the whole community feels bad."

By the "other sad thing," of course, he meant my mother, but didn't say it because we do not speak directly of the dead if it's at all avoidable, which it usually is. I looked into his honest eyes and thought that I'd consult him more from now on when I needed straight answers.

"I don't wish you anything but quick success getting this thing settled," he said. "But maybe you'll be here for the big party next Friday." He waved at the poster. "Good drum dancers. Good throat singers, maybe you heard 'em on radio, the ones from Cape Dorset? And the knuckle-hopper, he's the best I seen. You were just talking to Byron—he'll do the disc-jockey job for the modern stuff. Davidee used to have and I guess still has some rock and roll tapes. The idea is that Davidee, Byron, and a couple of others are supposed to set up the sound system if Davidee is back from hunting by then . . ."

That would be next Friday. A week from now. If I was still here.

As Lewissie turned away, Andy Arqviq appeared in the doorway to the outer lobby, off which branched toilets and stairs to the township offices and meeting rooms above. Some kind of a meeting was going on up there. I'd seen men and women taking the stairs when I came in. Andy didn't worry about where he had to go to find customers for one of his fifty-cent cigarettes. He was coming from there and dashed straight for me, his languid man-of-the-world manner, which I'd thought so ludicrous, given the rest of him, now abandoned.

"Sir!" he said. "You are wanted on the phone upstairs by"— the tone of voice was one of awe—"CBC Inuvik!"

I slid down off the stool. "Thanks, Andy," I said.

He looked surprised. "How you know my name?"

"I asked."

"Oh." He followed me up the stairs. I'm sure he would have stayed to listen to my side of the phone call, but some of the elders jerked their heads at him and pointed to the stairs.

"Hey, Andy," I called as he turned reluctantly to leave. "Thanks again!"

He shot a "take that" look at the elders and seemed to fumble for a proper reply. I thought he probably wasn't thanked for anything all that often. "*Amiunniin!*" he said. Meaning "it's okay" or "you're welcome," or maybe in this case, both.

"Matteesie here," I said into the phone.

"Hi," Maxine said softly, her voice teary. Her fondness for my mother was something we both knew. I thought of how Maxine and I had been for years, together so often, never often enough or for long enough, having a drink or two, laughing over one thing or another, comfortable as friends and lovers. If Lois knew Maxine existed, she'd never said so, but I think she would have, and maybe then would have divorced me.

"I've been talking to the funeral director about your plans," Maxine said, then, with spirit, "I wish to hell he'd stop referring to 'the remains.' But my problem is that I can't get off on Sunday for the funeral, just can't, we're so short-staffed, stretched so tight. Everybody takes their holidays around Easter when the kids are out of school here *and* it's my Sunday to be the lone hand in news. Anyway, I've got something worked out. I called *News/North* about something and our friend Erika was telling me she's in a bind, supposed to fly to Cambridge tomorrow morning to do a wrapup on that case Charlie Litterick has. Erika had a sitter all lined up for her two boys, and then it turned out the sitter couldn't come until Sunday. So I said I'd come there tomorrow morning and stay with her kids until Sunday and come back here for when I start my shift."

"You're a genius!"

"I thought so, too."

"See you tomorrow, then."

I had not been looking forward to spending that day alone. We didn't string out the farewells, just thought them.

When we hung up the elders were carefully not looking at me, as if they'd heard nothing and anyway it was none of their business. My people are like that. At least on the surface.

———

The next morning, Bouvier drove me to the airport. I carried shaving stuff, the clothes I'd been wearing when I left Ottawa, a feeling that I hadn't slept at all, nothing else. The storm was gone but a new snow was beginning to fall, not a lot yet, not too thick yet. The windshield wipers were pushing at big wet flakes.

Bouvier used part of the trip to recap his plans for the day. "I'll start out with the Co-op and check the money, as soon as it opens. Then I'll round up the three local girls, separately." He chuckled. "Tomorrow's Easter Sunday, services at the church and all. I'll tell 'em to come clean for the Lord."

The snow was falling heavier. I was thankful to see that the Citation had been sent for me, meaning a fast trip.

"Besides them," he said, "I'll get a line on Davidee and his hangout guys, the ones Barker had down as hanging out with Davidee a lot." He stopped, then turned to me and said, "You know what, Matteesie?"

"What?"

"We're going to get 'em. This is the week."

"You sound like a guy who has just bought a lottery ticket. Like, this is the week you get rich."

ELEVEN

So I flew to Yellowknife. At the airport there I was told there would be no flight to or from Holman until the next day, Sunday, so my brother hadn't arrived. At the funeral home I laid my cheek for a few minutes against my mother's cold face. She was lying on a slab, looking at peace. I talked to the man with the quiet voice, who was named Albert and who came originally from Holland. Everything was in readiness to fly me and my mother's body and Albert to Holman tomorrow.

Albert said, "Somebody named Maxine, a friend of yours, asked us to let her know when you arrived, which we did. I hope that's all right."

She was waiting in the lobby area when I came out. We hugged, her soft black hair against my cheek. "Like your haircut," I said. It had been long and thick and now was short and stringily curled. "I figured twenty years the old way was enough," she said. The years had fled by so fast. We stepped into the raw cold of the street. I held her arm hard against my side. Big wet snowflakes fell on our shoulders and stuck. We walked a bit toward the center of town.

"Where to?" I said.

She said, "Maybe you'd like a drink."

I sure did. I was feeling very tired. I didn't know what arrangements she might have made about keeping an eye on Erika's sons, but I could go to the liquor store and we could have a few drinks in my room. The last thing I wanted was to be alone.

"How about the hotel?" I asked.

"Ah, come over to Erika's place. Her kids will be just starting to watch hockey. I bought some of that Mount Gay rum . . ."

"A mind-reader!" I said. She laughed.

A little later, more quietly, abashed, almost to herself, she said, "In different circumstances you could call this the silver lining."

I couldn't think of anything to say to that, but it was true.

Erika's two kids, fifteen and fourteen, both fair-haired, Gabe and Peter, were watching a hockey playoff between the Los Angeles Kings and the Calgary Flames. Afternoon game, for a change. They got up and shook my hand. Even took their eyes off the screen for a few seconds to do so. Maxine poured me a very large slug of rum, turning her eyes toward me, smiling, "Ginger ale or Coke?"

"Ginger ale."

I was glad there was a game on. Maybe Maxine was, too. It meant we didn't have to talk much. The four of us, the boys and I on the couch, Maxine in a chair at my end, sat together and watched. I was so comfortable, getting relaxed, a state not hindered by the rum, that I almost forgot to call Bouvier. When I did think of it, the hockey game was near the end of the first period so I decided to wait for the intermission. The phone was in the same room as the TV. Somehow, I didn't want to interrupt the fun in favor of the reality.

The lively cries of the boys—"Fake! It was so in! What a body-check!"—filled and somehow soothed me through the next few minutes. Then the period was over and Maxine handed me the phone. I was thinking, two periods to go, lots of commercials providing many opportunities for pouring new drinks, I think I'm going to survive. As I heard the phone ringing in Sanirarsipaaq I hoped something good was happening, as Bouvier had forecast.

I thought of him alone, probably at the detachment, in that oppressive atmosphere I'd temporarily left behind. Oppressive because of all the parts of it that were weighing on my mind—my mother, Margaret, the wraithlike man who was Debbie's father and had been taken through hell by Davidee. I was glad that when we did have the murders wrapped up, I would leave and not go back for years, if ever . . .

Bouvier answered. He said that in his interviews with Leah, Sarah and Agnes, all admitted being in Dennissie's room from time to time while Thelma slept but otherwise said nothing that we didn't know. He said Sarah and Agnes were quite forthcoming but Leah was sometimes silent and hostile. Maisie had come back that morning and he had seen her in the hotel at lunchtime and thought from her eyes that she had been crying. Pelly had called to say that another urgent case had come up and he probably couldn't give us a final report for a few more days.

"And there was an interesting thing," Bouvier said. "Hard Hat came in here to see you. He didn't know you'd gone."

"What did he want?"

"I guess he wanted to repeat, emphasize, some of the things he told you yesterday. Like, that the day we saw them at the airport, he'd thought at the time that Davidee had changed while he'd been in prison and was a different guy than the one he had been, and they'd been friends in school, and so on. But soon Davidee was starting to push him and others around like he used to. Frankly, he was afraid. Didn't want to get involved. Was doing okay, he's a welder, and could see the whole pattern coming at him again, Davidee manipulating people. He said he wanted us to know that whatever we'd heard, he had tried to stay out of Davidee's way, and repeated that the night he'd been at Davidee's place, the night of the murders, he'd got out and gone to the rec hall and after our search there had gone home by himself, didn't hear about the murders at all until the next morning."

More or less what he'd told me, with some exclusions.

"I've done a report on it," Bouvier said. "But that's about it."

"You believe him?"

A pause. I could imagine him pondering. "Let's put it this way: true or not, he's trying to distance himself from Davidee."

"How about the money check at the Co-op?" I figured there'd

been nothing sensational or it might have been his lead-off item, taking precedence over Hard Hat.

It was sensational, all right. In reverse. "Drew a blank," he said. "The manager, Nelson, is an officious bastard. He says we'll have to have a search warrant."

"*What?*"

It must have been a pretty good "what?" Both of Erika's boys stared at me. "What's his number?" I said. "I'll call you back."

While I dialed I tried for a second or two to see Nelson's side of things, thinking I maybe should wheedle if necessary, be polite. So much for good intentions. "Nelson," I said, "I hear you want to see a search warrant?"

"It's company regulations!" he said. "Nobody looks at our books or our cash without head office permission!"

"*Bullshit!*" I said.

"Pardon me?" he said icily. Co-op managers are big deals in small settlements, not used to having their bullshit identified as such.

"I said, *bullshit!*"

"You don't have to yell," he said aggrievedly.

"I figure otherwise," I said, not yelling but not whispering either. "But I'll tell you what I'll do. I will get a search warrant sent to you by fax right now from Cambridge Bay, where Judge Charlie Ferguson Litterick has a case going. If we have to do that! Go to that extra trouble! We'll make sure that it gets in the paper that through *you* the Co-op, with many stores in the north, blocks a simple police request that might have helped in the murder case."

Of course, I didn't know if Charlie was still in Cambridge, or had gone home for the weekend, or what. But Nelson didn't know, either, and besides that, he was definitely on the run, a state not unknown among little tin gods.

There was a pause of a few beats, then a grudging "Okay, you can look."

I called Bouvier. He went straight to the Co-op and phoned me back a few minutes later. "Nothing," he said. "Also, I forgot to tell you, I got the pictures back of the crowd at the rec hall on the murder night. They don't tell us anything we didn't know."

That pretty well covered, we agreed, what we could do for now.

I put down the phone to find Gabe and Pete regarding me with somewhat more interest.

"You really told that guy!" Pete said. " *'Bullshit!'* . . . wow."

They both worked on shouting the word and laughing until they fell off the couch. Then Maxine told them okay, okay, we got the message. She also brought me a new drink, my second.

Earlier I had gathered by the trend of their cheering and groans that Gabe and Pete were Los Angeles fans and hoped they'd wipe out Calgary in the playoffs.

"Why Los Angeles?" I said.

"Because that's who Wayne Gretzky plays for," Gabe said.

They said, almost in unison, "We were Edmonton fans until Gretzky went to L.A."

"I'm a Marty McSorley fan myself," Pete informed me, with a sideways look. "That lunk!" said Gabe. "Pete just likes his body-checking, not his skating or shooting or anything else. That's the way Pete plays. But Pete is even dirtier than McSorley!" This last caused Pete to look rather pleased.

"There are a lot of McSorley brothers, in about four different leagues," Pete offered, his eyes lighting up. "Once they were all serving suspensions at the same time!"

Then he sneaked one in. "I'd really like to hear Marty McSorley yell *'Bullshit!'* " he said, and collapsed laughing.

The game went on, tied until the final seconds when Gretzky's pass to Jari Kurri set up a goal that won the game for Los Angeles, which was shorthanded at the time (Marty McSorley was shown on TV cheering from the penalty box). At the goal, the boys jumped and yelled and pummeled one another joyously. They kept cheering as the replay showed the sheer majestic skill of Gretzky luring defenders toward him until an apparently loafing Kurri went into overdrive, took Gretzky's dead-on lead pass, and shot high and in, all in one motion.

Another drink, the third (or was it fourth?), and I was feeling much better. The four of us stood at the window looking at the snow and traffic and talking about Florida and California, where this kind of weather didn't happen. Maxine told the boys about a case I'd been on where I shot a guy, a murderer, out in the bush south of where she'd come from, Fort Norman. They listened, a bit wide-eyed. Obviously they were more than a little proud to be hearing such things from the inside. Kids are like that. I thought of Andy Arqviq and winced at the comparison—these two missing a father, Andy missing the whole damn shooting match.

They hung on other cases we talked about, inside anecdotes. They mentioned haltingly that they were sorry about my mother. All the warm things Maxine said about her then got me reminiscing. An hour or two went by, with approximately one drink per hour, before I switched to beer. Maxine broiled musk-ox steaks to go with french fries done in the microwave. From time to time, somewhat fuzzily, but never mind that, I was thinking that, in addition to everything else, she's a good friend, Maxine. In company like this there would seem to be nothing between us except friendship and a kind of joking back and forth, a certain awareness of one another, our gratitude to Erika for this chance to spend this time together. As the evening wore on, Maxine and I decided quietly in the kitchen that I would go back to the hotel for the night, rather than spell out our relationship to two boys neither of us knew very well. Might not matter, but might.

It occurred to me, walking back to the hotel, that if Erika showed up in Sanirarsipaaq later to cover this case, I'd probably find her a royal pain in the ass, which turned out to be true. But her home's warm family atmosphere had helped a lot that night.

It was a melancholy day, Easter Sunday. On the flight from Yellowknife to Norman Wells and then Inuvik (where Maxine had to get off and go to work), we talked quietly. The final leg to Holman I spent with my mother's body in its coffin in the cargo compartment. The Irish co-pilot, Kieron O'Kennedy, had saved all his jokes that day. I imagined him valiantly resisting on the grounds of good taste the vast stock of Irish burial stories that I was sure lurked behind those usually merry eyes. At first I simply leaned against the bulkhead near my mother's coffin. Then Kieron produced a folding camp stool and the stewardess (same one) brought me tea and a box lunch. I didn't leave mother's side except on takeoff and landing, when I had to find a seat and a seat belt.

Father Lovering had boarded in the brief stop at Inuvik. Last night late I'd sat in the hotel room writing a few notes I thought might be a help to him. I handed them to him when we were landing at Holman. My brother Jopie met me coming down the steps and we hugged for a long time. We are the only two of Mother's many offspring who were born to our father, Mother's last husband, who had drowned during a hunting trip when we were very young.

Then I was in a dense throng of sorrowful friends and relatives and people I'd never seen before, all brought together to bid farewell to someone they had long valued. Some, including Annie and Jonassie, had flown from Sanirarsipaaq to Cambridge Bay to meet a charter from Igloolik that had made pickup stops at Gjoa Haven and Spence Bay before reaching Cambridge. I was told that two major native meetings, one an all-parties election meeting, had been canceled so people could come to pay their last respects to my mother.

The weather was raw and cold, about normal for mid-April, minus twelve Celsius, as the procession formed up for the drive to the nearby settlement where mother had lived. Every van in town and a few pickups and cars had been pressed into service to handle those from afar.

Jopie's musk-ox co-op four-by-four, carrying the coffin, led the long procession of vehicles, snowmobiles, three-wheelers, and four-wheelers to the burial ground. Babies rode in the hoods of their mother's *amautiks*. Little children were cuddled warmly, patted on the head or backside by passersby as we unloaded and walked up to the gravesite in a high place overlooking the sea. To the unknowing, it might have looked like merely an isolated place of stone cairns and wooden crosses set among tundra grass peeping through the snow. There were no flowers. As we gathered around the grave, Father Lovering, not using my notes, did a better thing. He led the hymns, all sung in Inuktitut, "Rock of Ages" (cleft for me), "O God Our Help in Ages Past" (our hope for years to come), "Eternal Father Strong to Save" (whose hand doth guide the restless wave). I thought that last one was a little odd, having heard it before mainly in funerals with nautical connections. On the other hand, if the choice of that hymn had been somehow an oblique bow to the pervasiveness of sea animals and the fish-woman goddess Sedna in our tribal beliefs, would it not have been "Eternal Mother Strong to Save"?

Then Father Lovering did a nice thing. After his own few minutes of talking about my mother as a representative of the women and ways that had carried Inuit out of dark ages and many hardships into the present, he asked others for their memories.

This being Easter Sunday, some of the more devout spoke of the resurrection of Christ. While no doubt well meant, this topic proved less than successful in linking the gladness of Easter Sunday with the long life of a woman to whom Easter had been as pagan a rite as our tribal beliefs were to many. Others, some almost my mother's age, spoke simply and lovingly in celebration of our people, using anecdotes, some funny, to illustrate what they were trying to say. One old man, Adam, nearly ninety himself, and rather garrulous, told a story of a night when both he and my mother, as children, had had what he called "our first shamanistic experience."

"We were two families," he said. "The hunting had been good and our families were very good friends so we built a double-size igloo where we could talk and eat and play games, for this was not long before the dark days and the hours of daylight were very short. You have heard many stories of hardships. This is not one of them. We had much food, much oil for the lamps and for cooking, so we were happy. This one night we all were playing games and laughing and talking when the snowblock in the entrance began to shake. Nobody was scared. Then there was a sharp knock and there was just a sort of haze at the entrance and a man no one knew appeared. He told us about the spirits who help him, ticking off their names on his fingers. Then he got down by the entrance place and pointed to his back and everybody in the igloo piled on his back, first one man, then a second man, and so on. Soon both families in the double igloo, Bessie and I and other children as well as adults, were piled one on top of the other against the stranger and then he stood up and shook everybody off, and the door shivered again and he was gone. My father shoved the snowblock out of the entrance and ran out to look for tracks that would show us where the stranger had gone. There were no tracks. That's what I remember."

After old Adam stopped speaking, a long silence grew in which many, I among them, tried to make that into a story that somehow would have an end. Then I realized that he was simply saying someone had been there, had played with them, and had disappeared without leaving a mark, and that was the end—the idea that they had been visited by a friendly spirit, and "there were no tracks." I noticed that Father Lovering did not look pleased with that story. I glanced at Jonassie. He winked.

Some near the front picked up handfuls of snow and tossed them into the grave. Jopie pointed to a yellow backhoe that I'd noticed standing off out of the way on the edge of the hill. "When we go, the backhoe will bring stone and earth and cover the grave," he said. The stone would be to discourage animals trying to get at the body. As the throng moved down the hill Jopie and I shook many hands and hugged many people. Jopie said that when spring flowers came, he would gather some and put them on our mother's grave.

In Jopie's home later we feasted on musk-ox, caribou, muktuk, fresh bannock. There was a pull-out bed in the living room for me. The next morning, Monday, not too early, Jopie and his three shy sons, whom someday I will get to know better, drove me to the airstrip in the musk-ox co-op's van. I flew to Inuvik where I caught the late-afternoon 727. I got back to Sanirarsipaaq around eight that Monday night in broad daylight, a fine clear evening. Bouvier met me, but we gave a lift into town to two friends of the mayor who didn't have transport, so we didn't have a chance to talk much. He dropped me at the hotel and went on with the other two. "We can talk in the morning," I said. "See you then."

T W E L V E

Maisie apparently had been out for a walk alone. She was just entering the hotel when Bouvier dropped me, and she waited to hold the door for me. "Hi, Matteesie," she said quietly. I replied, "Hi," and while I got my parka off reflected on how *hi* had so quickly replaced all other forms of greeting in the Arctic. For natives it was the very easiest English word of all time. You could be bilingual with only one word, two letters. Hi! Also, there were inflections. Thomassie Nuniviak's little boy Ernie in Inuvik was twenty-three months old and so far had never felt the need to learn another word. Once I saw Ernie haul a stool over so he could stand behind his father, who was cutting caribou steaks for dinner. Thomassie had shot the caribou the day before. Ernie, watching his Dad's hand on the knife, kept saying, "Hi? Hi? Hi?" meaning "Will you cut me a little piece please, Dad?" Which Thomassie did, from the tenderloin; he gave me a piece of the raw caribou, too.

Anyway, Maisie and I leaned against the wall a few inches from each other while removing our boots under the sign that read, "Leave boots here, this means *you!*" She lined hers up neatly, heels to the wall, and when I put mine alongside hers the bulk made my mukluks seem much bigger, but they weren't. Their toes and the toes of Maisie's classy leather snowboots lined up precisely the same distance from the wall. I'm a size eight.

She slipped into sealskin slippers. I kept my felt boot-liners on. Up the stairs and a few steps to the left she opened the door into the small apartment that she and her mother shared. It was at the opposite end of the corridor from my room and directly above the dining room.

The end of the room nearest the door was carpeted and furnished with a chesterfield, lounge chairs, end tables, floor lamps. They were grouped around a low square table that I judged to be walnut, and also judged to be a sawed-off onetime dining table from some period in Margaret's life. The top was scarred. The corners might once have been square, but had been rounded off. The legs swelled from ankle-size near the floor to rounded calf-size just under the edge of the table's top. Plain and yet somehow a beauty.

Margaret said, "You never seen a table before? Not for sale. Have a seat."

My opening guess that the table once had been a dining table was fairly accurate. That's not what we were here to talk about, but that's what we did proceed to talk about. I knew then that I should have arranged this meeting for the detachment instead of in these home surroundings. This was too bloody cozy altogether. Still . . . she told about the table.

It was the table from her first dining room suite in Lexington, Kentucky, she said. "It was full-size then and with six nice chairs and a husband to go with it, some of which, the chairs not the husband, I still have downstairs." Margaret liked talking. When she started moving from one city to another, she said, naming the places, well, the table had been cut down to its present height. That was when Maisie was just a child.

It was when Margaret was pointing to a small gouge near one corner and recounting the story of Maisie, just a toddler, falling into it and driving one of her baby teeth right back into her head, that I seized a small break and said, "I think we better get to the point."

"Ah, hell," Margaret said. "Just when I was getting into my life story. Oh, well . . . we'll get back to that sometime when Maisie isn't around to listen to the bedsprings jangling."

"Mo-ther!" Maisie said.

But Mother suddenly had her edge back. "Well, you don't think you're the only female who from time to time likes to see what a guy is really like, do you? What there is under that bulge in his jeans?"

Maisie looked pained. I thought it might be a hard life for a striking-looking but not especially self-assured tomboy-type young woman to have a mother who had sashayed her own way through forests of panting males, taking and rejecting, and learning a good deal from both.

"Just tell it the way you told me," Margaret instructed. "I mean, the way you *just* told me, not the version you told me first."

"Okay," Maisie said, glaring. "If you'll shut up."

Margaret held her lips together with a thumb and forefinger.

"All right!" Maisie said, looking directly at me briefly and then dropping her eyes in some confusion. "I liked Dennissie. From when I got here six months ago with what my mother calls a degree in Calgary Stampeder football players, which isn't fair, I only knew one and didn't sleep with him, I worked in the kitchen, first with a real crumbum who eventually took off, and then with Dennissie. The first guy was white and a pain in the ass—which he liked to put his hands on when I wasn't looking—and liked to say 'fuck' a lot, you know the type, stuck in some time warp, and Dennissie was the exact opposite." She smiled at some memory.

"In what way opposite?" I asked.

"He was fun to work with, always nice to Thelma, his granny, and he was really witty." She glanced at her mother. "Like when Steve Barker used to come in here for coffee almost every afternoon, and look like he was dying to get Mother to bed, she would butter him up, and Dennissie would mimic them both, with a little bit of Sadie thrown in, Sadie on the phone hunting for Steve . . . We'd be laughing out there in the kitchen fit to kill, even Thelma laughing at the same time she'd be whispering, 'Dennissie, stop! Stop!' "

"Besides that, he was good-looking," Margaret supplied.

I thought of the body and the foulness in his bedroom at the end.

"Yeah, he was good-looking. And I won't deny that him being

an Inuk made him . . . well, *more* good-looking, to me, different? Don't laugh."

Nobody was laughing. We were all just sitting. Monday night at home in Sanirarsipaaq.

"I mean so different from guys I'd known that he was like from another planet! Honest to god, until he started talking about maybe I should come home with him some night and listen to his music he'd never made a pass at me, even verbally . . ."

"All that fun they had in the kitchen is really an early part of making a pass, but she didn't know it at the time," Margaret explained in an aside to me, as if I didn't know.

Maisie ignored that. "So one night I thought, what the hell, he wants me so much, I'll go with him. But when we got there I was *so* nervous. I didn't really major in football players or any other kind of men, but I guess he didn't know that. We tiptoed past Thelma asleep on the couch, just like Dennissie said she would be, and up the stairs to his room, and at the top he put his arm around me like this"—she made a motion with her arm which ended with her hand clasping her breast—"and suddenly I, uh, lost interest! I just thought of Thelma waking up and finding me there and what she'd think . . . I didn't say anything, I just ran back downstairs and went in and shook Thelma.

"Dennissie came down right behind me and stood in the doorway looking I don't know what, amazed, I guess. But laughing, too. I'm saying, 'Thelma, it's me, Maisie! Just dropped in to say hello!'

"She woke up a little, but not very much, the poor dear. Then I left. Dennissie didn't try to stop me. The next morning when I reminded Thelma about me dropping in and trying to wake her up she said she thought it had been a dream."

It was a funny story, in a way.

"Did you go back with him some other night?"

Maisie started to cry, sobbing, "No, I wish I had."

Margaret was looking at me. I was looking at Maisie. Maisie was looking down at her lap, making weeping noises.

"She's been crying in her sleep," Margaret said, eyes brimming with tears of her own.

"So have you, the last couple of days," Maisie sobbed. After a minute or two, she calmed down. Margaret got up and put a kettle on and made coffee in the kind of pot where you push a perforated close-fitting round of metal down through the coffee grounds. It sure as hell beat the coffee from the instant jar downstairs. For a while then we just sat. I believed Maisie's story, as far as it went. It was too natural to be untrue, for that one visit anyway. It didn't even conflict with the idea of Dennissie as a ladies' man.

"You said you didn't go back another night," I said.

I was looking straight into those blue, blue eyes, and thinking about the latent footprints Pelly had mentioned, ones he'd thought might be a woman's, made while the floor was still clean.

The silence was not long at all, a second or two.

"No, I didn't," she said, and I was sure she was lying. I waited, giving her a chance to amend, or whatever. No amendment. Until I had more from Pelly, I decided to leave it at that, for now. I looked at Margaret, who showed no sign. So I switched.

I said to Maisie, "Did Dennissie talk much about other people he dealt with, like Davidee, Hard Hat, and so on?"

Immediately, her eyes were on mine. "Sometimes, but not in detail. He and Hard Hat had something going on, some business thing, I don't know what. After Davidee started showing up with Dennissie, usually at night, I met him and thought he was a creep, one of those good-looking guys who could turn it on like a tap. It seemed to me that Davidee arriving sort of pushed Hard Hat into the background. I asked Dennissie about that once and he just clammed up. But one other time when I saw them together they were arguing, I thought about money. I knew Dennissie well enough that I asked. He looked worried but said no, that it was something about a date that Davidee wanted him to arrange."

A shot in the dark. Sometimes shots in the dark hit something: "With you?"

"Not me! God, no. Davidee never looked at me twice. He likes people he could dominate, which ain't me."

"About one of Dennis's girlfriends, then?"

"Well," she said slowly, "there was one girl that Davidee was really gone on, Dennissie said . . . oh, hell, I got no right . . ."

"If it would help solve the murders, you got a right."

She thought about that. "This was a girl that Dennissie I think took home with him more than anybody else. He never told me in so many words but I got the idea she was somebody special to him and that right after Davidee met her he was always pestering Dennissie to set her up for him. Maybe that's what they were arguing about."

"Who?"

Reluctantly, she said, "Leah Takolik."

That was one of the names on Annie's list. I thought of the one small bloody footprint that Pelly had pointed out. I had sort of lost track of Hard Hat in this part of the conversation, but I didn't want to interrupt what Maisie was saying. Forget Hard Hat for now. Suppose Davidee had something on Dennis, and used it in a way somehow connected to Leah. How do Dennis and Thelma get killed out of all that?

Anyway, no harm in trying it on.

"Did Dennis ever make deals with other guys, like to double-date and go to his place?"

"Not that I ever heard about. I can't imagine it, I mean Dennissie just had this one small room. Two people could probably keep fairly quiet so as not to rouse poor Thelma, but not four!" Then she thought of something; her expression slowly changed. "Well, maybe something like it, I don't know."

"What made you change so fast from absolutely no to maybe?"

"One night when we were going snowmobiling Dennissie was so mad after talking to Davidee that he kicked his own snowmobile and hurt his foot. That was the night he told me that Davidee really had the hots for Leah. But that was all he said."

"The hots," Margaret mused, pouring coffee. "I rather like that."

So Dennis would kick his snowmobile angrily over something Davidee said or did. But really stand up to him?

I let that sit there. "When you went home with Dennis that one time, did he open his door with a key?" I stressed the word *one*, and watched. I'm sure she got it, but she didn't react.

"No. I don't think they ever locked the door. Thelma told me that once. Said, 'What have we got that anyone would want to steal?' "

"Do you know Leah fairly well?"

"Pretty well. I like her. When these kids up here get together sometimes, the girls, they giggle a lot. Always remind me of that song, whatever it's from, 'three little girls from school are we, fresh from the ladies' seminary,' or however it goes, and they talk about this boy or that and how they are in sex. But Leah isn't a giggler. Gives me the idea she doesn't do something without thinking, including sex. Of course, sex up here is treated as a really natural thing to do, no stigma for sleeping around, and so on, right?"

Drily I said, "I think we know what you're talking about."

"Speak for yourself," Margaret said.

"I know that Leah liked Dennissie a lot," Maisie went on. "I don't think she had other guys, too, like a lot of girls do. It wasn't like what anybody in the south would call having a steady, just that not many guys have the kind of setup that Dennissie had, fairly private, with Thelma sleeping like the dead the way she did . . . Aw, hell."

She stopped and shook her head. Tears began to well up again.

"Matteesie," Margaret said. "I think that's it, eh?"

I was ready. "Okay." The Leah-Dennis thing was interesting, with a little Davidee a question mark on the side. I thought I had opened a door, just a crack, but couldn't guess where it might lead. Why didn't I press harder when I thought Maisie was lying? That was instinct. All I could have done was hammer away. I had a feeling that the next time I brought it up, I would know more. Maybe from Annie. Maybe from Pelly. Maybe from Maisie herself.

The next morning, Tuesday, I beat Bouvier to the detachment. On the way I could see and hear the settlement coming to life, the yells of the sliders, girls in brighter, maybe Easter-bought, anoraks and pants. I remember once reading a piece in which a writer said he wished he had four lives. I forget what they were, but the idea surfaces in me once in a while, at times when one life, in the Arctic, would do me fine. Maybe as a hunter, with a son or two I could teach.

I shook myself back into the present. I was sure Bouvier hadn't made significant yards with the three native girls he'd questioned Saturday. When I talked to them again myself, maybe I'd get more, would expand upon Maisie's account. I went to the window and could see Jonassie walking down to the shore, appearing to be deep in thought. When he turned back he walked slowly, head down, toward Debbie's father and mother at the side of their house. The man, watching Jonassie approach, wiped his skinning knife on his pants. His wife put down the sharp *ulu* with which she'd been cleaning another skin. Jonassie seemed to speak first, then he and the woman both talked to the man, who stared down, apparently saying nothing. What was that about?

And how was it that Debbie's father and mother were working on seals? They must have come from a friend, someone who had hunted well . . . or from Davidee? Of course, I hadn't been around from Saturday morning to Monday night. Davidee and his playmates could have bagged a seal or two, then zoomed off again. The three-wheeled Honda was still in place, but no snowmobiles.

Perhaps this was my chance to talk to Debbie. She'd been on my mind off and on since Barker said she had not been home when her parents backed up Hard Hat's alibi on the night of the murders. I left a note telling Bouvier where I was going, and walked up the hill. Jonassie, leaving, called a greeting but kept going, not looking back. I waved at the other two. The woman waved back, not the man.

I knocked on the door. Debbie opened it a crack, then wider, and beckoned me in while putting one finger to her lips and nodding toward a store-bought wooden cradle where young Julie was sleeping. Inside, once the door was closed, I said quietly, "I want to ask you a few things about when Davidee starting sneaking back into town . . . what, a week or two ago?"

She smiled, a very small smile. "Try three."

"You mean as soon as he got to Cambridge and got parole permission to go as far as No Name Lake, he started coming here?"

She nodded, not smiling at all. "I heard that but didn't see."

"He didn't stay here, then?"

She shook her head. "Too close to the RCMP. No, he'd stay

with Hard Hat, probably. Has a little place of his own." She shrugged. "Now, of course, no need to hide, so he's back in his old room here."

"You talk to him much?"

"Not at all . . . So what else do you want to know? Early this morning he took off hunting. Tommy and Paulessie had been out sealing with him late Saturday. Maybe they went along with him today. I just heard the two snowmobiles taking off."

There was nothing basically suspicious about that kind of hunt at this time of year. With the weather moderating sometimes young men got restless and took their guns and snowmobiles and went out to bring home meat.

When that Friday storm hit they must have been holed up somewhere warm, like an igloo or a tent. Maybe they had come back Saturday in better weather; maybe they had sighted caribou and come to get provisions and go out again. Farther south, the caribou herds would be moving past the tree line into the open tundra to where the females had their favorite calving places. Here, hundreds of miles north of the treeline, the caribou had the same habits of calving in one secluded area. If hunters saw a herd, they went for them.

Meanwhile, Debbie. Her parents? I thought their wariness of me earlier would almost guarantee that they wouldn't come in. I thought of Davidee being back in this house. No matter what the courts allowed in their dumb idea of justice, honest to god, what could have been in their minds, a family reconciliation? Bullshit. But where could she go? From what Byron had told me, he and Debbie wanted a place of their own but did not have it yet. So she was here out of necessity. Necessity is something that my people have lived with for centuries, sometimes in worse circumstances than these, but it shouldn't be imposed on them by some dunces living in suburbs of Prince Albert, Saskatchewan, where Davidee had been in the pen.

I plunged. "The night of the murders, when Hard Hat was here, according to your parents, Barker told me that you weren't. And that you weren't around the next morning, either, when he questioned your parents to check on Hard Hat's story."

She watched me, listened, but said nothing. I picked my way with a certain amount of care.

"If you were here both times and backed up your parents on Hard Hat being here all evening on the night that the murders happened, I would have been inclined to believe you."

She watched my eyes, her own very big behind the round spectacles.

"Was Hard Hat really here that night?"

Her gaze didn't waver, but she said nothing.

"Put it a different way—you don't know whether Hard Hat was here or not?"

"That's not exactly right," she said with a little smile, but didn't go on, although various emotions crossed her face. She dipped water from a pail into a kettle and put it on the stove. She got out a small teapot. I was not jumping from one foot to the other waiting for the answer. I could guess how she was considering what I had asked. When a lawyer or a policeman or a judge is asking questions, there is a tendency among our people to figure out what answer the questioner would *like* to hear, and provide it. That way, you're less likely to get bullied. Conflicting sworn evidence is a constant bugbear in even minor cases in the north.

So as her silence dragged on, I let it. I was a native, too, sitting at a seal hole. Make the slightest false move, and no seal, or in my case no answer. I had all day. Davidee was one thing; I couldn't see her wanting to protect Davidee. Her parents' story giving Hard Hat an alibi was another thing altogether. She wouldn't want to hurt her parents by contradicting their accounts, if she could avoid it.

She was silent, moving around, gazing at her child. I thought she was getting ready to answer. Then someone passed by the window, heading for the door. She said hurriedly, "Not now. Not here. Tonight at the detachment," and the door opened behind me and Byron Anolak limped in.

"Hey, inspector," he said.

Damn the interruption!

Which might have been why I needled, "I thought maybe you'd be out hunting with Davidee." I said it to get a rise out of him, but I was astonished at the black fury that suffused his face.

He took a deep breath, two, three. His angry color receded a little. Only a little. "My girl and our daughter live in this house where Davidee now lives too, thanks to a justice system that doesn't know its ass from a seal hole! I don't hang out with those guys and you goddamn well know that! I don't hang out with Davidee *ever*. But I don't disturb the peace if I can help it."

"Okay," I said. I really liked that line "doesn't know its ass from a seal hole," and would make sure that the judge in question got that message. "However, do you know where they might have gone to hunt?"

Rather curtly he replied, "I could guess. Lewissie Ullayoroluk went south a day or two ago, down around No Name Lake, and got caribou."

At that moment the little girl's eyes opened and she smiled at Debbie and Byron, standing together, looking down at her. Debbie picked her up. I was thinking, with all that bloody happens around this place, and keeps on happening, the child woke up smiling. Byron reached for his daughter and sang a few lines of a song that I knew and apparently she did, too, for she laughed. I looked at Debbie. The question I'd asked still hadn't been answered.

"I'll see you later," she said. She spoke swiftly to Byron about him taking over the baby around nine or a little later. He nodded. She turned back to me. "Okay, after dark be in the detachment with no lights on. I'll knock."

Byron glanced at me and then at Debbie, laughing. "Say, 'yes boss' to the lady, Matteesie!"

"Yes, boss, lady," I said.

Exit, all laughing, including the baby. Outside, the parents, back working on the seals, were being studied soberly by two or three bundled-up children too young for school. The man stared at me sadly and then at the house and then looked back down to continue skinning the seal.

As I walked to the detachment I was thinking that, beyond tonight, when Debbie might tell me something, I needed a plan. If by then Davidee and those with him were still out on the tundra, what better place could there be to face them? Checking out Byron's No Name Lake guess would be a logical start. Maybe I could track them by snowmobile, but—the big *but*—following snowmobile tracks on the tundra is very low on any list of surefire projects. What I needed was a backup from the air.

I thought about that. It was routine for the force to pay for a charter to do a search, especially in a murder case. But I didn't want some pilot I'd have to explain things to—not only who we were looking for, but how long the charter might take, hours or days. Antler Aviation, flying out of Inuvik, came to mind. I knew their pilots. But right on the heels of that idea came another that for a lot of reasons was more personal and therefore suited me better.

While I was reading the note Bouvier had left on the counter, saying that he'd decided to go out to check garbage cans again for remnants of burned boots or clothing (my "new hobby," he wrote), I picked up the phone and called Komatik Air in Inuvik. Thomassie Nuniviak, who owned Komatik's three-aircraft outfit, had been my friend since we were both only seven or eight years old, shipped into Inuvik with a lot of other scared kids, away from our families for the first time to go to school.

As the phone at Komatik Air rang and rang, I remembered our first textbooks, ridiculously enough the standard Dick and Jane and Spot stuff—stories set in southern white family situations as alien and unknown to us as if they'd been set on the moon. But at the time that was how the government insisted every native kid learn to read, write, and talk in English.

They were regretting that now, with individuals in every native organization recalling publicly for the first time how they were mistreated. Some had been whipped if they were caught speaking Inuktitut. It was the old, old story, not exclusive to Canada, of the white establishment senselessly and systematically trying to wipe out ancient native cultures in favor of . . . what? The bullshit that whites know it all. The hatred and distrust bred in those days would not go away, and knocked hell out of the more understanding initiatives that slowly followed, the government was forced into reluctant reform only when the natives grew, matured, and fought back, as they learned that fighting back sure as hell beat turning the other cheek.

Finally, it must have been on the twentieth ring, Thomassie

answered. "Matteesie! Are you in town? Come on over. God, I'm sorry about your mother. Live that long and then die for being in the way of that shit, whoever did it!"

He had come home with me to Holman one springtime after school finished, when his parents hadn't come in yet from the winter hunt—either stranded or just late, I forget—so he knew, had known, my mother. Once he had tried to smoke her pipe and had gone so pale that she said, "Oh, Thomassie, I didn't know you were part white man!"

I told him where I was, not in Inuvik but Sanirarsipaaq, and that I needed somebody to do some flying. The sooner the better.

"It's about the murders?"

I said it was.

"Well, look, I got both the Beaver and the Cessna right here. You got a preference?"

"No, whatever you say. Any chance you could fly it yourself?"

He laughed. I could imagine him in that little office he had in an old 512 on the banks of the Mackenzie, electric kettle and tea bags and powdered milk at his elbow, two of his three somewhat timeworn aircraft sitting on the river ice out front. Last time I'd seen him his Cessna had been missing, flown by some fugitives who'd hidden it south of Fort Norman where I'd found it safe and sound.

"Sure I'm gonna fly you myself! You think I'd let anybody else fly you?" He thought aloud about the time element. "It's a little late for me to get there today but I could get part way. Can't fly at night into that landing strip you got there with forty-watt bulbs along the runway, but I should make Cam Bay and call you from there and maybe come on at first light in the morning."

After I hung up I thought that if Davidee did return on his own today and I didn't need an aircraft, I could cancel. But I had a strong feeling that Davidee was not planning a quick return. If I was right I had saved a day or two by laying on an aircraft now.

Bouvier had rushed in during the Thomassie call and headed straight for the bathroom, his business there broadcast by a sound like that of a hose filling a pail. He emerged grinning and drying his hands on a well-worn towel. Before I could ask him to fill me in on the days I'd been away, Bouvier, looking a little embarrassed, beat me to it, laughing, comically trying to both talk and light his cigar.

"Really weird thing happened Sunday. I had my Easter dinner at the hotel, a big spread, soup, fish, chicken, pie, you name it, and came back here to write a letter home but first I really had to go to the can. When I came out pulling my pants back up, not so easy in that bathroom, it's so damn small, I just happened to look out. What do I see but Davidee walking downhill across the open space, as if he's heading for the rec hall.

"It was still broad daylight, of course, and around Easter Sunday dinnertime, hardly anybody else around. Then I see Byron, going in the same direction as Davidee, but by a different route, like shadowing him, always keeping a building between him and Davidee."

I was thinking about Byron's angry flush and denial just a few minutes ago when I'd needled him about thinking he might be out hunting with Davidee.

"While I'm watching, just pulling my braces up over my shoulders, and Davidee is going by in front of the detachment, Byron takes a step from where he'd been shielded—right behind the corner of our building here—and, Jesus, he brings up a twenty-two Magnum he's been carrying sort of shielded by his right leg. He sights right on Davidee, had his finger on the trigger, couldn't have missed, clear shot, twenty-five yards or so, and holds it for maybe a second or two, and then drops the gun and turns. It all happened so fast. I grabbed my parka and when I got outside I could see Byron heading back toward his house pretty fast for a guy with a bum leg, and I yelled at him, 'Hey, stop right there!' "

"So he went faster," I suggested.

"Yeah! He looked back to see who had yelled at him . . . and *then* he broke into a kind of run. I went after him up past where Annie lives, until we got to his family's house, and he went in and as soon as I got there, so did I.

"The people there, parents and a bunch of kids, Byron's the oldest but I don't know how many brothers and sisters he's got, were eating their Easter dinner, for Christ's sake . . . uh, no pun intended . . . and there was an empty chair with that twenty-two Magnum leaning against it.

"I said who I was, policee Alphonse Bouvier, in case they didn't know, and that I was sorry to interrupt their Easter dinner, but that I had been following Byron who had pointed that gun . . . I pointed to the gun . . . at Davidee, and he'd come into this house. The man at the head of the table, I guess the father, nodded. He's about your size, Matteesie . . ."

"A veritable giant," I said.

"Yeah!" He laughed. "And he was chewing away at the wing from the big roast goose on the platter in front of him and gave me a little grin. 'Ayah,' he said. 'We see that man.' He didn't say Byron's name.

" 'I wish to speak to him,' I said.

" 'He not here.' The man's grin got a little wider. 'You come in front, he go out back.'

"Everybody around the table was grinning. It was a really strange feeling. Then it suddenly struck me like one of those old rerun comedies on the TV, one guy running in the front and another out the back. When I grinned, they started to laugh. And I suddenly relaxed, thinking, what the hell, he didn't fire the gun, there's no law against carrying one, and I knew Byron, of course, thin, wiry-looking, no mustache, ponytail, no chance of me mistaking his limp, I'd find him all right and ask what it had all been about.

"At that point the older woman, I guess Byron's mother—who has a really nice face, smiles a lot, hair parted in the middle, I found later her name is Mabel—got up and brought another plate and nodded to Byron's empty chair. The dad moved the gun and I sat down, seemed the thing to do. Now, I guess it wouldn't happen this way in a big-city murder investigation—but then she brings in another roasted goose, and the man cut some meat from it and I had some, would have been rude not to. And I drank some tea and we talked about one thing and another, and I didn't push, and when we're sitting there, eating goose, I did find out what happened. They'd been just starting their dinner, talking and laughing, when Davidee barged in without knocking and demanded money from Byron. Said it had been owed to Dennissie and now was owed to him. Also made some dirty crack about Byron and Debbie's little girl. That's when Byron grabbed the gun and Davidee ran out of there with Byron after him. What I'd seen must have happened right after that. When I got back I wrote a report and looked up Byron in the files. Never in trouble. So I just thought, well, I've made a report, entered it in both Byron's file and Davidee's, and that I'd tell you all about it when you get back, in case anything did come of it. But nothing did that we know of."

"No more at all?" I asked.

"No more than Byron getting mad when Davidee walked in and started jawing about Byron owing him some money, and bad-mouthing Debbie and the little girl. Maybe that's it, entirely."

He then told me that by now he'd checked just about every garbage barrel in town, some twice, and found nothing.

I told him about my plan to hunt for Davidee and company the next morning, probably going out very early by snowmobile and then, if everything worked, to rendezvous around No Name Lake with Thomassie Nuniviak of Komatik Air. I also told him about the meeting scheduled with Debbie later tonight.

I went to the rec hall after dinner. The usual people were there, plus Jonassie. I'd never seen him in there before. He was leaving when I arrived. I thought of what I'd seen from my window, his conversation with Debbie and Davidee's parents and planned to ask him about this when I had a chance to do so privately. The little guy, Andy Arqviq, practically adopted me and told me how he wanted to be a carver, and Jonassie had helped him a lot. Lewissie came over and talked. There was another hockey game on TV, Los Angeles and Calgary again. It was still on when I left and told a little white lie, as the saying goes, that I was going back to the hotel to get some sleep.

When I came out, the last light after sunset gleamed from the northwest through a slit like a narrowed eye between black and stormy clouds both above and below. The clouds looked heavy with snow. I went into the detachment and turned the lights out and waited. After a while I could see Debbie strolling along and heard her steps crunching on the snow and then her knock on the door.

There was still a little light from outside by which I could see her find a chair near the counter and drop into it. I heard her sigh. For a while we were silent, glancing back and forth at one another, staring out at the few passersby on their ways to or from the rec hall. I was waiting for her to talk.

The eye of the dark cloud bank suddenly closed and left us in deep dusk. The sound of far-off wolves blew in on the cold and cutting west wind.

When she spoke it was as if she'd made up her mind to tackle a hard task and wanted to get it over with. Her words tumbled out. "It's about Davidee and Hard Hat," she said. Her brother's name came out like a swear word. "I just want you to know something. On the night that Dennissie and Thelma were killed and your mother was hurt so badly, I was home only in the early part . . ."

She paused, swallowing hard. This was the crunch, one way or the other. Either she backed up Hard Hat's alibi or she didn't.

She didn't; she even dropped a bombshell of another kind. "Hard Hat was there for a while, but I don't know how long. So was Davidee."

"Davidee!"

We had done what we could earlier, asking around about whether Davidee had been seen in Sanirarsipaaq that night, but had drawn a blank. In all Hard Hat's efforts to distance himself, he sure hadn't mentioned seeing Davidee that night. But then not everyone was like Debbie, obviously ready to talk.

"He'd sneaked into town, down the back streets, parked his snowmobile over by the school. When he and Hard Hat got to our place I took the baby and went to Byron's parents' place. We were there until nearly eleven, and then Byron came back with me, carrying our baby, who'd woken up on the way, and we put her to bed. Neither Hard Hat nor Davidee were there then, and my mother said they'd gone out around ten, didn't know where, except she'd heard them talking and heard Dennissie's name mentioned."

I felt silly asking, but wanted to be certain. "You're absolutely sure of the times?"

Obviously she understood what I was getting at. She went through it again, being specific about times. "As I said, we got back around eleven and they'd been gone a while by then, and hadn't come back. It's a time, booze night, when Byron and I like to be together and let other people live it up. The hockey was over and my mother was watching something else and my father was asleep in his big chair. So we went upstairs and played with the baby until she went to sleep again and after that we were in my bedroom until Byron left around twelve. Another night he might have slept over, but not with Davidee in the house. He hates Davidee."

"All that time your parents were in the kitchen?"

"All that time. At the kitchen table where they always are. Nobody else came in or out. We would know, you can hear what goes on all through that house. I fell asleep as soon as Byron left. So if anybody came back after that, they were very quiet."

I thought about that. "Even if one or both of them had come back, it could have been after the murders," I said.

She nodded silently.

"So," I said, "the next day when Barker came around to check Hard Hat's alibi that he was here all evening before going to the rec hall late, you weren't home then either?"

"I was in the bedroom with the baby. I could hear the corporal in the kitchen asking questions and my father not mentioning Davidee at all but saying that Hard Hat had been here all the time until he went to the rec hall about midnight, which of course was a lie."

"And your mother?"

"I heard the corporal ask her the same question. I thought she didn't answer or I didn't hear it. I asked her later and she told me, ashamed, that she had nodded her head."

A sudden gust of snow came in on the wind, rattled the windows, slackened off, and came again as steady blowing snow, swirling across the open space. Far off upwind the wolves were howling, and dogs in the settlement were answering, as they sometimes do.

I mentioned the possibility Bouvier had referred to the first time we talked at length: the chance that whoever committed the murders could have gone somewhere long enough to change his clothes and *then* gone to the rec hall, fast enough to ensure an alibi. Maybe Debbie had thought of that herself. She made a hard line of her lips and met my eyes.

"I can only tell you what I know, that neither of them were there when we got there, nor when Byron left at nearly midnight."

I belabored the obvious, but I wanted to nail it down. Maybe there was more there that needed shaking out. "So your parents lied."

Her words poured out in a hard and angry jumble. "If he was yours and he had already disgraced the family and done things to us and others for years so that we knew what he was capable of, and he said that he would kill you if you did not say what he told you to say, that Hard Hat was there most of the evening, and not to mention Davidee being around at all, would you lie?"

"Maybe I would," I admitted, putting myself in their place, old and defeated and fearful.

"Well, I wouldn't!" she said. "But our parents would and did, because he said that he would kill them both if they said anything else."

"But do you really know that he said that? I mean threatened to kill them if they didn't say what he told them to say?"

Her voice was shaking. "Yes, I do know."

"How?"

"My mother told me. Please be careful. Lie about where you heard this. I don't want Davidee to think it was my parents who told you. Even more, I don't want him to know it was me. If he knew that, he could do anything! He could hurt my baby! If he was going to be caught anyway he wouldn't care any more what he did . . ."

The last few words were almost inaudible. She wept for a minute or two. I thought of putting my arm around her shoulders, but didn't. Eventually she went on, much quieter. "Our father, it has been worst for him, years when he didn't know what he would do next about Davidee! Other men, friends he had hunted with

long ago and grown up with, pitied him! Used to say, 'Poor
Ipeelee.' With pity, among men, there is always a contempt as
well. He . . .''

Her tone had changed. The heat was gone. Now she was speaking matter-of-factly. She could have been reading a story from
a newspaper, a segment of one of those sociological roundups
about family problems. "Exclusive! Our Family Problems reporter interviews parents whose offspring have threatened to kill
them . . .''

"My father, Ipeelee, is treated as a *nothing* in all of Sanirarsipaaq
when all he did was take in a boy who needed a home, as many
of our people do. But he couldn't handle what the boy had brought
along with him, the fears and lying and violence against girls who
wouldn't do what he told them to do. You've seen my father, a
man with no manhood left to him. I know he thinks of suicide. It
was known from the time of Davidee's trial that when I was a little
girl and Davidee was screwing me that my father did nothing to
stop it. He said in court he did not know, and it was true that
always Davidee and I were alone in the house when these things
happened. But I had told them and they did nothing. It went on.
In a little house those things are known.

"You can look at my mother now and believe what I tell you.
She told me that if she had it to do over and knew what was going
to happen she would have killed him when he first came to us
when he was eight and I had just been born. She told me that.''

I thought of what the judge had told me about Davidee being
adopted after being sexually abused. Sexual abuse has some terrible by-products, one being the repetition of the original abuse.
The way Davidee could exercise power over others, lead them to
follow him, could be another element of his old nightmare.

Debbie might have guessed my thinking, or maybe not. Maybe
she had lived with it so long that the very thought was a com-
monplace. She went on, as calmly as before: "When I heard my
father lie to the corporal about Hard Hat being there until late
that night, as soon as the corporal left and my father had gone out
I asked my mother what had really happened. She said Davidee
had promised to kill them both if they did not tell the corporal

that Hard Hat had been at our house all evening." She gulped in a deep breath. "Even now I am afraid of what I have said to you. There are terrible things Davidee could do."

"But it has to end," I said.

"Yes, it has to end," she said, turning away, getting to her feet, saying no more. When she was walking unsteadily up the hill to her home, I added it up. Davidee had been in Sanirarsipaaq at least early that night. He could have been involved in the murders himself. He had told his parents to lie or he would kill them. His parents had duly lied.

But I had to have more, and somewhere there must be more. I thought of Hard Hat telling me and then Bouvier that he wasn't really involved with Davidee anymore, but that change, if it was real, could have come after the fact. Nothing, so far, firmly connected either of them to the murders—unless the bloody footprints that Pelly had taken to forensics would do that. Bouvier's search of the settlement for discarded boots and clothing, turning out old oil drums and going through the half-burned contents, had so far turned up nothing of value. It didn't seem reasonable that Davidee and Hard Hat would overlook getting rid of anything incriminating.

Unless Davidee had taken it with him now out on the tundra where it might be found in ten years, or a century, or never. All the more reason for me to find Davidee wherever he was, or had been.

I wandered back over to the rec hall, getting there at the same time as Byron, whom Debbie had just relieved from looking after Julie. We stopped in the lobby before going in to where the crowd was.

"Byron," I said. "I'm told that you went after Davidee with a gun on Sunday after he interrupted your Easter dinner. Were you really thinking you might shoot him?"

He let out a long breath, dropping his eyes and muttering, "I guess I was, but I didn't." Then he raised his eyes defiantly to mine. "But if he ever did anything to hurt Julie or Debbie I *would* kill him! I'd shoot him down like a dog! So if that ever happens, you'll know where to look."

T H I R T E E N

When the knock sounded on my door early Wednesday morning, it came along with Margaret's voice, pitched low. "Matteesie!"

The east-facing window of my room had been full of the early sun most mornings. Now the wind had driven snow through cracks around the storm window, and some lay sticky and wet on the sill. When I hopped out of bed I landed in a wet patch on the floor. A glance beyond the window revealed no sun in sight, not even the jumbled building materials behind the hotel, nothing but a wall of snow. So much for Thomassie flying to meet me early, as I had hoped.

"Hey, you hear me?" Margaret said in the same low voice.

"Coming. Stay there."

I grabbed my parka and held it around me as I opened the door, the parka coming to just above my knees, my legs bare from there down. She was fully dressed, the red dress again. In different circumstances I might have kidded that this early in the morning I might have hoped for her in a nightgown . . . but it just crossed my mind, I didn't say it, and she said, "Phone for you. Cambridge Bay."

I padded along the hall and down the stairs, pulled on my boots (my feet were cold on the bare floor) and picked up the phone. Thomassie sounded disgusted. "Snowing there?" he asked.

"Heavy and wet," I said. "How about you?"

"The same. Just got in ahead of the storm last night. Weather guy says it's all over the place. Not supposed to clear until middle or late afternoon."

I swore, but only a little. It wasn't as if I had to waste a whole day, unless I just stayed here twiddling my thumbs. Wherever Davidee was, he wouldn't be moving much in this stuff, either.

"You got a map handy?"

"Right here," Thomassie said. "But hell, I don't need a map to find Sanirarsipaaq."

"Look on the map between there and here. See No Name Lake?"

Pause. "Got it."

"Best guess is that the guys I'm looking for are out around there somewhere. What we'll do is check again at noon. When we're sure enough of the flying weather I'll head out by snowmobile. We can talk details later. Call you at twelve."

Margaret went by and pointed, laughing, at my knobby bare knees above the boots and below the parka. She came back in seconds with a cup of tea. I called the detachment number and got an answer immediately, "RCMP, Bouvier."

"You at Barker's or the detachment?"

"Detachment. Couldn't sleep. Dogs got me up."

I told him about my air force being socked in at Cambridge, causing me to delay the search. Meanwhile, I had some time. "I'd like to see those three girls this morning."

"I'll pick them up in the van. Might take an hour. They're probably not up yet."

"See you at eight."

I was first in to eat—eggs, bacon, sausages, toasted fresh bread, and gooseberry jam from a jar that read "Product of Poland." The peanut butter jar said "Product of China." Amazing world.

Outside the snow was as heavy and wet as before, but thicker. Bouvier must have knocked some off the van earlier, but the heavy new stuff on the roof looked like whipped cream a foot deep.

Beating my way through the smoke screen from Bouvier's post-breakfast cigar, I greeted Sarah Thrasher and got my first look at Leah Takolik and Agnes Aviugana. Since Bouvier's one-on-ones with them hadn't been fruitful, I thought that maybe getting them together would strike sparks.

Talk about Arctic contrasts. Of the three, Agnes and Sarah had the most cheerful Inuit qualities. Look at either of them and you'd think, "Game for anything!" From the standpoint of a young man on the make, which was stretching my memory a bit, none of the three would drive anyone away.

Sarah and Agnes were dressed more or less alike, a mixture of jeans and store-bought padded parkas, the kind used in spring. It didn't feel like spring that morning, at minus five and snowing, but kids that age sometimes rush the season. Agnes told us, giggling nervously—Inuit teen-age girls do tend to giggle a lot, some kind of defense mechanism—that her real Inuit first name was Atsainak, which she had shortened and anglicized. She had a round face, a mouth full of good white teeth, and breasts that stood out like melons. In normal circumstances she would be one of those merry Inuit who were natural photo opportunities at big events, visits of dignitaries, or even *News/North*'s annual photo spread on the arrival of spring. In such shots it wouldn't be surprising to find the other girl, Sarah, as well, a bouncy item who also featured a nervous giggle. It rang out almost every time she was spoken to, or spoke.

Leah was different. No girlish giggles from her. I remembered what Maisie had said about both Dennissie and Davidee being hot on her trail. Strange, in a way, because although in white terms she was plainly a knockout this would not necessarily be the case among Inuit, who favor plump women. Her outer garment was a beautiful creamy white *amautik,* probably made from the soft skin of caribou calves. Versions of this garment's shape show up in Arctic drawings a century or more old: really a parka falling to the knees in half-oval flaps back and front, but cut upward on both sides to free the hips. Hers was heavily beaded, someone's loving work, across the front and at the shoulders and cuffs. Her legs were fragile-looking in wildly colorful tights and caribou-skin knee-highs. She had a fine-boned face unlike the more rounded features of the other two.

And all that to waste on two cops in beautiful downtown San-irarsipaaq at eight o'clock on a snowy morning.

"You were all good friends of Dennissie," I opened. "And you all occasionally went to his home with him late at night when Thelma was asleep, sometimes to make love."

Again Leah did not react like the other two, who just shrugged. Leah looked somber, even sad. I wondered about that, but if cases could always be solved by facial expressions, police work would be a lot simpler.

"Did any of you see Dennissie the night he was killed?"

I couldn't believe it. They were all nodding.

"In his bedroom?" I asked.

They had misunderstood the first question. Agnes and Sarah said or signaled, "Oh, no!" Leah said, carefully, "There were some of us at the rec hall early in the evening." The others nodded. "Dennissie also was there."

"Who was he with, particularly?"

"He did some talking with Davidee," Leah said. This was the first-ever reference to Davidee being at the rec hall, probably only briefly.

"Someone obviously went home with Dennissie that night," I said. "Any of you?"

Two head-shakes, answering no. I noted that Leah did not answer so positively, but I left that, for now.

"Did he have enemies?"

More shaking of heads in the negative, this time Leah's included. I wondered how much they could know about Dennissie's loan-sharking, which had been taking place that night as well.

Now I had to get down to it, apply some pressure in the way of a threat. "From all the blood left around after the murders we have footprints that are being examined by experts in Yellowknife and probably Edmonton."

At the mention of blood Leah had gone very pale.

"Some of the footprints were big, like a man's, but at least one was quite small, maybe a girl's, so if one of you was there and could tell us what happened, it would help."

They looked at me. Nothing. What I'd said so far they could have expected, if they'd thought about it. Now I was ready for heavier artillery. Get 'em out of the foxholes.

"I should also say that whoever was there, and knows what

happened, is almost certainly in danger now. Someone who is already a murderer and who knows that identification is possible will not mind murdering again to get rid of the witness."

To an extent, that worked. Now their expressions were all the same: scared. Looking from one face to another I had one of my insights, that all three knew or could guess who had been there, one by being there and the other two by knowing something I did not. I watched carefully. All stared at me. None looked at the others at all.

"I will be finding out," I said.

"You always find out, so the people say," Leah said, with a dismissive sarcastic edge I ignored. "This time too late."

I went on, "If any of you know something that you're not telling me now because you're afraid to . . . I want you to think of a way to tell me. Even without letting me know who is telling me, if you're that scared. A note, a message, anything."

Three pairs of black eyes were doing no more than paying attention. I was getting nowhere with this reasonable shit. But I didn't really put much planning into what came next.

"The two people who were killed and the one who later died, my own *amaamak,* had harmed no one . . ." Then suddenly I was hearing myself. So goddamn removed, civilized, on the very edge of pleading! Invoking my mother, for god's sake! Trying to make them so sorry for me that they'd spill their guts. I couldn't stand it! I stood up and shouted into their startled faces. "If any of you three silly bitches know and don't tell me now, when I do find out I'll see that you are in trouble."

Nothing. They had stamina. Then I thought, maybe they really don't know . . . kids, schoolgirls. Except Leah. She was older and much more composed.

I got myself under control and went on quietly, paddling up a few other channels. "Hard Hat was not at Davidee's home all that night, as he had claimed. We now are sure of that. We don't know where Davidee was."

Now all three looked somewhat scared, Sarah and Agnes glancing at one another, Leah staring straight at me, but pale.

"Also, we know there is money around with bloodstains on it, Dennissie's money, taken from him probably after the murder.

When we find some of that money we will be on the track of the murderer, or at least someone who got to Dennissie before we did."

That gave me an idea. "Let me see what money you have." Just in case. "Hand over your *maniusiqpik*."

They gave me their purses and I emptied all three. No blood-stained money.

"Also, I'm going to your parents and find out where each of you was when the murders took place."

At this, finally, a reaction. Inuit kids are like kids anywhere, when they have something to hide. They could get hurt by some parent. Had been hurt before. Had their asses kicked and their money cut off and other things just made generally difficult. Had even maybe been locked up at home when a big party was coming up, like the drum dance. Depended on the parent, but cop questions were bad enough.

"Who gave you our names?" Leah asked.

"I won't tell you that."

She made a derogatory sound, her lips briefly blown outward, a letting out of air.

"What's that for?" I asked her.

"I think that Maisie told you our names. She and Dennissie were"—Leah dropped her eyes and made a small face—"very friendly."

What I was hearing from her, I sensed, was the edge of jealousy and something deeper. Oh, hell, I thought, how long will so many of our people be like that? As attractive, even beautiful, as Leah was, even mentioning Maisie's name, her rival, she felt inferior.

"Maisie didn't tell me your names."

"Then why isn't she here?"

"I talked to her last night—"

Leah made the same derogatory sound. "Not with other girls listening, I'm sure."

"With her mother listening," I said. "Which hasn't happened to you yet, so don't be so goddamn superior."

I was sorry I said that, when it wasn't feeling superior that was her problem.

Could I goad her into saying more? I spoke to Leah directly.

"The one thing Maisie did tell me was that you were the one Davidee wanted. Not her."

Finally, her aplomb was shattered. Her lips came down at the corners. She burst into tears. "Dennissie told me that! I didn't believe some of the things he said . . ."

Agnes passed her some slightly used Kleenex.

When Leah composed herself she asked, "When will you talk to my mother?" She didn't say, our parents.

"Soon," I said. "But not this minute. I'm hoping that one or all of you will decide to come and tell me more before I have to do that."

They left together but soon separated, Sarah and Agnes going one way, talking and sometimes looking back, Leah going another, without looking back.

I sat and thought for a few minutes. I planned to see Leah again, preferably with her parents, check the couple of times she'd answered either not at all or at least less positively than the others. But while I was chasing Davidee and whoever was with him, giving her a day or two to go back over her answers, maybe worry a little or a lot, wouldn't hurt. Might even help. She hadn't struck me as being a worry-free liar, if she had indeed been lying here and there.

Meanwhile, snow was still falling heavily and there were two of the earlier interrogations that hadn't really satisfied me. I walked up past Annie's house and knocked on the door of number 4. And knocked. And knocked.

I knocked so hard that the huge white woman in number 5 came out and glared at me, said nothing, then slammed her door. I kept knocking.

Finally the door opened. The old man had just skulked in the background during my earlier visit, letting others do the talking. Now he waved me to come in. "A lot of snow," I said in Inuktituk, for openers. Turned out to be for closers, as well.

He grinned but said nothing. A woman, also very old, came partway down the stairs. I spoke to the man again. "I want to ask you again if you've remembered more . . ."

Then I caught an imperative arm movement from the old lady.

She was pointing to her ear, and then at the man. When that didn't register on me, she came the rest of the way down and reached into the man's pocket and produced a small hearing aid and handed it to him. He put it in his left ear. He explained that the earpiece was uncomfortable so when the TV was on, they turned the sound up full volume and that night had heard nothing else.

He wasn't any too loquacious, even with the earpiece in. No, they'd seen nobody going in or out until all the crowd came, policee and everybody. They were very sorry about Thelma and Dennissie and my mother. The woman kept nodding. I left.

Next door, the fat lady didn't answer the door to my knock, but roared through it, "I didn' see nothin'!"

F O U R T E E N

I spent the rest of the morning partly on the phone, partly writing a condensed version of what I'd been doing, and sending it by fax to G Division with a copy to Ottawa. Bouvier was screening all incoming calls and I took none of them. One was from Erika Hall in Cambridge Bay. She wondered if we knew of any charters coming this way that she might hitch a ride on. When Bouvier told me that, I hoped she wouldn't somehow find Thomassie Nuniviak and turn on the charm. Thomassie, I knew of old, was not impervious to charm.

From the detachment window I could see, as expected, that no snowmobile was parked at Debbie's house. Every hour, I called the weather office. I also did a lot of looking out of the window hoping to see the storm easing off. By ten thirty, that seemed to be happening. I went back to the hotel and asked Margaret if she would make me up a lunch, sandwiches, thermos of tea. By then I had done everything else necessary. Bouvier was getting the detachment snowmobile gassed up and loading a sled with everything I might need for a three-day trip (to be on the safe side). I called to see how he was doing.

"Good," he said.

"How long?"

"Half an hour, max. Most of it's loaded already except some of Sadie's heat-in-the-bag stew I'll get from her freezer."

I decided to call Thomassie ahead of the noon call we'd decided upon. If I got out of here in half an hour and the traveling wasn't real bad, I'd be something like five hours getting to No Name Lake. From Cambridge Bay Thomassie said the official weather word was that the storm had blown itself out north of here by now and that the clearing was moving steadily south.

"They tell me likely I can get off by three."

"Okay, let's figure on that. What I'll do is take a direct course from the airstrip here to No Name. What you do when you can fly is head straight for the lake area and see what you can see. Three or four hunters from here including the one I want most are out somewhere on two snowmobiles, and the best guess I can get locally is that they headed for No Name. You won't see any old tracks around there, the snow would look after that, but if you see a hunting party or signs of a camp before you see me, just keep on going until you do see me and can land. We'll figure it out from there. If you're at two or three thousand feet with your eyes open—"

"Nuniviaks never sleep," he interrupted. "Especially while flying."

"—and we stay on those courses and neither of us screws up, we oughta see each other all right around four."

Being Thomassie, he didn't ask what if we don't?

"I'll be on the detachment snowmobile, blue, towing a sled. When we see one another you find a place you can land and I'll follow to talk about what next, okay? See any holes in that?"

"No more than a million," he said cheerfully. "But it sure as hell beats flying guys across the Mackenzie Delta from Inuvik to Aklavik with cases of beer. That all?"

"All I can think of."

I hung up. Margaret was watching me. She'd heard enough to know what was happening. "You're crazy," she said.

For reasons that I knew very well, the excitement of going into action, I felt not crazy at all, but good.

Boarding the snowmobile to head out a little later, I was briefly tempted to go along the sea ice for a while, which might have been smoother. But that wasn't the course I'd given Thomassie, the straight line from Sanirarsipaaq to No Name Lake, so I didn't.

The temperature, I figured, was just around freezing. I was prepared for worse, if it came. Most of my heavy-duty cold wear had flown with me from Labrador last Monday. The rest I'd borrowed from Bouvier. I had on a thermal shirt next to my skin, down vest, pants of caribou hide with the fur inside, knee-high boots of caribou hide with rubber bottoms, a winter parka, fur hat, and goggles which at first I had to keep wiping free of the occasional flurry of wet snow until I soon tipped them back under my parka hood.

In the compartment below the seat was the detachment's two-way radio and a few tools and spare parts that the prudent northern traveler never leaves behind. A rifle projected from a scabbard by my right knee, one clip loaded, with extra clips in my parka pocket. A light tent, a box of cooking utensils and food, plus seven (to be on the safe side) red plastic gas cans, each holding five gallons, made up the main load on the sled. Also, I didn't go anywhere in the north without the little Swiss-made Silva compass I had hanging around my neck. The bearing I had to follow was a little west of due south.

I speeded up past a snow plow on the airport road and onto the empty landing strip. After a mile or two I was in terrain I'd never traveled before, so I didn't know what landmarks, if any, might exist. Once I reached the open tundra the snow had almost stopped. The wind was on my back. I opened the throttle again, this time to what I thought was a fair cruising speed for unfamiliar terrain, bumping along at probably ten miles an hour.

An hour and a half out I stopped to look around, check my compass, pour tea from the thermos in a holder alongside my left leg. I ate a sandwich, slices of musk-ox pot roast on thick brown bread spread with butter, mayonnaise, mustard, and lots of pepper. Finishing that, I pulled my binoculars from their pocket next to my body and scanned the horizon. Visibility, which had been zero when I woke and maybe a few hundred yards when I set out, was getting a little better all the time. I saw rabbits, one fox, one raven.

Ahead, I really didn't know what to expect. Davidee and company might not have gone as far as No Name, might have encountered caribou before that . . . but I'd seen no caribou signs at all. The wolf howls I'd heard the night before, a likely sign of caribou, had been coming downwind and could have been well west of my course. My thoughts drifted back to the people at mother's funeral, dozens of whom I hadn't seen for so many years; some who hardly knew me at all; the extended family, kin group, of half-brothers and half-sisters, mostly older than me, from this father or that, causing me to remember all the sometimes kind and sometimes cruel men who had subbed for my father in my mother's life after he drowned. The funeral had been a time of sadness and praise, along with occasional slow and even shy questions. It seemed that after the sadness had been expressed, the thought on every mind was, "When are you going to find who did this, Matteesie?"

So I went on with occasional stops to wipe condensation from my binoculars and scan the horizons. Once, with a jab of excitement, I saw well to the west what I first thought was a wolf, maybe an outrider for a caribou-shadowing wolf pack. Where there were caribou I might find the hunting party I was looking for. But closer up, exit excitement. Using the binoculars again I could see from the animal's distinctive running style, humping along like a small bear, that it was a wolverine.

Farther along I crossed the tracks the animal had left going east-to-west across my course. Tracks are always conclusive. Wolves, from the dog family, have four toes. Wolverines, from the weasel family, have five.

One thirty passed, then two. Nothing in front, behind, or at either side except the featureless tundra. A feeling I knew well stole over me. For much of my life I had felt this kind of euphoria on the trail, an inner peace that is difficult to describe. On one level I was alert to everything I saw—even the total sameness of what I was seeing, the mainly trackless snow, places where the going looked rough and rocky and should be avoided, the vast expanse of empty land ahead whenever I reached the top of a small rise and started down the next long stretch. On another level I was thinking of my mother and of the dog teams I'd driven long distances while hunting, of times in my late teens when I had brought game back to camp to happy hungry people and had been the honored one around the cooking pot. Then I would be given the best sleeping place in the igloo (in the middle, with lesser lights assigned to the cold outside walls). At other times, before I had been old enough to be counted a hunter, and when others brought in the meat, I could remember when I had to sleep on the cold end trying to cuddle close to the body next to mine—never young and female, the adults who laid out the sleeping arrangements always would see to that.

In some terrible storms, when the right kind of densely packed snow for igloo-building wasn't close to hand, igloos built hastily or carelessly had been known to collapse, sometimes causing death or injury to some inside. Once, when I was quite young, my mother and her man and I were traveling with two other families, a total of fourteen in all, when a mighty blizzard fell on us, bad enough that we knew we might not be able to move for days.

One old man in the group, not often heard from with the younger men around, suddenly was boss. In a few shouted words above the howling wind he made the fourteen of us into a team; pointing, explaining, pushing for speed and accuracy. All of us, even children my age, dug down to find the kind of snow suitable. Heavy blocks were cut and trimmed by the old man into great wedges for the foundations, smaller wedges as the walls grew upward. When the igloo was domed and complete, with him inside, he lighted a fire in the igloo then cut his way out and sealed the hole. I shivered, held close to my mother while she put her mouth close to my ear so I could hear above the gale as she explained: the fire inside would melt a thin layer on the interior of the snow blocks, this to freeze solidly into a structure strong and safe.

When the old man cut out what was to be the entrance tunnel and then entered and doused the fire, this freezing did happen, fast. All of us were inside by then, the women preparing their oil lamps for heating and cooking and spreading skins two or three deep on the sleeping ledges. The old man then jabbed his knife through the roof to make the essential tiny hole always left in an igloo's peak. The hole would let out the warm air from our lamps and bodies so that everything would not get damp within. Every time I built a snowhouse after that, I did it the old man's way.

———

At three the clouds broke, and the sun shone through. I was passing the eastern tip of a small lake that showed on my map as being a few miles north of No Name. I halted for tea and another sandwich and to sweep the horizon with my binoculars, checking the sky too in case Thomassie's Cessna might be a speck up there somewhere. It wasn't.

Then, around three thirty, a break. Close to the north shore of No Name my binoculars picked up a line, some kind of a trail. Standing beside it minutes later I found a fresh set of snow-mobile tracks, heading east. They had been made since well after the storm began—maybe about the time the snow ended, to judge from the drifting that had started, along with the quickly dropping temperatures and rising wind. The straight parallel lines of the machine's skis framed the hard-packed narrower path of the drive-belt. Far away to the east the trail seemed to come to a point, like an old movie shot of train tracks disappearing into infinity.

I thought it over for angles. Except for the possibility that this trail had been made by someone entirely separate, someone had left Davidee's hunting party. Why? And who? While I thought about it, I tried to raise Bouvier on the radio, but he didn't respond. Anyway, he hadn't called me so I could assume there was nothing new at his end.

And then I did hear the aircraft. Thomassie circled me, waved, and came in to land on No Name a few hundred yards away. I arrived alongside just as he switched off his engine and opened the door to hop out. We hugged one another. We are almost exactly the same size. A person who didn't know differently might have thought we were brothers, even twins, with our black hair, stubby build, slanted eyes slitted by the sun; the main difference was that he was dressed more lightly for the Cessna's heated cabin, while I was more like a modern version of the old skin-clad Inuit who had been traveling these climes for centuries, hunting food and shelter to survive. He got on the snowmobile behind me. We went back and inspected the tracks. He agreed that the recent minor drifting set a time frame.

"I could see the trail but no machine when I was coming in,"

Thomassie said. "If it went by here say two hours ago that would be time to get out of sight."

I tried to raise Bouvier again. "Bouvier? Matteessie here. Over." Got only static in reply.

I was doing some heavy thinking, or trying to. Traveling at speed due east, whoever drove that snowmobile might have been on his way back to Sanirarsipaaq, hoping for smoother going on the sea ice. But the who and why could not be answered. Davidee? Not likely—he'd been at pains to keep out of my way, for whatever reason. Hard Hat? From what Bouvier said about the talk Saturday and from Hard Hat's remarks, to me earlier he'd seemed actually to be too scared to do anything except deny that he'd done anything so far, trying to sell the image that as far as he was concerned there was nobody here but us chickens.

Then I noticed something. I drove my machine slowly until I was close to, and parallel with, the other machine's tracks, which I could see had cut deeper than mine.

Thomassie and I were talking mostly in the regional dialect, Siglit, which we both understood. I pointed at my track and said, "*Atausitchiaaq,*" meaning, that "only one" man, I, was on that machine. Then I pointed at the other track. "*Malruk.*" Meaning that I thought two had been on that one. He pondered that and asked, "*Suuq?*" Meaning in this instance something like, "Why? How many are there in all?"

"At least three, maybe four."

Our planning conference then was fairly heavy with the common Siglit words for "What should we do next?" In the end I suggested that Thomassie take off and make a sweep to the east to try to pick up the other snowmobile and maybe land and see who was aboard.

I would run west, backtracking to where the machine had come from. When either of us had something to report, we could communicate by radio. Thomassie started back toward the Cessna, turning after a few steps to call back, "*Anayanaqtuaq,*"—"Be careful."

I'd seen him bounce a few times after his skis hit. I told him to be careful, too, and asked, "How is that stuff for landing on?"

"Well, it ain't no Edmonton International," he said, which is pretty hard to say in Inuktitut, so he said it in English, and was gone. As he took off, my radio suddenly squawked. "Matteesie. Bouvier. Come in. Over."

"What's up?"

"I'm at the airport. Hard Hat is leaving on a flight in a few minutes. I asked him where to and he had some story about a relative being sick in Inuvik. Also said he hoped to get some welding work there. Obviously he didn't go out with the others. Should I hold him?"

This was a huge surprise. I had assumed that one of those with Davidee was Hard Hat, despite his earnest disclaimers to me that he was through with Davidee. That didn't alter what Debbie had told me about his movements on the night of the murders. But I wasn't ready to reveal what Debbie had told me—not with a vengeful Davidee still loose. I thought hard. "Tell him to register his whereabouts with our detachment in Inuvik," I said, "and that we might need him back here in a few days. If he doesn't show we'll get him picked up. Scare him. Let him know he isn't off the hook, wherever he is."

With that ticking over in my mind, a complication I hadn't foreseen, I headed west along the other snowmobile's track, dismissing Hard Hat for the moment. Whatever he had done or not done, Davidee had to be the key. We knew little or nothing so far about what kind of relationship Davidee had with Dennissie, and we hadn't had a chance to pin him down on threatening his parents into not mentioning him to the police. Obviously he had scared the hell out of a lot of people, including Hard Hat.

Then I went on to think about the stalwart and straight-ahead Lewissie Ullayoroluk's speculation that sometimes Andy Arqviq, the kid in the rec hall, might have been some kind of a dope runner. I wanted to track this down, in case dope turned out to have anything to do with the murders. I would have to press the kid. And what did it mean that Davidee had a powerful yen for Leah, the stunning-looking girl with the steady gaze and closed-in manner? Could that somehow be connected to what had really happened that night when the murders took place? But how? And how far could I get by pushing Davidee hard on his whereabouts that night without involving Debbie and putting her in danger?

Backtracking the other snowmobile now led me off the tundra onto the lake ice and straight across to what appeared to be an island, a low projection above what in summer would be the surface of the lake. The track came from behind the island. I could no longer hear the Cessna and was now a few miles from where Thomassie had taken off. I was approaching a danger zone. Then on the breeze, lighter now and westerly, I could smell something that was cooking, or had been cooked. I slowed to barely walking speed. I was almost upon the island.

As I rounded it close to shore, to my left I saw a small snow house, the yellow snowmobile, and Davidee. Simultaneously I heard a shot. Snow puffed and fell back a few feet to my right. Beside the snow house Davidee stood motionless, having lowered his rifle until it pointed at the snow in front of him.

I took my own rifle from its scabbard and laid it across my knees, steering with one hand as I drove slowly toward him.

He didn't make a move or a sound. He had an aspect of intense readiness, staring at me. I halted fifty yards away and dismounted, holding my rifle, ready to raise it quickly if he moved his.

"What the hell are you shooting at?" I yelled.

He laughed. "I thought it was Tommy and Paulessie coming back, just thought I'd give them a scare."

"Bullshit," I said. "You knew what their machine looked like, and even if you're colorblind their machine wasn't towing a sled."

"You don't think if I'd been shooting at you I would have missed."

I raised my rifle quickly and fired a few feet to his left. He jumped, raising his rifle again menacingly. I kept walking toward him until we were only yards apart.

"If I'd been shooting at you I wouldn't have missed, either," I said.

For long seconds we stared at one another, both sharply alert. I knew what I wanted. If he'd come out here partly to hide something that might be incriminating, bloodstained money, boots with blood on the soles, I'd find out.

Abruptly, his manner changed. "You come in that airplane I heard?" he asked.

That was not necessarily a dumb question, because he couldn't have seen and probably didn't know engine sounds well enough to identify a Cessna of a type too small to transport a snowmobile, let alone my sled.

"No. I came on the snowmobile. The aircraft is my backup against you doing something stupid."

"You're something new around here," he said mockingly. "I don't think Barker has ridden that machine five miles out of town in all the years he's been here."

"Maybe there was no need," I said. "Law-abiding place like Sanirarsipaaq."

He smiled at the sarcasm. "So what are you doing out here?"

"Looking for you."

"Why?"

"You can guess why."

He still hadn't moved. "You mean, I done something bad, coming out to hunt caribou? I didn't know I had to get permission. There isn't anything like the booze committee running hunting, you know, telling people when they can and when they can't."

Well, I couldn't stand there passing the time of day. I thought of my mother knocked down, sprawled and hurt when someone, maybe Davidee, or maybe somebody he knew about, had run her down.

"I think you either killed Dennissie and Thelma or know who did," I said. "You got no alibi that will stand up. You weren't supposed to be in Sanirarsipaaq on the night of the murders, but you were. Also you've got your reputation, which has half the town scared to stand up and say what a shit you are, and that something like killing two people for whatever reason or no reason at all is right in character for you."

He had remarkable composure. "You can't prove any of that."

"When I'm finished tracking down a few loose ends I think I can," I said. "For instance, when we find the other two guys who were here with you and hear why they ran out of here—probably, if they got any sense, because they didn't want to get involved in whatever it is that you're going to do next—we'd be a little closer."

I could see the flush of anger. "Those stupes. Out not two days, haven't fired a shot, and they get all screwed up about getting back . . ."

For a moment he seemed to be unraveling a little. But he must have felt that, too, and imposed his will. His next words were an almost funny attempt to act innocent.

"Who won the hockey playoff?" he asked. "We don't hear a thing out here."

"Get out of the way," I said, approaching with my rifle at my shoulder, but pointing down. "Put your rifle down. On the ground."

For a second or two he resisted. Rage flashed across his face. At that instant the drone of the Cessna sounded, growing fast. The Cessna banked into sight from behind the island, flying low with Thomassie visible, staring down. It roared overhead, as much as a Cessna 185 can be said to roar, circled once, and then set down on the lake and taxied in.

Davidee slowly and carefully put his rifle on the ground.

"I'm going to look in your snow house and search you and your snowmobile," I said, raising the rifle so that it pointed at him.

The Cessna stopped a few yards from us. Thomassie jumped down and looked at Davidee's rifle on the snow.

"What's doing?" he asked mildly.

I handed him my rifle. "Hold this gun on him while I do some checking. If he makes a move, don't wait, shoot."

Davidee was looking from one of us to the other. "You couldn't get away with it," he said.

"Don't bet."

I walked to the snow house, a tawdry affair, kicked down the entrance tunnel and crawled in on hands and knees, feeling vulnerable but trusting Thomassie to cover. Inside, a primus stove was still warm, under a pot half full of stew. A sleeping bag had been flung across caribou skins on a crude sleeping shelf.

I searched thoroughly. No boots, no nothing. No marks anywhere to indicate that anything had been hidden in the walls.

When I emerged, neither Davidee nor Thomassie had moved.

"Satisfied?" Davidee mocked.

"Not quite. Throw your parka on the ground."

He didn't argue. I knew then that he didn't fear a search at all. I searched his parka pockets, then patted him down as he stood absolutely still. There were no lumpy signs of anything hidden. In his pants pockets he had a few fives and tens, none showing any sign of blood, and two unopened packages of Accord Red cigarettes. I opened the seat of his snowmobile. It contained the usual spare drive belt, wrenches, screwdrivers, a fresh sparkplug still in its package, and a clean hunting knife of an ordinary store-bought variety.

"Nothing, eh?" he asked.

He was clean. He'd traveled over miles of tundra where he could have hidden almost anything but a battleship. The thought was depressing. But he'd had others with him on this trip, and if he'd hidden anything, he'd know that didn't mean it was safe. I took my rifle back from Thomassie and held it loose but ready. I knew that this was pretty well it, for now.

"What next?" Thomassie asked me.

"Nothing much. Davidee is going to come in with me and answer a few questions."

"I'm not ready to come in," he protested.

"How about I arrest you on a charge of obstructing justice by withholding or falsifying evidence about two murders?"

For a long minute or two he hesitated. He might have been weighing a possible escape—getting on his snowmobile and making a run for it, daring me to shoot. His snowmobile, with no sled to tow, was faster than mine. But he would know that he'd only be postponing. With an aircraft to shadow him, in the long run he wouldn't have a chance.

F I F T E E N

There was a certain shock value to our procession back into San-irarsipaaq just before sunset, which is a little after eight at that time of year. A fascinated throng (at least nine people) rushed out of the airport building to see us go by. One was the old Inuit lady who'd been ducking as the wingtip almost hit the window the day I arrived. She was wearing a bright calico Mother Hubbard gown over her parka. Beside her was Father Lovering, who had inter-rupted his annual visit with Jonassie to officiate at my mother's funeral and burial, and had now returned, as he'd told me he would, and was standing with Jonassie. All watched more or less transfixed as we chugged in past three parked aircraft, the dis-tinctive insignia of Aklak Air and Nahanni Air contrasting with the weather-worn Komatik Air marking on Thomassie's Cessna.

Among the locals one could almost discern in bubbles above a few heads, "Why the hell is Davidee driving policee's skidoo? And why is Matteesie driving Davidee's?" This had really been the only precaution open to me. On his own machine, Davidee might have outrun me if he'd felt like getting back first to strike the fear of God into anyone he thought might need to be told to keep their mouths shut—such as Hard Hat, who he probably didn't know yet had vamoosed out of there. On the slower police vehicle towing a heavy sled, he didn't have the option of outrunning me. I had the satisfaction of noticing that, for once, he looked worried. After one quick glance at the crowd, possibly to see if Hard Hat was on hand, he kept his eyes straight ahead.

When we pulled up at the detachment, I told Davidee that he was not to leave town or his parole would be revoked.

"You mean you haven't got a charge," he said.

"It means I'm not charging you right now," I said.

"Which means you know you couldn't make it stick."

I obviously had run out of the need for empty threats. I called up a line I must have heard once in a play or an old movie. Richard Harris, adjusting his naval officer's cap? Groucho Marx, stroking his mustache? "Let's wait and see, shall we?"

Davidee's parents were watching from up the slope as he got aboard his own machine, zoomed past them, parked, and, after a long look back at me, jerked his head at his parents to follow him inside.

Bouvier, appearing on the detachment steps in his shirtsleeves, had seen only the last part of this. I'd given him bare details by radio, with Thomassie adding an embellishment or two from his perspective as commander in chief of my air force. Bouvier followed me in, brimming with some excitement of his own. "A fifty-dollar bill with bloodstains on it has shown up at the Co-op," he said. "Apparently somebody took it in before we'd alerted them and didn't notice any staining—one side was clean—and tucked it under the change tray and forgot it. So it wasn't in the pile in Nelson's office when I checked."

I never have much of an idea where my own money goes, but expect other people to be more careful. "Seems strange to me that fifty dollars could be mislaid without that fussy bastard blowing his stack. Don't they check cash against cash register tapes?"

Bouvier grinned. "He's very defensive about that, going on about temporary help and kids who can't count and say their cash is balanced when it isn't. But anyway, he did call as soon as he found this fifty with the blood on it. Wanted to know what to do. I told him you were on your way back in and he shouldn't do anything until you got back tonight and he heard from you." Reminding me of one of my favorite song lines, "Do nothing till you hear from me."

We had tried to keep the hunt for bloodstained money reasonably quiet, figuring that if we brought the whole weight of our mighty two-man detachment into an open search, and somebody had more, they might decide to swallow, hide, burn or otherwise destroy the rest. Now with the fuss around the Co-op staff, the business about money with blood on it would be all over town.

"He's at his office now, waiting," Bouvier said. "They're closed, but I told him to wait."

The formerly unaccommodating Nelson Akpaliapik was a small, round and serious man. He had a lot more of the co-op spirit this time. I think he'd got into the swing of things, seeing himself becoming famous by helping the Mounties get their man. He obviously thought Bouvier had been slow off the mark in cautioning him to do nothing without my input. "The longer you leave a thing, you know, the more people don't remember," he complained. "But I can tell you one thing."

"What's that?"

"There's one guy in town you can rule out."

"Who?"

"Davidee Ayulaq."

What the hell did that mean? "Why rule him out?"

Nelson's normally benign expression flushed with annoyance. "The sonofabitch owed us money since before he went to jail, so when he did come back I told him he had to pay up. He kept telling me that he was getting some money soon, a guy owed it to him, but I told him no credit until it was paid. Not only that. I stuck a note at every cash desk that not only was his credit cut off, but if he ever tried to pay cash we were to take the money and apply it against his old bill."

So Nelson had put a candle to the devil, as our elders would describe it, and he'd got away with it.

"You're a hard man, Nelson."

"Thank you," he said modestly. "Of course, I figured out that when he wanted something real bad he'd get somebody to get it for him. His father came in a few days ago with a welfare check and bought things like ammunition, which I knew wasn't for him—he hasn't been out hunting for years—and cigarettes, Davidee's brand, Accord Red. The old man doesn't use cigarettes, smokes a pipe."

"Can I see the fifty?"

"Sure." While he fumbled with the lock to the top drawer of his desk he said, "Also, um, I'm pretty sure that Dennissie, the late Dennissie, poor guy, did something the same just before he was killed. He doesn't smoke, but one day before we even knew Davidee was back in this vicinity I happened to be around one day when Dennissie was buying Accord Red."

The father doing Davidee a favor under duress was one thing, but involving Dennis was something else. I turned that over in my mind. Davidee had told Nelson that somebody owed him money. The somebody could have been Dennis. That would fit with the way Davidee had demanded money from Byron and got chased with a gun for his pains.

Nelson handed the fifty across his desk to me.

Like most people, when I handle money I usually look mainly at the numbers. I had never really studied one of any denomination before. Now I noted that the main color of the fifty is red. One side of this one was mostly clean and crisp, showing a crest that from the top included the standard Canadian Anglo-French mix, the crown of England, a lion and a unicorn, a Union Jack, a fleur-de-lis, three red maple leaves growing off one stem, and the words *A Mari Usque Ad Mare.* In the middle was a red line of print reading "Fifty 50 Cinquante" and the word *Canada,* along with head and shoulders of a longtime and now long-dead prime minister, not identified by name on the bill but unmistakably (as I learned in school), William Lyon Mackenzie King.

There was very little stain on that side, only an almost unnoticeable blotch along the end that must have been in the bottom of Dennissie's pocket.

But when I turned the bill over, there it was. A blackish smear ran across the "Cinquante 50" message, as well as an irregular smudge across the bill's rear centerpiece, which is a perfect inward-facing circle of red-coated Mounties on black horses, holding their lances high, a depiction of the RCMP's famous musical ride, performed at many a formal ceremony in Canada, an old Mountie trademark.

"Can I use your phone?" I asked Nelson.

He shoved it over.

I called the hotel. "Margaret," I said, "when you paid Dennissie that night, did you give him any fifties?" Earlier, Bouvier had checked this with her. No harm in checking again.

Instantly she answered, "No."

"You're sure?"

"I am absolutely sure, because he asked me not to. He said he was going to need smaller bills, something about people owed him some money, he'd have to make change, I suppose that sharking he was doing. I gave him probably six or seven twenties but also smaller stuff . . ." Then, after a very brief pause: "Why? You got a fifty with blood on it?" I said we had and she immediately said, "On Davidee?"

I had to smile. So she suspected Davidee too. "No such luck." Nelson thought I was smiling at him—maybe thought the smile meant that I was getting somewhere with his valuable help—and he smiled back hopefully. Actually I was smiling because nothing in this case ever seemed to fit together.

Nelson stopped smiling when I told him I would have to take the fifty as evidence but would give him a receipt that he could turn in along with his bank deposit.

"Where the hell do you put a receipt from the RCMP into a bank deposit?" he asked.

A lot of people have wondered about that, from time to time when their money has been seized as evidence. Usually it is connected with a drug deal. Some guy, nabbed in a hotel room or parked car or something full of hash or whatever, the dealer nabbed with him, both redhanded, turns out to have a lot of cash on him. I've seen it happen. He's there to buy and now he's blabbering, "Ah ba, ah ba," as he tries to think of a plausible reason to be carrying that kind of a roll.

I told Nelson that the money would be returned to him.

I also wondered how much more might still be around.

"One thing you could do—" I began.

"You mean, besides explain to head office why I'm short fifty," he interjected disconsolately.

"—is tell all your cashiers that this bloodstained money has turned up and for them to look on both sides of any bills they take in for the next little while. And if they find any, I'll tell you what . . ."

"What?" Nelson said suspiciously. He apparently didn't see this anymore as a story to tell his grandchildren about how he'd once helped the Mounties get their man.

"Any more you find, I'll have to take that, too."

"For how long?"

"Until there's a trial and it's all over with."

"Oh, hell," Nelson said. "First the goddamn . . . I don't mean goddamn . . . I mean first the bodies in our goddamn freezer, and then this."

When I got back to the detachment through the deep dusk, I saw immediately that Bouvier had something more. I was becoming fond of the twinkle in those big owlish eyes when he had news. "Jonassie was at Davidee's house last night trying to do something for Davidee's father."

"How do you know this?"

"When you were at the Co-op Debbie came in and asked me to tell you. Jonassie and several others, you know how a shaman's intervention goes, some of the elders, including Annie and others from the Inumerit, were there when she got home last night and until daylight this morning."

"What 'something' was Jonassie supposed to do?"

"The old man was talking suicide. Debbie's mother called Jonassie in."

I thought of that sad-looking man whose latest worry must have been his lie on behalf of Davidee. According to Debbie, he had been living for years in a kind of long-running tragedy. A feeble excuse for a father, sure, but I felt ashamed that I'd seen only that as defining him. Sometimes when a person even seems suicidal to those close to him, the shaman is called in. I wondered if that was the case here; or if Debbie's father actually had tried to end his life.

Some try until they do succeed. Even considering what Debbie had told me about him, I didn't see her father as being that focused, but what did I know? One of my mother's childhood friends, grown old, unable to hunt, depressed at a feeling of uselessness, tried to hang himself on a rope pushed through the tiny airhole in the top of an igloo and tied to an oar resting as a brace on the roof. A son came home unexpectedly and cut him down, still alive. All the family told the old man that his strength would come back and he would hunt again, that they needed his presence and his advice. He must promise not to try again. He promised. The next time the hunters came home from hunting, again they found him hanging, same snow house, same rope, same oar, this time dead.

Maybe when he was younger, Debbie's father had thought his nightmare would end. Now, wasted away, he must believe it wouldn't, and his despair had caused his wife to call the shaman. I knew people in the force who at one time, maybe not now when I'd won a few, would have been scornful about me taking shamanism seriously. But the man must have been very afraid. How would Davidee be taking the news right now, knowing that he, Davidee, was the true reason for the shaman being called in? Should I go there immediately, or go to get Annie's reaction, or go to the shaman himself?

In the end, I chose none of those options. When I left the detachment I walked out into the tundra fringing the settlement; it was totally dark now. Hearing wolves in the distance and the occasional snore of a snowmobile in the town, I was thinking of shamanistic séances that I had witnessed as a boy and later. I put myself into the house where Debbie and her parents and Julie and Annie and others, perhaps Byron, last night had witnessed Jonassie fighting with age-old means the threat of the man taking his own life. It would be late, fully dark, all blinds drawn, only an eerie dim light showing those present in a circle as Jonassie, masked and with his body covered with skins and his own shamanistic charms, came out of the shadows, his leggings hung with rattles that sounded and danced as he summoned up his helping spirits.

Chanting and singing and dancing, he would have gone eventually into a trance in which he described spirit conversations he was having, beginning with his familiars, the gyrfalcon and the Arctic fox, dancing his intricate steps and shaking his charms and asking the spirits for help, then, over time, many hours, describing the trip his soul was making as he moved deeper and deeper to seek help from the greatest spirit of all, the goddess Sedna, who lives at the bottom of the sea.

In the chanting and dancing and suddenly fierce movements and cries depicting his passage to Sedna's presence, the words and incantations he spoke or sang would carry listeners and watchers along in their own trances until they felt they were watching Jonassie with Sedna, the fish-woman goddess of all the seals and sea animals, who has the power to cast out dangerous spirits and return an afflicted person to normal functioning on earth.

When I came in from the tundra I walked up the hill to Jonassie's home. This time I was going to see Jonassie uninvited. I wondered if he could or would tell me anything new and useful to the murder investigation. He had been forthcoming before. We sat in the room where he worked, under a hanging unshaded bulb. Again armed with tea out of his microwave, I asked, "Is there anything specific to the case that has made Davidee's father suicidal?"

"Perhaps," he said, "but nothing that he said in words. During my activities, he was downcast and silent. I thought several times that he was bursting to speak, but did not. I asked Debbie to let you know what we had tried to do, to bring him some peace, just so that you would know in case anything happens later."

That was all. After a lengthening silence I rose to go. He walked me to the door. There, with his hand on the latch, he said with a smile, "As you know, my brother, Father Lovering, does not approve of shamanism. Before he flew out just a little while ago, he renewed an old, old argument between us. He was trying as he always does to convince me that I am wasting my time, my life, when even now I could, like him, become a priest in an internationally recognized and accepted religion, instead of obeying crude tribal concepts based on an old and unverified set of superstitious beliefs."

"How did you answer?"

His eyes were merry in that huge leonine head. "I told him that no religion on earth depended on old and unverified superstitious beliefs as much as Christianity does."

It had been a busy night. I was tired. When I trudged back down the hill from his place, the shamanistic experience I had imagined filled my mind and weighed heavily in my body, bringing no knowledge with it—until, near the detachment, I saw someone lurking in the shadows. Debbie.

"Byron and I slipped out to take our baby to his place," she said hurriedly. "You know about the shaman and my father?"

"Yes. Bouvier passed on your message . . ."

"There's something you should know, I think. The shaman could not get through to Sedna. He kept trying for hours, singing his pleas through his helping spirits before at the end, near dawn, he gave up and said this to all of us there: 'I have failed, for a particular reason. I am being told that in this house, perhaps with the man I am trying to help, there is an object that does not belong here, maybe as a result of theft, and there is no more I can do until that object, whatever it is, is revealed and returned to its owner.' "

I was close enough that I saw Debbie shudder as she spoke. "It was getting light when he said that, and then left . . ."

"You have any idea what the object he referred to could be?"

"None! I have racked my brains! I must go, I mustn't be seen talking to you!"

Then she ran, not toward her own home but up the hill toward Byron's place.

At the hotel Thomassie and I ate the leftovers Margaret provided. He had been put into my four-bed room for the night, which suited me fine. We took a couple of cans of ginger ale to my room to go with the rum I'd bought in Inuvik.

I had one drink and then another, but I wasn't good company. Too tired. Confused both about the shaman's visit and the limited amount he had told me about it, and the mystery of what Debbie had said. The shaman's knife occurred to me, the only thing I knew of that was missing from where it should be, but from what I knew or could guess, certainly not taken by Debbie's father.

Eventually Thomassie said, "Do you need the Cessna anymore?"

That took me out of my reverie, briefly. "Let's make the charter day by day just in case."

In case of what, I didn't know.

Thomassie seemed instinctively to know the signs of my preoccupation. He turned in. I pretended to. I lay there wide awake, with all that had happened in the last few hours streaming through my mind. I gradually turned away from the brief encounter with Debbie and got back to the main event. Who must Davidee talk to, to guard against me making the essential links that I was sure were there if I could only find and identify them? I had a lot of information that I couldn't fit together. As long as his parents stuck to their silence about his presence on the night of the murders, he had that on his side, their word and his against what Debbie had told me so definitely about him being here on the murder night—information I had, which he didn't know about yet.

If it ever got that far, to trial, I could imagine the scene in the rec hall, which would be used as a courtroom.

His parents' testimony would say one thing and Debbie's, if she'd agree to testify, another. A defense lawyer would have been arranged for Davidee either privately, if someone put up the money, or through legal aid. I'd encountered enough defense lawyers in my time to know that Davidee's, whether legal aid or private, would be scathing about how much credence should be given to Debbie's evidence.

"Here you have," he'd tell the jury, "a young woman with, in her eyes, a legitimate reason to get even with her brother whatever way she can. How much of what she says is truth and how much is a desire to settle that old score, which my client paid for with four years in penitentiary? How can her story be taken as believable when her parents contradict it?"

No doubt he also would use whatever that prison psychiatrist in Prince Albert had put on paper to support the case that had been legitimized in that successful appeal: that Davidee had repaid his debt to society and would be no threat in the future if his freedom were restored.

All right, I was stuck. Debbie's evidence would cast doubt, but

I really needed an actual eyewitness or other evidence that would place Davidee in the murder house that night. It must be there, if I could only find it. At a little after two I abandoned the Debbie-versus-Davidee-and-their-parents scenario and tried the only other tack open to me. Who had Dennissie taken home that night who might be the murderer, or who might know who the murderer was? The small footprint in the blood that we'd guessed might be a woman's, whose could it have been? Leah's? Not Maisie's, too small. Whose then?

At that point I sat up in bed.

I said to a sleepy Bouvier on the phone at seven a.m., "Can you meet me at the detachment in a few minutes?"

"Okay if I come in my pajamas?"

I grinned. "Fast as you can, anyway."

I had tea on by seven fifteen, when he drove up in the van. It was about a three-minute walk from Barker's house, but he always drove. Maybe that was why he totaled at least a foot more around the middle than he should have.

"You know that kid who hangs around the rec hall," I said. "You said he was there when you and Barker checked there on the night of the murders. Andy Arqviq."

"Yeah?"

"What was his story?"

"As I recall, he said he'd been there most of the evening. I don't think we paid that much attention to him, not as much as to the bigger guys, anyway. Figured that mess couldn't have been done by anybody his size, I guess."

"He goes to school?"

"Don't really know. A lot of kids his age just quit and get jobs if they can, or go on the bum."

I called Lewissie Ullayoroluk's number. His wife answered. She was up, she said, getting ready for school. I told her who was calling. She said Lewissie had gone hunting. "He did okay down around No Name Lake a few days ago and figured we could use more caribou for the freezer. From what I hear about you going down there, Davidee didn't go far enough. Lewissie was away down past the south end of the lake when he hit caribou."

I like chatty women, especially ones who run libraries and teach school and have enough sense to marry an Inuk and live our life. I tried to imagine Lewissie living in her hometown in Nova Scotia. Didn't make it. But she seemed happy to have made her life here. Seemed to be thriving on it.

"Want him to call you when he gets back tomorrow, for the big party."

"Not necessary. The answers I need are about Andy Arqviq. Does he go to school?"

"No. Got thrown out. He was pushing dope right in the schoolyard. Lewissie was the one who caught him. Some dumb kid on Lewissie's youth hockey team stole some money at home, long story, but it turned out that Andy had started the kid on cigarettes at fifty cents each and then moved up a notch to something more expensive that made the parents finally notice that money kept disappearing."

"Was this known around town?"

"Sure. Barker knew about it. But what're you going to do with a fifteen-year-old in a place like this? The Inumerit took it on and Annie wanted to take him into her house, but I guess Andy didn't want to be quite that supervised. They're still talking to him but without much luck. He seems to be around all hours of the night, whenever I'm out anywhere. Is he in trouble again?"

"Might be," I said, and we both let it go at that.

I hung up and said to Bouvier, "We need a pair of Andy's shoes."

I was thinking: Number 5 in the row of townhouses, Andy, living with that woman who gets that subsidized house and money on the side to look after waifs and strays. Number 4, the people who might have heard the murder being done but stayed with their television, scared of what they heard. Number 3, two murders and the rundown of my mother resulting in her death. Number 2, Annie and her kids and for a while, my mother. Number 1, vacant.

"Wanta bring Andy in, too?" Bouvier asked.

"Just his shoes. But I'll do it."

I walked. Kids were out playing. I thought how hard it was to balance, get an insight into, why some kids could be chattering away and wrestling and running and yelling and throwing snowballs, having fun, rarely in big trouble, while another ran his life the opposite way. So much so that from what Lewissie had told Jonassie, just the sight of Andy around Jonassie's house had made him briefly suspicious until he considered, well, no problem, Jonassie's home. Not knowing that wasn't the case.

Answering the door at number 5, the woman was so big she blocked the doorway. I couldn't see past her. She glared at the RCMP badge on the front of my hat. When I asked for Andy, she said, "Either he's still in bed or he ain't home, anyway I haven't seen him . . ."

She called loudly up the stairs, "Andy!" Again, louder, "*Andy!*" No answer. "Is he in some kinda trouble again?" she asked.

"Would you go up and have a look, see if he's there?"

She pushed at her vast head of unmade hair, either gray going blond or blond going gray, glanced at the stairs, and sighed.

"How about I go?" I said.

She looked relieved. "Better you than me. His room is the one to the left of the landing."

I climbed the stairs. The door to the lefthand bedroom was open. I looked in.

The bed either had been slept in, or had not been made since the last time. The blind was drawn. I switched on the light.

From the bottom of the stairs, a contralto roar. "He there?"

"No."

"You shouldn' be up there then, should ya?"

I didn't answer, right away.

Apart from the bed the room was fairly neat, maybe because it was so empty. The clothes closet door was open showing on hangers one jean jacket, one cotton plaid work shirt, nothing else. On the floor was a pair of running shoes, Nikes, black with a white stripe.

I picked them up, and turned them over. The soles of both bore black stains that looked remarkably like the ones Pelly had taken back to Yellowknife, cut from the linoleum and rugs of the house two doors from this one.

I stuffed them into my parka pockets, one in each pocket.

From the bottom of the stairs I heard, "You coming down?"

"Right away."

When I got there, she hadn't moved. "You shouldn' go in his room when he ain't there."

"As part of what the government gives you this house and some money for, aren't you supposed to know where he is from time to time? Maybe help keep him out of trouble?"

"So report me to Annie," she said contemptuously. "I don't need the money that bad. Goddamn cops." So much for home influence.

At the detachment I showed the Nikes to Bouvier, who whistled and said, "Holy Jesus!"

I got through to RCMP Yellowknife on the phone.

"Kitologitak," I said. "For forensics, Pelly."

"Jeez, Matteesie," said Constable Emily Ford on the switchboard, "aren't we formal?"

"Didn't know it was you, Emily!" I said. "Honest!"

"Who the hell'd you think it was? Don't tell me that old bullfrog I'm relieving has a voice like me."

We usually have a man on the switchboard.

I was going to tell Pelly right away about the Nikes, but he came with a rush. "I was just going to call you, Inspector. We're overloaded, as usual, but I've got a fair amount and some of it you might like. Main reason for the delay was those latent no-blood prints I mentioned. I had to send them to Edmonton for evaluation, they've got better equipment or smarter forensic guys, I'm not sure which. Anyway the results were faxed to me overnight. Lemme tell you what I've got."

I'd been waiting days for this. Now I didn't want to interrupt. I'd go with the flow. I held the Nikes in one hand, the phone in the other.

"Commonly sold boots all over the north pretty well match the bigger footprints, but as we decided when I was there, half the men in Sanirarsipaaq wear those boots at one time or another. Like, if we had a definite suspect who wore that kind of boots, some with blood on them, or signs that blood had been removed but some minuscule bits that someone trying to clean them had missed, that'd be fine. Otherwise most of the boot tracks in the blood don't give us much. Might rule out very small or very big feet, but that's all. So a lot of the tracks must have been made by the murderer, and that's about as scientific as we can get right now."

This was shaping up like a textbook lecture, with a beginning and, I had no doubt, a middle and an end. He was doing aloud what I often do in my head, summarizing known facts, hoping an idea would jump out and pop me on the nose.

"As we discussed before, I think, a thorough check of boots the morning after the murders might have helped a lot," he said. "I'm not criticizing the police work but that's a fact, and also, with everything else going on, a man would have had to be a real, uh, genius, to have acted as fast as the murderer would have had to. So let's forget that one for now, the murderer's tracks. Then we have tracks in blood that were made by the murdered people, slipping and staggering around, and we can forget those, too, for the moment."

He stopped to consider something. Maybe notes. I heard a page turning.

"You with me?" he said.

"I'm with you—we can't draw any conclusions for now about the tracks made by the murderer and we forget the victims' tracks entirely."

"Right. Out of the six sets of prints, that leaves us three, the small bloody ones and the two sets of latents I mentioned to you that must've been done before the murders, as if somebody had tracked clean snow onto a floor, say . . ."

"Like those nagging tracks on the kitchen floors in a set for a TV commercial," I said.

He laughed. "Some Inuk bimbo with a mop showing how easy tracks can be wiped up with Glare, Bash, Purge, Stain-off, or whatever!"

"I won't interrupt anymore," I said hastily.

"Okay. First the two sets of latents. Edmonton says both sets were made by winter boots normally worn by women. Lighter than men's boots, narrower, a different shape. Different heels. We couldn't get any revealing tread patterns or trademarks, but Edmonton says the sizes are as accurate as we can expect: the larger ones would be size eights, and the small ones size six. That ring any bells?"

"The size eight, maybe." I was thinking of Monday night, standing with Maisie, noticing in passing that when we put our boots down side by side, hers were of equal length with my size eights. Small feet for a man.

"Who?" Pelly asked.

"Maisie Johanson, I don't think you met her. The size six I'll have to think about."

"Okay," he said. "Now the last one, the smallest footprint, is not in any of the categories I've mentioned. Could be worn by a male or female. Anybody that small probably would not have been strong enough to do all the damage that was done, but might just have happened into the scene during or after the murders."

Then he got to the meat. "Let me tell you what I have. That small print was made by someone wearing a size five shoe, like one of those common running shoes that a lot of people wear . . ."

"Like maybe a Nike?" I said.

"I was going to say maybe like a Nike. But how'd you guess?"

"I got them in my hand right now."

S I X T E E N

"Hi, Andy," I said at three o'clock that afternoon, when I finally found him after hunting everywhere else, including another visit to his foster home, where I was told, "He was here a little while ago but he isn't now, fuck off."

Andy looked at me bleary-eyed. He had been drinking either straight-world-type booze or vanilla extract or rubbing alcohol or shaving lotion, maybe mixed with the orange drink that had been in the pop can he was clutching. Or maybe he'd just had a dainty swallow of orange pop to cleanse his palate after sniffing glue or antifreeze or paint thinner or nail polish remover or any other poison he could lay his hands on.

"Hi, Matteeshie," he mumbled. He was lying flat on his back in those thin clothes with nothing beneath his parka, amid the ice and snow that had been blowing all winter into the space under this overturned boat, along with enough candy wrappers and cigarette butts to indicate that he used the place often. He was even sheltered from the afternoon sun, which today felt warm. I'd wanted to be on his trail earlier, but it had been nearly noon before I could get started. By telephone from Cambridge Bay the judge, Charlie Litterick, had said sure, he'd delay the Yellowknife-bound departure of the Supreme Court's Citation until Thomassie got there. This was so that the Nikes, carefully wrapped and carried by Thomassie in the Cessna, could be handed in Cambridge Bay to the sheriff's office man, Bob, who would be met at the Yellowknife airport by Pelly.

When I'd finally got down to looking for Andy, my procedures certainly would not have ranked with great Mountie get-your-man operations of story and song.

A special I knew in Sachs Harbor a few years ago always had a stock reply when being complimented on some job or other. "Eeee-eee," he would say, shrugging, and then in Inuktituk, "Like tracking a caribou with a nosebleed through a snowbank." For a while I felt like that, tracking Andy around Sanirarsipaaq. Everybody had seen him from time to time.

At the Co-op Nelson told me Andy had practically fallen in when the door opened at ten a.m., had bought a can of some orange drink, and headed for the rec hall.

At the rec hall the old caretaker, smoking ruminatively in his chair by the door, told me with a polite, "eee-eee," that yes, Andy had been there, mostly sitting in the furnace room, and had seemed okay but maybe had been drinking a bit or sniffing because, as the old man told me, there'd been a smell. He'd told Andy he didn't want that kind of stuff in there and Andy had said it was cough medicine and he'd go home and get the bottle to prove it. Then, the old man said, Andy had stumbled (*kunikaqtuaq* is the Siglit word) out of the back door of the rink. Going out by the front door would have been more public, if that meant anything.

I went to the rink's back door. That's where scrapings were thrown when the ice was cleaned. Nobody went that way normally unless he wanted a longer walk, or not to be seen.

Could Andy have known by then that I had taken his Nikes and would want to know where he had been the last time he wore them? So that he wouldn't want to chance running into me by passing in front of the detachment? There was only one way to find out.

I went back to number 5, where I found Big Mama laying for me. She had more to say than she'd had an hour or two earlier.

"I *thought* you was doin' somethin' up there!" she accused. "When he arrives he yells down and asks where the hell his Nikes are, really upset, musta wanted to sell 'em, and I yell back that the only guy up there was the little Eskimo Mountie. Then I thought he'd fainted it was so quiet up there and then he comes down and just goes out without saying a word . . . Did you take 'em, you bugger?''

She was glaring.

I glared back, thinking about the sequence of Andy's movements.

When he'd found his Nikes gone I was already working on getting Thomassie to the airport to start the shoes on the first leg of the way to Pelly and forensics. Maybe he even saw us take off in the van. That could have been when he bought something at the Co-op, then dropped out of sight.

I checked the rec hall again. He hadn't returned. This time I left his way, by the back door, and walked in widening half circles until I found amidst all the trampling in yesterday's snow an occasional small footprint heading down behind the hotel to the shore.

There they'd been easier to follow, the only prints since yesterday's snow. They had led me to this overturned wooden skiff.

I'd had to crouch even to see in where he was. As he lay there he was so out of it that his lower eyelids kept going up and meeting his upper eyelids coming in the other direction. It occurred to me that I could have taken him in just for being so smashed, but that was not really my line of work and would quickly get around— and I did not want anything to do with Andy to get around right then.

I looked the full length of him. His rundown cheap boots. The way his jeans hung forlornly against his skinny legs, the bones like sticks of kindling. The bravado of his shirt and parka both open showing the boniest chest in the Arctic. The pinched cheeks beneath a too-big woolen toque he'd acquired someplace. Knitted into the turned-up part of the toque was an arresting phrase: Costa del Sanirarsipaaq. In his own way, Andy had style.

It wasn't too difficult to sense that there was more to this now than locking him up and questioning him until he came clean about the blood on his shoes. What I wanted with Andy at the moment was an uninterrupted time to get him sober and get him to talk, to learn why he had been tracking around in that mess of blood, what he knew about that night that we didn't.

"Ish okay I call you Matteeshie, not Inshpector, or lord high?" he began, peering out at me and suddenly beginning to snore.

I went the rest of the way under the boat on my hands and knees. When I sat back against the far side I could not see out for more than a few yards. This boat was at the end of a row and thus sheltered from any casual onlooker. Nobody would go this far along the rough shore ice except on purpose, like me.

While Andy snored, one other development nagged at me a little. Erika Hall had phoned that morning from Cambridge Bay, where she'd been covering the end of the abduction trial Charlie Litterick had told me about, which had ended with the acquittal I had rather expected after talking to Charlie. I don't mean Charlie had his mind made up in advance. What I mean is that the tall young crown prosecutor I'd talked to in the Citation must have been unable to convince Charlie to reverse the amount of pre-judging he *had* done. There's a difference there that only lawyers and judges know.

Erika adrift in Cambridge Bay had a choice between flying home with the court people to Yellowknife and calling up people there that she otherwise would see only fifty-two weeks of every year anyway until death or snow blindness did them part, or hitching a ride to Sanirarsipaaq for whatever journalistic or other adventure the murder investigation might hold. The choice apparently had not resulted in a hung jury.

"Matteesie!" she'd said on the phone just as I finished talking to Pelly. "Wash your face! Iron your pajamas! I'm on my way."

That jauntiness was all part of her surface line, and I knew it. Right away she noticed that I wasn't playing.

"I shouldn't be joking," she said, "but I just thought of coming up there to see how you're doing, and hear about your mother's funeral."

What can you say when you want to get the hell off the phone without revealing too much of why?

"Maybe I got you at a bad time," she said tentatively, probing.

Her antennae were very sensitive. At that moment I was itching to get the final word from Cambridge that the Nikes were on their way. Then I could go after whatever Andy Arqviq knew. So far only Bouvier and Pelly and I knew that we might be on the edge of something. I didn't want Erika Hall to know anything. I wanted her out of there, but *not* flying back to Yellowknife with the chummy Supreme Court group on the Citation. Bob, the sheriff's office guy, carrying something in a brown paper bag, is exactly the kind of thing that would have made Erika ask, right away, "What's in the bag?"

"Oh, just something Matteesie wanted taken to Yellowknife."

"What?"

"Sorry, I can't tell you."

What difference would it make if she did manage to track down a pair of bloodstained Nikes and make a headline out of it on *News/North*'s Monday edition? Maybe none. But if I managed to have things happen at the pace I set, I would be happier.

"So what's new in the case?" she asked.

"Well, it isn't solved yet."

"Really? You losing your touch?"

"Could be."

"You sound too cheerful for that to be true."

"We must have a bad connection."

Maybe it didn't make any difference in the long run. There's no doubt that Erika's instinct would have told her that Sanirarsipaaq was a pretty good place to be right then. In some kind of a reflex action, knowing that she was on the trail, I phoned Maxine and told her there was nothing certain yet, but I thought I was getting close and would let her know more, when there was more. Whatever happened, I didn't want Erika Hall to scoop her. If that is managing the news a tiny little bit, so be it. I owed Maxine.

Anyway, what happened was that Erika did get a ride to Sanirarsipaaq with Thomassie and landed just about the time I found Andy Arqviq. I learned later from Bouvier that she was looking for me and not finding me when I was sitting well hidden under the overturned boat.

———

I am not great at talking to the young. Or so Lois says, anyway, and can produce chapter and verse in support of her own opinion. She says I talk too much to kids when I should be listening, and listen too much when I should not be letting the little demons (her phrase) dominate the conversation. All this might be true. But now I was in a situation not covered in Lois's or anybody's manual on how to be better at talking to the young.

I was neither talking nor listening. Sitting on the snow and ice under that boat while Andy Arqviq snored, I watched the dribble from the corner of his mouth, which he sometimes wiped at clumsily without opening his eyes. I wondered what he was like, inside. I couldn't even make a stab at answering that from what I'd seen in his room. Not counting the bloodstained Nikes, there was nothing personal there at all. Maybe he had nothing personal.

I remembered his cocky walk in the rec hall a few nights ago, the first time I'd seen him. I'd never seen a bantam rooster, had only heard the phrase and imagined a strutting little bird.

Maybe I really am no good at talking to the young, I thought. But I have a certain amount of experience with Inuit orphans, kids who had to scramble just to stay alive, few of them really fitting the common concept of childhood but often with a spark of decency in them somewhere. Maybe, I thought, the ones I am no good at talking to live in one of the yuppie parts of Edmonton or some other city and never have to do anything tougher than walking behind a lawn mower on nice green grass, or getting their driver's licenses routinely when they are sixteen so they can use the old man's car.

Maybe "spark of decency" would be too strong a phrase for Andy, but did he have something similar? Why would he get stoned? And here I am under an overturned boat, which is where this fifteen-year-old kid goes to be alone. I remembered reading once about another very small Eskimo orphan whose name, or the name people used, translated as "the Little Shit." Later in life he'd turned out to be a great hunter.

Andy's eyes came open again very slowly. He groaned when he saw me. He didn't speak. He was still not much more than semiconscious. His eyes closed again. Not only so young but so ludicrously small, he could have been a jockey if he'd lived almost anywhere in the world except where he did.

I knew where my thoughts were going and I didn't care, this was what was going through my mind under that boat with little Andy Arqviq, whose Nikes had bloodstains on the soles.

First, it was physically impossible for him to have killed Dennis the way it was generally conceded to have happened: beaten him to death. It was almost as impossible for him to have killed Thelma the way she had been killed, mainly with stab wounds but with a lot of physical strength involved as well. On the other hand, assume that at some stage in that wild night, before the police arrived, maybe even before the murderer fled, Andy had been in the house. Which would make him either a material witness to murder or an accomplice to murder.

I would be willing to accept that he had gone to the house with no knowledge of what was happening. But if so, why?

Andy's slow-moving eyelids were open again. I had to make up my mind. Either Andy and I crawled out of here and walked past the hotel to the detachment where he would be held and safe until he had answered the questions, or I let him go but kept a string on him while charges were decided upon. Not a murder charge. Maybe not accessory to murder. Maybe material witness.

"What are you going to do?" he asked, voice tired and far away.

"I'm thinking," I said.

One way of doing it would be to crawl out of there and yell at somebody to go and get Bouvier, and take Andy to the detachment for what we could call routine questioning.

Another way would be just to march off the shore with Andy as if I were right on the tail of the murderer and didn't have time to look to left or right. I didn't like either of those methods. Words suddenly streamed across my consciousness: He had nothing whatever to do with the actual murders! I was amazed to realize that I had reached that conclusion just by shivering under a boat looking at the pitiable state of this boy so full of illegal substances that it would have been a danger to low-flying aircraft to light a match in his vicinity.

So okay, he's not the murderer. I went on from there. As impossible as it seemed, he might have had some legitimate reason to be leaving his footprints in blood and then not volunteer what he did know that might have helped identify whoever did do it. Behind all this was my extreme reluctance to march him across what passed for Sanirarsipaaq's main square obviously in custody, perhaps for the only crime that was on anybody's mind right then. He might have to spend the rest of his life here with that image in the settlement's consciousness . . . and he was only fifteen.

Even to me, what I had in mind seemed like the strangest way in the world to conduct an interrogation. When his eyes opened again I was ready.

"You didn't kill Thelma or Dennissie, right?" I said.

His eyes did not light up appreciably.

"But you may have an idea who did, or how it happened."

He thought about that.

"Did you see Maisie or anybody else at the house?"

"No," he muttered.

"Suppose I let you go—"

I was going to go on to say that he could then tell me in his own time and his own words what he did know. But I didn't get the whole thought out before he interrupted, "Don't do that!"

Amazed, I asked, "Don't do what?"

"Don't let me go!" He was awake now, and very scared.

What happened then was that we both crawled rather slowly and painfully out from under the boat and walked a few feet apart through yesterday's now-slushy snow. We passed the hotel and headed toward the detachment while I tried to figure out where to go from there. Two words kept going through my mind: *protective custody*.

"You're afraid of somebody," I said. "Who?"

He just shook his head—but when we were passing the rec hall I noticed that he was stealing glances to his right where Davidee and his family lived. None of them were anywhere in sight.

Later on, in Annie's house, where I'd taken him, Andy played cards with Annie's two kids and ate ravenously and drank hot chocolate. Bouvier picked us up in the van about seven and the three of us drove to Barker's house, Andy scrunched down in the back, obviously not wishing to be seen.

"That reporter Erika Hall," Bouvier said, "she's been all over me asking where the hell you are and what's going on."

"What did you tell her?"

"Nothing."

He told me that Erika had heard about me bringing in Davidee from his hunting grounds the day before. That piece of information wouldn't have been hard to come by, with everybody in town talking about it. Maybe she got it from Byron.

"She asked me about you invoking his parole to order that he stay in town, and wanted to know what that was all about. I told her she'd have to get that from you."

"Does she know about the Nikes or the fifty with blood on it?"

"I don't think so. She didn't mention it. And she would have."

"How would she know about me ordering Davidee to stay in town?"

"Well, she has that connection with Byron. Also, she interviewed Debbie, Davidee, and their parents."

I continued to avoid Erika for the rest of that day on the grounds that as much as I did like her, I had no wish to have her threshing out the case in the next edition of *News/North,* including quotes that might start from my "no comment" and go on to interview "aroused townspeople" and "fearful parents" and even "puzzled shaman." She'd certainly get on to Jonassie, as her original story from Byron's phone call away back in Franklin House had mentioned shamanism.

If she ever lucked on to hearing any details about the shaman's missing knife and its menacing gyrfalcon handle, half the Western Arctic would go to bed scared.

That night in Barker's house Andy had a bad nightmare, babbling about a knife and screaming the name Leah and struggling as I tried to hold him. Bouvier went outside and came back with a cooking pot full of snow and we held handfuls of snow to Andy's face and neck. He finally came out of the nightmare, shivering with terror.

The next morning Andy didn't remember the nightmare, or said he didn't. I said, "You kept yelling Leah's name. Why?"

"Leah . . . ," he began miserably. I kept pressing him but he set his lips and refused to say anything more, or talk at all.

The next morning, a mild day when many people in town seemed to be out wandering around and enjoying the sun, several had congregated in the rec hall to prepare for the long-heralded entertainment and dance that night. Among them were Byron Anolak with Debbie and their baby, Julie, as well as Tommy Kungalik, Paulessie, Davidee, and several others. The three throat-singing women from Pond Inlet, well known because of an interview on CBC Inuvik, came in and looked around, chatting among themselves and with some of the older locals.

Davidee was giving a lot of the orders. I remembered Lewissie telling me he'd be running the tape machine. When I came in he instantly looked past me, behind me. Looking for Andy?

Some tension, or at least constraint, was noticeable among Byron and the other young men when Davidee was nearby. A couple of times when Davidee said something, the other three would react grudgingly, if at all. Davidee was haranguing first Paulessie, then Tommy Kungalik, and finally Byron. Once Byron pointedly turned and walked away from him.

Debbie ignored Davidee as she tacked some fresh bunting to a wall. The tape-playing machine seemed to belong to Davidee, or at least he was the custodian of it. He plugged it into a wall outlet and played a Willie Nelson tape apparently as a check. Then he picked up the tape player, and left.

Everything seemed to be in readiness. Big Paulessie, little Tommy, and Byron—Byron carrying the baby, Julie—went off together, Byron and Debbie chatting briefly before they left.

Debbie had glanced at me from time to time. With the place almost empty, she came over to me.

"Davidee is looking for Andy," she said. "Is he somewhere safe?"

"Yes," I said. I didn't say where.

She nodded and then spoke hurriedly. "Davidee was out to

number five, looking . . . He's never paid much attention to Andy before. Could Andy know something?"

I didn't answer. I could tell by her eyes that she noted this.

"There's something going on," she said. "I'm worried. Byron and Paulessie and Tommy Kungalik got something planned that might be bad. Byron told me about it. They've decided they're through taking all the crap that Davidee throws at them, and are going to do something about it at the dance tonight."

"Do you know what?"

"Davidee claims that they all owe him money that they borrowed from Dennissie, says that Dennissie owed him money, so he's trying to collect it from them. Tommy Kungalik got paid for some carpentry work he did in the shack at the airstrip, making a desk for Bradley Air. He's got a check that he could cash at the Co-op if he wanted to. Davidee shoved him around trying to get him to sign it over to him. And you know he's always on Paulessie's back and Byron's, calling Byron a no-good cripple and trying to get money or drugs from him—"

"Drugs?"

"That's what Byron says. Sometimes there are drugs here. Apparently the dealer don't trust Davidee but Davidee thinks he might trust Byron, so he tries to get Byron to get some for him."

"What drugs?"

"You know him, he talks big, cocaine or hash maybe."

"So what are they going to do? I mean, what can they do?"

She let out a long breath. "They know that none of them are good enough fighters to stand up to Davidee alone. What they're talking about is picking a fight with him tonight, just, you know, bumping him on the dance floor or something, and when Davidee goes at whoever does it the other two will get into it and the three of them will beat him up. They talk about teaching him a lesson so that he won't bully any of them again because he'll know that he has three to deal with from now on."

"You think that would work?"

She shook her head several times, for emphasis. "Tonight, who knows? But next time he gets one of them alone, which is always going to happen sooner or later, I hate to think about it."

When I left the rec hall it was still the broad daylight of early afternoon, with hours left before the big party was supposed to start. I intended to try Maisie again about whether the size-eight boots in the latent prints had been hers. Also, I would try Leah again. Bouvier had found out for me where she lived, in one of the houses along the airstrip road. She was one of the many conundrums in this case so far.

When questioned along with Sarah and Agnes she had admitted, as they all did, that from time to time she had gone home with Dennissie. Yet I'd had the feeling from the start that she was more complicated than the other two. For that reason—and on the grounds that, until I could get Andy to talk, which I was sure would happen eventually, I wasn't getting anywhere—I walked through lightly falling snow to the house Bouvier had pointed out to me. The house, like only a few others in Sanirarsipaaq, was one of the original 512s, one of the neater ones. There was no clutter of discarded or half-discarded building materials outside. A chained dog barked at me, but not with much fervor, almost as if he ranked as a pet. I said, "Hello, dog," and it wagged its tail as I approached the door. I noticed that, although a little snow had fallen for an hour or two around noon before the sun came out, there were no footprints approaching or leaving the door.

At my knock, the door was answered immediately by a youngish-looking woman, whom I correctly judged to be Leah's mother. There was a resemblance in the delicate features. She said nervously that Leah was not home, had gone out earlier and was not yet back.

"How long ago?" I asked.

"Maybe an hour," she said.

But leaving no tracks in the fresh snow, I thought.

Normally, if this had not been a visit by a man with the RCMP crest on his hat, I would have been asked in for tea. My people are hospitable, even to strangers. As it was, I thought that Leah's mother looked distinctly ill at ease and possibly was lying about Leah not being home. I couldn't force my way in, but I did mention that she must have left before the snow, because there were no footprints. The mother looked even more nervous, saying, "Well, it must have been longer ago, then, I've been . . . ," and let that trail off.

I left then, but knew I had some time before things started happening at the rec hall, so an hour later I tried for Leah again.

At Leah's house, there were still no footprints outside.

I knocked. This time Leah answered the door.

I had the feeling that she had seen me coming, for she immediately invited me in. The kitchen was spotless, although meal things were still on the table, including a bowl of stew that I recognized as rabbit, plates of bread and butter, and a jar of stewed fruit.

"Have you eaten?" Leah said.

I hadn't. I hadn't gone to the hotel, because it almost inevitably would have meant running into Erika Hall's questioning—even though I would rather have liked to hear what Erika had found out, in case it included things I didn't know. If it hadn't been that Bouvier was occupied keeping Andy safe and out of the way at Barker's house, I would have sicked him on Erika with instructions to listen but not talk about more than the weather.

Leah set out a plate for me. Her mother came in and poured tea and sat silently watching us both. There was no sign of a father. Leah volunteered that he was out hunting, smiling rather tensely. "For more than rabbits, we hope."

As she pushed the stewpot toward me it was not that there were any visible signs, hands shaking or teacup rattling, but there was something in her manner that suggested deep tension; the kind of tension one feels when about to admit frankly to an evasion, or lie.

The admission came immediately. "I was home before when you came, but I did not want to talk to you."

"I found her crying after you left," her mother said. She looked sad but somehow resigned.

"I knew that I should talk to you," Leah said. "I have hardly slept for days. If Jonassie had come to see me I would have told him everything . . ."

I didn't know exactly what was going on. When she mentioned

Jonassie it was as if at the mention of his name she had mentally crossed herself. Of course, that was nonsense. But the image persisted. And then I had a growing sense of what I was witnessing and now was part of. Imagine anyone with a deep religious conviction, one who believes that sins or transgressions should not be kept secret. That was the impression I was getting from Leah now. But I was equally certain that what motivated her was not the result of Christian teaching. I have met people, more of them old than young, who, although they might pay lip service to the teachings or church services of Catholic or Anglican missionaries, in their souls believe that only the shaman has a true connection with another world, the spirit world.

"I have been very troubled," Leah said. Her voice and her eyes looked it, and the strained expression in her mother's eyes confirmed it. "I knew that you were spending a lot of time with Jonassie, and that perhaps through the spirits that help him he would learn all that happened."

I thought: things that you could have told me but didn't.

It was as if she was reading my mind. Perhaps she was. Her eyes had never left mine. "Things that I could have told you but didn't," she said, her words precisely echoing my thoughts. "I will tell you now. Dennissie and I . . . He had other girls when I was away at school, which is natural, but not when I was here. And I went with other boys when I was away but Dennissie and I felt blessed when we were together. We talked of children we would have, and all this is why, because of the privacy we had there, sometimes I would go to his home when his granny was asleep."

I thought I knew what was coming, but was thinking that the only bloodstained small footprints had not been hers but Andy's. I had a sudden thought. "What size boots do you wear?"

She looked surprised. "Size six."

So now I knew about both sets of latent prints, hers and probably Maisie's. She went on as if I hadn't interrupted.

"The only trouble we had was Davidee," she said. "He sometimes followed me. Even on the street he would make gestures . . ." To describe the gestures, she held up her left hand with the thumb and forefinger touching, and made her right forefinger go back and forth rapidly through the circle her left hand had made. Then she held the circled fingers to her mouth and made her tongue go back and forth. Gestures not unknown elsewhere in the world.

"He offered me money, drink, drugs. Dennissie knew about that, but he was afraid of what Davidee might do to me or to him, so managed to deal with him the way he did, by paying him something, by promising to bring in liquor and give it to Davidee, I think even last week once giving him some cocaine that someone had given him as payment for a loan.

"Davidee knew from somewhere about girls sometimes going to Dennissie's place. On the night of the murders, Dennissie and I met and went to his room. He was very upset and told me Davidee had offered him money if he would get me to his room that night and then let Davidee come in.

"It was maybe the first time Dennissie had refused him, stood up to him entirely, I do not know, but soon after we got to his room, there was a knock on the door—the bedroom door!"

She sobbed, then controlled it, wiped her eyes and after a minute or two went on.

"Davidee must have got in and up the stairs without knocking on the outside door. They began to argue and then Davidee hit him and Dennissie hit him back, knocking him down . . . I was scared and ran down the stairs and out of there and came home."

"Crying," her mother put in.

"Yes, I was crying," Leah said. "I cried more when I found out what had happened. I wished I had stayed and died with him if I had to."

It was difficult to gather my thoughts as I walked back toward the rec hall. Certainly Leah had provided almost all the evidence I needed that Davidee had been in the house that night. Added to Debbie's, it should be enough to convict, even without a weapon being found.

I thought of Davidee beating and stabbing Dennissie to death and then, on his way down the stairs, perhaps hearing a noise, a groan, a question, from where Thelma was lying in the dark before the television set. Then the terrible battle between a strong young man and a strong but aged woman.

The question then was a fairly simple one. Do I arrest Davidee now, or do I wait just a little, maybe a few more hours, tell Andy what Leah had told me, get Andy's story. Because as close as it now was to being a locked-up case, there was more, and only Andy and Davidee knew what that more was. And maybe Maisie.

I found her alone in the kitchen of the hotel adding potatoes and onions and carrots to a pot roast that was simmering on the stove. Erika must have been out, maybe still looking for me. "Mother's out," Maisie said. "She said she was going for a walk with Erika and to do the shopping. She'll be back for dinner soon, though." I was glad both Margaret and Erika were out, lessening possible complications.

"It's you I want to talk to," I said. "You told me that you were only at Dennissie's house the once. We've found some footprints, not bloody, that are your size, eight. By picking up all your boots, which we'll do if we have to, we could be more sure. The floor was pretty clean before all the blood arrived, so they probably were made before the murders, maybe that very night. Now tell me straight."

She stared at me wordlessly, but her eyes looked stricken, near tears.

"Don't you cry!" I ordered. "You're a big girl now. Tell me exactly. What were you doing there? And when?"

She sat suddenly in one of the kitchen chairs, but when she spoke she seemed calmer. "It's so degrading, makes me look like such a fool! But I'll tell you. I was attracted to Dennissie, as you know. I thought about it all the time, day and night, worse at night. I kept thinking, if he wants me and I want him, why don't I? That night a little after ten I made up my mind. I said I was going to the rec hall, but I went straight to Dennissie's place. The front door was unlocked, as it had been the first time I was there. I could see Thelma asleep in front of the TV. I tiptoed to the bottom of the stairs and was just starting up when I heard some sounds from above, low sounds, but the house was so quiet I could make out the voices. One was Dennissie's and the other, I was sure, Leah's. I felt like such a fool! I could have let him know I was coming, and maybe he would have waited. But I hadn't and he hadn't. I just tiptoed back through the hall and out of the door and ran all the way home."

I believed her. Everything, including Leah's story, fitted.

When I left the hotel and reached the rec hall, Debbie had finished her chores and was heading away from the brightly lighted area near the front doors. It was still a few hours from party time. "Going home to eat and feed Julie and change," she said, seeming happy at the prospect. "Byron can do a lot of things, but feeding the baby is something I like to do myself."

"Anything going on here since I left?" I asked.

"Not a thing, thanks be to God or the shaman," she joked. "Hope they can both keep it that way through the night."

We were standing just outside of the doors at the entrance. Glancing over her shoulder, I saw Bouvier approaching in the van. He got out hurriedly, definitely excited. I looked past him into the van. No Andy. I'd left them together at Barker's house with instructions to stay there unless there was an emergency.

Apparently this was the emergency. Bouvier signaled to me with a jerk of his head. When I went over he said, "Andy has something he wants to talk about. To you. Nobody else."

S E V E N T E E N

As far as I could learn later, Andy had felt oppressively penned
up and ill at ease in Barker's house. The house itself was all strange
to him. He'd never been in one before with big chairs and television
and a telephone. He was forbidden to answer this phone, and he
heard Bouvier having conversations on it in which he sometimes
pretended to be answering from the detachment. Through the long
day he'd been unable to think through what he knew and what he
was strongly tempted to tell me. Against his desire to talk, the
thought of being hunted down by Davidee terrified him. I think I
know how he felt. Once in a dream long ago (and sometimes since)
I was a fox and had stepped into a leg trap that had not snapped
shut but was closing in slow motion. Andy knew that one way or
another his life was in danger because of what he knew, and that
it would be even more in danger if he told and Davidee, still free,
knew he had told.

He also felt that he knew safer and more familiar hiding places
than Barker's house, places where he could think through what
he should do and then either find me and tell his story, taking his
chances of Davidee finding out, or go to the hiding place under
the boat that he felt no one else knew, except me, convinced that
when the time came I'd look for him there.

Sometime during the day he had decided he had to get out. He tried to convince Bouvier that he felt okay and could be left alone, but I had told Bouvier to stay with him, so he did. By that time Andy knew that I was not easily available by telephone. Bouvier had tried the detachment a couple of times on the buzzer system we had between the two extensions, and had got no answer.

Which is what gave Andy his plan. He waited for a time when Bouvier buzzed the office and got no answer. He didn't want to go out and chance meeting Davidee or someone who might tell Davidee, but he knew he'd have to take the chance when it came. As it happened, Erika Hall phoned from the hotel and gave Bouvier a hard time about not being able to find me. Bouvier buzzed the detachment. No answer. Andy saw his chance. He told Bouvier he had something important to tell me about the murders. Right away! He wanted to talk! "But only to Matteesie. Find Matteesie!"

My part of this I thought out after Bouvier and I hurried to the house and, as I'd half expected, found it empty and Andy gone. Bouvier did not curse or swear at being tricked.

"Damn that kid anyway," was all he said, shaking his head. He knew a good con when he saw it.

"Think of it this way," I said, "if he was your fifteen-year-old in this kind of a fix you'd be pulling for him."

Bouvier, as if he'd been thinking along those lines too, said, "I better look for him." He noticed that I had not suggested calling out the Inumerit, Neighborhood Watchers, reinforcements from Cambridge or Spence, or indeed doing anything he couldn't do by himself. "I'll just cruise the streets, up to the airport, along by number five, and around."

"Not to the boat," I said. That would be mine, if needed.

He nodded, understanding. "If I find him, what?"

"Try to talk to him. If he doesn't run, bring him here to Barker's again. If he runs, let him go. Think of all those hungry mouths you've got to feed and that maybe when you're running after him, you'll get hurt or have a heart attack."

I didn't have to ponder what to do next. At least as important as finding Andy was the gang-up plan on Davidee. What Debbie had told me had a strong ring of truth, or at least of intent. It might happen any time. I wanted to be there when it did.

While Bouvier looked for Andy, taking the van, I went back to the rec hall, where a crowd was gathering around the entrance. I stopped on the fringes. In Sanirarsipaaq or any other small settlement in the Arctic, nobody hangs around home waiting for the fashionable time to show up. Byron, Paulessie, and Tommy went by me, nodding but not speaking. They looked much more resolute than just three young guys heading for a good time. Also, I got a whiff of them. It was booze day. They'd been drinking.

Then I got a whiff of something else. Davidee's father, the chronically forlorn Ipeelee, was walking downhill toward the rec hall—but not at his usual gait of slouching aimlessly along, eyes down, dragging each foot with every step. He was striding out, head up, turning his head from side to side, obviously searching. Then off to my left I first heard and soon saw Davidee's yellow snowmobile coming at speed from the direction of the townhouses. As he neared and slowed, his eyes were searching the clumps of people; I figured he'd be looking for Andy.

Ipeelee must have seen Davidee at the same time. He headed to intercept, holding up one hand, palm out. Davidee kept going. Ipeelee called out a few words and then stepped right in front of the snowmobile. Snowmobiles do not steer well on ice or hard-packed snow. Two or three people yelled, "Ipeelee! Look out!" Davidee had the choice of running down his father or jamming on the brakes. He came to a skidding stop, the forward tip of one ski touching Ipeelee's boot. Ipeelee did not flinch. People who had stopped in alarm shook their heads and kept on toward the rec hall, muttering about Ipeelee being soft in the head.

I had moved close to look at Ipeelee and hear Davidee, in effect, calling this apparently chance meeting to order, his opening remarks being, "You stupid old fucker, what do you think you're doing?" After that, for some reason he calmed down. Maybe in that instant he really looked into Ipeelee's face and saw what I was close enough to see and recognize: the look of a pushed-around human being who has had enough. I didn't move. I was afraid to break what bore some resemblance to a spell. For a moment, the three of us were in what had become a quiet and private space. Then Ipeelee unhurriedly took from his side pocket something small, wrapped in ordinary brown paper, and stepped to Davidee's side, holding it out.

"You gave this to me," he said. "I give it back to you."

Davidee's face reflected not anger but shock and fear. Then he saw me nearby and I assume he figured he could handle the situation better without me. He ignored the proffered parcel and suddenly revved the snowmobile while wrenching the handlebars into a left turn. As the machine began to move Ipeelee, with a cry, grabbed Davidee's arm with both hands, wrenched at him. He was the angry one now. As if the years of shame and bottled-up rage fueled his strength, he yanked Davidee's hand off the throttle and the machine stopped. As Davidee struggled to regain his balance, Ipeelee reached over and stuffed his small parcel into the space between Davidee's legs, then abruptly turned and headed for the rec hall.

Hell of a good idea, Ipeelee, I thought. Safer for you in there than out here. Falling in beside him as Davidee zoomed past us to park by the rec hall door, I said conversationally, "What was it you gave to Davidee?"

"Ask him," Ipeelee said, without looking at me.

When I looked at Davidee he was hastily tucking into an inside pocket the parcel Ipeelee had given him.

"Goddamn it!" I yelled. I'd had enough crap. I yanked Ipeelee's arm around so that he was facing me. Davidee had gone inside, glaring at us. "I'm not the one who made your life miserable all these years!" I said. "Three people dead and every way I turn nobody wants to talk!" I was tempted to add, "Even Sedna!" but that would have been hearsay, from Debbie, and Sedna is not a name to be taken in vain. "For God's sake!" I said. "Maybe it means nothing, the parcel, but it seemed important. What was it?"

Maybe it was my tone that caught his attention. Or maybe what he said to me then was just another step in his emancipation. As he said it, my immediate thought was for his short-term safety. The long term we should be able to look after.

"What I gave him and what he now has," Ipeelee said, "is the shaman's knife."

Walking a few feet behind him, I made my way slowly through the crowd. It was, after all, just a knife. We could have forensics check it out as the possible murder weapon, but after that, what? The course it had followed from Jonassie's shelf through who knew how many hands to land in Ipeelee's, who could tell? Ipeelee had said, handing over the parcel, "You gave this to me, I give it back to you."

Maybe its main provable importance right now was that its presence in the house somehow, supernaturally or otherwise, had caused Jonassie to abort his attempt to banish Ipeelee's suicidal depression. However, as important as that must seem in the family, him threatening suicide had to be strictly a side issue to the murders, in which any knife could have been used. Most important was to find whoever had wielded it.

If forensics cleared this particular knife of involvement in the murders, it simply would return to its previous state, an interesting artifact—which, I suddenly thought, I might buy if it was for sale. Why not?

Maybe it was due to the days of pressure, but in that crowd in the rec hall, with people eyeing me and no doubt wondering what I knew that they didn't know about the big murder case, my mind suddenly drifted into fantasy. Maybe I needed the therapy. Anyway, I thought, *that* knife, if it really was *that* knife, like Ipeelee said, could be my souvenir of Sanirarsipaaq! Wow! It could sit unobtrusively on my desk in Ottawa until someone on a tour, like a senator or something, or maybe the queen, after all she travels a lot, would pick it up and remark on the beautiful gyrfalcon handle, and I would go over to the fireplace, surely I would have a fireplace in my office by then, and lean my elbow on the mantel (I'd have to order a low mantel, or I'd look ridiculous), and say, "Well, Your Majesty, there's a story that goes with that knife . . ."

I'm afraid that at that point I was smiling. Anyway, when I suddenly came to my senses everybody was smiling back at me. Everyone who caught my eye nodded. But I conceded reluctantly that this had nothing to do with my daydream. They always preferred a smile to a frown—and also they were getting used to me.

To most natives, even when we were being tough, police were more dependable, even essential, than politicians, lawyers, spouses, and some employers. The smiles persisted.

I stopped by Jane and Lewissie Ullayoroluk, who had settled in two of the chairs along the wall and were sipping coffee from paper cups. Lewissie would be the master of ceremonies when things started rolling. Jane would play the piano for "O Canada," the national anthem.

I thought of telling them what had happened, the strange Ipeelee-Davidee encounter, the possibility that the small mystery of the shaman's knife would be solved, but hesitated.

"Davidee was here a few minutes ago but then left," Lewissie said casually. "Probably gone to get his tapes."

Davidee gone again? In my head, an alarm bell. "You haven't seen Andy around, have you?" I asked.

Lewissie's eyes showed surprise. "I was going to ask you. Last I heard about him, he was with you."

"He was, but he got away."

Lewissie made one of those mild grimaces sometimes seen when the half-expected actually happens. Should I go after Davidee? I decided not yet. If he didn't come back soon, I would.

Now the hall was full. Nearly the whole settlement had turned out. Maybe two hundred people milled around expectantly, from round-eyed and alert babies in their mothers' amautiks to elders who hobbled or were helped to chairs. There are ritualistic aspects to such a gathering. The older people and the pregnant and some young mothers congregate along the walls, filling the chairs. Some shed their outer clothing onto wall hooks or into a pile in a corner, some don't. Now some were lining up at the free coffee and tea table. Younger ones were putting coins into the soft-drink machine, the heavy clunks of dropping drinks sounding like a warmup to the drum dance. Young girls chattered in little groups.

Among them I saw Sarah, Agnes, and Maisie. Leah was standing in a human traffic jam with her mother. Both waved at me and smiled, causing me to reflect like the goody-goody I really am that confession is good for the soul. I banished the mildly uncharitable thought that they'd known I would catch up eventually. Copping a plea usually gets a person a break in court. I could only guess at what Leah had not been able to tell me, because she didn't know about it, questions to which there was maybe no answer. Why had Andy screamed her name in his nightmare? I wondered—a strange thought—if ragged little Andy had one of those adolescent crushes on Leah such as sometimes a young boy gets for an older girl.

Erika Hall looked daggers at me from across the room, where she was now moving in on Sarah and Agnes. That's another thing she probably had picked up, that I'd questioned them along with Leah. Erika would be trying the all-girls-together line, which she was almost as good at as she was at getting men to talk; both were effective journalistic skills when wielded by a woman with what one might call the right stuff.

Then, with some relief, I saw Davidee enter, standing well back and looking at the crowd, holding his tape-deck and a coil of wire. I wished I could read his thoughts.

The clock on the wall ticked over to nine. Lewissie walked across to the microphone at one end of the room, ritualistically blew into it, welcomed everybody, and announced that the evening would begin with the throat singers.

They moved together to the microphone a little shyly, three traditionally dressed women approaching middle age. Immediately the room was full of the remarkable sound that only throat singers can produce. The sounds are melodic to those accustomed to throat singing, a blending of moans and phrasing and gestures as old as our people's history. They finished to complimentary handclapping and a few whistles from younger listeners.

The form of the program had been to get the traditional concert items out of the way first. A fit-looking young man whom Lewissie introduced as a gold medalist from the recent Arctic Winter Games performed one of his specialties, the knuckle hop. With only his knuckles and the toes of his white rubber-soled athletic shoes touching the floor, he made mighty hops around the cleared part of the floor three times before collapsing comically to lie still for a few seconds then spring to his feet to take his bows.

Drum dancing was next. There were five drums, skin stretched tightly over wooden hoops about the size of barrel lids, which the drummers held by a small handle attached to the rim while they beat on the rim or skin with foot-long batons. Two of the drummers were old ladies, the others young men. They started out slowly with a series of mighty booms.

As they gained speed, almost all the young men in the place sprang into action, stamping their feet on the floor in unison with the sound of the drums, thunderous slams of feet as the dancers moved from one side of the floor to another and up to the stage and down the steps, louder and louder until the dancers were sweating and the floor seemed to tremble.

Nearly ten minutes went by with booming drums and hammering boots, until only two of the dancers were left, muscles straining, knees bending faster and faster on each step, competing for the honor of being the last one on his feet—until finally one gave up and the other performed for another minute of gradually slowing boot-banging and then stopped and bowed.

"The best drum dancers in the whole world!" Lewissie called in his deep voice over the thunderous applause.

"And now," Lewissie said, "we'll have a short intermission while the young men of our community set up the sound system for a different kind of dancing, the modern kind."

The crowd began to move around, younger people coming forward expectantly while older people moved their chairs back to make room. By then the hall reeked with tobacco smoke and the sweat of overheated bodies.

Davidee shoved through the crowd from the back toward where one of the snooker tables had been covered with a sheet of plywood. On that he set his tape deck, of the type known elsewhere as a ghetto blaster. In smaller spaces, one such machine will make all the noise any group of dancers requires. However, Davidee had with him also insulated wire and two amplifiers of the sort used by stereo owners.

Paulessie, Byron, and Tommy, holding small screwdrivers, joined Davidee to string wires from the ghetto blaster to the amplifiers. Davidee was carrying a Coke bottle with him and sipping from it occasionally. The way he was acting, the Davidee at his worst that I had never seen before, suggested there was more in the bottle than Coke. He shoved the others away peremptorily to inspect the connections.

That brought the first sign of open antagonism. He ripped off a connection that Byron had made, growling some remark as he reconnected the wire.

This byplay was not lost on the audience, which made a murmuring sound of disapproval. Byron limped away and picked up another end of wire, only to be stopped by Davidee telling him to leave it alone and let somebody do it who knew how. Byron said something inaudible to Davidee, who told him plainly, in a tone audible to many, to fuck off. Tommy Kungalik snapped something. Davidee made a threatening gesture at him with the Coke bottle.

That moment passed. Davidee shoved a tape into the machine and threw a switch, and loud music drowned out all else. Young folk surged onto the floor, an instant mass of gyrating bodies, some doing older dances like the twist, others looking like throwbacks to jitter-bugging of even older days, still others making up their dancing techniques as they went along. To anyone not paying close attention, many of the dancers seemed to be going it alone, staying only in the general area of their partners. The dancing was wild and energetic, and the nondancers around the sidelines beat time with their feet or hands. Elvis records, Rolling Stones records, Beatles records, U2 records, a Sinéad O'Connor song, a long, long Neil Young "Everybody's Rockin'," seemed to have been spliced together for that first long set.

The lights had been dimmed so that it was not easy to keep track of everybody I wanted to watch, Davidee mostly, but also those who Debbie had said would be his assailants when they saw the chance. Davidee danced with several different girls, sometimes leaving one in midsong to grab another partner. Once he tried to cut in on Leah, who shook him off and stayed with big Paulessie. Immediately Byron, dancing with Debbie, bumped Davidee. The two glared at one another. Debbie, having left Julie with her mother on one of the chairs against the wall, got between them.

It was not long after Davidee had changed the tape to another long mix of mainly rock and roll and some country music that—

in the midst of one wild surging dance that made the whole floor shake, rattle, and roll—some dancers knocked over one of the amplifiers. Their feet tangled instantly in the wires. A chain reaction brought the ghetto blaster to the floor, wrenched-off wires streaming out of it.

It was then that Davidee seemed to abandon altogether what until then had passed for at least minimal self-control. He screamed at Byron, who was trying to untangle one of the wires from around his ankle. Paulessie and Tommy converged and attempted to hold Davidee. Lewissie got between them. Davidee stopped struggling, seemed suddenly to go limp, took two or three deep breaths, and then made a gesture at the tangle of wires and—I had got close to back up Lewissie—said something about fixing the connections and getting on with it.

Lewissie and I stood where we were. Byron, Paulessie, and Tommy produced small pliers and began stripping some of the insulation from wires to repair the connections. They and Davidee shot insults back and forth. Many in the vicinity quickly moved back out of range. Davidee now could not miss the fact that the three were pitted against him.

That is when, almost insanely haranguing those around him about their clumsiness with the splicing, he yelled, "Get the hell away from here, I can do it myself!"

He was wearing a small leather belt attachment on which was the sheath of a hunting knife, under his overshirt. I'd noticed the sheath before, thinking it held his pliers and screwdriver. But when his hand came away, instead of the pliers the others had been using, he produced and brandished an ordinary hunting knife.

I can see yet in my memory the way the other three briefly fell back. Some girls screamed. The loudest shriek, full of terror, came from Leah. It was Byron, despite his crippled leg, who reacted first. Balanced on his good leg he lashed out with the other and kicked the knife out of Davidee's hand. As they began to wrestle, Byron grabbed Davidee's belt and yanked.

This shook loose from under his outer clothing another knife, the one with the gyrfalcon-head handle, the shaman's knife that old Ipeelee had forced on him. Now it was bare, unwrapped. It fell a few feet away and slid between churning feet and legs to disappear under the snooker table. The first knife was lying in plain sight, but only those of us closest could have seen the second knife. Only Lewissie and I among those nearby could have known that such a knife existed. From those close by came a scared gasp, a sudden, "Oh-o-o-o-o!"

This was the moment the three had been waiting for. They plunged in swinging their fists, kicking, butting, as Davidee wildly tried to defend himself. His attention seemed to be divided between trying to locate the shaman's knife and trying to fight back, when Byron threw the pliers he had in his hand. They hit Davidee high on his left cheek. Blood flowed instantly from a cut near his eye, streaking down into his mustache.

The audience had cleared a space around the struggling four, but many saw the blood. Some cried out.

Davidee put one hand against his cheek, and when he too saw the blood his eyes were murderous. The attack on him was continuing. Apparently he hadn't seen where the knife with the gyr-falcon-head handle had gone. Shouting imprecations and trying to protect himself against the blows raining on him, he kicked around the clutter on the floor as if looking for it. Then abruptly he turned his back on the fray and strode quickly through the crowd toward the door.

As he passed a few feet from Byron, his fury was concentrated in one shouted, snarling remark which, it turned out later, nobody could hear except Byron.

Byron the calm, Byron the man who had managed by and large to keep the peace with Davidee and his family in order to protect Debbie and their child, now dove under the snooker table and came up with the shaman's knife. Davidee was almost to the door, not looking back, everyone nearby was falling over themselves to get out of his way, when Byron, shouting, screaming curses, limped after Davidee and did what some people later described, with variations, as, "Well, Byron ran and caught up to Davidee and seemed to punch him on the back . . ."

But what Byron had hit Davidee's back with was not his fist, but the shaman's knife.

Still, not everyone knew. Someone cried out, "Turn on the lights!" Someone, obeying, hit the wrong switch and turned them out altogether. The only light for a few seconds was one near the door, so that Davidee could be seen plainly turning and picking up a chair and taking a couple of faltering steps toward Byron with it raised high. Byron grabbed another chair to defend himself. Then Davidee turned and stumbled out of the place.

I was one of very few who followed, so I saw him lurching as if drunk, badly hurt, or both, toward the snowmobile he had parked at the door. He tried to lift one leg to swing himself aboard, but instead fell face-down across the seat. When he did so I could see the black handle of the shaman's knife sticking out of the middle of his back.

Right behind me was Byron. When he ran toward Davidee he was sobbing. I thought he was going to attack again, but while I and everyone else stood back, Byron put one knee on the snow-mobile alongside Davidee, who was motionless, started it up, and swung it out of there. Davidee's head and shoulders were hanging over one side of the snowmobile seat, his legs dangling free on the other side. Byron, standing up in front of him with no room to sit down, opened the throttle to a moderate speed and took off . . . where? Not to escape, I thought. There was no place to hide, or to leave behind, ever, what had happened.

Seeing the direction he took, I made a logical guess. He was heading for the nursing station on the outskirts of the settlement.

The uproar subsided into stunned silence. People crowded out of the rec hall and stood around me in subdued groups. Those who knew what had happened were talking and those who did not were listening. In one of the groups I saw Leah, Erika, Margaret, Maisie, and Debbie. When Debbie saw me looking at her, she ran, holding Julie in her arms and crying out Byron's name.

One big unanswered question buzzed around me like a persistent deerfly: How had Ipeelee come into possession of the shaman's knife?

E I G H T E E N

It didn't take much thought, what I did next. There was no doubt
that Davidee was hurt, maybe badly, depending on the damage
the knife had done internally. I did not envy the woman at the
nursing station. Normally her cases would be cuts and bruises from
boozy fights or accidents, people with acute appendix pains or
blinding headaches, people in off the tundra with frozen limbs,
pregnant young girls or women who had ignored her urging to fly
out to Inuvik or Yellowknife where their confinements could be
monitored. Or who had not come to her at all.

At that moment I saw Bouvier cruising up to the rec hall in the
van, staring in astonishment at the milling crowd, his hunt for
Andy obviously in vain. I ran to the driver's side door as he wound
down the window. "What the hell happened?" he asked.

I told him. The short form, mainly Davidee, the shaman's knife,
Byron, and that I was not sure how serious the wound might be.

"You go to the nursing station," I said.

"That where Byron took him?"

"That's what I figure."

"Is Davidee likely to cause a lot of trouble there?"

"Don't think so." A full stab in the back with what Jonassie had
told me was a five-and-a-half-inch blade . . . depended what it hit.

"We'll have to pick up Byron but there's no hurry about that part." Pause. What else? A statement. "You haven't found Andy."

"Right."

I could see Erika Hall running toward us, her eyes wide with shock and excitement at what she had witnessed, and perhaps, to be charitable, only secondarily concerned with how it would look in print.

"You go with Bouvier," I told her.

She ran to the other door and they drove off, Bouvier honking his horn to make a way through people heading in the same direction. Some were hurrying but most, visible in the glow of the few lights holding back the cloud-blackened Arctic night, moved slowly, like a crowd leaving somewhere after a game, the excitement to be reflected upon, regretted or savored, but the result unchangeable. Heading for the nursing station . . . what else was there for them to do? This was not a place where you could go home and listen to the radio to find out what happened.

As I stood watching for a few seconds, among the walkers I could see Margaret and Maisie close together. Sarah and Agnes were with a larger group, Lewissie and his wife Jane nowhere to be seen, Jonassie the same. Leah and her mother were among those still milling around the entrance to the rec hall.

I moved out of the light from the entrance and soon found myself alone, all the signs of excitement behind me. Rather than risk being seen going directly toward the shore, I walked quickly to the right and down the slope where there was no road, through the ankle-deep snow. Passing behind the hotel, I wished I had brought a flashlight, but maybe it was just as well—the light would have been seen, someone might have followed. I wanted Andy to myself.

The dark line of overturned boats showed plainly against the snow. I stopped at the end one. I thought I could see recent footprints in today's noon snow. I leaned over almost double to peer in, but could see nothing.

"Andy," I said.

No answer.

"It's Matteesie," I said.

Still no answer, no stirring from under the boat.

"Davidee has been stabbed with the shaman's knife," I said. "It happened at the dance. He's badly hurt."

His unbelieving voice came from only feet away. I still couldn't see him. He was hiding as deeply in the shelter of the boat as he could get. "You're just trying to get me to come out."

I could hear his teeth chattering.

"I wouldn't do that."

He crawled out on his hands and knees.

"We have to talk," I said. "We'll go to the detachment. You're safe now. I promise."

He stood up, his tiny body shivering uncontrollably. I realized he still didn't know what had happened, how Davidee probably was no longer a threat to him. We walked out of there behind the hotel, behind the rec hall, past the door to the rink where the ice-scrapings were piled all winter. He stayed close to me as if trying to make one shadow out of two. We walked up the slope between the rec hall and the detachment and crossed a few yards of open space before I unlocked the door and turned on the light.

He was the one who locked the door behind us. Then he went to the window facing the house where I'd first laid eyes on Davidee and Debbie and their family. The house was dark. He was still there staring out while I made tea and hunted through the scanty rations in the refrigerator, finding bread and margarine and a can of soup. I put the soup into a bowl and into Bouvier's microwave to heat, cleared a place on Barker's desk, laid out bread, margarine, Bouvier's jar of peanut butter, a half package of cheese slices.

At the same time, speaking largely to his back, except once in a while when he turned to glance at me, I told him what had happened: the fight, the appearance of the shaman's knife, the stabbing by Byron.

"Byron?" he asked incredulously, coming to sit down. "Shee-it!"

He wolfed the bread and cheese, gulped the soup. Sitting across the desk from him, I phoned the nursing station. Busy signal. I put down the phone, waited, tried again. Still busy.

Then I turned on the office tape recorder and said to Andy, "Now you're safe. You accept that?"

He nodded.

"So I want the whole story. No more running away, right?"

He nodded again.

"How come your Nikes had blood on the soles?"

He gulped, but after a few seconds answered in a mixture of dialect and English, faltering, "I have to start farther back."

"We've got lots of time. Now's the time to tell it."

He let out a long breath, paused, then met my eyes. "Well, one time when Jonassie was away buying stone, but I didn't know that, I went to his house. I did that because sometimes Jonassie has been kind to me when other people weren't. I knocked on the back door. There was no answer. I tried the knob. It was open, so I went in."

I had to keep remembering he was only fifteen. I wanted to ease him along, let him set his own course, interrupting only when I had to, in short, soft rather than hard questioning—as long as that worked.

"Then what?"

He shifted uncomfortably in his chair, but in a few seconds went on.

"Well, I was inside so I looked around. Sometimes when we talked he told me about the old days when it was like one for all and all for one, and if a person came to the door or came to a snow house out on the tundra and had no food to eat or skins to sleep on or boots that were not worn out, it would not be that he was coming to beg [*tuksiaqtuaq*], but he would be treated for a time at least as one of the family to be fed and looked after as long as he behaved himself. I was hungry so I found some caribou dry-meat that I knew he dried himself and while I was chewing that I went around the place looking at his stuff. Just looking. I thought he might come in any time, but didn't think he'd be sore at me as long as I didn't do anything bad."

"What kind of stuff were you looking at?"

"Well, masks, and a lot of carvings, mostly finished. He introduced me once to a black-haired woman from Winnipeg Art Gallery he said comes nearly every year and buys carvings. Many of the carvings were large and would sell for a lot of money, I think, but I just cruised around in there and began to think I might take a small one if I could find one, and maybe he wouldn't notice."

"So that's when you found the shaman's knife?"

An instant glance of surprise that I knew, then a nod. "I saw it tucked away at the back of a shelf. The handle was black stone, carved to the head of a bird, I didn't know what bird, something like a hawk [*qilriq*] or an eagle [*tingmiaqpak*] that I have seen in many drawings. I thought that this knife would be easy to sell, and probably Jonassie would never miss it, or I would tell him I had taken it. So I took it. Only later did I find that the bird was a gyrfalcon [*kidjgavik*].

"I knew that in the spirit world the gyrfalcon is one of the spirits of death. This is all not long ago, maybe a month."

"So for a while you had the shaman's knife. How did Davidee get it? Did you sell it to him or he took it from you or what?"

Andy sighed. I could tell this was a bad memory. "One night at the rec hall before he was even supposed to be back here, he was after me for twenty dollars I had borrowed from Dennissie and was supposed to pay him back twenty-five in a week. Dennissie asked me for it and I said I didn't have any money, so a few days later he sent Davidee to collect. I still had no money but Davidee scared me and I showed him the knife and said that it was worth fifty dollars."

At that he looked exactly like anyone who didn't like remembering a bad deal, his eyes showing the kind of deep regret well known among some used-car buyers.

"I was surprised—he took it from me and gave me twenty-five dollars change! He seemed very excited about the knife, as if he had seen it before, or knew about it, and right away I knew I had not asked enough, but then it was too late. I know it was wrong, but I thought that when I had fifty dollars again I would give it to Jonassie and tell him what happened, but I have never had fifty dollars since."

I had to push a little, needed to know the rest as fast as possible and get to the nursing station. "Did you ever see Davidee with the knife, or did anybody else know about it?"

"Not that I know. The next time I heard about the knife was

on the night of the murders. I was in the rec hall and Davidee wasn't but some of the others were laughing about something that had happened the night before."

I thought he might be straying. I didn't have time for digressions. "Something connected to Davidee? What?"

Then what Andy said turned out to be precisely the other side of what Leah had told me about earlier.

"Why they were laughing was that some of them had heard Davidee trying to get Dennis to set up Leah at his house. It was known that Dennis and Leah had gone there before fairly often. The difference this time was that Davidee had offered Dennis fifty dollars to get Leah there the following night and leave the front door open so that when Leah and Dennis were uh . . ."—he looked ashamed—"finished, Davidee would get a turn at her.

"I didn't laugh when I heard that. Leah is one of the people who is good to me. If I think of an angel, I think of Leah. But what the guys were laughing at was two things. Dennis had told Davidee that he already had spoken to Leah and she couldn't come that particular night. But someone had seen Dennis and Leah together that night, going to his house. Because nobody likes Davidee, when he came to the rec hall they laughed at him and told him that he had been made a fool of. I was there to hear all this. Davidee had been drinking but didn't seem real drunk. When everybody was laughing he just listened, looking mad as hell, and then walked out, fast, without a word."

"Did you talk to him then at all, where he was going, or anything?"

He pressed his lips close together, a hard straight line. "Not then. But the next time I saw him it was just about twelve, maybe a few minutes earlier, the rec hall was supposed to be closed but on booze nights rules were broken. The thing I noticed was that he wasn't wearing the same clothes he'd had on earlier. Probably his other ones had blood on them . . ."

"How would you know that?"

"I didn't, right then. I figured it out later. Anyway, he pulled me off to the side and said he'd been in a fight with Dennissie and it had got rough and now he found that he had lost the knife. He told me to go to the house right away and find the knife and bring it to him and he'd give me fifty dollars. He said it would probably be in the living room, maybe in or around the chesterfield. He grabbed me by the shoulders and pulled me up tight against him and said, 'I'll kill you if you ever say a word about any of this.' "

I could imagine it.

"So you went to the house."

"I didn't know anything about the murders then, not a thing. At the house, that's when I found out. I get up there. The police had just arrived. People were gathering. The old lady I later learned was your mother, Matteesie, had been taken next door to Annie's house, and . . ."

I was feeling more than a little sick by then, about murder, my mother, everything I knew about that night—including some sloppy police work. I didn't want to believe what I now was imagining.

"You mean you went into the house then, nobody stopped you?"

"There was a lot of confusion. I almost got sick from the amount of blood I could see even from the door. I didn't know what had happened but the blood made me think what would happen if I came back to Davidee without the knife. The house was pretty dark inside, bad lights. I heard Barker saying to Bouvier, 'What the hell do you mean, you didn't bring flashlights?' Anyway, I am small, and when Barker went upstairs and Bouvier went next door to talk to your mother, I slipped in. Some of the blood was dry, but I almost fell stepping into a sort of pool of it. I could see that Thelma was on the couch. I couldn't see well enough to know that she was even hurt. I said, 'Don't yell, Thelma, it's just me, Andy,' and meanwhile I'm trying to see what's on the floor and I do see a gleam of light and it is the knife. I pick it up and get out just as Barker was coming downstairs."

"Jesus," I said. The only thing I could think of.

"Someone outside must have seen me, I don't know, but after all I just lived two doors away, they were used to me."

Well, I thought, we're getting there, slow but sure.

"So now you had the knife," I prompted.

"There was blood on it. I ran a little and cleaned it off on some

snow and took it back down to the rec hall, where Davidee was
pacing around waiting for me, not talking to anybody. When he
saw me I went to the toilet and got into one of the stalls. I had
been in a stall with him before doing drug deals. He followed me
in and I gave him the knife and he gave me a fifty-dollar bill. I
told him about cleaning the blood off the knife and he said, 'Oh,
I hit Dennissie and he got a nosebleed.' Then he took some more
money from his pocket, mostly twenties and tens, a little with
blood on it, not even all dried, and gave it to me and said, 'Is your
man out there?' I knew he meant a dealer, a guy who came in
once in a while but wasn't known to the police. I said I thought
he was still there.

" 'Cocaine,' he said. 'Get back here fast.' Then he went out,
but instead of leaving fast I stood there almost crazy, wondering
what the hell I'd got into.''

"How long before you went out, then?''

"Just a minute or two. I looked at the fifty he'd given me and
one side had some blood on it. I didn't want any money with blood
on it so in the money he'd given me I found two twenties and a
ten for myself that were clean. Then I put the fifty he'd given me
with seventy more, with only the clean side of the fifty Davidee
had given me showing, and I went and I found the dealer and I
bought a cocaine packet for a hundred and twenty and took it
back in to the can with Davidee right behind me. He took it right
away, sniffing it off the side of his hand, and then he practically
ran out of there.

"Left the rec hall, too, you mean?''

"I heard his snowmobile go. I was back out with the others for
a while before the police came and lined everybody up and checked
for bloodstains. If they had been able to check the dealer's pocket
they would have found some, I'd given all the bloodstained stuff
to him.''

"But he'd already left when the police arrived? He wasn't in the
pictures Bouvier took.''

"He'd gone by then. I looked for him the next day but he'd
flown out on the first morning flight. Guys like that know when
to disappear. I was wishing by then I could have gone with him.

Then when one of the cashiers at the Co-op found she had a fifty with blood on it, and Nelson was in an uproar, I knew the dealer must have bought something there on his way out of town."

He stopped talking for nearly a minute, dropped his head, stared at the floor. The fear hadn't left him. "I haven't felt safe since that night," he said. "Every time I saw Davidee again it all came back that if I talk, I'm dead." Apprehensively, he asked, "How bad is he hurt?"

I explained as much as I knew: that he'd been stabbed and practically collapsed across the seat of his snowmobile.

"That knife would go through me and come out the other side," Andy said, and shuddered. "I knew all along he'd have it hidden somewhere, either carrying it hidden, or hiding it where it wouldn't be found in a search. I don't know where. I hope he's dead, I'll sleep better . . .

"Oh"—this was an afterthought—"two days after the murders, that Sunday, he showed up with a note. I don't know where he'd been. He told me to pin it up on the notice board at the rec hall when nobody was around. I read it fast, something about the shaman causing the murders. I knew that was crazy, but he'd told me to pin it up and I did.

"That's all I know," he said. He looked deathly tired.

I had no more questions. I had what I wanted.

I wrote out quickly the main elements of his story. With Leah's account, backing up the presence of her footprints in the house, and Maisie's story about being there when she heard Leah and Dennissie upstairs, it should be all the evidence I'd ever need.

I read it to him.

He nodded. "Okay, sign it," I said, and he did.

This document, labeled exhibit something or other, I forget exactly, and backed up by the tape, later appeared in my overall report in a section headed: "Andy Arqviq's Story."

I asked if he wanted to come with me to the nursing station. He said no, he would go home now.

"No," I said. "You'll stay here. I don't want to lose you again. I'm going to lock you in. There's the cot over there. Don't answer the phone or the door. I'll be back when I can and we'll go back to Barker's house for the night. But right now, can you sleep?"

"I think so," he said, and, looking like a small ghost, fell asleep in his chair. I lifted him onto the cot. I've lifted much younger kids who weighed more. I unzipped one of the detachment's sleeping bags and laid it over him like a blanket. He didn't move.

I thought about maybe disturbing him if I used the phone, but then decided no way and dialed Maxine at her townhouse in Inuvik. I was thinking of her moving to answer it from wherever she was: reaching from bed or from her hassock in front of the TV, or more likely just reaching out a wet arm from the bath. This was her bath time, I'd learned from sometimes letting the phone ring ten times before I'd just about give up and then she'd answer. For her forty-fifth birthday I'd given her an extension phone with a thirty-foot cord that she could carry with her into the bath.

"Maxine here."

"This is the RCMP on our new view-a-phone. You don't look very decent to me."

Her chuckle always made me feel good. "For you I don't have to be decent."

"I've got news. You got a pencil and paper there in the bath?"

After a few seconds, she said, "Fire away."

"I think I'm just about finished here," I said. "But Erika Hall is beavering around and I thought I should tell you. You remember Davidee Ayulaq from here? That rape case?"

She did.

"Tonight at a dance he got stabbed and he'll be charged tomorrow, two murders, one manslaughter. I'm just going to the nursing station now to find out what shape he's in. Can't give you the name of the guy who stabbed him until we decide what to do about it, but the main thing is that to all intents and purposes the case is closed except for the wrap-up."

"Can I quote you as saying that?"

I thought about it. "Yes. I've gotta go now. What do you pay your stringers?"

She laughed. "For you, guess."

"If you call me tomorrow I should have it all."

———

Trying to recall the time I spent getting to the nursing station after I had locked the detachment door, I am reminded of . . . what is it? Anyway, a line: Where did you go? Out. What did you do? Nothing.

The nursing station was only four or five hundred yards away. I walked all over Sanirarsipaaq to get there. I had a strange reluctance to go and actually find out what was happening with Davidee.

On that near-midnight walk I thought of how Leah's story fitted so closely into Andy's: she running out as soon as the fight between Davidee and Dennissie started; Andy's background story about Davidee trying to pay Dennissie to set her up for him in what would have been another rape; the blood on Andy's shoes as he earned his fee for recovering for Davidee the knife he had stolen in the first place; the blood on some of the money, including the fifty that Davidee had used to pay Andy, and that Andy had used for the cocaine, the fifty that had turned up at the Co-op. Davidee must have started taking Dennissie's money and then taken only part of it, for whatever reason.

What else? More thoughts: The rec hall guys who'd been laughing at Davidee, maybe starting his murderous rage. Andy could identify them as backup witnesses to what Davidee had in mind for Leah that night. Then there was Andy himself as an example of what could happen to an orphan kid left to do what he thought he had to, to stay alive. The drug dealing in the can at the rec hall could be an investigation of its own, leading to a later arrest. Maybe. You can never be sure.

But what I really wrestled with was Davidee. The fury that I'd had originally, personally wanting to get whoever ran down my mother and eventually caused her death, had been largely forgotten in the nuts and bolts of trying to put the case together. Now my anger was back, full strength. Three people had died because of him. Leah mourned Dennissie, many friends and relatives mourned him and Thelma, and I mourned my mother and always would.

"I was wondering if you were coming," Bouvier said, outside the nursing station. "It's been a madhouse around here."

"What kind of shape's he in?"

"Alive, so far."

I walked up the wheelchair ramp and inside. Davidee was lying face down on a stretcher with the gyrfalcon handle of the shaman's knife still sticking out of his back through his layers of clothing. His anorak's sleeves had been cut off and there were two intravenous needles in him, traces of red foam on his lips.

"Hi, Matteesie," the nurse said, looking up. She was just standing by, as if to watch and do anything that suddenly needed doing. I could see the sweat on her uniform under her arms and bloodstains down the front. A little blood showed around the hilt of the knife where it stuck through Davidee's clothing. His father and mother sat in one corner of the room. Not Debbie. I had an idea that she'd have been torn, in a way, about leaving her parents on their own, but more concerned about what was happening to Byron. Erika was taking notes, sitting unobtrusively against one wall.

Bouvier entered behind me. "What about Byron?" I asked.

"Lewissie picked him up. He found Byron just walking with his father. His father was right there, you know, when it happened. He walked up here and went straight to Byron, who was still sitting outside on the snowmobile when I got here, his head down, I'd guess in shock. Tell the truth I didn't notice when he and his dad left, but then asked Lewissie to watch for him, we probably had to charge him. He and his father had just gone for a walk, and to talk. They were walking back along the road from the airstrip when Lewissie found them and sent a message with Paulessie to say he'd go home with them. They're at Byron's home. Debbie and Julie are there, too."

"Never handled anything like this before," the nurse said to me. "Hope I never do again." Her fair hair was mixed with gray. She was stocky and strong-looking. A badge clipped to the front of her white uniform read: Elizabeth Homfray-Davies, Registered Nurse.

"Have you kept notes?" I asked.

She tapped a pad beside her.

"Could I read them?"

"Maybe I'd better read them to you," she said. "Or you ask what you want to know. Funny, this is something we're taught to do, have notes we can consult if we have to give evidence in court, but it's the first time it's ever been necessary for me. Yet, anyway."

She had an English accent. I'd been going to talk to her about the night my mother was hurt, but never got around to it. If this case got to court, which it almost certainly would when Byron was tried, she would have to give details of her training, experience, any degrees she held, where she had served, and so on. I'd been through that with doctors testifying, never with a nurse.

"Okay, will you read what you've got?"

"It's pretty formal," she said. "I thought I'd better make it that way, like we're told to do."

I can stand formality better than I can sloppiness. "Formal's fine," I said. "I'll take notes. Now, tell me off the top."

She began in her precise English voice, sometimes consulting her notes. "Yes, well, here it is, then. I had a phone call about eleven o'clock from Lewissie Ullayoroluk. All he said was that an emergency was coming in right away. I'm all alone here, my backup is in Florida, so I couldn't go to the dance and was in bed here reading. I was just into my clothes when I heard a snowmobile coming and went out and saw Byron driving the snowmobile and Davidee lying across the seat on his abdomen . . ."

"Nobody else with them?" Dumb question, I knew immediately, unless some Olympic sprinter was around who I didn't know about.

"Nobody else right then," she said, "but soon, I assure you! People by the dozens began arriving, the younger ones running. I had to tell them for God's sake to get out of the way and let me do what I could, but there was still a crowd around me when I was trying to see what we had here."

"Did he say anything?"

She shook her head decisively. "Never, so far. He was breathing, but only just. Of course I could see why, that knife." She jerked her head at the knife sticking out of his back. "I got help from some of the young men, Tommy was one of them, to help me with a stretcher, and we wheeled him up the ramp and in here just the way he is now, knife and all. He's hardly changed since he got here. You can see yourself, blue around his mouth, frothy blood drooling out from his nose and mouth."

"Any sign of consciousness at all since?"

"Not a stir out of him."

"So what happened after you got him inside? Now I guess I need any technical stuff."

"I examined him. His pupils were dilated. There was very little reaction to my light testing, no response to verbal command. I tried mild pain stimuli, jabbing a small needle shallowly into his hand. He didn't react. When I checked him with a stethoscope his heart rate was very faint and rapid, so much so that I could not count it. Also, the air entry into his lungs was very poor, very shallow, probably meaning badly damaged lungs. The knife is in the middle of his back just below the shoulder blades, I think that's where, just a little to the right side from the midline, anyway, wouldn't be able to be certain without undressing him."

"Did you try for any advice, like call a hospital or doctor?"

"I tried to get a call through to the doctor on call in Churchill, but couldn't get her, left a call, she was on the line to some other nursing station, so I went ahead doing what I had been doing. While Tommy kept trying Churchill for me, I cleared his airway, put an airway in, and sent a message out to get two of my local health-aides in to help.

"They were on their way anyway, they were at the party and saw some of this happening." She waved a hand at Jane Ullayoroluk and an Inuit women I knew by sight. "They've been a big help. Then I tried to start intravenous infusion. That was very difficult but on the third try I got a very small needle in. When the doctor in Churchill called me back her advice was don't remove the knife but try to start two intravenous infusion lines running at the maximum and to keep the airway open. She said she would call for a medivac flight right away."

I sighed. Medivac several days ago for my mother, and now medivac for the guy who knocked her down.

"But you got the intravenous going all right."

A brisk nod. "It took me quite a while. I haven't got the time exactly when I did start it."

"Is it making any difference?"

"It has to, but there's been no noticeable effect. I can still hardly get any pulse or blood pressure, can hardly observe any breathing, pupils still dilated, no reaction to light, in fact I've thought he was gone two or three times, but he seemed to stabilize just before you came in. He might just make it. So that's where we are now.''

I sat down at her desk and from my notes wrote in longhand a summary of what she'd said. When I read it to her, she said, "Yes, that's about right," and signed it. This statement later appeared in my final report under the heading of, "Nurse Homfray-Davies's Account."

Bouvier claims, and he might be right, I was not functioning all that well by then, that when I was folding up her statement and sticking it in my pocket, I looked at her and said quietly, "Thank you. You're a bloody star!"

"What on earth do you mean?"

"Keeping this guy alive so we can try him for murdering Dennis Raakwap and Thelma Pukwap and causing the death of my mother," I said, having trouble with the last few words.

And then I said something that Bouvier insisted on laughing about later. He even phoned Maxine to tell her, figuring she would appreciate it.

"You're standing there, Matteesie," he said. "The guy is almost dead. About one breath away from eternity, wherever that is. And you're standing over him telling the nurse, 'It would have been a bloody miscarriage of justice if he checked out unconscious and never had to sit in court and listen to what an asshole he really was.' "

Soon after that, Davidee died. Slipped away, with no sound, more like a cessation of sounds. The nurse swiftly checked and looked to me, shaking her head. "Gone," she said.

I stood looking down at him for a moment and then for some instinctive reason I went over to his ravaged-looking mother and father. She was motionless, expressionless, staring nowhere, as if in a trance. I put my hand on Ipeelee's shoulder. He looked up at me and slowly, faintly, smiled. Either the shaman trying to help him, or maybe the shaman's knife right there, sticking out of Davidee, had made a difference.

Then I went over to Erika, standing against one wall taking

notes. "Phone me in the morning," I said. "I'll answer any questions you've got, on one condition."

"What's that?"

"Find out where Barker is staying in Honolulu and fax him a copy of your story. Put a note on it saying it's with Matteesie's compliments."

"You're a bastard," she said. "It's a deal."

I drove to the detachment with Bouvier. While we carried Andy to the van and later into Barker's house, he mumbled sleepily and then was gone again. We laid him on a bed and took off his lousy cheap boots.

"Byron?" Bouvier asked.

It had to be done. "You stay here," I said. "I'm going over there now."

The whole family had gathered, brothers, sisters, parents, Byron, Debbie, Julie. Plus Lewissie. I stood just inside the door.

"I have to charge you," I said to Byron. "I'll let you know in the morning what happens next. Get a good lawyer."

Debbie cried. "You know what Davidee said to Byron in the rec hall, that he was going to kill Julie!"

I had wondered. Now I knew. But I only said, tiredly, "Be sure Byron's lawyer gets that. It'll help Byron in court."

I don't know when I got back to the hotel. Margaret let me in and hugged me. I hugged her back. Maisie hugged me, too, just about cracking my ribs, crying a little, either over her narrow escape from being more involved, or from a lingering wish that she had stayed around to throw another male creep out of a second-story window.

Thomassie was sitting in our room, smoking his pipe. He'd heard all about the action by now but had missed being an eyewitness —he hated rock music, and had left when it began. He had done rather well with the rest of my rum, but had saved one drink for me. I told him that, with Davidee dead and everything else done that could be done, I wanted him to fly me and Byron and maybe somebody else to Inuvik in the morning, once I had a chance to think things over and talk charges with Yellowknife. There are holding cells in Inuvik.

"What other passenger besides Byron?" Thomassie asked.

"Andy. I'll ask him, anyway. Just want him to see somewhere that isn't Sanirarsipaaq. Broaden his horizons. He can use that."

Actually, Andy and Maxine got along fine. He made her laugh a lot when he was mimicking me marching around his town looking important. But soon he got homesick for Sanirarsipaaq. He just wanted to know what was going on there. He didn't want to be away when he had a chance, maybe his first, to be the center of attention. It was probably the right thing for him. Annie took him in. I might do more about him sometime. But so far I'm not sure exactly what.

E P I L O G U E

There was no avoiding the original charge against Byron, first-degree murder. Mr. Justice Charlie Ferguson Litterick heard the case in the rec hall at Sanirarsipaaq. Maxine flew in to cover the trial. She told me she'd just got word back about the directors' course she'd applied for, giving me one of her more radiant smiles. "I didn't get it, and now I'm relieved." She waved around the rec hall-cum-courtroom, jammed full with the Inuit community, men, women, babies, parkas, knee-highs. "Who'd want to leave all this behind?" I'd felt that way often, too; still did.

Among dozens of witnesses, the most important were Andy and Leah, with Hard Hat a close third. What made him decide so precipitately to leave Sanirarsipaaq was that he had overheard Davidee making a second muffled call to the hospital at Yellowknife to ask about my mother's condition, and had drawn a conclusion that filled him with terror.

The judge agreed with Byron's counsel, with the assent of the crown prosecutor, to allow the charge to be dropped to manslaughter because of extreme provocation, Davidee's threat to kill little Julie, who was in court wearing the sunglasses with the heart-shaped rims.

When Byron pleaded guilty to the lesser charge, the judge sentenced him to three years with a recommendation for early parole, and also ordered the court clerk to return the bloodstained fifty-dollar bill to the Co-op, and to have the shaman's knife returned to the shaman, who gave it to me. "A souvenir, Matteesie," he said. A real mind reader.

Byron served a year and was granted parole in the minimum time allowed by Canadian law, one-third of his original sentence. With the active help of the Inumerit, fully supported by the community, he and Debbie and Julie got their own house.